CASSIE EDWARDS

THE SAVAGE SERIES

**Winner of the *Romantic Times*
Lifetime Achievement Award for Best Indian Series!**

SAVAGE EMBRACE

As Blazing Eagle gazed at Becky, she was acutely aware of the slope of his hard jaw, his bold nose and strong chin, of his lips that seemed made to be kissed.

Her whole body trembled as his hands were suddenly on her throat, framing her face. His thumbs lightly caressed her flushed cheeks, his mouth a feather's touch from her lips.

Suddenly he surrounded her with his hard, strong arms, pressing her against him as his mouth seized her lips in a frenzied kiss, a kiss that stilled all of her doubts and fears.

Her arms crept around his neck and answered his hunger with hers. She knew that she must not allow this, yet she could not stop it once it had started. She felt all of her reserves melting away into something beautiful, something sweet.

SAVAGE SECRETS

CASSIE EDWARDS

LEISURE BOOKS NEW YORK CITY

A LEISURE BOOK®

August 1995

Published by

Dorchester Publishing Co., Inc.
276 Fifth Avenue
New York, NY 10001

Cover art by John Ennis

Printed in the United States of America.

With much love I dedicate *Savage Secrets* to my beloved Cheyenne great-grandmother, Snow Deer. Although she joined her Great Spirit in the heavens many years ago, she is still alive inside my heart.

I would also like to dedicate *Savage Secrets* to the following people with whom I have made special friendships: Craig Tharp, whose fascination with Indian lore matches my own; also Cathy and Mike Globe, Harrett and Ernest Cargile, Donna Cohrs, Kathy Hersey, and Nancy Livingston.

Also to two people who mean the world to me—Virgil F. and Mary Kathryn Cline, my parents.

SOARING HEART

My heart soars, as if on eagle's wings,
Soaring on the winds of the seasons,
Summer, winter, fall and spring.

Looking north, south, east and west,
Searching for more than just a place to rest.

Being carried over mountains, hills, valleys, and
        streams,
Forever clinging to the eagle's wings that
Will carry me closer to my dreams.

Not ever wanting to give up the flight,
My heart will continue the search,
With the sun by day, and the moon's glow by night.

Knowing in my heart that there is a place of rest,
My search will not be over, until I find
The special place where two hearts nest.
        —Linda Waterfall Maroney, (Sokoki band of
        Abenaki, Siksika band of Blackfoot, Cherokee
        and Micmac)

This poem, written by Waterfall, is being published in
her memory. She has joined her Great Spirit, her search
now over for that special place in heaven.

        —Cassie

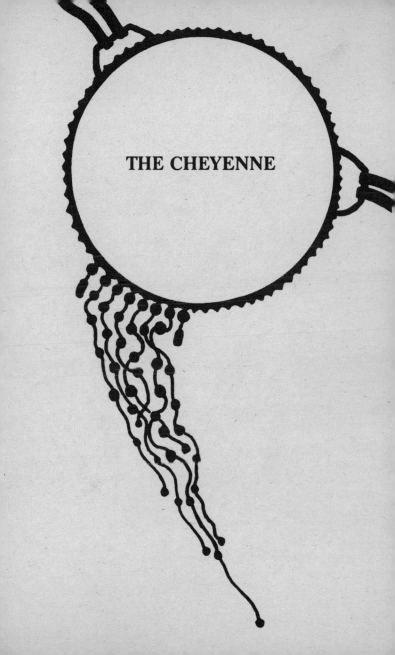

THE CHEYENNE

Chapter One

Shaiyena Country—1849

Halfway through her journey across the sky, Sister Sun bathed the land in amber light. Dust rolled upward behind their mighty steeds as two Cheyenne warriors rode along a narrow trail, their long, waist-length black hair fluttering in the breeze over their bare shoulders.

Dressed in a brief breech clout and moccasins, Chief Black Thunder yanked at his reins and wheeled his horse to a stop. The sight before him made his spine stiffen.

His companion, Young Bear, also saw it. A young brave of perhaps nine winters was wandering aimlessly toward them. There were blood stains on his clothes and face.

Chief Black Thunder said, glancing at Young

11

Bear, "Do you see how he stumbles as he walks? He has been injured."

"This child is more than likely from a neighboring Cheyenne village," Young Bear said tightly. "Our enemy the Crow surely are responsible for his injuries."

Chief Black Thunder and Young Bear sank their heels into the flanks of their horses and rode hard toward the boy. "The Crows would not have done this, Young Bear," Chief Black Thunder said, his eyes never leaving the child, who continued staggering along the narrow path through the waist-high grass. "They only steal Cheyenne horses. They do not seek glory in harming children.

"Palefaces are responsible for this boy's plight," Black Thunder said, his voice tight with rage. "Are we not constantly troubled by the vast number of bluecoats and gold-hungry whites swarming into the best hunting ground of the sacred Cheyenne homeland? The bluecoats have thundering wagon guns that overpower the weapons of the Cheyenne. They can raid a camp and go on their way unharmed. They may have raided this child's village."

Silence fell between them when they reached the boy and drew their horses to a shuddering halt, then dismounted. Chief Black Thunder reached for the boy, quickly recognizing him. "Blazing Eagle," he gasped, taking the youth into his arms. He studied the face of the young brave, a brave whose father was Laughing Elk, a powerful Cheyenne chief in his own right. Dreaming Sky was his mother.

Black Thunder gripped Blazing Eagle by the shoulders and held him at arm's length as he gazed down at him. *"Naha*, speak to me," he said gently. "Tell Chief Black Thunder what has happened. Who did this to you?"

Blazing Eagle said nothing as he stared mindlessly up at the chief. His eyes were void of expression.

Seeing that the child was not going to respond to his question, Chief Black Thunder slowly searched him for wounds.

"He has not been injured as we first suspected," Black Thunder said, casting Young Bear a glance. "The blood comes from someone else's body."

He swallowed hard, looked down at the child again, then again drew Blazing Eagle into his comforting arms. "Young Bear, this child may be the sole survivor of an attack on his people," he said, stroking the child's long hair. "Ride ahead, Young Bear. Get several warriors and ride to this child's village. See what awaits us there. It must not be good, for the young brave has been badly affected by it."

Young Bear's gaze lingered on Blazing Eagle a moment longer; then he nodded and leapt onto his horse and rode away.

Black Thunder lifted the child into his powerful arms and placed him on his saddle. Still the young brave said nothing, only stared ahead as though seeing nothing.

"Young brave of nine winters, your silence says more than words ever could," Black Thunder said, swinging himself into the saddle behind him. Slipping an arm around the boy's waist to secure him against his strong body, Black Thunder inhaled a quavering breath at the thought of what his warriors would find at Blazing Eagle's village.

A massacre.

It tore at his heart to think that any man, white or red-skinned, could be responsible for such heinous acts against other human beings. It was something he could never understand, or get used to, this greed that had been introduced into the lives of his people when the white man invaded their land.

Yellow rock, *gold*, was the cause.

To the Cheyenne, the gold was a part of the land. It should not be disturbed. It was something that belonged there—not in the pockets of white men!

Shifting his thoughts back to the child and what was best for him, Black Thunder nudged the sides of his horse with his knees and slapped his reins.

Whirling the steed around, he rode back toward his village. Until now, his mission today had not been a serious one. He had just wanted to ride with his friend to enjoy the loveliness and tranquility of the land which sent his heart soaring with gladness whenever he gazed upon its grand vastness. What was not yet invaded by the whites still remained as pure as a newborn babe. He relished it, this land of blowing grass, mountains, and animals.

As he rode onward, he caught sight of a herd of buffalo running over a slight rise of land, a mass of black, like a huge shadow cast onto the ground by a clouded-over sun. He was proud to see the buffalo, to know they were always there to supply his people with food and hides for clothing and blankets.

"They, also, will soon dwindle," he whispered angrily to himself. "Why must it be that the white man steals not only our dignity, but also our means of living?"

He felt guilty to be thinking of himself when Blazing Eagle suddenly shifted in his arms, reminding Black Thunder of what had happened to him and his people.

"Young brave, soon you will be in my village," Black Thunder said, even though the child made no indication that he heard. "There you will be taken to my lodge. You will be bathed, clothed, and fed. My bed will be yours tonight. I shall sit beside you and be there should you suddenly awaken with memories that might tear at your very soul. I shall be there to comfort you."

When the child still did not respond, Black Thunder was overwhelmed with a deep sadness, not only for this young brave, but also for himself. His wife had died many moons ago, when Black Thunder had been a young leader of his people. She had died of a mysterious illness only a few weeks into their marriage, and he had vowed then never to love another, not even if it meant that he would never be a father. He could not bear to think of losing another wife, and therefore a good portion of his heart. His people had become his life. They had become his family.

Only recently, when Black Thunder had begun to have strange, searing pains around his heart, had he truly regretted not having a son to follow him into chieftainship when he was forced to step down to make way for someone younger and more vital.

This child, this young brave, had been taught the ways of a chief by his own chieftain father. Black Thunder shook his head when he realized where his thoughts were leading him. How could the boy be prepared for chieftainship when he could not even remember how to speak his name or show emotions?

"Sadly, it cannot be," Black Thunder mumbled, lifting a hand to stroke Blazing Eagle's thick, black, waist-length hair. "My *naha*, my son . . ."

He paled when he realized that he had spoken to Blazing Eagle as though he were talking to his own son.

There were dangers in that. He *had* no son. He never would have.

He rode onward, relieved when his village came into sight. He gazed wistfully at the lodges, the smoke spiraling from their smoke holes. How peaceful his village seemed, spread out along a winding river with its covering of cottonwoods.

He gazed up at a butte where sentries were always positioned to protect his village.

"Are they enough?" he whispered, knowing that should the bluecoat pony soldiers decide to attack, nothing could stop them. Had the soldiers attacked Blazing Eagle's village? Or had it been money-hungry settlers who wished to have the run of the land?

"Young brave, will I ever truly know who did this to you?" Black Thunder said softly. "Will you ever regain your memory enough to point an accusing finger at those responsible?"

Blazing Eagle still did not respond. He just sat

lifelessly on the horse, Black Thunder's arm holding him in place.

As Black Thunder rode into his camp, men, women, and children surrounded him and followed him to his lodge.

Waterfall, a young maiden the same age as Blazing Eagle, gazed up at Blazing Eagle as Black Thunder dismounted.

"Oh, no—it is Blazing Eagle," Waterfall said, paling at the sight of the boy and noting how he continued to stare straight ahead as though she were not there.

She looked quickly at Black Thunder as he lifted Blazing Eagle from the horse. "When Young Bear rode into our village and told everyone about Blazing Eagle, I did not want to believe it," she said softly.

"Believe it, sweet maiden," Black Thunder said as he carried Blazing Eagle toward his lodge.

Waterfall entered ahead of him, the fringes of her snow-white doeskin dress wrapping about her ankles in her haste. "I shall help you," she said, pulling aside the entrance flap for Chief Black Thunder's entrance.

She made way for Black Thunder inside the lodge. She had just added wood to the fire and had hung a large kettle of soup that her mother had made for Black Thunder over the flames.

Her heart ached for Blazing Eagle as she watched Black Thunder lay him on his bed of furs. Tears burned her eyes when she saw that Blazing Eagle continued to stare vacantly straight ahead.

"Child, bring me a basin of water and a clean

cloth," Black Thunder said over his shoulder. "Add plenty of yucca to the water so that we will have enough suds to remove all the blood from this young brave's body."

Waterfall nodded and ran from the lodge, reentering soon with everything that Black Thunder had asked for, and even more. She had an older brother, yet by only one winter. His name was Fish Hawk. His build was similar to Blazing Eagle's. She brought one of his buckskin outfits fresh and clean and dry from a washing at the river.

She stood back, not at all modest as she silently watched Black Thunder bathe Blazing Eagle. She had seen her brother nude many times in the river. There was nothing about a young man's anatomy that was a mystery to her. It was just that they were built differently from her.

After Black Thunder cleaned Blazing Eagle and replaced his soiled clothes with clean ones, Waterfall ladled some soup into a wooden bowl and took it to Black Thunder.

She poured some sweet root tea into a wooden mug and handed it to Black Thunder. This Indian medicine was used for all kinds of healing.

Then she knelt down beside the bed of furs and watched as her chief fed the young brave the soup. She smiled with relief when her chief was able to get Blazing Eagle to drink the medicinal tea, glad at least that he willingly swallowed both. That made her feel as though he might be all right once he was able to accept whatever had stolen the power of speech from him.

"What do you think happened to Blazing Eagle?"

Waterfall blurted out. "I have never seen anyone like this. He is nothing like before. He was always so friendly. He was always laughing."

She gazed at Blazing Eagle's perfect facial features, and her insides grew warm. He was handsome, like all Cheyenne braves, yet more than the others. She had always admired him when he had come with his father for a council. She had loved it when he had looked her way and smiled.

Now he seemed to have forgotten how to smile.

The sound of horses stopping outside Black Thunder's lodge drew Black Thunder around. Waterfall's question was forgotten in the commotion as Young Bear came in a rush into the lodge.

"They are all dead," he said, panting hard as he tried to get his breath. "No one was spared." He gazed down at Blazing Eagle. "He is the only survivor. Only he."

An icy chill spread through Black Thunder at the realization that one whole village of Cheyenne had been annihilated. Their past and future had been taken away in one heartbeat.

He looked down at Blazing Eagle. Even if the boy grew well and his mind returned to full function, there was no one left for him to return to. His only future seemed to be in another village, with another clan of Cheyenne. With Black Thunder's.

"From this day forth, Blazing Eagle is my son," Black Thunder said, his voice breaking with emotion. "He has been taught the ways of a chief by his chieftain father. When he emerges from his dark void and understands the things around him, he shall then be taught *my* ways. He will follow me into chieftainship as though he was made of my own seed."

Young Bear gaped openly at Black Thunder, then relaxed his shoulders and smiled at his chief. He placed a comforting hand on Black Thunder's shoulder. "You have been too long without a son," he said gently. "Now it is no longer so."

"I am certain that Blazing Eagle will adjust to being a part of the Fox Society," Black Thunder said, giving Waterfall only a half glance as she slipped from the lodge. "He learned from his father why we are called the Fox—because the swift fox is a beautiful animal and fleet of foot, never letting its prey escape it."

"*Ne-hyo*, Blazing Eagle will adjust to this, as well as to being your son, for it is the best of two worlds for a young Cheyenne brave," Young Bear said, smoothing a gentle hand over Blazing Eagle's black hair.

Waterfall came back into the lodge. Holding a long-stemmed blue daisy, she knelt down beside Blazing Eagle again. "Blazing Eagle, I have brought you something," she murmured. She laid the flower beside him, close to his hand. "I promise you that I will always be here to care for you. I will be a sister in every way. I will try everything possible to bring you out of your saddened state. When I am older, I will be your princess."

Her eyes widened and she smiled at Black Thunder when Blazing Eagle's fingers circled the stem of the flower and grasped it.

"Black Thunder, he *heard*," Waterfall said excitedly. "Do you see? He now holds the flower. And he knows that it was I who placed it there."

Slowly her eyes moved back to Blazing Eagle. "He hears, but does not want to speak," she said softly.

"At least not yet," Black Thunder said, sighing deeply with relief. "But he will, and *soon*. The Great Spirit will make it so!"

Chapter Two

Saint Louis, Years Later—1869

The breeze blew Becky Veach's black veil around her face as she maneuvered her horse and buggy down the bustling streets of Saint Louis, Missouri. She had only moments ago left the silence of the cemetery where she had buried her father. Except for friends, she was now alone in the world.

Her true mother had died giving birth to her.

A few years ago her stepmother had died of consumption.

Her brother had mysteriously disappeared after the Civil War.

Lost in thought, Becky recalled her many conversations with her father these past months after discovering that he had a brain tumor that would soon kill him.

"Now, Becky, you'd best get out there and find a young man and get married," he had said more than once before he became too ill to talk. "When I'm gone, it's best that you have a husband to look after you. You're twenty. You're wasting your life on this old man. Forget me. Find a handsome young man and get married."

Her father had never urged her to marry a *rich* man. He knew that when he died she would be rich in her own right. Since no one knew where her brother was, should he even be alive, her father had willed her everything.

She had never met that perfect someone with whom she would share the rest of her life. She now wondered if she ever would.

Becky turned her horse and buggy into a long drive that was lined on each side by tall, stately poplar trees. She gazed at the two-storied stone home that stood at the far end of the drive.

Her father had worked diligently during his fifty-five years and had become rich. He had started out as a real estate agent in Saint Louis. He had invested his money well and had ended up owning a great deal of property himself.

Now it was all hers, and she was not sure what she was going to do with it. She did not aspire to dabble in real estate. Yet she did not want to sell off the investments, either. Deep in her heart she'd always hoped that her brother was alive and would return to Saint Louis to claim what was rightfully his.

As Becky drew her horse and buggy up before the house, a deep melancholy swept through her.

As she stared up at the house, she dreaded going inside. It was filled with too many memories. The good had been erased of late by the bad, as her father had lain in his bed crying out with pain, his memory gone as the tumor destroyed his brain. He had wasted away to skin and bone.

Becky had watched it all, her heart tearing away a piece at a time, until her father took that last breath that finally gave him peace.

"Oh, Father," she said, easing the black veil up so that she could wipe tears from her eyes. "I don't think I can stay one more night in this house now that you are gone. But where shall I go? What shall I do?"

Becky stepped from the buggy and wound her reins around a hitching rail. Slipping off her veiled black bonnet, she again gazed at length up at the house. She blinked her eyes nervously. For a brief moment, she thought that she had seen her father standing in his upstairs bedroom window where he had ofttimes watched her come home from some social function or another through the years.

Oh, how his eyes had twinkled as he had watched a gentleman bring her home after a ball or a picnic in the park.

Even when she had only gone horseback riding alone and had returned, feeling lighthearted and gay from the freedom riding always afforded her, her father would be there with a wave and a smile, happy when he saw her happiness.

She swallowed hard and looked quickly away. He was not there. It had only been her imagination, a part of her that had not yet accepted his death.

Sighing heavily, she lifted the hem of her black silk dress and walked slowly up the gravel path that led to the porch. She had asked that friends not return home with her after the funeral with their offerings of food and consoling glances and conversation.

This was her private time.

She wished to keep it that way.

She had never approved of get-togethers after funerals, where people consumed too much food and disrespectfully talked and laughed, too soon forgetting why they were there in the first place.

After climbing the stairs and reaching the door, her hand trembled as she placed it on the knob. Just inside, to the right of the entrance foyer in the parlor, had been where her father's casket had sat for viewing the past few evenings.

That was another reason she did not want to stay in the house. She would never forget the sickening, sweet aroma of the many vases of flowers. How could she forget the crowd as, one by one, they viewed her father's corpse? She had cringed when they whispered comments to one another about his appearance.

She had vowed then and there that before she died, she would make arrangements that her casket would be closed. No one would look at her and comment on her appearance after she was dead. She shivered at the thought.

Going inside, she stopped and paled as she quickly became aware that something was wrong. To the right of her, in the study, and to the left of her, in the parlor, all of the furniture and precious keepsakes had been removed.

Her knees weakened when she took a quick step toward the study. She almost collapsed at the door when she discovered that nothing had been left in the room.

The shelves had been stripped of the priceless collection of rare books. The great oak desk where her father had spent countless hours was gone. Even the sleek satin draperies that had graced the windows for years were gone.

While she had attended her father's funeral, someone had entered the house and had stripped it bare!

"Even upstairs?" she cried, rushing back out into the foyer to peer up the dark steps.

Dropping her bonnet and gathering the hem of her dress into her arms, she bolted up the stairs. She stopped and gasped when she saw that the thieves had robbed her of all her possessions.

"Even my bed is gone!" she cried, feeling faint.

She went from room to room. She stopped and gaped openly at the emptiness of her father's bedroom. The bed on which he had lain all those months through his suffering was gone too.

"How can this be?" Becky whispered. She took slow steps into her father's bedroom. The antiseptic smell of medicine met her approach. She had thrown out the countless bottles of medicine after he died. Would the thieves have also taken them? she wondered bitterly.

Going to the window, Becky stared down at the long, narrow gravel drive. When her father bought this house she had worried about it sitting so far back from the street. It was so isolated, so vulnerable. It was a perfect place for thieves to do their dirty work without being noticed.

But through the years there had only been one robbery. Since then, her father had hidden his money beneath the floorboards in his study.

Becky's heartbeat quickened and her eyes widened at the thought of the money downstairs. What if . . . ?

She half stumbled over the hem of her dress in an attempt to turn around to leave the room, then rushed to the staircase and ran down the stairs. She was breathless as she entered the study.

Her gaze settled on the floorboards that had been hidden beneath her father's stately oak desk. With the desk gone, they now lay exposed, but to her relief, they were still in place.

But that did not necessarily mean that the thieves had not discovered the loose floorboards and lifted them to remove the stored cash. If they had, they would be rich enough to retire for the rest of their lives, for her father had never believed in banks.

Becky fell to her knees and placed her fingernails beneath the edges of one of the boards and pried it up, then another and another, until she was finally able to see into the metal container that her father had built there to use as a safe.

She went limp with relief when she discovered that the money had not been disturbed. It was still there in snug, neat stacks. The musty smell of the money rose from the safe and wafted to her nose. It was familiar to her since she had been responsible these last months for adding to the stacks as money came in.

Heaving a sigh, she replaced the floor boards, then got slowly to her feet.

Again she looked around the room. All visible signs of her father were gone forever—the valuable paintings and books, even his prized collection of pipes that he had collected as he traveled around the world when she was away at boarding school.

She moved to the dining room. Her heart sank, and she felt sick to her stomach when she found that the china and silver had also been stolen. They were more of a loss to her than the furniture. They had been in the family for generations.

Anger replaced her shock. She had to do her best to find out who the thieves were. And the only way to do that was to go into town and make a call on Sheriff Dolson. If anyone could track down a thief, he could do it. He was known wide and far as the best sheriff in the area. A decorated hero from the Civil War, he was admired by everyone.

Except for Becky. To her he was an aggravation. He had pestered her to death in his attempts to court her. She had never liked his gruff ways, nor did she wish to marry a man who came face to face with danger every day. She had lost enough loved ones during her lifetime. She most certainly did not wish to become a widow.

Becky went back upstairs to her room. She swung the doors of her chiffrobe open, then placed her hands on her hips, laughing bitterly. At least they had not taken her clothes!

Determined to find those responsible for having

turned her life upside down, Becky hurried into a riding skirt and white cotton blouse. After tying her long golden hair back with a ribbon, she hurried down the stairs.

She ran past the horse and buggy to the stable and grabbed a horse from a stall. She led it outside, then quickly saddled it.

"Let's go, boy," Becky said as she swung herself into the saddle. She nudged the steed's flanks with her heels and urged the horse into a gallop up the long, narrow drive.

She rode hard until she reached the outskirts of Saint Louis. Riding as skillfully as a man, she guided her horse through the heavy traffic of the city, then stopped when she reached the city jail.

After securing her reins to a hitching rail, she strode into the sheriff's office. She cringed when he stared back at her as he always did, as though mentally undressing her.

"What brings you here so soon after your father's funeral?" Sheriff Ted Dolson asked, rising from the chair behind his cluttered desk.

Becky took a step away from him as he sauntered from behind his desk, a pistol hanging at each of his hips. He was a tall and lanky man. His rusty-colored hair was thick, as was his bushy mustache.

"Ted, while I was at the funeral, someone came and took everything from my house," Becky said, her eyes anxious, her heart pounding. "How could anyone be so crude and heartless? The thieves had to know where I was. Can you imagine anyone being this low-down? To rob someone whose father was being buried?"

"Yup, seems I can," Sheriff Dolson grumbled. He walked past Becky and lifted a pot of coffee from the top of his potbellied stove. He poured two cups, then turned and offered one to Becky.

"No thanks, Ted," she said, stiffening. "I didn't come here for a social call. Didn't you hear what I said? I was robbed. Everything is gone. Everything!"

"Doesn't surprise me none," Sheriff Dolson said, then took a sip of coffee and set the cup aside on a table. "I told your father more than once that your house is too isolated. It's a perfect place for such a crime. Who would see a wagon coming to take the loot away? Nobody."

"Where's the respect?" Becky said, her voice breaking.

"Thieves don't think 'respect,'" Dolson said. His eyes locked with hers. "Becky, you shouldn't stay out there all alone. Move into town. I'll find you a place. Marry me."

"Marry you?" Becky stammered, eyes wide. "Ted, this is a crazy time to be talking about marriage. Anyhow, I told you before. I don't have any intention of marrying anyone now, perhaps *never*. I'm afraid I'd just be setting myself up for another hurt. First my brother disappears, my stepmother dies, and now my father." She swallowed hard. "When you allow yourself to love someone as I have loved my family, and then lose them all, the hurt is just awful. I fear it will never go away."

"In time it will," Dolson said. "Becky, I won't rush you. But I do wish you'd consider movin' into town."

"I have," Becky said softly, then turned quick eyes up at him. "But not because you suggested it. I don't want to live in that house. It is too full of hurtful memories. That's the only reason, Ted. It has nothing to do with you, or anyone else, for that matter. I've my life to get on with. And I intend to do it alone."

"Gets mighty lonely livin' alone," Ted said, frowning at her.

"It seems I was born lonely," Becky said wistfully, her thoughts going to a mother she had never seen. So often during the lonely hours of night, she had tried to envision her mother being with her. She would always end up feeling guilty, thinking that perhaps she had caused her mother's death. Her mother *had* died shortly after giving birth to Becky.

Becky gasped and her eyes fixed on a wanted poster on the wall behind Sheriff Dolson. She paled and felt lightheaded when she recognized the face. She had no doubt that the man pictured on the poster was her brother, Edward! He had gone south during the war to fight for the Confederacy since their earlier lives had been spent in the Carolinas. He would now be twenty-nine. She had never heard from him since he left, and thought he might have died at the hands of the Yankees. But deep inside herself, she had never let go of the hope that he might somehow be alive!

Now that she knew that he was, she was jubilant, but numb to realize that he was a wanted man. Her brother had always been a gentle, caring man. To be an outlaw, a man had to be hardened and heartless!

"Ted, it's *Edward*," she cried, her pulse racing. "Ted, don't you see? The man on that poster is my brother!"

When he didn't respond, but lowered his gaze to the floor, a sudden rage engulfed Becky. "Ted, you *knew* it was Edward," she said, her voice tight. She glowered at him as he turned his eyes slowly up at her. "Ted, I demand to know why you didn't inform me when you received this poster. You *had* to know that it was Edward's picture. You were his best friend. How could you not have told me that he was alive? How long *have* you known? You even kept this from my father."

"In *my* eyes, Edward was dead the minute he went south to fight for the rebel cause," Sheriff Dolson finally said, his face furrowed into a deep frown. "He was a traitor. And now he's an outlaw. Twice he is a traitor to his country. Why should you even care about him? I know your father would never have wanted to hear about a son who is a hardened outlaw."

Her brother was an outlaw, Becky thought, cold inside at the very word. Had Edward actually killed men and women in cold blood?

She brushed those thoughts from her mind and studied the poster again. It stated that he had last been seen robbing trains and stagecoaches in the Wyoming Territory.

"Wyoming?" Becky said, arching an eyebrow. She turned to the sheriff. "Why did you receive a wanted poster if my brother's activities are mainly in the Wyoming Territory?"

She found it very hard to talk about her brother

this way. Discussion lent reality to the horrible realization that Edward was a wanted man.

Still, she could not help wanting to find out everything that she could about her brother's new way of life. Nothing would change the fact that he *was* her brother. He had been the sort of big brother any young girl would want. When he had left to fight for the southern cause, a piece of her heart had gone with him.

"Posters are sent far and wide for the most wanted criminals, as they are generally on the run," Sheriff Dolson said nonchalantly. "Your brother must be a real hard case, or I wouldn't have received a poster on him."

"I'll never believe it," Becky said, raising her chin. "Not *my* brother."

"You are the most stubborn, bull-headed woman I've ever run across," Dolson said as he slouched down into his chair. He flung a hand in the direction of the poster. "There it is, plain as day about Edward, and you still don't believe it. What's a man to do?"

"I know what *I'm* going to do," Becky said. Not folding under his glower, she placed her hands on her hips. "I'm going to go and look for my brother. And by damn, I won't stop looking until I've found him."

"You don't have a chance in hell of findin' him," Dolson growled.

"I *will* find him," Becky stormed.

"Okay, say that you *do*," he said, laughing beneath his breath. "What will you do with him? He's a criminal. A lowdown, stinking criminal."

"I plan to bring him to his senses," Becky said, her voice breaking under the sheriff's sarcastic smile. "*And* I will bring him back home with me."

She took a bold step forward and yanked the poster from the wall. At her action, Sheriff Dolson pushed himself quickly from his chair.

"What the hell do you think you're doin'?" he shouted. He reached for the poster. "Give it back to me."

"So that the whole city of Saint Louis can know about my brother?" Becky said, holding the poster behind her so that the sheriff couldn't get it away from her. "Never, Ted. And if you would allow yourself to stop and remember the good times you had with my brother, and recall how kind he was, you'd not be so anxious to display this damn wanted poster of him on your wall, either."

"He's getting his just desserts, that's all," Dolson grumbled. "And you're askin' for trouble, Becky, with your fool-dang notions of going to the Wyoming Territory."

"Ted, I'm *going*," Becky said. She gave him one last stare before she rushed from the jail.

When she reached her horse and swung herself into the saddle, the poster held tightly in one hand, she collapsed in tears. She had been strong with the sheriff, but that had only been a front. Knowing about her brother had knocked the spirit clean out of her.

Her brother was a wanted outlaw!

Oh, Lord, how could she live with the knowledge?

Yet he *was* alive. She was glad for that at least.

The thought of seeing him again would get her through the next days, weeks, and months while searching for him. She would pack a few things and leave on the next steamboat up the Missouri, then take the Union Pacific Railroad from Omaha to Cheyenne. Her destination was Fort Laramie on the Platte River. The posters had been sent from Fort Laramie. That had to mean that her brother was somewhere in that vicinity.

As she wheeled her horse around and rode in the direction of her home, a fearful thought came to her. The land on which Fort Laramie had been built was originally Cheyenne land.

Her eyes lit with fire. "Let the Cheyenne just try and stop me," she whispered to herself. "Nothing will keep me from searching for my brother! Nothing!"

Chapter Three

Light cascaded over the land outside the railroad car. Becky watched from the train window, mesmerized by the scenery that stretched out before her. Though weary from the long boat and train ride, she could relax now and enjoy the landscape that so differed from her homeland of Missouri. She had not far to go now before she would arrive at Fort Laramie.

She leaned closer to the window and stared up at vultures that rode the warm air currents rising from the land. Her gaze shifted as a prairie falcon came into view, a silhouette of grace and speed as it soared across the sky.

Her eyes traveled elsewhere, to a lone deer that romped away from the noise of the train that rumbled along its iron tracks.

Her golden hair cascaded across her shoulders

and down the back of her pale blue silk dress as again she looked heavenward. Everything was so peaceful. She felt a desire to climb, to touch the sky.

But the memory of why she had traveled this far, to a strange land where Indians were a constant threat and where outlaws would cut a stranger's throat as soon as look at him, made her heave a deep sigh and stare blankly down at the bonnet that rested on her lap.

Her brother Edward was the only reason she had uprooted herself from her life in Saint Louis.

"Penny for your thoughts," a deep, masculine voice suddenly said.

Becky looked quickly over at the owner of the voice as he sat down on the seat beside her. It was obvious that he was a man of wealth. A diamond stickpin glistened from the folds of his ascot. The dark suit that fitted him well was expensive. His brown hair and mustache had been groomed to perfection. Yet the glitter in his pale blue eyes as he looked at her unnerved her. It was the look of someone who knew well the art of flirting.

Not wanting conversation with anyone at this time, especially a smooth-talking stranger, Becky only smiled weakly at him, then looked out the window again.

She had only one thing on her mind—Edward. She had to mentally prepare herself for what she might endure in the upcoming weeks, perhaps months, while trying to find him.

He was an outlaw, she thought, still finding it hard to believe that Edward had taken the unlawful road of life.

"I'm sorry, sir," she finally said, forced to speak when the stranger persisted in trying to catch her attention. "I didn't quite hear what you said."

"I said I'll gladly give you a penny for your thoughts," Thad Patrick said, smiling ruefully at her beneath his thin mustache. "You look so serious. Don't you realize that you're on a most magnificent train? You should be enjoying it. You look as though you are headed for a funeral."

Becky's spine stiffened and she paled.

Thad's smile waned. He leaned toward Becky. "Did I speak out of turn, ma'am?" he said apologetically. "I hope you *aren't* headed for a funeral."

Becky shifted uneasily in her seat. She didn't like being reminded of having just recently buried her father. And she feared the fate of her brother. Outlaws were surely gunned down every day in this uncivilized Wyoming Territory.

"Sir, why don't you just return to your seat and leave me be?" Becky said, casting him an annoyed frown. "I will soon be arriving at my destination. I am sure you will be also arriving at yours."

Becky's fingers tightened on the rim of her bonnet when he gave no indication of leaving.

"My name is Thad Patrick," he said, offering a gloved hand her way. "It would be a great pleasure to know yours."

"Becky," she said, knowing that she had no choice but to be at least this courteous to him. "Becky Veach."

She most deliberately looked away from him to stare from the window again, to prove her lack of interest in him.

He lowered his hand and spread his long, slender gloved fingers on the expensive wool fabric of his breeches. "Ma'am, I am a major stockholder of this great Union Pacific Railroad on which you make your travel today," Thad said, drawing Becky's eyes quickly his way again. "Do you see this train? You might say that it is mine."

He showed the pride of an owner as his gaze took in the design of the passenger car. "Did you ever see anything as grand as this?" he boasted, then went over the fine points of the car. "Do you see the dazzling fittings? The sea-green velvet curtains? The shining brass? The wood gleams as darkly brilliant as the surface of a pool of oil."

Becky gazed upward at places in the ceiling, finding it hard not to admire the frescoes in olive and silver. But she wasn't about to say anything to lead him into further conversation. She only nodded, then looked from the window again.

"Traveling in the grandeur of such a train is much better than enduring others that are cramped and dusty," Thad continued to brag. "It is a pleasant diversion from the monotony of the scenery one tires of so quickly here in the Wyoming Territory."

Becky cast him an agitated stare. "I find the scenery outside quite breathtaking," she said, breaking her silence.

Thad smiled slyly at her. "So she does talk, does she?" he said, chuckling beneath his breath. His gaze swept slowly over her, stopping momentarily at her generous breasts that pressed against the fabric of her silk dress.

Becky blushed and turned her eyes away from

him again, knowing that to totally ignore him was the only way to get him to leave her alone. She did not need an arrogant man such as he to complicate her life at this time. His sort always rankled her. If she were ever to fall in love, it would be with a man who was gentle and caring, whose every thought was not on himself.

"Ah, yes, once I put my lips to the intoxication of rail, I was a slave to it for life," Thad said. "Even when I was a mere child, I felt the craving in my bed at night when I heard the long whistle of trains going places. I love the lickety-split and the bustle of train travel."

Thad leaned closer to Becky, even though she kept her eyes glued on the scenery outside, obviously ignoring him. "Of course you have been in the diner car," Thad persisted. "We try to keep the prices reasonable. We charge only a dollar for a meal."

Thad paused, then continued talking, more to himself than Becky, for she heard nothing else that he said. Her eyes were wide when she thought that she caught sight of Indians riding on horseback on the far horizon.

When she finally realized that it was only a herd of buffalo rumbling their way along the land, she sighed with relief.

She turned slow eyes to the seat next to her, smiling when she discovered that it was empty.

When she felt someone staring at her, she looked across the aisle and found Thad glaring at her with angry eyes.

She looked quickly away and again watched the land moving by outside her as the great train whirled onward with dignity of motion.

Chapter Four

Riding a sorrel horse through the heart of Shaiyena Country, the Cheyenne Homeland, and dressed in only a breechcloth and moccasins, Blazing Eagle was browsing the countryside with several of his warriors. He was now twenty-nine and had been named chief of the Fox clan of Cheyenne after the death of his beloved adopted father, Black Thunder.

Remaining silent and alert, using all of his senses, he constantly scanned the horizon, sniffed the air, and listened to every sound while watching for the iron trail of the tracks that the pale-skinned white men had run through The Cheyennes' hunting ground.

White men had even built their log lodges and carved roads through their sacred country.

Although resenting the white man's presence,

under Blazing Eagle's leadership the Cheyenne had generally not interfered in the settlers' lives. Blazing Eagle had spoken often to his people, saying there was no honor in fighting the white man. It disrupted the harmony of the Cheyennes' world and it would bring them only pain.

As for Blazing Eagle, enough pain had been inflicted on him when his mother, father, and all of the people of his village had been slain all those years ago, and he had been the only survivor.

Blazing Eagle had not yet recalled what had happened on the day of the massacre when he was but nine years of age. He only knew about it from those who had gone and seen the aftermath of the tragedy. He was content with his blank memory. He feared that if he ever remembered, it might be too horrible to live with.

Not ever wanting the past repeated, when an entire band of Cheyenne had been wiped from the face of the earth, Chief Blazing Eagle was a peacemaker. He was known wide and far as being generous in disposition, liberal in temper, deliberate in making up his mind, and a man of good judgment.

A good chief, he gave his whole heart and whole mind to the work of helping his people.

He was a very brave man. He had captured many spotted horses from other tribes.

But although honest, generous, and tender-hearted, when occasion demanded, he could be stern, severe, and inflexible of purpose.

Such a man commanded general respect and admiration, and he got it.

Fish Hawk, Blazing Eagle's best friend from childhood, sidled his steed closer to Blazing Eagle's. "Do you see it?" he said, bringing Blazing Eagle's thoughts back to the present. "Up ahead, Blazing Eagle. Four white men. They are working on the iron path."

"They make it easy for the monstrosity they call a train to move farther onto our land," Blazing Eagle said. He drew his steed to a shimmering halt as he stared down at the railroad tracks from a slight butte.

Fish Hawk drew rein beside Blazing Eagle, the other warriors edging close on both sides. Some lagged behind purposely, to keep watch behind them for any interlopers into their pleasant, carefree ride this day.

With a hand, Fish Hawk shielded his eyes from the sun and watched the white men below as they hammered at the rails, then lifted new ties in place.

Then his eyebrows forked as the white men boarded a small sort of car and began pumping it strangely, making it move on the tracks.

"Do you see . . . ?" Fish Hawk said. Blazing Eagle interrupted him.

"*Ne-hyo*, yes, I see the white men on what they call a handcar," Blazing Eagle said, then chuckled. "They are not wise in how they choose to ride across our land. The hand car moves slowly. They would do much better on a horse."

"They cannot run from us should we attack," Fish Hawk said, drawing Blazing Eagle's eyes to his. "We can go in all directions on our proud steeds. They can go only backwards or forwards.

Shall we prove our ability to them? Shall we stop them?"

"I do not wish to harm them," Blazing Eagle said solemnly, not wanting to cause trouble between his people and the white pony soldiers at Fort Laramie. His village lay too close to the fort, on the North Platte River.

His eyes gleamed into Fish Hawk's. "But we *can* have some fun at their expense," he said, his eyes smiling.

"And how can we do that without bringing harm to them or our warriors?" Fish Hawk said, looking around at the many warriors who were showing their restlessness as they waited in their saddles.

Blazing Eagle's mouth became set in a straight, determined slit, his dark eyes filled with a sudden contempt at the thought of the white eyes whose only God was gold. "We will wreck their car, that is all," he said. He nodded toward Fish Hawk, then looked at his men. "Come! Follow me! Do as I do!"

He snapped his reins and nudged his horse in the flanks with his heels. His horse rode in a hard gallop down the slope of land, through scattered stands of scrub pine and cedar, mule deer scattering on either side. They left the spotted bighorn sheep and cougar behind them in the higher elevations.

The sun and wind hot on his face, Blazing Eagle yanked his reins and sent his steed toward the shine of the tracks a short distance away. His eyes filled with amusement. His heart pounded at the thought of humiliating the white men on the handcar. He wheeled his horse to a stop beside the tracks and quickly dismounted.

His men, following his lead, used their horse ropes to drag big logs across the tracks and lash them down. They pulled up several spikes and with much effort pried loose a small portion of the tracks, then removed several ties and laid them aside.

Standing chest-deep in prairie dock, Blazing Eagle turned to his warriors. "The shining rails have probed into the heart of our land," he said, firming his jaw. "They have brought secrets from the other world beyond, where whites know nothing of the red man. We care not for their ways, nor do they ours. Let us show them now in this small way how little we think of them."

Fish Hawk moved to Blazing Eagle's side. "I shall ride only a short distance with several of our brothers, then hide behind brush," he said, his eyes dancing with excitement. "We shall rush out and frighten the white men to distract them from seeing what we have done to their demon tracks."

Fish Hawk gestured with a hand toward the sky. "When they collide with the logs, they will soon find themselves flying through the air like birds," he said, laughing at the very thought of it.

The other warriors laughed, then turned their eyes back to Blazing Eagle when he spoke.

"Your mind travels the path of mine, for that was my plan also," Blazing Eagle said, resting a hand on Fish Hawk's bare shoulder. "I shall go ahead with the rest of the warriors and taunt the men."

His waist-length hair blowing in the hot breeze, his shoulders bare and gleaming beneath the pounding rays of the sun, Blazing Eagle swung himself into his saddle.

After everyone was mounted, he lifted a fist and gave a whoop. "Let us ride!" he cried. "Let us give the white men something to tell their grandchildren when their hair is white!"

Laughing, the Cheyenne warriors rode off toward the advancing handcar. When they finally reached it, and Blazing Eagle slipped his rifle from its gunboot at the side of the horse, so did the others. Firing their firearms into the air, never intending to actually shoot anyone, they rode beside the handcar.

They whooped and hollered as they chased the handcar down the tracks, and the white men showed their fright by how their faces paled and their eyes became wild and wide.

"Pale faces, your horse is slow!" Blazing Eagle shouted in the English that he had been taught by his adopted father. The English language was required to live among those who spoke it well—the cunning, trickster white men! Now that Blazing Eagle was chief, he had ordered his people to practice the language by using it most of the time, even while speaking among themselves. Only during holy times were they required to speak in the Cheyenne tongue.

Blazing Eagle laughed as he again fired his rifle in the air. "If you white men do not go faster," he shouted, "the Cheyenne steeds will trample you!"

"Get out of here!" one of the white men shouted back at Blazing Eagle. "Leave us alone!"

"It is you who trespass on the land of the red

man!" Blazing Eagle shouted back at him. "It is you who must get accustomed to whatever the red man chooses to do to you."

"This land belongs to the railroad, not the Indians!" the man shouted back, then screamed with fright when Fish Hawk and his companions jumped out and began riding alongside the handcar, whooping at them as they waved their rifles in the air.

Frenzied by all that was happening and what they saw as a threat in the Cheyennes' behavior, the railroad men did not see the logs in time. They collided. Their handcar tipped over, tossing the four men in all directions.

Yelping, the men rushed to their feet and ran away from the Cheyenne. They soon became hidden in the tall, swaying grasses that spread out on both sides of the tracks.

Laughing throatily, Blazing Eagle slipped his rifle back into his gunboot. Content enough for the fun they had enjoyed at the expense of the white men, and feeling they had not done all that much harm, he waved at his men to follow him as he rode onward.

Still following the path of the tracks, he rode past the wreckage. Aware of some sort of hum in the tracks, he dismounted and leaned an ear against them.

He turned smiling eyes up at Fish Hawk. "An iron horse draws near," he said.

He mounted his horse and rode away from the tracks for a short distance, then kept them in sight as they rode onward, his mind whirling with a plan.

Chapter Five

Through the air came the haunting whistle of the train. Blazing Eagle wheeled his sorrel to a stop and looked skyward. Billows of smoke momentarily turned the color of the sky to inky black.

His gaze shifted and he watched as the train came into sight, whirling onward along tracks that glistened in the powerful heat of the afternoon.

A slow smile tugged at his lips as he envisioned the train becoming derailed when it reached the tracks that he and his warriors had only moments ago rendered useless.

"We have always wanted to see the insides of a train, have we not?" Fish Hawk said as he sidled his horse closer to Blazing Eagle's.

"*Ne-hyo*, and today our curiosity will be satisfied," Blazing Eagle said, smiling at his friend.

"Do you think that it would be best to distract

those white people who ride the black iron demon so they will not notice the ruined tracks ahead?" Fish Hawk said, his fingers clenched tight to his rifle.

"*Ne-hyo*, but we must make special efforts not to harm anyone," Blazing Eagle said, watching the trail of the steam engine's smoke as it wafted toward him on the breeze. "Never have the pony soldiers imprisoned us for only taunting their people. They want no trouble from us as we wish none from them."

"They have tormented our people enough times by their interference," Fish Hawk grumbled. His eyes squinted angrily as he mentally measured the space between the train and where the tracks lay strewn about.

"That is so," Blazing Eagle said, his voice tight. He had always wondered if the pony soldiers were responsible for the slaughter left behind at his true village those many moons ago.

Or had it been white men who wore no uniforms, who instead wore clothes of those who came from far away to build their homes where they were not wanted?

"You are deep in thought again, my friend," Fish Hawk said, his gaze now on Blazing Eagle. "You think of unpleasant things always when you see the presence of white eyes on Shaiyena country. It is because of your childhood loss."

"Again you know my mind," Blazing Eagle said, turning a smile Fish Hawk's way. He leaned over and clasped a hand on his friend's muscled shoulder. "True friends can see deeply into each other's souls. That is the way it is between us, Fish Hawk. May it always be so."

Fish Hawk nodded. He squared his shoulders proudly to know that he was Blazing Eagle's best friend. A bond had formed between them many years ago after Blazing Eagle had been brought into Fish Hawk's life following the massacre of Blazing Eagle's people. Fish Hawk had lent Blazing Eagle his heart as a friend then, and now they were bonded as though they were brothers.

"But let us talk no more of friendship when unbridled excitement awaits us," Blazing Eagle said, yanking his rifle from his gunboot. He gazed over his shoulder at his men. "Let us give chase! After the iron horse monstrosity can go no farther, we shall make the white people wait outside in the heat while we enter the strange domain they call a train."

Blazing Eagle looked from man to man, pausing long enough to hold his eyes steady with each of them. "But remember well, my brothers, we do not kill unless forced to," he said sternly. "We do not do this today to leave death scattered along the ground as food for vultures. We do this for amusement only!"

His warriors responded by nodding. He smiled, his heart warmed by the willingness of his men to follow his every whim, fill his every desire. But they knew that he would tolerate no less from them. He was a powerful leader.

Yet his heart was big and filled with love for all of his people.

The lonely echo of the train whistle drew Blazing

Eagle's eyes around. He followed the train's movements as it came closer and closer. His heart beat with excitement. His eyes gleamed as he raised his rifle in the air and led his warriors to meet the train's approach.

They spread out and scattered along the full length of the train on each side. Hollering and whooping, they rode beside the two passenger cars, one freight car, and the smoke-spewing engine. The spanking new, bright-red caboose stood out from the rest like a brilliant sunset.

Blazing Eagle winced and ducked when one of the men in the engine shot at him while shouting obscenities at him.

When neither Blazing Eagle nor his warriors fired back, only showing the threat of their rifles as they waved them in the air, the train's crew ceased firing at them.

But the white men continued to shout and jeer at the Cheyenne. They laughed boisterously when the engine went full throttle and soon left Blazing Eagle and his warriors behind.

Blazing Eagle was not going to be discouraged this easily. He sank his moccasined heels into the flanks of his steed. He slapped his reins.

Soon he and his warrior caught up with the caboose of the train. More white men were there to shout and laugh at the Cheyenne, making fun of their attempt to keep up with the train.

Proving the mighty strength of his steed, Blazing Eagle leaned low over his sorrel and rode past the caboose.

He looked over his shoulder as his warriors kept up behind him.

Soon they reached the engine of the train and rode beside it at a hard gallop. They whooped again, to keep the white men's attention from the wrecked track that lay ahead of them. Blazing Eagle had his heart set on seeing the inside of this monstrosity, perhaps to see what lured white men into it. To Blazing Eagle, it was a smoking demon that ate up land that belonged to the Cheyenne!

Succeeding at distracting the white men, Blazing Eagle looked past the train and saw that the wreckage of the tracks now lay only a short distance away.

Not wanting to take the chance that he or his warriors would be crushed, should the train topple over on its side, he shouted the command that led his men away from it.

They stopped and watched with laughter in their throats as the train grew closer and closer to the scattered ties.

A loud blast of the train's whistle and the sound of screeching brakes proved that the white men had finally seen what lay ahead, but they were too late to do anything about it.

A mighty rumble and splintering sounds filled the air as the engine plowed into the logs, railroad ties, and uprooted tracks. The engine swayed dangerously from side to side for a moment, the cars behind it slowly, precariously rocking from one side to the other.

Soon the entire train came to a trembling halt in clouds of steam, leaving a momentary strained silence in its wake.

"Surround the train!" Blazing Eagle then

shouted as people came stumbling from the train. "Disarm those who carry weapons!"

In a matter of moments, everyone—men, women and children alike—had left the train and stood together, weaponless, their eyes wide with fear.

Scarcely breathing, Becky watched the Indians as they dismounted their horses. With astute perception, she singled out the leader. She could not help but notice his pleasing features and how tall and broad-shouldered he was.

Surely he was Cheyenne, she thought to herself. The Cheyenne warriors had earned the name "beautiful people" among their red brothers. And never had she seen anyone as handsome as this warrior.

While attending school in Saint Louis, she had studied Indian culture, fascinated by it. She knew that eagle feathers were the emblem, or insignia, of a chief.

This man who so fascinated her wore an eagle feather. And she was glad that the feather was worn straight up from the back of his head, instead of through the back lock of his hair, from left to right.

Worn straight up signified peace.

Worn through the back lock of hair, from left to right, meant war.

To her relief, it seemed that these warriors were only out for fun today, not a massacre.

With building interest in the one warrior who appeared to be the leader, her gaze followed him. He was somber, yet intriguing as he tossed out one command after another, the others quickly obeying.

When this warrior went inside the train, Becky strained her neck to get another glimpse of him at the windows as he slowly passed through one of the passenger cars. She sighed when he stepped out of sight.

The sun was scorching hot as it beat down on Becky's bare head. Her bonnet had been tossed from her lap into the aisle of the train upon impact. She had not worried about that simple loss when she had seen the warriors lining up alongside the train. It was then that she realized that they had caused the train's derailment.

She became unnerved when she looked slowly around her and saw the warriors standing guard, a rifle aimed threateningly at the innocent victims of the derailment. Although she had heard that it was safe enough to travel on the train through the heart of Shaiyena country, she could not help but be frightened to have come face to face with Indians.

Yet she did prefer them over a gang of outlaws. She had heard too many tales of the heartless behavior of outlaws toward travelers.

It ate at her heart to think that her very own brother was among those who were considered the most lethally dangerous to all of mankind, white *and* red-skinned.

Her face throbbing from the heat, perspiration trickling down her brow, Becky shuffled her feet nervously as she waited to see what the Indians had planned for the passengers after they had finished with the train.

The firearms aimed at her, the dark eyes of the Indian warriors glaring at her and her traveling companions, sent chills up and down Becky's spine.

"I won't let anything happen to you," Thad whispered as he edged closer to Becky. "I have a derringer hidden in my inner coat pocket. I'm waiting until I can catch the savages off guard. Then I'm going to take my derringer and—"

Becky paled as she looked quickly over at him. "If you try anything with that small thing, you'll get us all killed," she whispered back, harshly interrupting him. "Don't be foolish. You are no longer on your train. You are no longer in charge. Just let it be. I'm not quite ready to die."

"Quiet!" one of the warriors shouted in plain enough English as he glared from Becky to Thad. "Do not speak unless ordered to!"

Becky swallowed hard, then lifted her chin defiantly.

Trembling, Thad inched away from her.

When Blazing Eagle heard Wind Walker, one of his most devoted warriors, shout something at the white people outside the train, he hurried to an open window and stared from it.

His gaze quickly locked on a beautiful white woman whom he had not noticed before in his eagerness to board the train. It was apparent that it was she who had drawn angry words from Wind Walker. He was glaring at the woman, whose confident tilt of her chin proved that she was brave in the face of what she surely saw as a dangerous encounter.

Blazing Eagle took the time to study the woman at length. She was a beauty with flashing green eyes and a creamy complexion. He was taken by her glimmering golden hair, her lithe body, the long skirt of her dress billowing about her shapely legs.

His gaze lingered on her swelling bosom, then he looked at her face again. His pulse raced at the thought of how soft her skin must be to the touch. He allowed a moment to think about how it might be to kiss her shapely lips, how it might be to taste her with his tongue.

"Blazing Eagle, come and see what we found in the travel box next to this one," Fish Hawk said, breathless as he ran into the car. "We have already removed all sorts of supplies from the other travel boxes. We have maple sugar, ginghams, and beads. But in the next car we have found strange foods."

Blazing Eagle wrenched his eyes from the woman, yet still saw her in his mind's eye and felt her deeply within his soul as he followed Fish Hawk to the diner car.

When he stepped inside, he stopped and gazed in wonder at the food that lay on tables covered in white linen. He eyed a bowl of fruit, puzzled by most of it. He guardedly reached a hand toward a long yellow fruit. When he touched it, it felt smooth to his fingers.

His warriors watched as he picked it up and placed it to his lips. Without peeling it, he took a bite.

Finding the fruit bitter, curling his tongue, Blazing Eagle gagged and spat it from his mouth, dropping what was left on the floor.

Curiosity moved him onward, from plate to plate, to examine the food spread out on them. He enjoyed the buttered carrots, but spat out a bite of steak, finding it tasteless and unpleasant.

When he reached for a sweetbread and lifted it to his nose before taking a bite, he found no reason not to eat it. It had a pleasant aroma.

He consumed it in quick bites, the sweetness of it making him eat another.

Then he knew that he and his men had already overstayed their visit on the iron horse. Not wanting to be there if pony soldiers happened along and found the captives standing outside the train, Blazing Eagle rushed outside with his men and went to stand before the white men and women as his warriors loaded their horses with the belongings they had stolen.

Slowly, Blazing Eagle walked before the huddled, cowering people, their eyes showing their fear.

But when he stepped up to the beautiful woman, his heart once again jumped with a quick wonder at her loveliness, and he was taken anew by the impudent glare that she continued to give him.

When she spat at his feet, Blazing Eagle's powerful, buckskin-clad figure tensed. He stood straight and tall as a statue over her, his eyes aflame with anger.

Without further thought, he twined his fingers through her golden curls and yanked her face close to his.

Their eyes locked in silent battle.

Chapter Six

Becky was momentarily rendered speechless by how quickly the warrior had grabbed her by the hair. His eyes were like molten lava as he peered into hers. The anger was there, so intense that she could almost feel the heat of it as his breath brushed her cheeks and stirred the locks of her hair.

She felt that she must do something quickly. What if he was so angry that he went for the heavy Bowie knife that was thrust into a sheath at his waist? Was that even why he was holding her by the hair? Was he envisioning it waving from his scalp pole?

The thought weakened her knees. She could feel her stomach churning, yet she reached deep inside herself and found enough courage to speak in her own behalf. She must show him that she was not afraid of him.

In truth, at this moment she feared him so much, and her heart was pounding so hard that she felt dizzied by it.

"Let go of my hair, you—you—" She stopped herself just short of saying the word 'savage'. She suspected that word alone might cause the warrior to quickly end her life.

"You show no respect to Chief Blazing Eagle by spitting at his feet," he said. His throat was dry—not so much from anger now but from his fascination with this woman who did not seem at all threatened by his presence.

His eyes went to her hair, mystified by the sunshine that seemed to live in it. Yet he had seen golden hair on whites before—one in particular, whose outlaw ways had wreaked havoc on the lives of both the red man and white settlers. Too often blame was cast on the Cheyenne for what that savage outlaw had done!

Blazing Eagle's eyes were forever searching for this golden-haired outlaw. Although he never took white people's scalps, he *would* take that one, if given the chance. He would proudly hold it up for his people to see. With the death of that white man would come a measure of peace for the Cheyenne people.

Becky's eyes widened. She knew for certain now that this warrior was a powerful chief. She saw much about him that made her wish he did not have such contemptuous feelings toward her. His face was sculpted perfectly. His hair fell free to his waist, except for a band of otter fur at his brow which held it in place. He wore armlets of brass and copper wire and a necklace of elk teeth, while the other warriors wore deer teeth and fish-bone necklaces.

As Blazing Eagle relentlessly held her by the hair, Becky once again looked defiantly into his eyes. She was only vaguely aware that everyone was staring, waiting to see the outcome of this confrontation. She knew that Thad Patrick and the other men were cowards, or they would have stepped forward and demanded her release.

It was up to her, she thought bitterly, to fight her own battle.

"I showed you no respect?" she said tersely. "You came with your warriors and forced everyone from the train to stand in the hot sun. What else can you expect from us but loathing?"

She winced when he tightened his hold on her hair.

"You white eyes came and forced the Cheyenne to relinquish claim on much of their land, forcing us also to learn the dreaded language of the white man to survive among them. What can *you* expect?" Blazing Eagle said, his voice drawn. "Would you prefer to see the Cheyenne without honor, even though the Cheyenne walked upon this earth, drank from this river, and breathed from this sky before the white eyes ever set foot upon this land?"

"I don't see how your honor is threatened by the white man's presence in the Wyoming Territory. From what I have seen of this land, there is enough room for everyone," Becky said, then glared at him. "Turn me loose. Now! You are already in enough trouble for having derailed the train. Surely you know that the authorities at Fort Laramie will make you pay for this."

"The pony soldiers have done far worse to the Cheyenne," Blazing Eagle grumbled.

"I am certain you deserved no less from them," Becky spat out.

Blazing Eagle gazed down at her from his greater height, unable to stop himself from admiring her. He admired her courageous impudence. He liked a woman filled with fire, with daring. Such a woman could make love exciting.

Not liking where his thoughts had taken him and knowing that he must not waste time on such thoughts at such a time as this, he released his hold on her hair. He must flee this place where he and his warriors had perhaps gone farther than they should in their fun today.

"White woman, you let anger rule your tongue too much," he said, their eyes holding a moment longer.

Then he wrenched himself away from her and moved on down the line to gaze at the other white people. Their behavior was much different from that of the golden-haired woman. In their eyes they showed their fear of the Cheyenne.

And he felt that was good; that was important. The more whites who were frightened of the Cheyenne, the more might decide to return to the homes they left behind to come to Shaiyena country!

But he knew it was only a dream to believe that the land might belong to the Cheyenne again.

Progress, as the white eyes called it, had begun, and nothing could stop it.

Blazing Eagle stepped back and stood with his fellow warriors. His gaze again studied the huddled few, shifting slowly again to the golden-haired woman. She seemed misplaced there. She was not their kind. She had been born into a strong-willed family.

And he had to wonder what she was doing on the train alone. He knew that she traveled with no one, or she would be standing with them, protecting them with her fiery attitude.

"What do we do with the people now that our fun is over?" Fish Hawk whispered as he leaned close to Blazing Eagle.

"They are of no further use to us," Blazing Eagle said, needing no more time than that to speak his mind. "We shall leave them."

Blazing Eagle's gaze held on the golden-haired woman. His pulse raced at the thought of taking her captive. And who would be the wiser? No one on this train knew which tribe of Indians had rendered them helpless—except the golden-haired woman.

By the time the white men had repaired the tracks and continued their journey to Fort Laramie and the pony soldiers, then sent scouts out to find her, he might already have released her to freedom again. He hoped with every fiber of his being that once he knew her more deeply, his fascination would wane.

He wanted to have no feelings for a white woman.

In a sense, all whites but a select few would always be the enemy!

And from her head to her toes, she was white!

Shaking the thought of taking her with him from his mind, Blazing Eagle stalked to his horse and swung himself into his saddle.

After his warriors were saddled and ready to ride, he took another lingering look at the woman. His loins ached with a passion he had not felt for many moons. He had lost faith in women long ago.

His wife—she had caused it!

Lifting his reins, Blazing Eagle wheeled his horse around to ride away, then swung his steed back in Becky's direction. He rode toward her, stretched out an arm, and swept her onto his lap, then positioned her in his saddle in front of him.

Becky was so stunned by what he had done, that he was riding away with her, his arm locked possessively around her waist, before she realized what had happened. She was powerless to do anything.

Then it came to her in a flash. He was taking her captive. "Let me go, you beast!" she screamed. She grabbed at his arm and tried to release it. "You can't do this! Let me go!"

Blazing Eagle ignored her protests. He did not flinch or reveal to her the pain that her fingernails inflicted as she dug them into his arms in an attempt to get free. He looked past her fluttering golden hair, and sent his horse into a harder gallop.

He even ignored the stares from his warriors as they each came to his side to look at the woman, then silently questioned him with their eyes about this strange behavior of their chief.

Never had he taken a white captive back to his

village. Especially not to his lodge, where they expected her to be kept.

Yet none argued the point. Their chief's decisions were his own to make. He was their leader, and they trusted his judgment in all things.

Until now, they had never been given cause to doubt him.

Fish Hawk edged his horse closer to Blazing Eagle's as the other warriors dropped back and followed. "My friend, the woman is trouble," he said, feeling free to voice his opinions since he and Blazing Eagle's hearts beat as one, yet speaking in his own tongue so the woman would not understand.

"Perhaps," Blazing Eagle said, casting Fish Hawk a quick glance. "Perhaps *not*. We shall see."

"What are you saying about me?" Becky demanded. "If you think I come willingly with you, you should know I'm going to make your life miserable until I find a way to escape."

"Again you speak when you should be silent," Blazing Eagle said to her when she turned and glared at him. "Be quiet. Sit still. I will have it no other way."

Becky felt defeated. "Why are you doing this to me?" she cried softly. "I've done you no harm. Please release me. I've so much that needs to be done. Please free me."

"Silence, woman," Blazing Eagle said, his face shadowed with a frown. "I prefer you more when you are showing courage than when you are whining like a wounded pup."

Becky's mouth opened in a gasp. But he had achieved his goal. She couldn't find the right words to express how she truly felt at this moment. Fear was mingled with a strange sort of excitement that overwhelmed her.

Before her father's death, never in Becky's wildest dreams had she thought of traveling alone in a faraway land hundreds of miles from Saint Louis—or that she would be forced to fight such daring verbal battles.

Not until she had seen the wanted poster of her brother.

At that moment something snapped in her mind.

She recalled acting like a hellcat with the sheriff. She smiled at the thought of how she had put that coward Thad Patrick in his place when he had toyed with her on the train.

And now? To have been so bull-headedly arrogant to this Cheyenne chief? No, it was not like her at all.

But she liked the new person she had become. And she liked the excitement of facing all her tomorrows without flinching. Never again would she be that frail little thing who meekly attended all of Saint Louis's social functions along with the rest of those pinch-faced, boring women!

She settled in and waited to see where Blazing Eagle was taking her. Surely she would soon know what his true intentions were toward her. She reached a hand to her hair. It was blowing in the breeze and had become tangled.

She combed her fingers through it, still wondering if her hair might be the reason she was there. What if the Cheyenne were waiting until later to scalp her so that no white man or woman would be a witness?

She shuddered at the thought.

Having no choice but to submit to her situation—for now—Becky rested her arms on the Cheyenne's bronze, muscled arm. She stared at it, finding it hairless and smooth. She could even smell the fresh, out-doorish scent of him, liking the smell. She looked further, at the muscled thighs of his legs as they gripped his horse on each side.

Then she gave him a quick glance over her shoulder, glad that he did not notice her gazing at his beautiful copper face and his fathomless dark eyes. She could not help wanting to touch his face, to feel the smoothness. She saw no hint of whiskers and wondered how he could get such a close shave, for there seemed to be no hair at all on Blazing Eagle's face.

Blazing Eagle felt her eyes on him. His pulse raced as he shifted his gaze downward and found her looking at him. He had seen women look at him like that countless times. It was a look they wore when they were fascinated by him, when they wanted to share their blankets with him.

Many had wished to be with him in that way.

Only a few had he actually bedded.

Blushing when Blazing Eagle caught her admiring him, Becky quickly turned her eyes away from him. Her heart pounded as she forced her attentions elsewhere and looked instead at the scenery on all sides of her. Pronghorns dashed over the grassy knolls, their white rumps shining in the hazy afternoon brightness as though giving off their own light, independent of the sun. Sage sparrows were perched in trees. A mule deer doe and two fawns scrambled away.

After riding for some time, Blazing Eagle led his horse up an incline so steep that its hooves clicked on the rocks and it grunted as it humped up the steep slope.

When the land finally leveled off toward a ridge, Becky saw a valley down below where cottonwoods grew thick beside a river. Blazing Eagle rode down into the valley toward the river. When flat land was reached, he nudged his sorrel into a trot.

Becky's eyes followed a hawk with black-tipped wings that drifted in slow circles high in the sky. Then she went cold inside when she discovered camp guards—Cheyenne sentries stationed atop a knoll.

Her gaze shifted and she stiffened when tepees appeared. The village was pitched in a great horseshoe shape within a thick growth of willows. A large lodge stood near the banks of the river. Becky had to surmise this was the chief's lodge—this was Blazing Eagle's home.

She was impressed. She had learned enough in her studies of Indians to know that the size of a lodge was determined by the number of horses possessed by the lodge owner, by the owner's wealth and position in the community. If a man had but a few horses, his lodge was small. Becky recalled having read also that one hundred elk teeth were worth one good horse.

She noticed, as her studies had taught her, that all lodges were set up to face the rising sun each morning, the west always at their backs. At the top, two flaps served as windbreaks. From the fires in the center of the tepees smoke even now escaped through the opened smoke flaps of the lodges, joining the clouds in the heavens.

Strange vibrations shook Becky when she envisioned a lovely Cheyenne maiden kneeling beside Blazing Eagle's lodge fire, keeping a pot of food warmed for her husband's return.

That thought sent her eyes over her shoulder to look at him. Was there an eagerness in his eyes as he cast them homeward? Was he envisioning his woman beside his lodge fire? Was he longing to take her into his arms and kiss her?

Jealousy had never been a part of Becky's consciousness—until now. Even though she resented with all of her might this Indian's power over her, there was something more that she could not help but feel about him. She was drawn to him passionately. She wished that he might feel the same about her. She prayed that was why he had brought her to his village—not because he desired to have her golden hair on his scalp pole!

The sun was lowering along the horizon. The breeze was cooler when they rode into the village. Becky's heart raced when the children stopped playing and stared at her.

She looked guardedly around her and saw that the women paused at their work cleaning buffalo hides to gape openly at her.

She looked at the tepees, dying a slow death inside to see so many people filing from them to see what had caused the sudden silence in their village.

Becky was thankful when the people's fascination toward her was diverted as the warriors dismounted and began distributing to everyone what they had stolen from the train.

As Blazing Eagle lifted Becky from his horse, she noticed a young brave standing back only a few feet from Blazing Eagle, suspiciously watching her. Blazing Eagle motioned for the young brave to come to him. The boy quickly obeyed and soon took Blazing Eagle's horse's reins.

"This brave is my son. His name is Whistling Elk," Blazing Eagle said. "My son, this is . . ."

Blazing Eagle paused and forked an eyebrow as he turned to Becky. "White woman, no name has been mentioned between us."

"You did not have the decency to ask," Becky said, boldly lifting her chin. "You were so intent on taking me captive, nothing else mattered."

"Your name," Blazing Eagle said flatly, frowning at her.

"Becky," she said, taking an unsteady step away from him when she saw that she had angered him. "Becky Veach."

She gazed down at the boy, who stared up at her with silent wonder. This boy was Blazing Eagle's son. He appeared to be about eight years old. And to have a son, she thought, one must have a wife.

She did not like the realization that this Cheyenne chief's being married made her so jealous. She felt foolish to feel anything but fear of him.

She still did not know his reason for bringing her to his village, especially now—now that she knew he had a wife. His reason could not be a sexual one.

She lifted a hand to her hair when she once again saw Blazing Eagle's eyes shift to it. Oh, Lord, he was surely going to scalp her soon! That *had* to be his reason for abducting her! What else could it be? She was surely useless to him otherwise.

Whistling Elk continued to stare at Becky, her golden hair mesmerizing him. He wanted to know why his father had brought her home as his captive. Never had his father done this before!

Yet Whistling Elk knew not to question his father's judgment about anything. Blazing Eagle was his idol, and he prayed that one day, he too would be as powerful a Cheyenne leader as his father.

Whistling Elk said nothing more to his father. He yanked the horse's reins and walked away with the sorrel toward a cottonwood stockade, a crude corral of buffalo-hair rope.

But curiosity caused him to look over his shoulder at the woman. He stared, his lips parting as his father ushered her into his private lodge.

Becky scarcely breathed when Blazing Eagle led her to a cushion of blankets and pelts beside the central fire and shoved her down on them.

When he sat down across the fire from her, his eyes never leaving her, she was suddenly more fearful than ever. There was something new in his eyes. She could tell that he was relaxed in this situation where she was the captive, he the captor. His eyes showed intense approval of her. His jaw was no longer tight. There even seemed to be a slight smile on his lips.

She shifted her weight on the blankets. She nervously clasped her hands together and placed them on her lap. She could feel something happening between herself and the Cheyenne chief. It was the way she had felt from the beginning, from the moment she had first seen him, but had tried to fight as something foolish and unwise.

She could not deny this instant passion that she felt for this man.

It angered her to realize that she was unable to think past this passion, when she wished only to be angry with him for having interfered in her plans to find her brother.

And she feared where these feelings might take her and the Cheyenne chief.

Except, she reminded herself again, there was nothing truly to fear from him.

He had a wife already.

Her eyes now adjusted to the dim light from the central fire, Becky looked slowly around the interior of the tepee. When she saw no signs of a wife, she turned questioning eyes up at Blazing Eagle.

Slowly smiling, he gazed back at her.

Becky suddenly bolted to her feet. She turned to run, but he was there too quickly, his hand on her wrist, stopping her.

"Do not be foolish," he uttered threateningly.

Scarcely breathing, Becky gazed up at him, then slowly nodded.

Chapter Seven

Whistling Elk was Becky's reprieve. When he came into the lodge, his eyes wide and fearful at what his father was doing, Blazing Eagle saw his son's reaction and quickly released Becky's wrist.

Father and son sat down beside the fire. The yellow flames licked the logs and black smoke rose skyward through the smoke hole.

Becky glanced quickly toward the entrance flap, then at Blazing Eagle, thinking about escape again. Yet she knew that such thoughts were futile. Even if she *did* manage to leave this lodge, she would get no farther. Blazing Eagle would be there just as quickly as before to stop her.

Sighing resolutely, knowing that for now she had no other choice, Becky went quietly to the blanket upon which she had been forced to sit earlier and eased herself down onto it.

A strained silence filled the lodge.

Becky smiled weakly at Whistling Elk as he cast her a quick glance, but her smile faded when he turned his eyes back to the fire.

Not knowing what to expect next, wishing that Blazing Eagle would say something—anything—to break the silence, Becky's gaze shifted to the Cheyenne chief. He had brought her to his lodge, and now it seemed that he was at a loss as to what to do with her.

Still Blazing Eagle neither did nor said anything. His brow furrowed, he stared into the fire.

Becky jumped when he suddenly turned to his son. "Go and see that food is brought to us," he said, his voice soft, less a command from a chief than a request from a father.

In his voice, Becky heard gentleness and patience. This somewhat eased her fear of him, yet she realized that if Whistling Elk left, she would be totally alone with Blazing Eagle. Was this a ploy to get his son away from them long enough for Blazing Eagle to do as he pleased with her?

Whistling Elk scurried from the tepee. Becky swallowed hard and looked guardedly over at Blazing Eagle again. "All right," she said, her voice quavering when she had hoped to make it thick with sarcasm. "Your son is gone. What will you do with me? Kill me? Rape me? Scalp me? What?"

She swallowed hard again, fighting back this fear that crept higher and higher into her throat the longer she was forced to puzzle over why she was there.

"Just get it over with," she said, her voice breaking when he still said nothing to her. "Or . . . or let me go. Please let me get on with my life."

Becky winced when he turned his midnight-dark eyes suddenly her way.

"What brought you on the iron horse to Shaiyena country?" he said. "Where is your man? I have never seen a white woman traveling alone before."

"Perhaps I am not just any ordinary white woman," Becky blurted out, the words slipping across her lips without much thought. She was normally not so outspoken.

"It seems not," Blazing Eagle said, his lips tugging into a smile.

Surprised that he actually seemed to believe that what she had said was how she truly felt made Becky stare frustratedly at him. He even seemed to have found some humor in it.

She was surprised at herself. How could she feel comfortable enough to banter with Blazing Eagle? He was a powerful Cheyenne chief!

Feeling more confident as the moments passed that she was safe with him, Becky smiled weakly back at him. She was glad that, thus far, he made no move to harm her in his son's absence.

And she was glad that he spoke the white language so well. That had to mean that he had aligned himself with the white people enough to have learned their language.

Then surely he did not see all white people as his enemy. Perhaps *she* was, somehow, more to him than that. In his eyes now, as he gazed at her, she could see a softening, perhaps an understanding of why she chose not to answer his questions.

Becoming flustered by his continuing stare, Becky looked quickly away from him. Yet strange feelings were assailing her that she did not understand. Confusing to her as it was, he did not seem like a stranger at all to her. The longer she was with him, the more she felt as though she had known him forever.

In awe of her confidence, even though she was his captive, Blazing Eagle questioned her no more now to discover the secrets of her inner self. He had plenty of time before she would be reported missing. By then he should have all the answers that he was seeking, and perhaps even more. The longer he was with her, the more he fell into the trap of wanting her.

Her golden hair, her mysterious green eyes, her lips that he wished to claim as his, her courage in the face of what she surely considered danger— these things were making him more captive to her than she was to him!

And he would not believe that deep within her soul she was the sort that normally spoke with a spiteful tongue. Now was different. She had cause to. She was a captive. She had no idea what her future held for her. It was only natural that she should fight back with verbal assaults if her only weapon was her tongue.

Relieved that the Cheyenne chief did not force answers from her, Becky felt herself relaxing by degrees. She had heard him tell his son to go for food. Her stomach told her that it was time for her to eat. She hoped that Blazing Eagle would share his food with her. If he made her watch him and his son eat, offering her none, her stomach growling unmercifully, she would hate him with a passion!

Passion, she thought to herself, a strange thrill coursing through her veins as she recalled his muscled, bronze arm holding her possessively on his horse. Although she should hate him for having abducted her, her body and her thoughts responded in a much different way when she allowed her fear to waft into something more sensual.

To shake such thoughts from her mind, feeling foolish every time she thought of this Cheyenne chief in such a way when she should hate and resent him with every fiber of her being, Becky began slowly looking around her to see how he lived.

There were two beds. She remembered well her teachings in Indian culture and knew that the mattresses on the beds were formed of willow rods almost as thick as a man's forefinger, and strung on long lines of sinew. These were flexible and thus could be easily rolled up.

Mats loosely woven of a certain bulrush, known to the Cheyenne as *mo-um-stat*, were spread on the mattresses. Food was stored between the edges of the beds. There would be sacks of pounded meat, dried corn, dried roots, and fruit. In parfleches—the Cheyenne trunk—were ornaments, wooden bowls and dishes, and small horn spoons for eating.

She gazed more intensely at the beds. They had been made comfortable by coverings of well-tanned buffalo robes and other skins.

A shield hung on a tripod at the foot of one of the beds. She had not read anything about shields in her studies of Indians. She hoped to one day know the meaning of the objects that were attached to this one. To say the least, they were intriguing.

Again she looked from bed to bed. One was surely for the son. The other, larger one would be for the man and wife.

She stared at the larger one and fought off the vision, in her mind's eye, of Blazing Eagle making love to a beautiful Cheyenne princess.

She could almost feel his hands trail along the thigh of the woman as though it were his hands on *her* flesh. She could almost feel his fingers on her breasts, kneading them until they throbbed with pleasure, his mouth covering her lips in a passionate kiss . . .

Her pulse racing and her face flushed, Becky wrenched her eyes from the beds and gazed elsewhere. The fireplace had been dug in the form of a cross. The equal arms pointed in the four cardinal directions, and a fire burned softly in the center of the cross.

She looked around her and admired how beautifully the lodge had been painted.

"In a dream I was advised by a buffalo to paint my lodge in this manner." Blazing Eagle suddenly spoke having looked up in time to see her interest in the paintings. He had seen in her eyes a warm admiration of what she saw. This might give him reason for conversation, which he felt he needed to break the silence between them. Conversation would not be filled with questions that obviously troubled this woman's mind.

"A dream?" Becky said, interested.

"Many things come to the Cheyenne in dreams," Blazing Eagle said, his gaze moving past Becky to the paintings. "We follow their guidance."

When he began to explain the painting to Becky, she felt a strange sort of bond forming between them, a bond so natural that she felt her anger and her frustrations slowly ebbing away into nothingness.

For this moment she pretended to be as one with him, as if they were soul mates. The feeling gave her a wondrous sense of peace, of serenity, that moments ago she would have thought impossible.

She followed his gaze and looked once again at the paintings as he continued to explain them to her. A great snake-like animal was painted all about the lodge, the head on the left side of the door, the tail on the right.

Close above the body of the snake were paintings of many buffalo-cow heads. A night owl was painted on either side of the door. A crescent moon was over the door, and also at the back, just below the smoke hole, and over the pole to which the lodge was tied.

The explanation was drawn suddenly to a halt when a beautiful maiden entered the lodge, carrying a black pot. Becky's insides tightened and she scarcely breathed as she watched the beautiful girl hang the pot on a tripod over the lodge fire. An aroma wafted from it that made Becky realize how hungry she was.

But hunger was not on her mind as much as discovering who this maiden might be. Surely she was Blazing Eagle's wife!

Jealousy swept through Becky, leaving her shaken, when Blazing Eagle rose to his feet and gave the woman a warm hug. This jealousy was something new for Becky.

But never before had she had a reason for such feelings. She had never been intrigued by any man until now. Yet she knew that her interest was wasted on this man. He belonged to someone else.

"Waterfall, I have brought you something from my adventure today," Blazing Eagle said. "Stay. I must go and get it. I will bring it to you."

Whistling Elk gave Waterfall a hug, then stood arm in arm with her as they both stared down at Becky.

Waterfall asked Whistling Elk something in their own tongue. Her soft and lilting voice showed no jealousy toward Becky.

Whistling Elk frowned at Becky as he replied, then turned questioning eyes up at Waterfall.

Waterfall shrugged and took a step away from Whistling Elk and extended a hand toward Becky as though to touch her hair, then dropped her hand to her side as though she had thought it best not to.

"Such beautiful hair," she said instead, in hesitant English.

"Thank you," Becky said stiffly.

Realizing that the woman seemed more friendly toward her than angry, Becky was puzzled. How could any wife not be jealous of a strange woman being taken into her husband's lodge?

And what had Blazing Eagle meant when he had told Waterfall to stay? Surely she had been cooking the evening meal outside by the large communal fire and had returned now to stay as a wife should at her husband's side.

And why had Whistling Elk called his mother by her name instead of "Mother?"

Becky's thoughts were interrupted when Blazing Eagle came back into the lodge, a gold necklace dangling from his fingers. She surmised that he had taken this from someone's travel case on the train. She did not want to label him a thief, for he seemed not the sort to make a living by stealing.

Yet he *had* stolen many things today.

Including *her*.

"For my convenience, since I was traveling with a captive, Fish Hawk kept what I chose to take from the train," Blazing Eagle said, slipping the necklace over Waterfall's head. "Waterfall, is this not beautiful?"

Waterfall's eyes shone as she reached down and held the gold locket out for her eyes to feast upon. "I have never seen anything as beautiful," she sighed, then frowned up at Blazing Eagle. "But it does not truly belong to me. Blazing Eagle, you took this from a train?" She shifted wary eyes Becky's way. "You took *her*?"

Blazing Eagle shrugged. "*Ne-hyo*," he said. "Have not the whites over the years taken more than these from us? It is not even a fair exchange."

Waterfall once again admired the necklace, then turned wide eyes up at Blazing Eagle again. "You have never done this before," she murmured. "You never stole from a white man's strange iron horse. Always before you only stole horses from our Crow enemies."

"That is so," Blazing Eagle said, nodding.

Becky sucked in a wild breath when she heard a strange huskiness come into his voice as he looked at her. Her eyes locked with his, then she turned slow eyes to Waterfall.

Waterfall turned to Blazing Eagle and gave him a long, affectionate hug. She whispered something that Becky was certain meant "I love you," but of course such a private thing should not be heard by the white woman. "Thank you for bringing me such a wonderful gift." She stole a quick glance over her shoulder at Becky, then gazed into Blazing Eagle's eyes again and asked him a question.

"Time will tell," Blazing Eagle said mysteriously. He gave Waterfall another kiss on the cheek, then stepped aside as she hugged Whistling Elk, then left.

Becky wanted to ask where this woman was going, this *wife*. She wanted to ask why she did not share the evening meal with her husband and son. She wanted to ask if Waterfall would be returning to spend the night with her husband while a strange woman slept close by.

But her questions left her mind when Blazing Eagle handed her and Whistling Elk a wooden platter, then took a platter on which he would place his own food.

With a sharpened stick, Blazing Eagle took meat from the pot and placed portions of it on each of the platters. Then he dipped out corn and potatoes and placed them on the plates beside the meat.

Becky flinched when Waterfall came back into the lodge with a platter of fried bread, then left again just as quickly.

So hungry her mouth almost watered, Becky eyed the food questioningly.

"I see that something I placed on your platter is unfamiliar to you," Blazing Eagle said as he picked up a piece of the meat with his fingers. "Might it be the lungs of the buffalo? They have been cut open, dried, and roasted on the coals, then boiled with corn." He placed the meat in his mouth and heartily chewed it.

Becky winced at the mention of buffalo lungs. She had never eaten buffalo, let alone their *lungs*.

She gave Blazing Eagle a slow glance as he continued eating. She looked over at Whistling Elk. He was eating as though starved.

"Eat," Blazing Eagle said, lifting some meat toward Becky's lips. "It is nourishing. It will give you strength."

Strength for what? Becky wondered, her heart pounding at the thought of what he might be thinking. If his wife remained outside the lodge, would he take this white woman to his bed as a substitute wife for the night?

Her face turned crimson at the thought.

She gasped when he placed a piece of the meat against her lips, forcing them open. She sucked the meat inside her mouth and began chewing as his hand lowered slowly away from her lips.

"Soon you will enjoy the taste," Blazing Eagle said, smiling.

"Bread is also good," Whistling Elk said as he offered Becky a piece of fried bread. "Eat. You will see that Waterfall is a wonderful cook."

Cook? Becky wondered, her eyebrows forking.

She wanted to ask Whistling Elk if she wasn't more to him than a mere cook. Why did he still not call her "Mother?"

She took the bread, nodding her thanks since her mouth was still filled with the tough, tasteless meat. She eyed the fried bread. While studying Indian culture, her project for the class was to make fried bread at home and bring it to the class to share with them. She had made it of flour, baking powder, salt and water and had rolled it out like doughnuts, then had fried it in hot grease.

She was glad when she could fill her mouth with the bread to take the taste of the meat away.

Finally the meal was over, but then Becky had to face something much worse. Where was she going to sleep, and . . . and with *whom*?

She glanced over her shoulder as Whistling Elk went to his bed and stretched across it.

She looked over at Blazing Eagle, who looked proudly at his son and watched him until he was asleep.

Then he directed his attention Becky's way again. She stiffened inside. Her pulse raced. A strange melting inside warned her that something more was happening to her as the Cheyenne chief's eyes stayed on her as though he were seeing into her heart. Somehow he knew she was fascinated with him.

She jumped with alarm when he suddenly spoke.

"Again I ask you, why were you on the iron horse?" he said, his voice soft as though he spoke this way so that he would not disturb his son's sleep.

Becky still refused to answer him. Even *she* now wondered about her carelessness at having traveled alone.

Yet had she not, she would have never met this man—a man who held her very destiny in the palm of his hand. She no longer feared him, nor any choices that he might make for her. She wished to stay long enough with him to know many things about him and why he made her heart react so strangely when no other man before him had.

"You do not yet wish to open your heart to this Cheyenne chief?" Blazing Eagle said softly. He stretched out on his side and rested himself on an elbow as he looked through the flames of the lodge fire at her. "It is of no matter. There is time enough for me to wait."

He shifted his gaze and stared into the dancing flames of the fire. "For so many years now the Cheyenne have been squeezed from within and without by those seekers of yellow metal," he said, seemingly more to himself than to Becky. Yet she knew that his words were meant for her to hear.

"Our hills are even now being ripped apart to uncover the yellow metal," Blazing Eagle said. "White men leave a trail of blood behind them as they fight among themselves for the yellow metal."

His gaze shifted. His eyes locked with Becky's, making her knees grow weak.

"The iron horse brings these evil men to our land. The first time I saw it, it was like looking at a big snake crawling across the prairie. In the sky I saw a stream of black smoke following the snake."

He paused for a moment to roll a log into the

fire, then went on. "This thing the white man calls a train became a great curiosity to the Cheyenne," he said. "My people climbed high in the hills to watch the iron horse run along its tracks. We listened to the strange noises it made. When we saw that it ran on an iron track and could not leave it, we became braver and came in close to better examine it."

He smiled slowly. "Never have we been as close as today," he said, chuckling.

Then he frowned. "The whites have taken too much of Cheyenne country, disturbing our habits of life and introducing decay and disease among us," he said, his voice hollow with emotion. He sat up and glared at her. "And it was for this my father made war. Who could blame him?"

He rose to his feet and went to her. He took her hands and drew her up before him. "But I, chief of my people, walk the road of peace," he said softly. "Only by traveling this road will the Cheyenne avoid total annihilation."

Becky wrenched her hands from his and took a shaky step away from him. "Do you see wrecking trains and taking a captive a way to show the peaceful side of your nature?" she said. She boldly lifted her chin. "I think not. The authorities from Fort Laramie will come for you. They will take you back with them. They will hang you and your warriors for stealing away an innocent woman."

He started to reply, but his attention was drawn quickly to Whistling Elk as he cried out in his sleep. He rushed over and sat down on Whistling Elk's bed and cradled him gently within his powerful arms.

"My son, what makes you cry in your sleep?" Blazing Eagle asked, gently rocking his son in his arms as Whistling Elk sobbed against his father's bare chest.

"I dreamed of my mother who is no longer with us," Whistling Elk whispered in his own language so that Becky would not hear. "She left me, father. She left me when I was but one snow old. Did she not love me?"

"I have told you often, my son, that she wished to take you with her. I would not allow it. When she chose to return to her parents' lodge those many moons ago, when you were too small to understand the ways of the heart, she went alone," Blazing Eagle whispered back. He did not wish for Becky to hear. It was a humiliating moment not only in his son's life, but also in Blazing Eagle's. "A son's place is with his father. Are you not content with your father?"

"Yes, but I cannot stop dreams," Whistling Elk said, pleading up at his father with tearful eyes. "Even though I was too young to remember her face, in my dreams I see her with arms outstretched toward me. Something holds me back so that I cannot go to her."

"Not something, some*one*. That someone is your father," Blazing Eagle said. "Accept what you have, my son. And always remember that one day you will follow my footsteps into chieftainship."

"I do not wish to be with you only for the power and glory of one day being chief," Whistling Elk said, flinging himself into his father's arms again. "I love you, Father. I wish to be with you. I only wish dreams of my mother would stop."

Becky strained her ears to hear what was being said since she saw so much emotion being exchanged between father and son. But she could not understand the few words she did hear. And she thought that might be best for her. She might not want to hear what would make a young boy cry in the early hours of the night.

She glanced toward the entranceway. Why wasn't the boy's mother there to comfort him? Why did she choose to sleep elsewhere?

"My son, dreams lead one into the future," Blazing Eagle whispered to Whistling Elk. "You might have a mother in the future. Perhaps *soon*. A new mother who will replace the one who left us."

"*Who*, father?" Whistling Elk asked anxiously. "Who? I hunger so for a mother. Soon I will be a warrior who will be too old to be held in a mother's arms. I will have missed so much, father. So much! I see my friends' mothers hugging them. I always wish I were there to receive the love of a mother."

"It is something you will have to be patient for," Blazing Eagle murmured. "Listen well, my son, to what I have to say. This phase of your life occupies but a small part of your existence. One day dreams of a mother who chose a life without you will be behind you. You will walk with your chin high, as *chief*. But do not be anxious to chase your childhood away just to get to that point in your life. Childhood is a special time. Savor it."

Becky continued to watch. Although she could not know what was being said, she was very conscious of the devotion between this father and son and was touched deeply by their closeness.

More and more she found cause to admire, to feel so much for this Cheyenne chief. Yet she must put these feelings behind her. She didn't want to feel anything for Blazing Eagle but loathing.

But she did. She couldn't fight the want that was building inside her, the need to know this man better, to give him cause to know and like her.

When Whistling Elk was asleep again and Blazing Eagle stood over Becky, his midnight-dark eyes burning into hers, she took a slow step away from him.

"Why are you looking at me like that?" she asked in a quavering voice, her insides strangely warmed by the desire that she saw in his eyes.

Tired of bantering with this woman and tired of not getting to the point of why he had brought her to his lodge, Blazing Eagle grabbed her by her wrists and yanked her against his rock-hard body.

Becky's senses swam as his lips bore down upon hers in a heated, passion-filled kiss. She was stunned by how the kiss affected her. She wanted the kiss. She wanted to be held in his arms!

Just as she began surrendering to him, consumed heart and soul by her passion, he wrenched himself free.

She stumbled clumsily beside him when he took her by a wrist and forced her outside his lodge, then led her to the large outdoor fire.

"You stay here," he commanded. "You sleep here."

Becky's eyes were wide as she looked wildly around her, realizing that she would be alone if he truly meant to leave her there.

She started to plead with him, but he was already back inside his lodge.

Sobbing, Becky sat down beside the fire. She hugged herself and gazed overhead. The night was a clear, velvet black, studded with stars. Bathing her in a silvery light, the moon hung overhead like a great luminous rock.

She sucked in a wild breath when she heard an owl's mournful cry, followed by the whisper of leathery wings as they stroked the air somewhere above her in the darkness.

When Blazing Eagle left his lodge again and walked toward Becky, a sudden hope leapt into her heart that he had changed his mind. It was not that she wished to sleep with *him*. She just did not wish to be forced to stay outside alone where anything or anyone might happen along and do what they wished with her.

But her hopes were dashed that he might have changed his mind when he dropped a blanket down beside her.

"This will warm you," he said gruffly.

Blazing Eagle stalked away from her, his heart hammering inside his chest. He was torn. He was remembering his son waking up with dreams of a mother who thought nothing of abandoning him. He was remembering the humiliation of a wife leaving him.

He was afraid to love again.

Chapter Eight

A full day had passed. Becky had been left virtually alone except for when Waterfall had brought her food. Otherwise she had stayed outside as people walked past her, staring.

There was one thing that she was grateful for. She had been allowed to sit under a tree, where she had found a welcome reprieve from the sun.

Pushing herself up from the blanket spread on the ground and wishing that she could have a bath, she stared at the river that shimmered along the outskirts of the village. The tepees had been pitched where the water was not deep. Since dawn she had watched men and women go to the river. The women had gone there for water. The men had gone farther downstream where the water was deeper and they had privacy while bathing.

Becky's skin seemed to crawl from having not

bathed. All night, as she had lain between the blankets hardly sleeping at all, she had swatted off mosquitoes and other tiny creatures that found their way between the blankets.

Becky gazed toward Blazing Eagle's lodge. She could not understand what he had in mind for her. Why was he holding her captive if only to make her sit alone away from everyone else? Surely he had more in mind for her than that.

When would he let her know what it was?

Why had he kissed her?

She turned and peered into the dark shadows of the trees behind her. It would be easy to escape were it not for the sentries who stood in strategic places, guarding the village. One of them would surely see her run into the forest. She had felt ill at ease those times she had gone there to relieve herself. She had hidden herself behind bushes and had seen to her necessities quickly, in case one of the warriors came to see what she was doing.

Seeing the women of the village doing something Becky had never seen before, she strained her neck to watch. The women were pulling out of the ground all the pins that held the hides of their tepees in place.

This left the tepees loose around the bottom. The forked ends of box-elder branches were placed through holes around the edge of the tepee to hold the edges up, much like an open umbrella.

Becky surmised that they were doing this because today was much hotter than the previous day. The air would be welcomed in the tepees. Yet the women stayed outside. Some were making moccasins. Some were sewing leggings and other wearing apparel.

Farther from the lodges, in the shade of towering oak trees, men were making rawhide ropes for their horses and saddles. Others were making hunting arrows, shields, and war bonnets. Children ran around and played, dogs yapping after them.

Of all the activity she saw in the village, she had yet to see any at Blazing Eagle's lodge, except for Whistling Elk leaving to join the children at play and Waterfall entering the lodge with food; soon after, she left and went to another lodge not far from Blazing Eagle's.

Weary of being held against her will in the Cheyenne village, Becky sat back down on the blanket and waited. And waited.

She watched the sun move slowly in the sky, shadows shifting with it.

She watched the women go back inside their lodges.

She envied the children as they ran to the river and splashed themselves, playing and running through the water.

Again her eyes shifted to Blazing Eagle's lodge. Her insides stirred sensually when she finally saw him leave.

But he did not turn his eyes toward her once. He went to the warriors who stood beneath the shade and talked with them.

She recognized another face among them—the warrior who seemed to be Blazing Eagle's friend. She struggled to remember his name.

When a child squealed that he had caught a fish

between his hands, the name Fish Hawk popped into her mind.

She watched how Blazing Eagle and Fish Hawk laughed together, now occasionally glancing her way.

Feeling as though she was the cause of jokes between friends, Becky tightened her jaw and firmed her lips. She glared at Blazing Eagle, her eyes boring into his bare back, glad when he turned and caught her angry stare. She smiled slowly when his smile waned and their eyes locked again in silent battle.

But when he sauntered away in the other direction, Fish Hawk at his side, Becky saw that she had not achieved anything by showing that she was angry with him, except to be further ignored.

"Why?" she whispered, nervously raking her fingers through her tangled golden hair.

She gazed down at her soiled and wrinkled silk dress and groaned. She had never been as disheveled, nor as uncomfortable. She lifted her eyes heavenward.

"Lord, deliver me from this!" she said beneath her breath. "Please?"

Becky scrambled to her feet when Waterfall came toward her with a platter of food. Her pulse raced at the opportunity for company, no matter whose. This time she would demand answers until Waterfall gave them to her! Even if she had to grab the Cheyenne maiden and shake the answers out of her, she *would* get answers!

But Waterfall's sweetness and her gentle smile made Becky change her mind. Waterfall seemed to be the only one she could depend on in the village. It was apparent that the pretty Cheyenne maiden wanted to be friends.

Becky would use this friendship to her advantage.

But only when she felt the time was right.

One more day. She would wait one more day for Blazing Eagle to make his move, to reveal to her why he had brought her to his village.

Becky smiled a thank-you to Waterfall as the maiden handed her the platter of fruit and meat. She started to speak to Waterfall, to ask her to stay and become acquainted, but Blazing Eagle came into view and motioned for Waterfall with his hand, sending her quickly to him.

Too hungry to ignore the food, Becky sat down and began eating the wild strawberries. Her eyes never left Blazing Eagle and Waterfall as they talked, occasionally looking her way. When Blazing Eagle gave Waterfall a generous hug, Becky choked on the juice of the strawberries as it trickled down her throat.

Feeling strangled, she coughed and gagged. Unable to get her breath, she struggled to her feet. She could feel the heat of her face as her distress worsened.

Then strong arms enfolded her. She gazed up at Blazing Eagle, her eyes wild.

Waterfall rushed to her with a drink of water. Becky tried to drink it. It would not go down.

Blazing Eagle turned her back to him. He gave it a couple of gentle slaps. Finally she was able to get her breath, exhausted from the ordeal she had just experienced.

She swallowed over and over again, then took several breaths. When she was finally able to speak, to thank Blazing Eagle and Waterfall, they walked away from her, once again leaving her alone.

Disgruntled and embarrassed at having needed their assistance, Becky sat back down on the blanket, yet shoved the food aside.

After arranging her dress comfortably around her legs, she drew her knees before her and hugged them.

She passed the day by watching everyone around her. She had never felt so lonesome and frustrated as she did now.

Some women were returning to the village with baskets of gathered roots, having left earlier armed with their root diggers. Some old women dragged out the animal hides and spread them on the ground. Others pounded berries under a shade tree.

Curiosity caused Becky to watch some young men who devoted much of their time to their personal appearance. Standing outside their lodges, looking into small mirrors, they plucked out the hairs from their eyebrows, around their lips, and across their cheeks. They rubbed bear grease into their hair, then combed it and braided it. They seemed to be preparing themselves for some special event. Perhaps they would be courting the maidens tonight when the moon was mellow in the sky.

Such thoughts sent Becky's eyes back to Blazing Eagle. She was stunned to see that he was outside his lodge, likewise busy plucking hair from his face and then his bare chest.

Now she knew why his face was so smooth and hairless. He took much more time with it than she could remember her father or her brother taking. Her heart pounded at the sight of Blazing Eagle. He was dressed only in a breech clout, his bronzed, lithe body gleaming beneath the waning rays of the sun.

Everything about him was muscled. As he bent to retrieve the tweezers he had dropped, she watched the rippling play of those muscles. She knew, from being held by him, that there was much power coiled in those muscles. She thrilled to feel him against her once more. At this moment she could not help but want to possess him!

Blushing at where her thoughts had taken her and so badly wanting to hate Blazing Eagle, not love him, Becky started to turn her eyes away.

But she had not done it soon enough. He turned and found her staring at him. She saw strange lights moving in the depths of his eyes as his gaze burned into hers.

She forced a mutinous look into her eyes, wanting to prove to him that she was his enemy, not a woman he might soon totally possess, for she now knew, by the way that he looked at her, that this was what he wished of her.

Her stomach weak with a passion she could not fight, Becky moved slowly to her feet. She thought that he might come to her finally and explain things to her. Instead, he wrenched his eyes from her and disappeared once again inside his lodge.

"Damn him," Becky whispered to herself, at that moment truly hating him for playing this game with her that she could not understand. She plopped down on the blanket again and angrily folded her arms across her chest.

As the sun fell and it grew cooler, horses were driven in from the hills, followed by great clouds of dust that rushed down the bluffs into the village. Gagging, Becky covered her nose and mouth with a hand.

Earlier in the day, Becky had watched the horses grazing in pastures closer to the village. They were gentle, and she had been amused to see how black-birds stayed around the horses when they were feeding, getting their own meals as the horses scared up myriads of grasshoppers which the blackbirds easily snapped up. Sometimes there were several birds perched on a pony's back at the same time.

As darkness settled over the village, the skirts of the tepees were again lowered, and bright firelight soon shone through the yellow lodge-skins. Sparks came from each smoke hole as the fire was mended or fresh wood was thrown upon it.

After everyone had retired inside their lodges, Becky was left alone with only the neigh of a colt, the barking of dogs, the musical laughter of the women, and the yelp of some sportive boy who had not yet entered his parents' lodge for the evening meal.

A shiver rode Becky's spine when she heard the sudden shrill howl of coyotes, wondering how close they were. Was she going to be safe tonight, or dragged away as food for wild animals?

Gulping hard, Becky drew a blanket around her

shoulders. Again she eyed the river. The reflection of the moon made the water glitter like jewels. The splash of the water as it rolled over rocks tempted her. She still so badly wanted a bath, or at least the opportunity to splash water on her face to refresh herself.

When her stomach growled, Becky turned longing eyes toward the platter of food. For the most part it had been left untouched.

With eager fingers, she plucked a strawberry between her teeth and, recalling the mishap when she had eaten earlier in the day, this time took her time as she ate.

After the platter was empty and her stomach felt comfortably full, she started to lie down but stayed in a sitting position when there was a sudden activity outside the lodges. A huge fire was built and then, in the coolness, the people gathered outside, leaning against their tepees. There was much laughter and cheering when some young braves participated in foot races. Blazing Eagle cheered his son onward, his chest swelling when Whistling Elk won one of the races.

Becky watched Blazing Eagle sullenly. Not once did he turn toward her. It was as though she was totally forgotten.

The thought of staying another full night and day like this mortified and angered her. How dare this Cheyenne chief do this to her!

Then her eyes widened when other braves arrived on horseback and paraded around the camp on their horses, their eyes lingering on the pretty girls who were watching them, giggling.

Becky was fascinated by the way the braves and their horses were attired. The men appeared to be wearing their best clothes. Eagle feathers were tied to some of the horses' tails and on the braves' own foreheads. Over and over again they paraded around the village in front of everyone.

Finally everyone retired for the night. Becky stretched out beneath her blankets. But her skin itched incessantly. She swatted at mosquitoes that buzzed around her head.

Suddenly, she tossed aside the blanket and rose to her feet. Without much thought as to who might stop her, she stamped toward the river. She was determined to take a bath. She had to refresh herself. She could not spend another night feeling so dirty.

When she reached the river, she turned and looked slowly around her. She seemed to be alone. Even the dogs were asleep outside the tepees. The only sounds she could hear were an occasional horse's neigh or the hoot of a distant owl.

She shivered involuntarily when in the distance she heard the solemn, lonely sound of wolves baying at the moon.

This hurried her onward. She knelt down beside the river. The moon gave her a good view of the water. It rushed between two white shores and plunged into a dark chasm of almost black spruce.

The water seemed darker and purer because everything else was without color. It danced and frothed in a rocky bed.

Leaning low over the water, Becky lowered her hair into it. She ran her fingers through her hair, wrung it out, then looked around her again to see if she was still alone.

When she discovered that she was, she slowly unbuttoned her dress and slipped it over her shoulders. After removing her slippers, leaving on only her underthings, she stepped gingerly into the water.

Sighing, finding the cool water deliciously sweet on her flesh, she bent over and splashed it all over her. She was not aware of someone watching her. All that she cared about at this moment was the way the water felt as it trickled across her weary flesh.

Blazing Eagle had not been able to sleep. Just as he had stepped from his lodge, he had seen Becky run toward the river. He had stayed behind long enough for her to get in the water, then had crept closer to make sure she did not get the idea of traveling farther down the river.

Although he had decided to deliver her to her people tomorrow, because he saw the wrong in what he had done by abducting her, Blazing Eagle did not want her to leave on her own. The Cheyenne village was too far from the fort and white settlers' cabins. He would not allow her to be foolish enough to take off across land unfamiliar to her, especially on foot.

He watched now, mesmerized by her. Yes, he would return her to her people tomorrow, but he would never forget her. And once he discovered where she made her lodging, he would approach her as a man approached a woman he wished to court. He had thought seriously about his feelings for her, and decided that he *would* have her as a wife. He would give her time to learn to love him and accept his ways.

But he would never take no as an answer from her. She was as much a part of him as the breath he drew into his lungs each day.

Her smooth, white thighs flashed pale in the darkness of night in the shallow pool of water. He watched her as she splashed herself, up and down her arms and across her shapely legs. He inhaled a quavering breath when she splashed water over her well-formed breasts.

When he took another step closer, the crisp snap of a twig alerted Becky that she was not alone.

She turned with a start.

She felt weak when she found Blazing Eagle standing nearby, watching her.

Chapter Nine

As Blazing Eagle moved stealthily closer to Becky, his eyes locked with hers, she inched backward in the water and her heart cried out to her to be afraid.

Be afraid!

She was scarcely clothed. He was a man whose intent was becoming more clear by the minute as his eyes swept over her with a silent, urgent message.

Becky's senses reeled with her own raging hunger—a hunger she had never felt before.

Fight it! her heart cried out to her.

Fight these emotions that are so dangerous!

She was a captive, she frantically reminded herself. Captives were forced to do many things they did not wish to do.

Yet as Blazing Eagle stepped into the water,

dressed in only a brief breechcloth, and he came closer, gazing at her now with a fierce, possessive heat, she knew that if he drew her within his arms, it would be because she wished it to happen.

She was experiencing desire for the first time in her life.

Sweet currents of warmth that she could not deny were sweeping through her.

She wanted him. She wanted his kiss, his arms, his . . . everything.

As she continued to retreat from him, Becky's thoughts were so chaotic that she paid no heed to what might be in the way of her feet. Suddenly she tripped over a large rock and fell backwards, landing with a jolt on the rocky bottom.

Blazing Eagle took one more step, then stood over her and stared down at her. He saw her as nothing less than a vision in the moonlight. His passion was fueled by her skimpy attire that enabled him to see so much more than he had before.

And he was not disappointed. There was the slimness of her body below the swell of her breasts that he had envisioned as he had sat by the fire thinking about her.

There was the gentle curve of her stomach that led to the supple broadening of her hips.

There was the slim, sinuous body that seemed to cry out to be caressed.

The soft glimmer of her golden hair spilled over her shoulders and tumbled down the perfect line of her back.

Her skin was exquisitely creamy, and he could make out the soft pink crests of her nipples as they pressed against the thin, wet fabric of her under-garment.

Becky's backside ached unmercifully from the fall. Rocks jutted into her buttocks even now as she sat there mesmerized by how he stood over her, his face finely chiseled, his eyes lit with points of fire.

When he bent over and reached a hand out for her, the muscles moved in sinuous ripples down the full length of his lean, bronzed body.

"Do not be afraid," he said softly. "I came to tell you that you will be escorted to Fort Laramie to-morrow. Does that please you?"

Becky was at a loss for words to hear that he was going to set her free. Would he ever tell her why he had taken her captive in the first place? Dared she ask?

"Yes, that pleases me," she said, her voice break-ing, to realize that a big part of her never wanted to say good-bye to him.

She saw an instant hurt leap into his eyes. Had her words caused this? Did he truly care that she was leaving? Could he be feeling the same strange foreboding that he would never see her again after tomorrow, as she felt about not seeing him?

There had been so much in his presence that had awakened her to feelings she had never before felt. There had been so much in his eyes every time he had looked at her.

And there had seemed to be a strange bond be-tween them that she could not deny. And tomorrow that bond would be broken. He had a wife—a beau-tiful wife.

But even knowing that Blazing Eagle had a wife,

Becky was not sure she could ever turn her back on him totally. She knew that she would return to his village, if only to get a glimpse of him.

He was in her blood.

He was trapped within her very soul!

She had thought so much about Blazing Eagle during the two days of her captivity that she had almost every inch of him memorized. As he gazed at her, she was acutely aware of the slope of his hard jaw, his bold nose and strong chin, of his broad shoulders, of his lips that seemed made to be kissed.

As though his eyes commanded her to, Becky reached a trembling hand toward him and allowed him to wrap his fingers around hers. He gently helped her up to stand before him.

Her whole body trembled as his hands were suddenly on her throat, framing her face. His thumbs lightly caressed her flushed cheeks, his mouth a feather's touch from her lips.

Suddenly he surrounded her with his hard, strong arms, pressing her against him as his mouth seized her lips in a frenzied kiss, a kiss that stilled all of her doubts and fears.

Her arms crept around his neck and answered his hunger with hers. She knew that she must not allow this, yet she could not stop it once it had started. She felt all of her reserves melting away into something beautiful, something sweet.

Blazing Eagle was on fire with needs so overwhelming that they stunned him. He had loved before. At that time, he had thought that it was a special love.

But what he felt for this woman now made what he had felt for his wife when they first discovered love pale in comparison.

But then something began interfering with the bliss that he found within Becky's arms. In his mind's eye he was seeing things that made his head spin with despair. For the first time since the massacre at his village, when everyone but he had been slain, he was seeing white men dressed in soiled buckskins racing through the village firing their rifles. He could see smoke billowing from the tepees!

Suddenly he wrenched himself free of Becky. Hoping to block out the memory of the bullet entering his mother's heart, he cried out and closed his eyes. He held his temples within the palms of his hands. He held his eyes tightly closed and gritted his teeth.

"No!" he moaned, as in his mind's eye he saw his mother fall to the ground, her arms outreached for him. He saw arrows whizzing past, sounding like angry hornets. Some Indian tribe had joined forces with the white men to kill the Cheyenne!

Horrified, Becky watched Blazing Eagle. She took guarded steps away from him. The way he groaned, cried out, and gritted his teeth—it was as though he was battling some demon inside himself.

Was it because of her? Did he wish this badly not to have feelings for her?

Was it because he felt guilty over having kissed another woman besides his wife?

Or had the kiss been that disappointing to him? She still reeled from its effect on her. It had been paradise on earth! She felt as though she were truly alive now for the first time in her life!

And now, if he hated being with her this much, these feelings that she had allowed herself to feel were surely for naught.

Blazing Eagle's eyes opened, the nightmarish memories passing as quickly as they had surfaced.

Becky was relieved when she saw that Blazing Eagle seemed to be coming around. She was more concerned over him than about the fact that she was standing ankle-deep in water only half-clothed. Placing a gentle hand on his arm, she gazed up at him.

"Are you all right?" she murmured, daring to ask. "What happened?"

Blazing Eagle stared down at her and gave her a puzzled stare. He could not help but wonder why kissing her had brought to his mind things that he had not remembered since he was nine winters of age. What was the association between being with her and remembering that part of his past?

He feared the answer with every fiber of his being, for now, after tasting the white woman's sweetness and holding her supple body within his powerful arms—and knowing that she returned his feelings—how could he ever totally resist her?

"What happened," he said, gazing guardedly down at her, "is not something that can be talked about."

Her lips parted in a gasp when he turned and left. She watched him until he disappeared from sight among the shadows of the trees.

Then, trembling, feeling a strong urge to cry over the tumultuous feelings that were assailing her,

Becky left the river and hurried into her clothes.

Her spirit gone, she went back to her blankets and stretched out between them. She gazed at the communal outdoor fire as it burned slowly into glowing orange embers.

She looked then at Blazing Eagle's lodge. Should she go there and try to get him to tell her what had caused his change in mood?

But, no. It was best left alone. Tomorrow she would leave him. She would direct her thoughts solely on finding her brother. He should be her only concern. She would force herself to remember this.

Blazing Eagle moved to his haunches on a butte that overlooked his village. He strained his neck to see if Becky had gone safely to her blankets, glad to see that she was there, stretched out for sleep.

He wondered if she would truly be able to sleep after what had transpired between them. He wished to be there now with her. He hungered to wrap his blanket about her and claim her as his for all time.

But now was not the time. For many reasons, that had to come later.

He watched her as she tossed and turned in her blankets, understanding her restlessness. He doubted that he could sleep himself, and not only because Becky was in his blood forever now.

It also troubled him that he was beginning to remember his past. He had fought to remember so often as a child, then had grown used to thinking it was best to forget the darkest day of his life.

"Why *now*?" he cried to the heavens as he opened

his eyes and looked upward. "Why did I recall these things when I was in the arms of the woman of my desire? Why? Why?"

When there seemed to be no answer, and thinking about it only confused him more, Blazing Eagle broke into song. He had always found comfort in songs. He sang now of something tender, something beautiful. A woman.

Becky rose quickly from her blankets when she heard someone singing from afar. It was a man's voice—deep, resonant, and hauntingly beautiful. She took several steps away from the shadows of the trees behind her and found herself gazing up at a butte, where a man was silhouetted by the moon's light.

She trembled with ecstasy when she realized this was Blazing Eagle. She could not hear the words.

But the melody was enough. It touched her heart. It stirred sweet feelings within her that made her feel warm and wonderful.

She knew at this moment that her heart was lost to this man.

Totally lost.

This saddened her. For the first time in her life she was in love, and it was a forbidden love.

"Oh, why must you be already married?" she whispered in a sob.

And he seemed filled with demons. She puzzled to herself, shuddering at the memory of how he had behaved only moments ago. What secrets did he hold within himself? What savage secrets? For they seemed to fill him with torment.

Wanting to go to Blazing Eagle, to follow the pleading of her heart, yet knowing that she shouldn't, Becky stretched out on the blankets again. She listened to the beautiful songs as she watched the stars in the heavens.

She flinched when a star suddenly streaked downward toward the horizon. Her stepmother had always told her that a falling star was a sign of things to come.

"Mother, whose face I have often seen in the stars, what sort of sign have you given me tonight?" she whispered, tears splashing from her eyes. "Where do I belong? With whom?"

Blazing Eagle watched Becky as she finally became still amidst her blankets. She was asleep. He wondered what her dreams would be about. Would she dream of him kissing her? Of him holding her?

The Cheyenne believed that everything that had ever happened was still part of the present, that all time flowed together. All things that happened made the world what it was today.

"My woman, we shall be a part of the future together, as the past is now a part of us," he whispered. "I have battles to fight within my soul, that is true. But they will not keep me from *you*."

Chapter Ten

Becky awakened after a fitful night of scarcely sleeping. She had not been able to get Blazing Eagle out of her mind.

And she had the journey to Fort Laramie to take today. She was anxious to see what she might discover about her brother.

Drawing the blanket around her shoulders, Becky leaned up on one elbow and peered around her. The sun had not yet risen. She shoved the blanket aside and rose slowly to her feet. Yawning, she started toward the river. She needed to refresh herself before she headed out on her long journey to the fort.

She looked over her shoulder as the voice of the village crier began shouting out to the camp the commands of their chief. Unlike most everyone else she had met, the crier spoke in the Cheyenne tongue instead of English, making it impossible for her to understand anything that he said.

Becky turned and gazed toward Blazing Eagle's lodge. Smoke was spiraling from the smoke hole.

She looked at the other tepees. She could smell the pleasant aroma of breakfast being prepared over the lodge fires. Jealousy splashed through her when she wondered if Waterfall was in Blazing Eagle's lodge, preparing his meal.

Or had she prepared it in another lodge, as she usually did? If so, whose?

Sighing, still wondering why a wife would sleep in a separate lodge from her husband and cook meals in a different lodge from that which she should occupy, Becky turned and walked slowly toward the river.

She gazed down at her dress and shuddered at how soiled and wrinkled it was. Once she returned to civilization, she would delight in taking a sudsy, perfumed bath. She would choose a dress that smelled fresh from starch and shone from ironing.

When she reached the river, she knelt and splashed some water on her face. Then, as she had done the night before, she dipped her long hair into the water and washed it as best she could without soap.

Then she cupped her hands full of the water and gulped it down in long, thirsty swallows.

Feeling somewhat better, Becky pulled her hair back from her face, sat down on the ground, and drew the skirt of her dress up past her knees so that she could give her feet a soaking.

As she dangled her feet, she looked over her

shoulder again. She listened to the crier still making his announcements as he moved slowly around the circle of tepees on his horse. He began at the opening of the circle, which faced the rising sun, and rode around within, but closer to the lodges. He rode first to the south, then to the west, then to the north, and so back to the east again.

As he called out the news, he seemed to repeat his announcements—this time in English.

Becky strained her ears to hear what he was saying. First he told the warriors they were not to disturb the buffalo that had meandered closer to the village than usual. He told his people that a neighboring village of Cheyenne were having a dance tonight.

Her ears perked up when the crier announced that the white woman would be leaving them today, that their chief would escort her half way to Fort Laramie, then point the way so that she could travel the rest of the way alone.

"Alone?" Becky whispered, her eyebrows lifting. She knew nothing of this wilderness!

Even if Blazing Eagle pointed the way to the fort, could she truly find it? Out here, where everything was unfamiliar to her, all things looked the same.

Thank God she knew how to ride a horse. At least that was in her favor. As a child, the most exciting moments of her day were when her father went horseback riding with her and her brother.

Then, when her father had gotten too busy to go with them, she had enjoyed riding with her brother. She and Edward had grown as close as a brother and sister could be. Oh, how she had missed him when he had left.

She wondered if he ever thought about her.

But how could he have forgotten? How could he allow her to believe that he was dead, perhaps buried somewhere on a battlefield along with thousands of others who had died during the senseless Civil War?

Becky shook her head in an effort to think of things besides a brother whose loyalty to her had been forgotten.

She turned around and faced the river again. She leaned over and rubbed water up and down her legs and between her toes, not sure when she would get the chance to get a true bath.

"Come to my lodge and eat the morning meal with me and my son and then I shall escort you from my village," Blazing Eagle said suddenly behind Becky, startling her.

She scrambled to her feet and smoothed her dress down her wet legs, her eyes wavering as she gave Blazing Eagle a weak smile.

"I want to thank you for allowing me to go," she said, her heart thudding inside her chest as he gazed down at her with his midnight-black eyes.

She could smell the freshness of his skin and the wetness of his hair. He had been to the river himself, but surely before she had awakened or she would have seen him. When she was awake, she was conscious of his every movement!

"I should not have taken you captive in the first place," Blazing Eagle said softly.

"Why did you?" Becky dared to ask.

She became unnerved when he did not reply,

only looked at her in that way that always weakened her knees as his gaze slowly swept over her.

Blazing Eagle could not help but be again taken by her loveliness. He stared at her soiled dress. He had thought to ask Waterfall to lend Becky a dress, but had decided not to. He would not want to be humiliated by her saying she did not wish to wear a dress that had been sewn by a Cheyenne maiden.

After she knew him better, and after she had accepted his proposal of marriage, only then would he offer her the clothes of his people, as well as beautiful beaded necklaces and bracelets.

His gaze went to her hair, envisioning it in braids, with otter skins woven into them.

Ne-hyo, she would be even more beautiful if she took on the look of his people.

The golden hair, the fair skin, the green eyes would set her apart always from the Cheyenne. But in her own manner, once she learned all things Cheyenne, she would fit in well enough and be accepted by everyone as his wife.

Reaching a hand to Becky's elbow, glad that she didn't recoil at his touch, he ushered her away from the river.

"Waterfall prepared a tasty meal for you to eat before you embark on your journey that will take you back among your people again," he said.

When Whistling Elk came and fell into step on his other side, Blazing Eagle turned to him. "My *naha*—my son—you will ride with me as I escort the white woman halfway to Fort Laramie," he said, affectionately patting his back.

Whistling Elk looked around his father and stared up at Becky, then looked up at Blazing Eagle again. "*Ne-hyo*—yes, I would like that, father," he said, nodding. "Why do we not take her all of the way to Fort Laramie?"

"My *naha*, if you think about it, you will come up with the answer without me giving it to you," Blazing Eagle said, feeling Becky's wondering eyes on him as he gave this strange answer to Whistling Elk.

Blazing Eagle's eyes jerked around and locked with Becky's as she continued to stare at him.

"Why *don't* you escort me all of the way?" she then blurted out. "Or don't you truly care whether or not I *do* arrive there safely?"

"It is not that at all," Blazing Eagle said, ushering her inside his lodge. He led her to a blanket that he had spread before the fire and gave a nod. "Sit. Eat. While you eat, you also think about this question both you and my son have asked. I am certain that you will be able to come up with an answer."

Becky sat down, Whistling Elk on one side of her, Blazing Eagle on the other. She took the bowl that Blazing Eagle handed her. It was piled high with boiled buffalo meat, turtle eggs, and fried bread.

Starved, she began eating, not at all happy about Blazing Eagle's suggestion. It made no sense at all why he didn't come straight out with answers instead of making not only her, but also his son, figure them out.

Wanting to draw Blazing Eagle into conversation, knowing that might be the only way she could get from him the answers she wished to have, she looked around her to find something to question him about.

Her gaze stopped on the beautiful shield that hung on a tripod at the end of Blazing Eagle's bed. It was beautiful, with feathers and animal claws, and painted red.

"The shield at the foot of your bed is so beautiful," she said, turning to Blazing Eagle.

"That was my adopted father's war shield," he said gravely. "It is now mine. When I pass to the great beyond, it will become my son's."

"Do the various things on the shield, and the paintings on it, have special meaning?" she asked.

"This circular shield, made of dried and toughened bull-hide, has very strong power and is the most important part of the equipment of a Cheyenne warrior," he explained. "No one can handle it without my permission. And *ne-hyo*—yes, what you see on the shield does have meaning. The four claws of a grizzly bear, in two pairs, is a symbol of great strength and courage. The bear is hard to kill—therefore, the man who carries this shield will have strength and courage and likewise be hard to kill. The turtle tail is attached because turtles know how to hide. The round leaden bow on the shield turns aside the bullets of the enemy. The feathers of the eagle and owl give to the man who carries the shield the power possessed by those birds. The bundle you see gives the owner of the shield much medicine."

He paused and gazed with pride at the shield. "If my shield falls to the ground, it may not be picked up at once," he said. "It must be covered with a skin or a blanket and allowed to lie on the ground for a time. When taken up, some of the medicine—crushed leaves—from the bundle tied to the shield is sprinkled on a coal, and the shield is then passed through the smoke. After this, the shield is hung on the tripod as before."

Now Becky hoped that she could ask him another, more important question: she still wanted to know why he wouldn't see to her safety at the fort.

But before the words slipped across her lips, something came to her in a flash. If he went on into Fort Laramie, they could arrest him, for while she was with him, she was proof that he had committed more than one crime against the white people.

He and his warriors had torn up tracks and wrecked a train.

And they had stolen from the train.

They had abducted her.

It was obvious to her now that he should not be seen with her.

But did he trust her so much that he did not worry about her telling the authorities that he was responsible for all those things?

Or had their brief, sensual moments together revealed to him that she could never turn against him?

She eyed him as he handed her a wooden cup of water. She looked over the brim as she took a long drink. This man filled her with so many emotions. And to think that he trusted her—so much that he would release her, knowing deep inside himself that she might bring the pony soldiers back to him to arrest him—made her love him even more.

She gazed at him, overwhelmed by her feelings for him, then turned her eyes away, sad all over again that she could never truly be free to love him.

"You have eaten. It is now time for us to leave," Blazing Eagle said, rising to his feet.

He held a hand out for Becky. She set her bowl and cup aside and placed her hand in his, her insides melting at his mere touch.

Wanting to remember everything about him on those long days and nights when she would be hungering for him, she let her eyes trail slowly over him.

Today he was dressed in fresh fringed buckskins, the shirt intricately beaded. His hair was not braided, but hung long and free down his powerfully muscled back. His moccasins were beaded in the same design as his shirt. He wore his Bowie knife thrust into a leather sheath at his waist.

He grabbed a rifle as they walked toward the door.

Becky stopped and gazed down at her feet. "My shoes," she said. "I must go and retrieve my shoes from where I slept."

"They do not matter," Blazing Eagle said, going to the rear of the tepee. He picked up a pair of moccasins and took them to Becky. "Waterfall brought these for you. They are a gift from her to you."

Becky's eyes widened as she took the soft moccasins in her hands. "For me?" she said, stunned by Waterfall's generosity.

"Rarely has she seen or been around white women," Blazing Eagle said, smiling as Becky bent over and slipped her feet into the moccasins. "She feels affection for you. The moccasins are a gift from her heart to yours."

"Will I get the chance to thank her?" Becky said, finding the moccasins wonderfully soft and comfortable.

"She is gone with the other women this morning into the hills to dig more roots and gather herbs," Blazing Eagle said matter-of-factly. "But you will see her again. Then you can thank her."

"I will see her again?" Becky said guardedly. "When? How? Where?"

"I cannot say," Blazing Eagle said, lifting the entrance flap and gesturing toward it. "Come. Horses are ready." He nodded toward Whistling Elk. *"Naha,* go and get the horses. Bring them to us."

Whistling Elk ran past them.

Becky stepped outside with Blazing Eagle. She looked slowly around the village. It seemed that no one cared one way or the other about her leaving.

Except for Blazing Eagle, only Waterfall seemed to care a whit about what became of her.

She turned with a start when Blazing Eagle left her and went back inside his lodge. Then she looked quickly around, and Whistling Elk was suddenly there, leading three horses on ropes behind him.

He stopped and said nothing to her as they waited for Blazing Eagle to emerge from the tepee again.

Becky became restless as she waited, now realizing that she was being watched from most of the entrances of the lodges. She had been wrong to suppose that the Cheyenne would not notice her departure. Women and children stood quietly eyeing her. Dogs were held back as Blazing Eagle came again from his lodge.

The warriors stood in the shade of the trees, solemnly watching, their eyes intent on Blazing Eagle, then on Becky.

Blazing Eagle stepped up next to Becky. Draped across his outstretched arms was a beautifully designed Indian blanket.

Becky stared down at it, then moved questioning eyes up at Blazing Eagle when he handed the blanket to her.

She looked quickly at Whistling Elk when Blazing Eagle told him to give Becky the reins of a beautiful strawberry roan horse. She nodded a silent thank-you to Whistling Elk and took the reins, then turned to Blazing Eagle and allowed him to place the blanket across her arm.

"There is always a prize for a thing of beauty," Blazing Eagle said quietly. "The horse and blanket are yours as payment for your capture."

"What?" Becky gasped, her eyes widening.

"It is true, they are yours," Blazing Eagle said, turning to take the reins of his sorrel from his son. "The saddle also is yours. It will make your journey more comfortable as you return to your people."

Becky was stunned by his generosity, yet when she thought about the inconvenience he had caused her, she concluded that these gifts were well deserved.

Yet, in truth, she had gained more than a horse and blanket from her capture. She had gathered much more knowledge about the Cheyenne, and she had fallen in love with a great and powerful Cheyenne chief. These things she would carry within her heart forever.

Whistling Elk swung himself onto his horse and edged his steed next to Blazing Eagle's. Becky hung the blanket across her saddle, then mounted the horse. She sat straight in the saddle and rode from the village with her chin high.

Blazing Eagle cast Becky occasional sidewise glances. He had been young and foolish when he had taken a Cheyenne bride from another clan. It was no disgrace then when she left him, for her elderly parents needed her more than her young husband did.

Blazing Eagle was not sure if this was the time to take a chance with another woman. He was a revered chief and must, at all cost, protect and preserve his noble presence, his dignity, his pride. To rule, one must have cause to hold one's chin high.

Yet nothing would keep him from loving this golden-haired woman with eyes that hypnotized. And in time he would have her!

But first he must learn more about her. He would watch her. He would see with whom she associated herself. He would discover the answers to the questions she evaded now every time he asked her what had brought her to Shaiyena country. He would know why she had been on the iron horse. He would know why she had been traveling alone.

He gathered from this fact that she was not married and was free to marry anyone she chose, even a Cheyenne chief.

"You will still not tell me why you were on the

iron horse?" he asked suddenly, startling her.

Becky still did not feel free to answer this question. And why should she when he did not share his deep thoughts with her? Two could play this game! She was proving to be good at it.

She so badly wanted to ask him why he had turned from her and behaved so strangely after kissing her.

But glancing over at Whistling Elk, she knew that she could not question Blazing Eagle about that withdrawal, for it would reveal to his son that he had kissed the white woman.

No, it was best they kept their savage secrets to themselves. It was worthless, anyhow, to delve into them when he had a wife.

Yet she loved him. And she could almost bet that he loved her!

She focused her thoughts elsewhere as they rode onward, along a small gully that grew into a steep valley meandering between crumbling walls. Rubber rabbit bushes and gum weed flowers were buttons of yellow in the grey landscape. A creek became divided and divided again into tributaries that disappeared up the precipitous canyon walls. The air was pungent with the scent of sage. On a summit, a bighorn stood, transfixed.

Becky steadied her horse when it caught sight of a garter snake lying by a muddy puddle of water, gorging itself on tadpoles.

They rode onward. She watched the shadows shifting as the sun moved slowly from the midpoint of the sky.

After many long hours, Blazing Eagle drew a

tight rein and stopped. Whistling Elk reined in beside him.

Becky stopped her horse and stared at Blazing Eagle with a silent question. Was this it? she wondered.

"You are truly going to leave me here?" she blurted out. "I *do* have to make the rest of the journey alone?"

Blazing Eagle's pulse raced at knowing that he must bid her farewell at this point in the journey, for he did not want to. But for his safety, and for the sake of his people who depended on his leadership, he saw no other choice.

He reached for a parfleche that he had earlier placed on his horse and offered it to Becky. "In here you will find food and water," he said, his voice drawn.

He reached inside another bag and brought out a small, pearl-handled pistol. He handed it to Becky. "This will get you safely to Fort Laramie," he said, holding his eyes steady with hers, already missing her. "Do not hesitate to use it on anyone who becomes a threat."

"I wish that you could go with me, at least until we see Fort Laramie in the distance," she said, her voice breaking. "Please, Blazing Eagle? I promise to speak in your behalf if the soldiers see us together."

"Your word would not carry much weight if the pony soldiers wished to cast blame on this Cheyenne chief," Blazing Eagle said. "You are but a woman."

He then wheeled his horse around and rode away

without saying any more to her, or saying good-bye.

Becky stared at him and Whistling Elk riding away from her until tears pooled in her eyes.

She flicked the tears away and looked away from Blazing Eagle. She rode onward, nervously watching the sun lower in the sky. Fear crept into her heart as the breeze cooled and the purple-and-gray haze of evening set in.

"I've never been so afraid," she whispered to herself.

When she saw riders approaching, it was too dark to tell if they were white-skinned or red; friend or foe. All she knew was that she was not practiced at defending herself against highwaymen or renegade Indians.

She prayed that they were soldiers from Fort Laramie. Her heart pounded in unison with the pounding of the horses' hooves as the riders grew closer.

Silently she cursed Blazing Eagle for placing her there in the eye of danger!

Chapter Eleven

When the four horsemen came close enough for Becky to finally see them, she recognized the blue uniforms of soldiers. Grateful, knowing that she was safe, she heaved a sigh.

As they drew rein in front of her, she smiled and eased her horse toward them.

"Ma'am, Lieutenant Fred Dowling at your service," the lanky, sallow-faced soldier said, tipping his cavalry hat to her. "Might I ask your name?" He looked past her for other riders. "Are you traveling alone?"

"Yes, I'm quite alone," Becky said quickly. She avoided telling him her name just yet. She did not want him to associate her with the train wreck and Blazing Eagle, who was responsible for it. The longer she waited to disclose who she was, the more time Blazing Eagle would have to return safely to his village.

"Your name," the lieutenant persisted.

"Just please direct me to Fort Laramie," Becky said. "I will talk to your commander when I arrive there."

"I don't mind if you don't want to tell me who you are," the soldier said, shrugging. He leaned closer to her, his eyes locked with hers. "I'd wager a month's pay, though, that you're Becky Veach, the woman who was abducted from the train by a band of renegades. You fit her description to a T. But what I don't understand is why you don't want to admit to it. Unless . . ."

His eyes traveled over her soiled dress and uncombed hair. "Unless you are trying to protect someone's hide. I know you're the woman who's spent the past two days with Injuns. Just look at you. You look no better than an Injun yourself."

He sneered. "Whose hide you tryin' to protect?" he said, laughing derisively. "Don't tell me you're an Injun lover. Protecting their identity makes you no better than them."

Becky's heart thudded at his reference to Indians, afraid that he might already know who had abducted her and was only playing games with her.

Although she was furious and humiliated by this soldier's attitude toward her, she fought to keep her temper at bay. Her response was silence and a boldly lifted chin.

The soldier, whose red hair blew in the evening breeze as he rested his hat on his knee, looked past Becky and kneaded his long, narrow chin. "Hmm," he said, cocking a shaggy red eyebrow. "I'd say from the direction you were traveling, you might have been with the Cheyenne."

Becky paled.

Yet she still sat stubbornly quiet, knowing that should she speak now, her voice would reveal that she was not as sure of herself as she pretended.

"Cat got your tongue?" the soldier said, peering into her face. "Well, it don't matter. It's up to the major to decide which Injun is going to pay for the damage to the train and its tracks, and for what was stolen from the passengers." He sneered again. "And for taking *you*, pretty lady."

She was glad when the soldier finished disrespectfully toying with her and snapped his reins and rode off, the others following his lead.

Knowing that she had no other choice and definitely not wanting to spend a night out in the wilderness alone, Becky soon caught up with them and rode with them into the quickly falling darkness.

By the time they reached the fort, she was bone-tired. She found her head bobbing as she occasionally fell asleep in the saddle, a nudge on her right side awakening her as the red-headed soldier found her dozing.

After they entered the courtyard of the fort, she looked guardedly around her. Soldiers were standing outside raw wooden barracks, gaping with impersonal curiosity at her.

Elsewhere, the air around the parade ground echoed with the clatter of low rumbling voices and occasional snorts from the horses that milled about in the corral. She was led to a good-sized building that stood in the center of the courtyard.

"Dismount and follow me," Lieutenant Dowling said, not offering to help her from her horse.

She dismounted and followed him into the major's office. She became uncomfortable when she saw him stretched out on a cot in a dim corner. He wore no shirt. His suspenders were hanging awkwardly across his thick-waisted breeches.

Becky was ushered to a chair. She gladly sank into it as the red-headed soldier went to the officer and gently shook him by the bare shoulder.

"Sir," the soldier said, again giving the man a shake. "She's here. We found the woman."

Becky felt safe now, yet she was uneasy knowing that the major would soon be plying her with questions. She hoped that he wasn't like drill sergeants she had heard about who sometimes broke the spirit of men during the Civil War, even before they had fought one battle.

If he questioned her about who had abducted her, she was resolved not to speak Blazing Eagle's name. Although what Blazing Eagle had done was wrong, she now knew that he did not make it a habit to take captives—or wreck trains.

"Who's here? What woman?" Major Kent grumbled as he staggered from the cot.

"She won't tell me her name," the Lieutenant growled as he cast Becky a look over his shoulder. "But I'd wager she's the one the Indians abducted."

When Major Kent caught sight of Becky sitting beside the desk, the dim lamplight showing how wilted she was, he arched an eyebrow. She reminded him of the petunias that grew in his mother's flower garden back in Indiana during the hottest part of summer.

He hurriedly slipped his suspenders up and over his shoulders and grabbed a shirt, his fat fingers having trouble with the buttons as he tried to get himself looking like a respected military officer.

Becky rose from the chair as he stepped up behind his desk. The dim lamplight revealed a heavy-set man whose gray eyes seemed bottomless and whose gray beard and mustache hid most of his face, especially his lips, as he talked.

She thought that he smelled pleasant enough, as though he might have taken a bath recently.

"Are you Becky Veach?" Major Kent asked. He splayed his fingers across the top of his map-strewn desk, leaning closer to her so that he could get a better look.

He let his gaze travel over her, tsk-tsking at her appearance. "So you aren't one for conversation, are you?" he said, slowly easing into the straight-backed wooden chair behind his desk.

He nodded toward the chair that Becky had been ushered to earlier. "Sit down," he said, his voice warm and caring. "Now, why don't you tell me everything. I'm here to listen."

"I bet she's been with the Cheyenne," the lieutenant said, smirking down at her as Becky cast him a frown.

"I imagine you bet on most anything, and most times lose," Becky said sarcastically as she stared into the lieutenant's icy glare. She was unable to stay silent any longer. This lieutenant rankled her to no end. And if he didn't shut up, he would surely cause this major to send his soldiers to Blazing Eagle's village.

"Lieutenant, you're dismissed," Major Kent said, glowering at him. "Leave the lady to me."

"Yes, sir," Lieutenant Dowling said, coming to attention and saluting the major. He gave Becky one more insolent look, then left the room with his long strides.

So tired she could hardly stand any longer, Becky eased herself back down into the chair. Running her fingers through her tangled hair, she waited for the next blast of questions.

"You are Rebeccah Veach, aren't you?" Major Kent asked, placing his fingertips together as he gazed over his desk at Becky.

"Becky," she said, sighing. "Most call me Becky."

"Which tribe of Cheyenne kidnapped you?" Major Kent asked, his voice drawn.

Still not wanting to reveal this to anyone, Becky's throat went dry. Her gaze shifted past the major. She gasped and stared at the wanted poster tacked to the wall. It was Edward's face. Seeing it again made her stomach feel as though it was sinking.

"That outlaw," she said, using this opportunity to direct the questions away from Blazing Eagle, at least for now. "Do you know his whereabouts?"

"The hellion is still in these parts," Major Kent said, looking over his shoulder at Edward's poster. "He's grown rich robbing trains and stagecoaches."

He turned slow eyes to Becky. "Why do you want to know about the outlaw?" he asked.

"I've come from Saint Louis to buy property, perhaps between Fort Laramie and Cheyenne," she said, holding her voice steady. "I'd hate to think that I'm not safe here from outlaws."

"We—the military—do our best to protect innocent settlers, not only from outlaws but also from renegade Indians," he said. "You've experienced some inconvenience at the hands of Indians, but they weren't renegades, were they, Miss Veach? They were Cheyenne, led by Chief Blazing Eagle."

Becky's eyes wavered. She swallowed hard. "Why do you think it was Blazing Eagle?" she asked.

"I'm aware of Blazing Eagle's recent restlessness," Major Kent said, reaching for a half-smoked cigar that rested in an ashtray. "And I don't blame him. It seems that somehow or other the treaties with the Cheyenne keep getting broken."

"You sound as though you respect Blazing Eagle," Becky said, yet fearing that he might be trapping her into talking about her experience with the Cheyenne. She was careful not to say too much.

"Yes, and he has given me cause to," Major Kent said, now puffing on the cigar. "Blazing Eagle is a man of honor. He has morals most white men don't even know exist."

He took the cigar from between his lips and gestured with it toward Becky. "Take you, for example," he said. "You were taken captive, yet you were not touched, were you? I'm not sure what he tried to prove by taking a captive, but the fact is, you are here, unharmed. A bath will clean up all signs of your having ever been with the Cheyenne, wouldn't you say?"

Becky still felt as though he was trying to trap

her by pretending to be an ally of Blazing Eagle. "Sir, I *am* in dire need of a bath," she said softly. "Was my luggage rescued from the wrecked train? Do you possibly have it here at the fort?"

"Yes. Your belongings, as well as the other passengers who suffered the train robbery, were brought to the fort," Major Kent said. He nodded to a darker corner of the cabin. "Your luggage sits over there."

"The other passengers?" Becky asked, rising to go to her luggage. "Are they all right? Did they have to stay long in the unbearable sun before it was discovered that the train had met with a mishap?"

"They stood there one full day," the major told her. "The men at the depot, who are responsible for the train's schedule, were drunk. They didn't even notice that the train was a full day late."

He shook his head back and forth. "Lazy, drunken bastards," he grumbled. "Then it took them a full day to get the train back on the tracks. *That's* why no one was alerted that there was a captive taken—not until the train made it finally to Cheyenne."

"Well, there is no need to worry any further about me or who may have inconvenienced me for a couple of days," Becky said, raking her fingers through her hair to draw it back from her face. "I'm fine now. *And*, sir, I'd like to ask about the property in this area. I'd like to purchase a small plot of land, let's say large enough for a small garden of vegetables for myself. I'd like a comfortable cabin."

"I think both can be arranged," Major Kent said, puffing again on his cigar, his eyes never leaving

Becky. "Once you are settled in a cabin and have a garden planted, what are your plans? What truly brought you to these parts? It ain't much of a place for a lady."

"My father was a real estate broker in Saint Louis," she murmured. "He recently passed away. I didn't care to stay where memories overwhelmed me. I heard of settlers coming to the Wyoming Territory. It sounded alluring. So I came with plans of following in my father's footsteps. After I am here a while, and *if* I decide it is a place for me, I shall begin buying and selling real estate myself."

She was proud of how she had managed to make her interest in buying property seem legitimate, even though she had no interest at all in it. At least the major had no cause to think otherwise.

"It won't be easy going for you, ma'am," the Major said. "Especially since you have no husband. Women don't usually live alone out here, where there is murder and mayhem practiced every day. Why, you're as lucky as sin that a peaceable Indian took you captive."

Becky did not reply, her heart crying out to see Blazing Eagle at least one more time.

"I'm certain it was the Cheyenne," Major Kent said, crushing his cigar out in the ashtray. "I'm not going to send any soldiers out to arrest Blazing Eagle and his warriors. The Cheyenne chief set you free. The train tracks have already been repaired. Neither the train nor its cars were irreparably damaged." He shrugged as he rose from his chair. "Sometimes the military has to put up with the Cheyennes' ways. The Cheyenne have been forced to put up with the white man's interference since our arrival."

Becky knelt down beside her embroidered bags. She lifted one into each hand and turned to the major. "I'd appreciate it if you'd show me where I may spend the night," she murmured. "I'd also appreciate a large tub of water."

"I know of a place that might interest you, since you've money to spend on property. It's even furnished," Major Kent said, slipping on a coat that was resplendent with gold buttons at the shoulders and up the front. "It's not inside the fort, but it is close enough for you to be able to come to us quickly if you find yourself in trouble and have a need for protection."

"I'd appreciate seeing it tonight, if you don't mind," Becky said, envisioning a sweet little log cabin with a wide stone fireplace and nice furniture.

"It'd be my pleasure, ma'am," Major Kent said, taking her bags from her.

She followed him outside, where a full moon dappled the ground with white. He swung her two bags into the back of a buggy, then helped Becky up onto the cushioned leather seat. He tied her horse to the back of the buggy, then sat down beside Becky.

As they left the walls of the fort behind, Becky's thoughts returned to the dreadful wanted poster of her brother. Then her mind drifted once again to Blazing Eagle. She was relieved that, even though the major had guessed accurately that Blazing Eagle was responsible for the recent train robbery and abduction, he was not going to bring the Cheyenne chief to the fort for prosecution.

She was glad to know that the major admired the Cheyenne chief. This supported her own conclusion that Blazing Eagle was a special man.

Yet he was a man whose love for his wife was inconstant. The fact that he kissed another woman, a white woman at that, made her doubt his moral character.

They drove for a while, then Becky's thoughts were brought back to the present when the major guided his horse to the right and the property came into sight.

"There it is," Major Kent said. "It's not much, but at least it'll be a roof over your head."

Becky's heart sank when she discovered beneath the bright rays of the moon that her pretty cabin was a sod shanty—an actual round, moss-grown hut! She grimaced as the horse and buggy stopped close to the soddy and she saw its total disarray.

Yet knowing that she had no other choice at this time but to live there, she stepped from the buggy and went to the door, the major behind her.

She flinched when the door opened slowly on flimsy leather hinges. When she stepped inside, she looked upward. The board roof not only let in moonlight, but also the wind. And she could hear the distinct hungry cry of a coyote as he slunk through the grass nearby.

As Major Kent lit a single candle for light, Becky shuddered to know that she would be staying alone in this shack. It was made of nothing more than sod, boards and tar paper, and it smelled of wood smoke, stale grease, rotted food, and dirty clothes.

"Like I said, the soddy isn't much, but it's the only place that I know about that's vacant at this time," Major Kent said, shrugging.

"Who lived here?" Becky asked.

"A couple of men who discovered they were not close enough to the gold fields," Major Kent said, covering his mouth and coughing when Becky smacked her hand against an overstuffed chair, sending clouds of dust everywhere.

"I knew no woman could have lived like this," Becky said, leaning over the fireplace and sniffing at food left inside a large black pot hanging over the cold ashes. She choked on the vile scent and took a quick step backward. "Lord. That smells no better than a skunk."

"You don't have to stay here," Major Kent said, as he went and stood in the doorway. "I'll find sleeping quarters at the fort, if you wish."

Not wanting to have any more contact with the soldiers than necessary, Becky turned quickly toward him. "No, I'll do just fine here," she said, clasping her hands behind her. "But one thing. I don't see a washtub. Do you think you might bring me one early tomorrow?"

She smiled weakly at him. "And I'd love to have the largest piece of soap you can find," she murmured. "It might take forever to get the stench out of this place."

"I'd be glad to," Major Kent said, stepping outside.

Becky forked an eyebrow. "There is a well nearby, isn't there?" she was almost afraid to ask.

"Out back," the major said, nodding.

Becky half stumbled over her bags as she followed him outside. "Also, sir," she said, as she stood in the brisk breeze and moonlight. "Tomorrow I'll pay you what you ask for this place. Also, I'd like to buy a rifle and ammunition, as well as ammunition for my small pistol. Would you please see to these for me? I'd truly appreciate it."

"I'd be happy to," he said, climbing aboard his buggy. "Livin' out here alone, I'd say you'll need all the protection you can afford to buy."

"Thank you," she said, smiling up at him. She was feeling more and more comfortable with him as each moment passed. She could understand now how he and Blazing Eagle had come to some sort of an understanding. Like Blazing Eagle, this major was a likeable man.

"Something you might consider, ma'am, is looking over the men at my fort," he said hesitantly. "Most aren't married. You'd have your pick. It'd be best if you had a man to care for you. Living alone like you plan to can be hell."

"Yes, I'm sure it can be," Becky said, again smiling at him. "But I don't plan on marrying anytime soon."

Her thoughts went to Blazing Eagle. If only he were not married.

"I'll see you early in the morning with the supplies," Major Kent said. He nodded, then rode away.

Becky went back inside the soddy. She dreaded sleeping on the bed, yet at this moment she knew that nothing would keep her from it. She was so tired, she felt as though she might drop.

She first went to the window, unhappy that there was no glass there to keep pesky mosquitoes or other creatures out of the shack. She gazed in the direction of Blazing Eagle's village. She missed him so much that her heart ached.

Then she shook herself back to reality. She was in the Wyoming Territory to find her brother. Nothing more! She must put Blazing Eagle from her mind and get on with finding Edward.

Her eyes heavy with the need of sleep, Becky went to the bed and threw herself across the lumpy, smelly mattress. Just as her eyes drifted closed, a noise outside the soddy drew her quickly awake again. She stiffened with fear.

Grabbing the pearl-handled pistol that Blazing Eagle had given her, she inched from the bed and toward the door. When she stepped outside, she found a small mixed-breed pup standing there, staring up at her with pleading eyes and whining. She felt an instant pity for the pup. He was so gaunt. He was so obviously hungry.

Slipping the pistol into the pocket of her dress, Becky reached down and lifted the small dog into her arms. Her nostrils flared; his scent was anything but pleasant. "I don't know who needs a bath worse," she said, laughing softly. "You or me."

Carrying the tiny thing in the crook of her left arm, she went to her horse and removed the bag that Blazing Eagle had given her. She swung the bag over her shoulder and went back inside the shack.

Gently she placed the pup on the floor, then sat

down with him and fished through the parfleche bag until she found some beef jerky.

As she took it from the bag, the pup reached his nose to it and sniffed, then hungrily yanked it from between Becky's fingers with his teeth and began gnawing on it.

"You poor thing," Becky said, stroking its spotted fur, wincing when she found several fat ticks clinging to its skin. "Tomorrow I'll bathe you and get those ticks off you."

Her eyes drifted closed and she slouched over, to awaken again when the pup began licking her face. Becky looked around and found no signs of the beef jerky. She smiled to know that the pup had eaten it and seemed content enough now to play.

"I'm sorry, sweetie, but I can't oblige you with a romp tonight," Becky said, lifting the pup into her arms again. She carried him to the bed. "Now you'd better be as kind to me as I was to you. I need a good night's sleep to be able to function tomorrow. And I've lots to do tomorrow besides bathing each of us. I plan to begin my long search for my brother."

The pup whined and edged close to Becky as she stretched out on the bed. The moon rippled through the window onto the dog. Becky gazed at the pattern of the spots on the pup's fur. They resembled pebbles at the bottom of a stream.

"Pebbles," she murmured. "I shall call you Pebbles."

Pebbles whimpered and placed a paw on Becky's arm. Becky watched his eyes close and knew that she had made a fast friend.

She closed her eyes, smiling, now not feeling so alone and so far from the home she had left behind in Saint Louis. As she fell into a soft sleep, she entered a frenzy of dreams.

First she was with Blazing Eagle.

Then she was with Edward.

Then she was with neither one. She was standing between them, and their arms were stretched out toward her, each beckoning her toward him.

When she made no choice, not wanting to hurt either of their feelings, Edward drew his firearm and aimed it at Blazing Eagle.

"No!" Becky screamed as she awakened in a sweat.

Chapter Twelve

It was noon the next day. Thanks to Major Kent, Becky had a house full of supplies, which included several bars of soap, a rifle and ammunition, canned foods, fresh fruit, and many more household items that he had been thoughtful enough to bring.

To Becky's amazement, Major Kent had even been kind enough to make arrangements for her to purchase the soddy and the many acres of land that surrounded it.

It was the first time that she had ever purchased property, and even though the wretched soddy left much to be desired, it felt good to know that she now owned land besides what she had inherited in Saint Louis.

Now she could understand her father's pride, his obsession, over owning so much.

But she would not get carried away with this. The property was only a way to look legitimate in the Wyoming Territory while she searched for her brother.

As soon as he was found, she would turn right around and return to Saint Louis with him at her side, and be damned to this wild land that meant nothing to her except that it had lured her brother into a life that had turned him wicked!

Proud of what she had accomplished this morning, Becky smiled as she gazed at the soddy. She had scrubbed her fingers raw until she had the hand-hewn furniture spanking clean. She had yanked the mattress from the bed and aired it out, determined one day soon to stuff it with more feathers to make it more comfortable.

The tin dishes and cups were now sparkling clean on the shelves over the kitchen table. The pot that she had found hanging from a tripod above the cold coals in the fireplace had been replaced by a black cast-iron pot that the Major had brought from the trading post at the fort.

She had even torn apart one of her lacy petticoats and stitched curtains by hand for both the windows after having placed cheesecloth over the openings.

With Pebbles at her heels, his tail wagging contentedly, Becky hurried into a riding skirt and shirt. She then plopped a narrow-brimmed straw hat on her head and secured it with a ribbon tied beneath her chin.

She sat down on the edge of the bed and struggled with the leather boots that she had always hated and only wore while on her outings on a horse.

Then she slipped her fingers into butter-soft gloves and smiled down at Pebbles. "Young man, are you ready to accompany me to Cheyenne on the first leg of my journey to find my brother?" she asked, smiling down at the dog, whose trusting brown eyes seemed to smile back at her.

She had made good use of the parfleche that Blazing Eagle had filled with food for her journey to Fort Laramie. She had cut it into two flat pieces of buckskin, and then had stitched them into a sort of sling in which she could carry her pup on her horse.

She had already grown attached to Pebbles and wanted to make sure nothing happened to him. She most certainly wouldn't leave him behind on their first day of becoming acquainted. She did not want him to venture away, to become the target of rattlesnakes or wolves.

And heaven forbid that any more ticks found their way onto his tender flesh. She shivered at the thought of having plucked so many blood-filled ticks from the pup's body today. Afterwards she had bathed him and placed alcohol on the sores. His fur was spanking clean now and soft, his spirits lifted.

Becky swept Pebbles up into her arms and fitted him into the sling. Then she lifted her rifle in her free hand and went outside, where she had earlier readied her horse for the long journey ahead.

First she slipped the rifle into the gun boot at the side of the horse, then swung the pup's sling over the pommel, making it possible for the pup to hang comfortably at the right side of the horse.

It was just past noon when Becky rode away from the soddy. The sun was so hot that it crinkled her skin. The air smelled of scorched grass. She rode in a gallop to the creak of saddle leather.

She knew that it was risky to wait this late in the day to travel to Cheyenne. She might even have to spend the night in that wild and woolly town. She hoped that it might have at least one decent hotel in which to rest her weary soul and aching bones.

She was certainly not going to waste another day in waiting and wondering whether or not she might discover a way to find her brother.

"I *will* find him," she whispered to herself.

And she would. No matter what it took, or no matter how far she would have to travel. He *would* eventually give her the answers that she sought!

She rode for many hours.

Sweat poured from her brow and across her cheeks.

Her perspiration-soaked blouse clung to her breasts, defining the tight nipples beneath the white cotton cloth.

Two red-tailed hawks soared overhead, their eyes watching Becky. A kestrel yelled "ki-ki-ki" from a roost in a cliff's side. A turkey vulture came into sight, its wings set back in a wide V shape.

Becky rode onward.

Chirping sparrows gathered gravel alongside the narrow path she traveled. A streak of yellow moved quickly from pines to cottonwoods at her left side, and she recognized the fluid song of a tanager.

She stopped to give her horse and pup a drink in a small stream. Taking delight in the feel of the water as she splashed it onto her face, she took deep gulps of it down her parched throat.

Becky then relaxed and watched fish playing in the cool pools, some hovering in the shade of floating leaves, some darting between shadows. Her gaze followed the path of minnows, chubs, and suckers.

Then Pebbles came to her and licked her hand. "It's time to go on, isn't it?" Becky said, stroking her hand through his soft, curly fur.

She lifted him, placed him back in the sling, then mounted her horse and rode onward.

Bison grazed and dusted themselves in a prairie dog town. Shadows formed, moved, and disappeared, as though a thousand shadowy figures lurked in the sandstone wall that loomed at her right side. The shadows gradually grew soft and purple as the flaming sunset softened by degrees.

"When will I get there?" Becky worried aloud, having followed the signs and the road cut out of the wilderness.

She shivered at the sight of a bone sticking out from the mud in the road as she rode past it, knowing that it was a fossilized bone of some unlucky creature that had not reached its destination.

A tortoise shell, smooth and elliptical, lay partially exposed to the sun.

She stopped and let her horse snatch a mouthful of grass, then rode onward.

Then, up ahead, outlined by the lowering sun, lay a town. "Cheyenne," Becky whispered. "It has to be Cheyenne."

Never had she been so glad to see signs of life.

She had met no travelers on the road and had wondered if most were too afraid now to travel, knowing that they chanced being accosted by outlaws or renegade Indians.

Becky was quite aware of the dangers herself. But deep down she almost wished that her brother might happen along and take *her* for someone to rob! That was a sure way of finding him and his hideout!

She couldn't imagine her brother being heartless enough to shoot to kill before robbing an innocent passerby.

What a surprise he would have gotten had he ridden up to rob her and discovered that she was his very own sister—a sister he had forsaken for this ungodly way of life.

She also knew the dangers of someone besides her brother accosting her. She had managed to care for herself these past years when her father had been too ill to be the man of the household. Yet out here, away from civilization as she had known it, everything was different. She was far, far from Saint Louis and the gentlemen who rode its streets.

Out here, in the Wyoming Territory, each day men staked everything they had for gold. Some toiled far beneath the surface of the earth by the dim light of candles. Others hunted for gold by the light of pitch-wood fires, playing fierce streams of water against gravel banks through the long hours of the night. She had read about miners on mountain streams sluicing tons of earth for their one ounce of gold.

She knew that many of these men came down from the hills to the bright lamps of the saloons and dance halls—and the stimulus of liquor and reckless spending. It was a land of bachelors, whose only love was pouches of gold and whatever woman they might pay for while taking a reprieve from their hungry search for more gold.

Soon these women-hungry men might start drifting into Cheyenne for the night. She had perhaps one hour of daylight left to search the faces of the men in Cheyenne for one she recognized.

She wondered if her brother was daring enough to ride into Cheyenne for a quick drink.

Sadness swept over Becky to know that her brother's life was ruled by chance. But it had been his choice. *Why?* she again wondered.

She gulped hard when she rode slowly past a small cemetery at the side of the road. Many graves were marked with rough wooden crosses or primitive stones. But she noticed that even more graves were unmarked, except for mounds of stones, or slight depressions where the earth had settled. What if Edward was there, in an unmarked grave?

The thought making her feel ill, Becky sank her heels into the flanks of her horse and rode onward.

When she rode into the crowded, unruly settlement of Cheyenne, she drew a tighter rein and looked guardedly around her. Tents were pitched in the middle of the street. Bullwhackers and riders pushed between canvas and people.

Her fingers tightened on the reins, her eyes ever watching for that familiar walk, that familiar face, that taller height, and most definitely those familiar eyes that mirrored her own. There would be no way of ever mistaking them.

She navigated the rutty, rocky road. The buildings, which consisted of claims offices, saloons, general stores, a hotel, and more saloons, were built with false fronts, architecturally designed to make a single story look like two, and a two-story structure appear to have three.

Shadows on the buildings were short and accented along the logs' vertical stacking. Yellow lamplight shone from shaded windows. Behind the weathered wood buildings, slopes of ponderosa pine rose skyward.

She reached for her hat and pulled it lower over her brow when she found herself being stared at by men on horseback and those who were browsing along the thoroughfare. They were dressed in all sorts of clothes. Some wore frock coats, checkered trousers, and capes. Those were obviously the men who wanted to be bigger and more important than they really were.

Then there were those who were burly-looking. She surmised they were mountain men—hard men whose weather-beaten, bronzed, leathery faces looked as though they might break if they tried to smile.

Becky rode onward down the snaking roadway between tree stumps and potholes. The street was packed with jostling men, horses, mules, oxen, wagons, and coaches.

Again she glanced toward a saloon when the bat-winged doors swung suddenly open and a man was tossed out onto the street. She could tell there must be much lawlessness in this town where whiskey flowed like water for men on their way to and from the mining fields.

She now realized that this *was* the sort of town her brother might seek out for his worldly pleasures—if not to drink his night away in the arms of a woman, perhaps to rob a bank!

Her eyes sought out the bank. She looked over her left shoulder. She had passed it already. Lamps were being taken from the front windows, and the shades were being drawn for the night.

Riding onward in a slow lope, Becky searched through the men who rode past her and again looked closely at those who strolled along the boardwalks.

One tall man in particular, who was riding a horse only a few yards away from her, drew her attention. He sported two revolvers holstered at his waist with their butts forward and wore a long blue denim coat over his soiled buckskin trousers. Becky's heart leapt. From beneath the sides and back of his wide-brimmed hat flowed shoulder-length golden hair. The hat shaded his face, but the hair! The straight, proud back! The muscled legs and tall height of him! He so resembled her brother!

Sudden gunfire scattered her thoughts as the man she had been studying was suddenly joined by several other men on horseback. Firing their pistols in the air, they rode away from her down the middle of the street.

Someone from the bank came out and shouted that the bank had been robbed. Becky turned and stared at him as he yelled for someone to stop the thieves!

One of the men, who Becky now knew was an outlaw, turned and shot the banker.

Becky's horse was spooked by the gunfire. She tried to steady herself when the horse reared and whinnied. But she couldn't hang on. She was thrown. She fell to the ground and hit with a hard thud just as Pebbles was tossed out of his carrier by the jerking of the horse's head and fell at Becky's side, yapping and howling.

Dazed, Becky leaned up on one elbow. Pebbles shook himself, then licked Becky's face.

A lean copper hand reached down for Becky. She looked up at the man who offered her help and was stunned to find that it was Blazing Eagle.

Her eyes locked with his, Becky reached for his hand and moved slowly to her feet.

"You are a foolish woman," Blazing Eagle said, frowning down at her. "No woman should be alone in this town of whiskey-crazed men and bank robbers. Why are you here?"

Blazing Eagle had worried constantly about Becky since he had said farewell to her. She had not seen him, but he had followed her to the fort and seen her taken to the soddy. He had spent the night not far from her lodge, to make sure she was out of harm's way.

He had stayed the morning watching from afar as she cleaned the filthy white man's dwelling, while reflecting that a tepee was much more desirable in every way. When she saddled her horse, he had hoped he might discover why she had chosen this land in which to make her residence. He had followed her. He had entered the town behind her.

But he had not been quick enough to warn her of the dangers of the gunfire. It had happened too quickly.

"What are *you* doing here?" Becky asked, easing her hand from his. She brushed dust from her clothes. "I cannot see how it might have happened by pure accident. Were you following me?"

She was well aware that a look of amusement had entered his eyes as he gazed at her hat, which was hanging awkwardly at the side of her head, the tied ribbon having kept it from being tossed off when she fell. She busied herself untying the ribbon, then retying it once the hat was positioned back atop her head.

"And if I were?" Blazing Eagle said, his gaze shifting to the small pup that snarled at him as it edged protectively closer to Becky. "Would you mind that I did?"

Blazing Eagle had watched her take the pup into her lodge the prior evening. He had watched her pick the ticks from its flesh today, then lovingly bathe the animal in a tub outside the soddy.

Although often Becky pretended to be something she was not—tough—he knew the gentle side of her.

"I . . . I . . ." Becky stammered, her eyes wavering. She was at a loss for words. What *could* she be expected to say to him? That she wished to take up with a married man? That she wished that he would never leave her, that they would never have to say good-bye again?

She did not want to shout at him that he was married, that his attention should be on his wife, not *her*.

But she couldn't find the words. She didn't want to give him cause to turn away from her. Since her father's death, she had been overwhelmed at times by loneliness.

Only since she had discovered that she was in love with Blazing Eagle had those feelings somewhat subsided.

She was finding it hard to play the angry woman, when in truth she wanted nothing more than to feel Blazing Eagle's arms around her.

At that very moment, she made a decision that she hoped would not destroy her life. She decided to take from this man what he would offer her.

She would block thoughts of Waterfall from her mind!

And even though Becky knew that she would be living in sin, at least she would have a part of this man whose mere presence melted her clean down into her shoes.

When she had left him, and he had not even said good-bye, she had thought she would never see him again, that she had lost him forever.

Yet he was here, looking out for her welfare as though they belonged together, their hearts intertwined. How could she not be touched deeply that he cared so much?

"You have nothing to say to Blazing Eagle?" he persisted, his eyes locked with hers.

"What *can* I say but thank you for being here for me," Becky finally said, her voice soft.

"You could have been injured by the gunfire," Blazing Eagle scolded. "This town is no place for a lady. I shall escort you safely home."

Becky looked quickly over her shoulder in the direction of the fleeing outlaws. Her heart sank when she thought of just how close she might have been to finding her brother. She was almost certain that the man she had seen just prior to the bank holdup was Edward.

If things hadn't happened so quickly—if she hadn't been thrown from her horse in the frenzy of the gunfire and the galloping escape of the outlaws—she would have gone after them, and to hell with the danger of doing anything so foolhardy!

"I hope your dog does not take as long to accept my friendship as it has taken you," Blazing Eagle said, laughing softly as the pup continued to snarl and bare his teeth at him.

Becky turned quick eyes up at him. "How do you know Pebbles is my dog?" she asked warily. "Unless you did not just happen on me here in Cheyenne, but instead *were* following me."

"I never said that I was *not* following you," Blazing Eagle said, their eyes meeting again in silent combat. "I will tell you now that I was with you always, from the moment I left you to find Fort Laramie on your own, until now. Do you think that I trusted this lawless country and the men that inhabit it to allow you to travel safely alone?"

"I don't know what to say," Becky said, astonished that he had gone to such lengths to protect her. "If you planned to do this, why didn't you tell me you were going to? It would have been a comfort to know that I wasn't alone."

"I felt it best to do it in this way," Blazing Eagle said. "I sent my son home to instruct Fish Hawk that I would be gone for a few sunrises so that Fish Hawk could watch over my people in my absence."

"Did Whistling Elk know where you were going?" Becky asked softly, in her mind's eye recalling how often she had caught Whistling Elk silently studying her, trying to understand what his father's interest in her was.

"It was best not to," Blazing Eagle said. "It is best that he gets to know you gradually, to give him time to accept that I have another woman in my life besides his mother."

Becky paled. She again was at a loss for words. This man was blatantly pursuing her while he had a wife. He had finally admitted it!

She had studied the Cheyenne in school, but was not sure whether or not the warriors took more than one wife.

Was this Blazing Eagle's plan? To eventually take her into his lodge to make her his second wife? Or would she be expected to live in another lodge away from him, as Waterfall obviously did?

Confused, now afraid even to ask what his true intentions were, Becky bent and lifted Pebbles into her arms. "There now," she said, stroking his thick fur. "Blazing Eagle isn't going to hurt you. Calm down. He's your friend."

Blazing Eagle whistled for Becky's horse. Having once been Blazing Eagle's favorite steed, it knew to follow the command of his whistle and came to him in a soft gallop. When it stopped at Blazing Eagle's side, it nuzzled at his hand and softly whinnied.

Becky placed Pebbles in his sling at the side of

the horse, then turned to Blazing Eagle. "I had planned to stay in town the night, but . . . but if you truly don't mind escorting me home, I'd appreciate it," she said softly. "I've had enough of this town for one night."

She had failed this time to make contact with her brother. She must be content to wait until another time, another opportunity, which she hoped would not be filled with as many risks as today.

"It would be best if you never come again," Blazing Eagle said, taking her by her waist and lifting her into her saddle.

As she grabbed her reins, he still stood there watching her. "You still did not say what lured you to this town," he said.

Becky's eyes wavered into his. "Please don't ask," she said softly. "It is something I would rather not share with anyone . . . at least not yet."

"In time you will?" Blazing Eagle said, arching an eyebrow. "You will share your reasons with Blazing Eagle?"

"When you are ready to share your secrets with me, then I shall share mine with you," Becky said, slapping her reins and riding away from him.

Blazing Eagle watched her for a moment, then mounted his sorrel and rode after her. As he sidled his horse close to hers at the edge of town, he turned to her. "In time we shall share everything," he said, knowing that she had referred to how he had behaved after he kissed her.

He could not speak to her about it until he understood the meaning of his sudden remembrances of that fateful day, after having them suppressed all these years.

The kiss they'd shared had caused all of the pain of that day to return to him, and he could not understand why.

What could the connection be? he worried again.

He had to know.

And he *would*.

He would kiss her time and again.

If each time he kissed her, the past came back to him in such a way, then he would take that as a sign that she was not good for him and he would have to turn his back on her forever.

If that was ever truly possible.

She was a part of him now, their souls having surely been blessed as though they were one from the beginning of time, when they both were only an invisible seed waiting to be planted inside the wombs of their mothers.

They rode until the inky blackness of night fell all around them. Becky's stomach ached with hunger, but she did not want to stop until she was back inside her soddy and Blazing Eagle had gone his own way.

If they stopped along the way and were totally alone beneath the moon and stars, without any chance of interference from a son or a wife, who was to say what would transpire between them?

Becky did know that her insides cried out for him even now that he was so close.

To be kissed by him again—oh, to be kissed by him!

But dangers lay in such a kiss, even in an embrace, with no one there to stop them from exploring their feelings completely.

She had never been with a man sexually.

But by the way she ached where she had never known she had feelings before, she knew that this ache was the ache of a woman in love!

Dawn began to creep along the horizon when Becky finally saw her soddy a short distance away. She was so sleepy that she could hardly hold her head up. Pebbles was the lucky one. He was asleep in his sling.

Finally at her home, Becky welcomed Blazing Eagle's arms as he lifted her from the saddle.

But that closeness was all that it took to awaken her.

She drifted into his arms.

His mouth covered her lips with a gentle kiss.

His hands set her afire when he molded her breasts within them.

Sighing, she twined her arms around his neck.

He started to carry her inside when Pebbles let out a loud howl at having been forgotten in the sling.

Becky was brought back to her senses by Pebbles. Wide-eyed, she staggered backwards from Blazing Eagle. Her heart was pounding so hard from ecstasy that she was dizzy from it.

Pebbles howled again.

Becky smiled weakly up at Blazing Eagle, then rescued her pup from the sling.

The sound of a horse's hooves drew her quickly around. Her heart in her throat, she watched Blazing Eagle ride away toward the rising sun.

When he turned and waved at her, his smile bright as the leap of her heart, she waved back and smiled at him.

"I love you," she whispered into the air as feelings that were deliciously new to her overwhelmed her. "My Cheyenne warrior, I shall always love you."

She frowned as she walked into her soddy, wondering if her love for him was strong enough to share him with another woman.

"Never!" she cried. "How could I be expected to? I would never be able to go to bed apart from him when he would be in the arms of another woman. It would tear me apart. I would want to die!"

She plopped down onto her bed without first undressing. "Pebbles, what am I to do?" she whispered, hugging him to her. "I knew that my life would not be simple once I left Missouri. But I never expected these sorts of complications."

Her thoughts went to Edward. "Edward," she softly cried. "Was that you today? Was I truly that close to you that I could have reached out and touched you?"

Chapter Thirteen

Becky had slept a full day and night away and had awakened more refreshed than she had felt since leaving Saint Louis. Even then, she had missed many nights of sleep sitting at her father's bedside those last weeks of his life.

After drying the last breakfast dish, she stared at a small box that she had taken from her travel bag. She had not yet opened it to take out the tintype of her brother to place on the mantel over the fireplace. She wanted it near to remind her of how her brother had once been—so sweet and caring, so gentle to all.

She wanted to remember that he had been everything to her before the war and before turning outlaw.

Yet she feared placing the photograph where others might see it. If he was recognized, and she was forced to say that he was her brother, her every move might be watched and the authorities might think that she would lead them to her brother's hideout.

"They wouldn't believe me if I told them that I don't know where he is," she said, her gaze shifting as Pebbles stretched out at her feet.

Her jaw set determinedly, Becky tossed her dishrag aside and lifted the box from the table. Her fingers trembled as she removed the lid and stared down at the small image of her brother set in a silver frame.

Tears pooled in her eyes as she took the framed picture and held it out to take a lingering look at it.

"Edward, I doubt that I shall *ever* understand," she murmured. "Even if I find you and you try to explain, I shall never be able to understand what drove you into the life of an outlaw. It makes no sense. No sense at all. You had everything a boy would want. And as a young man, the girls almost camped on your doorstep."

She hugged the photograph to her bosom. "Will I ever see you again?" she said, tears streaming from her eyes.

Not expecting anyone to come calling this morning, she placed the tintype on the fireplace mantel. She stood back and gazed at it again, wiped the tears from her eyes, then lifted a hairbrush to resume brushing her hair.

She dropped the brush when she heard the sound of horses arriving outside the soddy. Her heart leaped into her throat at the thought that it might be Blazing Eagle coming to check on her welfare since he seemed to have assigned himself her guardian.

She glanced down at her drab skirt and blouse. She had dressed in work clothes so that she could scrub some more on the wood floors. Never in a million years had she expected that anyone would see her. Especially not Blazing Eagle!

Then the color drained from her face when she looked across the room at the picture on the fireplace mantel. She had to hide it! She couldn't allow Blazing Eagle to see it. If he recognized it . . .

A persistent knocking on the door drew her eyes back around to stare at the door.

She glanced at the tintype again, then rushed to the door. She would step outside quickly and talk with Blazing Eagle there. Under no circumstances could she allow him, or anyone, to see the picture of her brother.

Her heart racing, her knees weak, Becky unlatched the door and shoved it slowly open.

She stiffened when she discovered who was standing there. It most certainly was not Blazing Eagle!

"You," she said abruptly, eyes wide. "Thad Patrick. What are you doing here?"

She glanced at Major Kent, her jaw tightening when she saw a distinctly mischievous glint in his eyes.

"How good it is to see you again, my dear," Thad said, lifting his hat from his head and bow-ing. He straightened his back and smiled down at her from his lanky height. The diamond stickpin in the folds of his cravat glistened in the morning sunlight. "When that savage rode away with you—well, I . . ."

Becky lifted her chin angrily and placed her hands on her hips as she glared up at him. "Savage?" she said, interrupting him. "Yes, you would label an Indian warrior a savage, wouldn't you? You and your fancy trains that now occupy so much of Shaiyena land."

She paled and took a step away from them when she realized what she had said in defense of Blazing Eagle and his people. She smiled awkwardly past Thad at Major Kent, then lowered her arms to her sides.

Pebbles inched his way outside the house, sidling close to Becky's skirt and whining. She bent and stroked his fur for a moment. When he grew quiet, she straightened herself again and looked stiffly from man to man, wishing they would leave.

"Thad came to the fort asking about your welfare," Major Kent said dryly.

"I was headed back to New York by train when I recalled the misadventure of the other day and wondered if you had been found," Thad said, circling his hat between his fingers. "It is good to see that the sa—Indian did you no harm."

"Thad, I truly appreciate your concern," Becky said, nervously raking her fingers through her hair, lifting it back from her face.

"It will be a while before the next train arrives.

Perhaps we could share some further conversation over a cup of coffee?" Thad said as he strained himself to look past Becky into her soddy.

Recalling the tintype and knowing that Major Kent would quickly recognize her brother, and truly wanting nothing more to do with this Thad person, Becky took a sidewise step which centered her in the door.

"Things are not yet presentable for visitors," she said, her voice drawn. She nodded toward the mud-and-grass roof. "As you see, this is not the most desirable of houses. It will do, though, until I have another house built on my property. Or move elsewhere, when more suitable lodging becomes available."

"We've both seen worse in our lives, haven't we, Thad?" Major Kent said, taking a step closer to Becky. "I'd sure enjoy that cup of coffee, ma'am."

Pebbles growled and bared his teeth at the major, causing him to take a quick step backward.

"Where'd that mutt come from?" he said, glowering at Pebbles.

"I found him at my doorstep my first night here," Becky said, bending to pick Pebbles up into her arms. She smiled devilishly at the Major, and then slowly over at Thad. "He's my watchdog. Although small, I think he could take a good chunk of skin off a man's leg."

"I think we'd best go," Thad said, swallowing hard as he slapped his hat on his head. "Nice seeing you again, Miss Veach. I'm glad you made it through your ordeal unscathed."

Major Kent tipped his hat to Becky, gave her a

lingering stare, then swung around and mounted his horse. He waited for Thad to mount, then they both rode off in the direction of Fort Laramie.

"Whew!" Becky said, carrying Pebbles back inside her soddy. "That was a close call, but I got out of that one, didn't I, Pebbles? I thought for certain they weren't going to take no for an answer when they asked to come inside for coffee."

She gazed at her brother's picture. "Edward, you came close to being recognized," she said, placing Pebbles on the floor. "And it's not the best of times to admit to being your sister."

Pebbles broke into a fit of barking and growling behind Becky. She tensed, knowing that if he was this upset, someone else had come for a visit this morning.

And the way Pebbles was acting, this person might even be *in* the soddy!

Swinging around, Becky gasped when she found Blazing Eagle standing just inside the door, his shadow long and lean across the boards of the floor.

"Blazing Eagle!" Becky said, her heart skipping an anxious beat. "I didn't hear you arrive on your horse. How did you get here? Why *are* you here?"

"I have still been keeping watch on you, to make sure that you are all right. I saw the two white men come to talk to you. One was Major Kent. The other man I recognized from the day I abducted you from the train."

"That man owns part interest in the train," Becky

corrected. "He came with Major Kent to check on my welfare."

"Nothing more?" Blazing Eagle said, taking a step closer to her.

Color and heat flooded Becky's cheeks. "Well—yes, I guess you could say that," she murmured. "He and Major Kent wanted a cup of coffee."

She didn't want to tell Blazing Eagle that she knew from Thad's behavior on the train, and this morning, that he wanted more than mere conversation with her. He saw her as vulnerable and innocent, someone who needed a husband.

She looked past him, then up into his eyes. "Where is your horse?" she asked. "As I said, I didn't hear you arrive."

"I thought it best to hide it in case other white eyes happened along," Blazing Eagle said. Studying her belongings, he began walking around the room. "If they knew I was here, in a white woman's house, the whole army would come in your defense."

Becky's heart skipped a beat when she remembered the tintype on the fireplace mantle. She had to remove it. She couldn't let him see it.

She inched her way toward it, but stopped when Blazing Eagle turned on a heel and looked her way, then past her, over her shoulder, at once seeing the framed picture.

His insides clenched and jealousy overwhelmed him when he saw that it was a man's face inside the silver frame.

Becky died a million deaths when she realized that he had seen the tintype. She nervously clasped her hands together behind her. She scarcely breathed as he lifted it from the mantel.

She watched his expression change from a strange sort of bitter jealousy to something dark and frightening. His fingers tightened on the frame as he drew it closer to his eyes. Then he looked contemptuously at Becky, making her cringe and take a slow step away from him.

"What is this man to you?" he said, having recognized the man in the tintype to be the golden-haired outlaw.

When Becky said nothing, Blazing Eagle took one step closer to her, his fingers tightly gripping the framed image. "Did you travel far on the iron horse to Shaiyena country to see this man?" he said, his eyes narrowing. "An outlaw hated by both red and white skins?"

Sparks of anger glinted in his dark eyes as he leaned down to speak into her face. "Speak!" he demanded. "Give me answers!"

Becky stammered, unable to find the words to tell him that this man in the picture, this outlaw, was her brother! How could she? She was too ashamed to ever tell anyone, especially Blazing Eagle. She didn't want to give him cause to hate her.

Unsure about how to explain her brother to Blazing Eagle, she turned her back to him. Her heart sank when he circled around in front of her and shoved the portrait into her hand. Then, without another word, he stamped out of the house.

She wanted to go after him, for this time she felt

as though she *had* lost him forever.

When she got to the door and ran outside, she didn't see him anywhere. It was as though he had disappeared into thin air.

Numb, she slumped down on the ground and beat her fists against it, sobbing. "Edward!" she cried. "Damn you, Edward!"

Chapter Fourteen

Back at his village, Blazing Eagle sat before his lodge fire, staring into the dancing flames. No matter how hard he tried, he could not get Becky off his mind.

Even though he now knew that she had an association with the golden-haired outlaw, he could not force her out of his heart. Each heartbeat told him that he cared for her more than he had ever cared for any other woman.

And the way she had returned his embraces and kisses had revealed to him her true feelings for him.

"Then what is this man to her?" he whispered, tortured by his worries. Becky's and the outlaw's hair coloring was the same. Could they be brother and sister? Or, if the outlaw was her husband, how could she *love* someone like him?

If he was her brother, how could she have the

same blood flowing through her veins as that ruthless, murdering criminal? Deep inside her somewhere, might she carry the same evil traits?

No, he thought, sinking his head into his hands. She was not capable of violence.

She was a spirited woman who stood up for herself in a time of crisis. But that was a trait most people admired. It did not label her a renegade only because she spoke her mind and had the courage to do so.

Weary of thinking about what Becky's relationship was with the outlaw, Blazing Eagle determinedly set his jaw and rose quickly to his feet. He slipped into his fringed buckskin breeches and shirt, then yanked on his moccasins.

In his frenzy of trying to find answers, he had finally come to a conclusion. He would fight for this woman. No matter if the outlaw was a husband, lover, or brother, Blazing Eagle would make her turn her eyes from the man whose heart, whose very soul, was black! As evil as the man had proved to be, he might be dangerous even to Becky.

And, Blazing Eagle thought with a pounding heart, it was time for him to love again—and to trust.

Needing more than himself in this time of tumultuous feelings, Blazing Eagle left his lodge in eager steps toward Young Bear's lodge. Young Bear was the village shaman and had powers in affairs of the heart. Young Bear was Blazing Eagle's special friend.

Blazing Eagle let the early morning sun warm his tired bones. The breeze carried with it the aroma of cook fires and the river. The sound of an eagle's cry as it soared high overhead made him realize the true wonders of this day, yet his heart was heavy. His mind was too troubled to enjoy anything.

As he reached the shaman's lodge, he stopped and gazed at it. Positioned somewhat outside the circle of tepees, this lodge was painted red and tattooed with the secret and magic totems of the tribe.

Nearby was a tribal scalp pole, displaying the hair of their enemies in the wars long since gone. The scalps hung there always to remind his people that warring was not something taken lightly.

Warring meant death.

Warring sometimes meant annihilation of one's tribe!

He grabbed at his temple and swayed when the pounding began as it had when he kissed the white woman. He winced and groaned as the flashes of memory came to him again. He closed his eyes and gritted his teeth as in his mind's eye he saw rugged white men racing into his village on horseback on the day of the slaughter of his people.

He saw rifles firing.

He saw . . .

His eyes opened wildly with a memory that tore at his very being! As before, he recalled seeing Indians scattered among the white men, their arrows hitting their targets as they sank into the chests and backs of Blazing Eagle's beloved people.

In his mind's eye, he saw something else. He gasped and shook his head to clear his thoughts when he envisioned a woman among those men who had unmercifully killed his people. He saw her hair! It was . . .

"Blazing Eagle?"

Someone speaking Blazing Eagle's name drew him out of his dreaded remembrances. Young Bear reached for Blazing Eagle's arm and steadied him.

"My son, what is it?" Young Bear said, his old voice weak. "I heard you groan. Are you ill?"

He ushered Blazing Eagle through the entrance way, over which hung a strip of buckskin. "Come in out of the sun," he said, taking Blazing Eagle into the cool darkness of his lodge. "You seem shaken by something. Would you want to tell Young Bear about it? Is that why you are here? You need to empty your heart of something that troubles you?"

Blazing Eagle sat down in the center of the lodge. There was only a low fire within the circle of rocks, which gave the lodge a ghostly air.

Breathing hard, Blazing Eagle reached inside himself to remember what had only momentarily surfaced. But, as always before, once he was wrenched back into the present the visions he had seen in his mind's eye were gone again.

He knew that one day he would remember it all. From what he could already remember, he was not sure he wished to know it all. He now knew that there would be much pain associated with these recollections.

If only it could have remained locked up somewhere inside him, and never surfaced!

But one thing was good about remembering today—it had not happened while he was embracing the woman of his heart! What had caused him to remember this time? The scalps that hung from Young Bear's scalp pole? He had been looking at the scalps just before remembering.

A tap on his shoulder and the feel of a pipe's warm bowl against the back of his hand, brought Blazing Eagle completely back to the present.

"We shall smoke your troubles away," Young Bear said, handing his long-stemmed pipe to Blazing Eagle. "We shall smoke, then we shall talk."

Blazing Eagle smiled at Young Bear. The elderly shaman had been there for Blazing Eagle when Blazing Eagle was a young brave of nine winters who had lost everything. He had given him comfort in his words.

He still made life more easy for Blazing Eagle. He was always there for him, to confide in over problems of his chieftainship.

Blazing Eagle had sought understanding from Young Bear when Blazing Eagle's wife, Star Shines, had chosen to return to her parents' lodge instead of staying and helping raise their son of one summer.

But never had Blazing Eagle brought talk of love for a white woman to this gentle shaman. Would he understand? Could he offer advice on a subject he would surely rather not discuss?

Young Bear's thick gray hair flowed over his shoulders. His eyes were no longer a deep brown, but instead had faded to an almost gray color. He wore a brief breechcloth, revealing his bony chest and arms.

Young Bear's eyes intense on him, Blazing Eagle touched his lips to the stem of the pipe. He drew out only a small measure of smoke, yet it was enough so that the mixture of red willow bark and tobacco leaves glowed brightly in the red earth ball of the pipe. He exhaled rapidly, then handed the pipe back to Young Bear.

Before Young Bear smoked, he ceremoniously pointed the pipe stem in the direction of the sky, the ground, and the four directions.

"Spirit above, smoke," he said softly. "Earth, smoke. Four cardinal points, smoke."

The smokes to the four cardinal points were offered to the spirits who dwelled in those quarters. The pipe was straight, made of the shank-bone of a deer. It was cut off at both ends, the marrow punched out, the mouth end pared down and made smooth.

He then emptied his pipe and restored it to its red cloth container.

"Now, my *naha*, tell me what is in your heart," Young Bear said, reaching to rest a hand on Blazing Eagle's shoulder. "Today your face is marked with a frown. Your eyes tell many stories, none of which I can read. Do you wish to share them with me?"

Blazing Eagle nodded. "I chose to come for one purpose, then it became two when I had a vision that shook me clear to the very core of myself," he said. "You are wise like the owl. I came to ask your advice about a woman. Then, just as I arrived at your lodge, something else came to me that needs to be spoken about."

"A woman?" Young Bear said, studiously gazing at Blazing Eagle. "The captive white woman?"

Blazing Eagle's eyes widened as he stared at the old shaman. "How did you know?" he said, his voice drawn. "Do you see inside my heart that easily?"

"I observe," Young Bear said, nodding. "I take

from my observations and know many things others do not. I saw you with the white woman enough times to see how you looked at her and behaved toward her. I saw her return the look of infatuation." He shrugged. "You love her. She loves you. That is my conclusion."

"And does that dissatisfy you?" Blazing Eagle dared to ask. "Can you accept that Blazing Eagle, a Cheyenne with copper skin and black hair, loves a woman whose skin is white and whose hair is golden? Can you accept that the blood that flows through our veins is so different?"

"My son, I have watched you grow from a child into an adult whose courage and knowledge made you into a powerful chief," Young Bear said, his eyes gleaming proudly into Blazing Eagle's. "Your judgment about all things is trusted. If your life path joins with that of a white woman, so be it. Follow it. Marry her. And should your children have pale skin, so be it. The child will have been born into this world for all of the right reasons. The child will have been born of love. I respect your wishes, my son. So will everyone else of our village."

"From the bottom of my heart, I thank you for saying these things," Blazing Eagle said humbly. He paused, looked away, then turned his eyes back to the shaman. "But I have not yet told you everything."

"You wish now to speak of that something else that you mentioned?" Young Bear said, folding his arms comfortably across his chest.

"No, I still wish to speak of the white woman," Blazing Eagle said, his voice drawn.

"Then say it," Young Bear said softly. "Bring it all to me today so that tomorrow you can go about your business without a heavy heart."

"This woman is somehow associated with the golden-haired outlaw," Blazing Eagle blurted out. He tensed when he heard Young Bear gasp and saw alarm leap into the elderly shaman's eyes.

"In what way?" Young Bear asked warily.

"I do not know," Blazing Eagle said, sighing as he slowly shook his head back and forth.

Then he firmed his jaw and gave Young Bear a stern, determined look. "He is either her brother, lover, or husband," he said, his voice ragged with frustration.

"If she is married, then you must look the other way and find another woman," Young Bear said solemnly. "If this man is her brother or lover, then I say that you should save her from this man."

Young Bear kneaded his chin. "I saw in her eyes that she loves you, yet there is this man who might be her husband?" he said softly. "Perhaps white people sometimes take two husbands to their beds?"

"I am not aware of such a practice," Blazing Eagle said. "But if so, and she is married to this outlaw, then I will turn my back to her." He paused. "You still give me your blessing about this woman?"

"I trust your judgment in all things," Young Bear said, placing a hand on Blazing Eagle's knee. "Be careful, my son. The outlaw with the golden hair is the worst of his kind."

"That I know is true," Blazing Eagle said, nodding.

"Now what else have you brought to me this

morning that needs to be spoken about?" Young Bear said, again folding his arms across his chest.

"I am having occasional recollections about my past that I never before could remember," Blazing Eagle said.

"That is *good*," Young Bear said, smiling. "Now it can be put to rest inside your heart."

"It is not that easily done," Blazing Eagle said, his voice drawn, his eyes weary. "I only remember in bits and pieces. It is torture, Young Bear, when I am remembering that day of my youth when everything was taken from me."

"Let it come, then you can bury it outside your heart, rather than carry it deeply within your soul like a festering sore that will not heal," Young Bear said, then looked toward his entrance flap when he heard the approach of a horse outside in the village.

Blazing Eagle also heard. His heart leapt at the thought that perhaps it was Becky coming to explain about the man in the picture and to tell him that she loved him.

Young Bear and Blazing Eagle rose to their feet. Blazing Eagle lifted the entrance flap and peered outside. His heart sank when he saw that Becky had not come.

Yet he was glad to see who had come to pay a visit. Judge Roy Newman. Blazing Eagle called him a friend. He admired the judge for standing up for what he believed. He saw that the judge's decision to hang the most vicious of criminals was the true way to rid this land of vermin!

Blazing Eagle stood just outside the shaman's lodge, Young Bear at his side, and watched the children rush to greet Judge Newman, whom they had nicknamed "Many Sweets Man." He always brought candy to the children.

Even now he was reaching inside his coat pockets for the candy, then giving it out by the handfuls as the children gathered around him.

"He is a good man," Young Bear said. "He is a man with a good and generous heart."

"Yes, he is a good man," Blazing Eagle said. "He is a true friend."

Blazing Eagle gazed at Judge Newman. He was a tall, big-boned man with broad shoulders, piercing blue eyes, a mustache and goatee, and a square-set jaw. He always wore a coarse black suit with a narrow black tie. He had served two years in the white man's Congress and had always displayed a sympathy for the Indians.

He had became known as the Indians' best friend because of his interest in Indian affairs.

He was in the Wyoming Territory to try to help bring law and order. His first murder trial had ended with a long, bitter denouncement of the prisoner. In a cold voice he had repeated three times that he sentenced the man to hang by the neck until he was dead, dead, dead.

He meted out justice as he saw it. He did not hesitate to pronounce a death sentence. He had said often to Blazing Eagle that those criminals he had judged to die had taken human life, had sent a soul unprepared to its maker. He said that the criminal had defied God's law and deserved the rope around his neck.

The candy gone from his pockets, Judge Newman turned laughing eyes toward Blazing Eagle, then came to him and clasped his hand in friendship, and then Young Bear's.

"What brings you to my village besides being generous to our children?" Blazing Eagle said, slinging an arm around the judge's shoulders and ushering him toward his own lodge as Young Bear slipped away, back inside his lodge.

"My friend, it seems I have a mixed bag of news today," Judge Newman said. "The bad news is that a wagon train of settlers were found slaughtered."

Judge Newman paused just outside Blazing Eagle's tepee. "I don't have time for a smoke today, Blazing Eagle," he said solemnly. "I have business that awaits my attention back at Fort Laramie. I just came to pass along the information that I felt you need to hear."

"What else besides the slaughter of more white settlers do you have to tell me?" Blazing Eagle said, turning his back to his entrance flap. He folded his arms across his chest and gazed into the judge's eyes.

"The slaughter was made to look like Indians did it," Judge Newman said. "And since the slaughter was closer to Shaiyena land than to that of any other tribe, some say that the Cheyenne are guilty of the crime."

"Blazing Eagle's Fox clan of Cheyenne walk a path of peace," Blazing Eagle said, his voice tight. "Should we be wrongly accused, those of us who were not incarcerated would be forced to follow the path of warring. I would not wish for this to happen. But if they are given no other choice . . ."

"Not wishing to show you any disrespect, allow me to interrupt what you are saying to tell you that although Major Kent might be forced to come and arrest you, the chief, to appease the townfolk of Cheyenne and the nearby settlers, don't worry about such an incarceration. I have the power to set you free again."

"One day or night of my incarceration would be too much for my people to tolerate," Blazing Eagle growled. "My warriors would come for me, for we are innocent of taking lives."

"I urge you not to worry about incarceration," Judge Newman reiterated. "I would not allow you to stay behind bars for even one hour, let alone one full sunset. And everyone knows that I am fair to everyone. I only hang those who I know are guilty of crimes accused. I know that you walk with a warm heart and with peace in each of your footsteps."

Giggling, several children inched closer.

"Well, business done, I think I just might have some more candy in my saddlebag," Judge Newman said, winking mischievously at Blazing Eagle.

Blazing Eagle went with him to his horse. He stood aside as the judge brought another handful of candy out and placed it in the tiny outstretched hands.

Content, the children ran away, laughing.

Blazing Eagle turned to Judge Newman, his smile gone. "Do you know anything of the history of the golden-haired outlaw?" he asked warily. "Where he is from originally? About his family? Does he perhaps have a wife?"

Judge Newman laughed sardonically. "All I know

of that man is that he's surely the devil's son," he said, swinging himself into his saddle.

Blazing Eagle's insides tightened. He reached a hand of friendship toward Judge Newman. "Peace be with you," he said thickly.

"And with you," the judge said. He eased his hand from Blazing Eagle's, then rode away.

Still wondering how the beautiful, sweet white woman could care anything for the renegade outlaw, Blazing Eagle went to his sorrel. He needed to take a long ride. He could think more clearly on his horse.

He took the reins, mounted the sorrel, and rode off. He could not help but wonder if the white woman could be blinded to what the outlaw did. Or did she even know that he had turned bad?

He wondered if such a man could have ever been good.

He rode from the village, Judge Newman long gone from his sight.

A kestral flew by and swallows chattered overhead. Then a prairie falcon came like a phantom from the pines, looped overhead and darted west.

Blazing Eagle's eyes followed and led them to two golden eagles, soaring in tandem, one over the other. They were the precursor of a vision.

"Give me a vision that lifts the weariness from my heart and soul!" Blazing Eagle cried to the heavens.

Chapter Fifteen

Blazing Eagle found himself drawn in the direction of Becky's soddy. He would question her further about her relationship with the outlaw. He would prove once and for all to himself that she was a good woman, worthy of being loved by a Cheyenne chief.

He did not want to believe that his love for her was wasted. Each of his moments on this earth was important. It was imperative that all of his decisions were accurate and not a waste of time, whether in council with his warriors or with a woman of his choosing.

Blazing Eagle's horse's mane fluttered as the wind blew through the sea of grass on each side of him. Cone flowers danced with lupine; blue flax reflected the sky and shimmered like small, suspended pools of water. There were butterflies on the bergamot and clovers, and mountain bluebirds flew in and out of the grass.

He rode onward, his gaze on the soddy a short distance away. A red-breasted nuthatch yelled "ink-ink" in its peculiar nasal twang as it flew overhead. A warbler sat in the dark foliage of pine trees at Blazing Eagle's right side, and sang.

When Blazing Eagle saw Becky leave her soddy and place her dog in the sling at the side of her horse, then swing herself into the saddle, he yanked his reins to one side. He led his steed into the dark shadows of the pines and waited for Becky to ride past.

As she grew closer, her free-flowing golden hair seemed to be the reflection of the sun. When her riding skirt lifted in the breeze past her knees, revealing a portion of her thighs, Blazing Eagle's body grew warm with want of her.

A part of him wanted to hail her and get on with the business of setting things right in their lives as a pair.

He wanted to listen to her explanation about the outlaw with an open heart.

He wanted her to feel free to speak openly with him.

Another part of him told him to follow her this morning. She seemed intent on something. Her chin was lifted stubbornly. Her eyes were filled with a determined fire.

"She must have a planned destination," Blazing Eagle whispered to himself, his fingers tightening around his reins as he continued to watch her.

He hoped that she would turn her horse in the

direction of his village. He hoped that it was her purpose to go to him to make things right between them.

His heart sank and he inhaled a disappointed breath when she swung her horse suddenly to the left and rode off through the tall grass away from the road in the direction of a low mountain range in the distance.

Blazing Eagle's eyebrows rose as he puzzled over her outing today. Although she was new to these parts, she seemed to know exactly where she was going.

Had she always known the location of the outlaw's hideout after all? he wondered. Even when she was a passenger on the iron horse, had she known?

Had she carried a map tucked into her possessions that the outlaw had sent to her?

The outlaw *did* seem to be her prime purpose for being in Shaiyena country.

Angry at himself for even caring, yet driven to find the answers so that he could either cast the woman from his life or take her into his arms and keep her there forever, Blazing Eagle rode off in the same direction and followed her.

He kept far enough back so that she would not know that she was being followed. The distance was so great between them that he had a hard time keeping her in his sight.

The distance was necessary, for should she turn around, he had to be certain that she would see nothing but the shifting of light and shadow beneath the brilliant dancing rays of the mid-morning sun.

Becky had fought a battle this morning as to where she should go. To Blazing Eagle's village, to apologize to him for being so evasive and to finally explain what Edward was to her? She didn't want to lose Blazing Eagle. She loved him with all of her being!

Yet a part of her fought to continue her search for Edward today. Each day that passed when she had not yet been able to find him and reason with him was a day lost to them both forever. She had the urgent need to meet him face to face to prove to herself that he was, or was *not*, the outlaw that everyone dreaded.

Until she was absolutely certain that this *was* Edward, a portion of her heart still hoped that it was all some horrible, ghastly mistake. She would rather he lay in a grave somewhere down South, having died valiantly defending his beliefs, than here, a dreaded outlaw. She wanted to think of him as a hero, not someone who killed for the pleasure of killing!

"Edward, Edward," she whispered to herself. "Why did it have to be this way? Why?"

Determined to search high and low for her brother's hideout today, and remembering the direction the outlaws had taken when they rode from Cheyenne after the bank robbery, she sank her heels into the flanks of her horse and thundered onward across the waist-high, waving grass.

Pebbles yapped as an eagle swooped low, its mighty wings casting a shadow over them.

"Don't be afraid," Becky said, reaching to pat her pup. "The eagle's eyes were not on *us* for lunch. It has surely spied a field mouse running from the hooves of my horse."

She laughed to herself when she soon discovered that she was right. The eagle swept gracefully down at her left side and flew up again with a mouse hanging limply in its sharp talons.

Sighing, seeing how quickly life could be snuffed out, Becky was even more determined to find her brother in an effort to save him. Each day that he rode with his outlaw friends he chanced being killed. One person's accurate aim could be the end of her brother.

Becky looked heavenward. "Good Lord above, please give me the opportunity to speak with my brother," she softly prayed, her voice breaking. "I've got to know what happened to turn his life in the wrong direction. Please give me the chance. I shall forevermore be grateful. Amen."

She continued onward, riding through scattered stands of scrub pine and cedar, glimpsing mule deer and wolverines. She heard the song of the lark, the whistle of the willow thrush, the harsh calls of the hawk and grebe.

Then her spine stiffened when she thought she heard something else. It sounded like horse's hooves. Was a horse following her?

Without stopping, she looked quickly over her shoulder. She studied everything along the horizon, seeing only the shimmering, fuzzy haze of the morning's heat.

Shrugging, satisfied enough that her imagination was working overtime and playing tricks on her, Becky turned her eyes forward again. She rode on at a gentle gallop and was glad when she found a road that wove among towering spruce trees, up into welcome cooler air. She wiped a bead of perspiration from her brow with her gloved hand.

Then her insides went cold when she heard the distinct sound of a cougar's cry not far away. She gripped her reins more tightly. Frightened, Pebbles barked and struggled to be free of his sling.

Becky patted Pebbles and stroked his fur. "Pebbles, you have cause to be skittish this time," she murmured, her eyes moving warily from side to side, ever searching. "Sweetie, I'm not that brave myself right now."

She slowly moved her hand away from the dog and lowered it toward the rifle at her horse's right side. Her fingers were trembling as she clasped them around the butt of the rifle and slowly slid it out of the gun boot.

Now finding the trees that surrounded her a hindrance, she frowned. They kept her from seeing what might be there that could jump out at her.

The cougar cried again.

Becky's spine stiffened, for she realized that the animal was much too close. It was surely following the scent of her and the horse.

Lord, it might jump on her at any moment!

Becky knew that she could not outrun the cougar on her horse, so she chose to stop and ready the rifle for firing.

Her heart thudding like a thousand drumbeats, she aimed the rifle first in one direction, then in another.

When the cougar cried again, this time more

shrill and threatening, Pebbles managed to jump from the sling. Yapping, he ran off, retreating in the direction Becky had just traveled.

"Pebbles!" she cried. "Oh no, Pebbles. The cougar will surely follow you since you are making such a racket!"

She whistled for the pup, yet did not turn to go after him. She knew that the best place for herself was to stay poised, ready for the attack, should it come.

"Pebbles," Becky whispered, tears pooling in her eyes. "My sweet Pebbles."

Then Becky's heart skipped a beat when she knew that this time she definitely heard the sound of an approaching horseman. She now knew that before, when she had thought she was being followed, her instincts had been correct.

But *who?* she wondered, frightened now more than before when she only had the cougar to be concerned about. Now she had the cougar and perhaps an outlaw or a renegade Indian to deal with.

She felt trapped.

She jerked her head from one side to the other, first watching for the cougar, then for the horseman. As the moments passed, her knees grew weaker and her throat drier. She envisioned her home back in Saint Louis and the serene life she had led. She would trade the excitement she had found in Shaiyena country for even one moment of solitude in her Saint Louis house with sweet memories of her father and brother there to embrace her.

Becky was suddenly aware that she no longer

heard the horseman approaching.

Nor did she hear any sounds from the cougar!

Was she going to be lucky enough to escape the dangers of both?

She slowly lowered her rifle, then rested it on her knee as she took several deep breaths.

"I think all is well after all, except . . . except for Pebbles," Becky said, gazing over her shoulder at the road. Her pup was nowhere in sight. And she could no longer hear him barking.

"He's lost to me forever," Becky whispered, knowing that to go and search for him in this vast land would be futile. If she and her pup were to be reunited, it would have to be up to Pebbles. He would have to find his way back to her.

"I've got to move onward," Becky whispered, slipping her rifle back inside its gun boot. She looked over her shoulder again. "Or should I return home? Haven't I had enough excitement and danger for one day?"

Her jaw firmed stubbornly. "No, I *won't* give up that easily," she whispered to herself. "I have set out today for a purpose. I shall still search for my brother's hideout."

Just as those words brushed across her lips, the cougar sprang into Becky's path, its green eyes luminous in the mid-morning brightness.

Becky's insides went weak. Her hands were frozen on her reins. She was unable to reach for the rifle. She had been foolish to slip it back inside its gun boot!

The cougar suddenly bounded away, startled, as the horse neighed, lowered its head, and reared in protest.

Becky screamed as she was thrown to the ground, landing so hard on her side that her breath was knocked out of her.

For a moment she saw nothing but a black haziness.

Blazing Eagle had caught Pebbles and was riding now to Becky's rescue. He drew his horse to a shuddering halt when someone else appeared on a horse from the dark depths of the spruces and drew rein beside where Becky lay on the road.

Blazing Eagle's eyes widened, and his heart seemed to stand still as he watched this man whom he recognized lean low on his horse and sweep Becky up from the ground onto his lap.

It was the golden-haired outlaw! He watched Becky's reaction to the outlaw as her eyes opened and she realized in whose arms she was being held.

Becky's heart raced as she stared up at her brother. She was filled with many emotions. The most wonderful was that she had finally found Edward! Here he was in the flesh, as real as the very heartbeat that hammered inside her chest. He was alive!

She gasped and stared at the deep, livid gash of a scar that ran from the corner of his left eye well past the corner of his mouth. She had always marveled at his clear, flawless complexion, at his absolute good looks.

It hurt deeply to see him scarred in such a way. She wondered just how he had received such an injury, and at whose hands?

She flung herself into his arms, sobbing. "Edward," she cried. "It *is* you. I've found you."

Edward held her close, one hand stroking her long hair. Tears shone in the corners of his eyes. "Becky, what are you doing out here in this god-forsaken land so far from home?" he managed to say, almost choking on his own emotions.

"Edward, father died a few weeks ago," Becky said, wiping tears from her eyes as she gazed up at him, loving him so much that her insides ached.

"No," Edward gasped, paling.

"Before he died, he wasted away to nothing," Becky explained, finding it hard to say the words. The burial had not been very long ago. She would never forget the horror of dirt being shoveled on her father's casket.

"God," Edward choked out, turning his eyes from her.

Becky placed a finger to his chin and directed his eyes into hers again. "Edward, I traveled from Saint Louis not only to find you, but to see if there was anything I could do to turn your life back around again, to what it was before the war."

"How did you know where to look for me?" he asked.

"When I returned home after father's funeral, I discovered that someone had robbed me of all of our possessions," Becky said bitterly. "I went to report it to the sheriff. I saw the wanted poster on the wall. *Yours*, Edward. Yours."

"God," Edward said again, nervously raking his fingers through his golden hair. "The news has spread as far as Saint Louis, huh? I never thought it would. What can I say, Becky?"

"Tell me the truth, Edward," Becky pleaded. "Tell

me you aren't an outlaw. I . . . we . . . father and I thought you had died during the war. We mourned you as though you *were* dead, Edward. The church gave a memorial in your honor."

She lowered her eyes. "They honored you as though you were a hero, Edward," she gulped out.

When he neither said anything, nor offered any explanation, Becky placed her hands on his cheeks. "Sweet brother, I can't believe that you have done all that is said about you. You were such a gentle man before the war. Did the war change you this much? Is that what drove you to this—this madness?"

Edward's eyes wavered into hers. "Sis, I've got to go," he said, his voice breaking. "I only came today searching for you when I heard that you were in the area. I have come to tell you to go home. Sis, you don't belong here."

He took her hands and held them tightly to his chest. "And, Sis, don't follow me," he said, his voice drawn. "Don't ask any more questions that I can't answer. Go home, Becky. Go home! You don't want to associate yourself with me, Becky. I'm no good for you."

"Edward," Becky said, a sob catching in her throat. "How can I leave you like this? Please come back with me to Saint Louis."

"I can't," Edward said, his eyes steady with hers. "I *won't*. This is my life. Let me live it."

"Oh, Edward," Becky said, again flinging herself into his arms. She hugged him tightly. "How can I say good-bye? How can I turn my back on you? I love you, Edward. No matter what you've done, I still love you."

"As I shall always love you," Edward said. He released her hands, his eyes lingering.

"Tell me you aren't an outlaw," Becky pleaded one last time.

There was a long pause between them, then Edward said in a quavering voice, "I can't tell you that."

With that he placed his hands at her waist and lifted her to the ground and turned her toward her horse, which was now grazing a short distance away.

Becky turned quickly and took uneasy steps away from her brother. "Edward, please," she begged, gesturing toward him with her outstretched arms. "Please stop this life of crime. Come with me. I'll speak in your behalf to the authorities. I'll explain about the war, that it did something to you. Please, Edward? Let me do this for you."

Edward gave her a lingering look, then swung his horse around and rode off.

Becky watched him disappear into the trees.

Feeling empty, her emotions drained, she went to her horse and placed a foot in the stirrup, then stopped and turned around with a start when she again heard the approach of a horse.

Her heart leapt with hope that Edward had changed his mind.

She turned with a smile on her face, then paled when she discovered Blazing Eagle there. In his eyes she saw utter contempt. She shifted her gaze as he set her pup on the ground, then wheeled his horse around and rode away.

She stood there for a moment, motionless, then began calling Blazing Eagle's name. "Blazing Eagle, don't go!" she cried.

She now knew that he had witnessed her moments with Edward. Yet surely he had not heard what had been exchanged between them. Or why would he show such anger toward her? He would understand a sister pleading with a brother!

He had surely viewed them from afar and had thought that she was saying words of love to a husband or lover!

"Blazing Eagle, please listen!" she cried.

When he paid her no heed, she went limp and leaned against her horse. All seemed lost to her now.

Her brother.

The man she loved!

Her reason for living.

Chapter Sixteen

Becky picked Pebbles up and hugged him to her breast. "It seems everything I have done since I left Missouri has been wrong," she murmured. Pebbles nuzzled her neck with his nose. "Except for you, sweet pup. You seem content enough."

She could not help but think of Blazing Eagle again. The look of contempt in his eyes hurt her to the very core of her being.

He had seen her with Edward. He had recognized her brother as a notorious outlaw. How could he *not* think that she approved of the life of crime that her brother led, since he had seen her throw herself into Edward's arms?

"Why didn't Blazing Eagle give me time to explain that Edward was my brother?" she softly cried, cuddling Pebbles closer. "Yet what does it matter, anyhow? He has a wife!"

"I have no wife," Blazing Eagle said suddenly from behind her.

Becky turned with a start and looked over her horse at Blazing Eagle. He had returned. He was on foot. Apparently he had tethered his steed elsewhere. She was stunned to see him there after he had ridden away so angry.

Then what he had just said to her finally sank in. "You . . . have no wife?" she murmured, eyes wide.

"As you have no husband," Blazing Eagle said, stepping around the horse to stand before her.

"But what of Waterfall?" Becky stammered. "She seems to mean so much to you. She is so . . . so devoted to you *and* Whistling Elk. I don't understand."

"My clan of Cheyenne is of the Fox Society. We are a military society," he softly explained. "The military society chooses a soldier girl, one who is like a sister to the men in the society and who is called each time the society goes into council. She is treated with great honor because she brings the men good luck."

"Waterfall is your clan's chosen princess—a soldier girl?" Becky murmured.

She felt full of joy to know that Blazing Eagle was free! She could give him her heart and she could have his!

"Yes, she was chosen," Blazing Eagle said. "Our Fox Society chooses the best-looking girls and those of the finest character. Waterfall is both those things, and more."

"This is why she isn't married?" Becky said. "She

196

is too devoted to you and your society?"

"This is her choice, not something forced upon her," Blazing Eagle said. "But once she chooses to marry, the man must be worthy of her and have riches more than a common man. He must pay well for this special woman, or he will not have her as a wife."

Blazing Eagle took Becky's hands in his. "You are as special in my eyes as any Fox Society princess," he said warmly. "I could not stay away. I had to come back to seek answers for my questions. Perhaps I already have them. I heard you say out loud that the outlaw was your brother."

"And so now you know," Becky said, lowering her eyes.

Then she looked up at him, her eyes brimming with tears. "For many reasons, I did not want to reveal that truth to *any*one," she said, her voice breaking.

"You came to Shaiyena country to search for your brother?" Blazing Eagle asked. "Not to join him in his exploits?"

Becky paled and gasped. "Heavens no," she protested. "If my brother is that outlaw everyone accuses him of being, I could never approve of what he has chosen to do with his life, much less ride with him. I only came to the Wyoming Territory to find him and get answers from him—and to try and talk sense to him." She swallowed hard. "I so badly wanted to take him home with me to Saint Louis."

"Why did he leave his home?" Blazing Eagle persisted. "When did he leave? How did you know where to look for him?"

"The Civil War took him away from our family," Becky said sadly. "He never returned." She hesitated. "I . . . recently saw a wanted poster on him in the sheriff's office back home in Saint Louis. Only then did I even know that he was alive. Only then did I know that he . . . was a wanted criminal."

"And now that you have found him, what will you do?"

"It seems there is not much I can do but pray for him."

"Your God answers all prayers?"

"Only those He sees fit to."

When Blazing Eagle took Pebbles from Becky's arms, his dark eyes heavy with desire, a thrill soared through her. Her whole body reacted to the wonder of the moment, to know that she was free to love Blazing Eagle and he to love her.

"You have a son," she said, as he took her hand and led her through the tall, waving grass, toward the shine of a stream only a short distance away. "To have a son, one must have at one time had a wife." She turned questioning eyes up at him. "Did your wife die?"

Blazing Eagle's eyes wavered, then he reached deeply inside himself for the courage to reveal the truth to Becky. It was a truth that he still felt made him look weak and not so virile in others' eyes.

"My wife, Star Shines, is not dead," he confessed. Not wanting to see the surprise leap into Becky's eyes, he stared past her.

"You said . . . you had no wife," Becky said, stopping, slowly slipping her hand from his.

He turned and gazed down at her. "She is no

longer my *true* wife," Blazing Eagle said. "Our divorce was final long ago when she returned to her parents to live with them."

"She chose to leave you?" Becky stammered out. "How could she? Why?"

"At that time, when I knew that my adopted father would soon die and that I would soon be chief of my clan of Cheyenne, my whole time was spent learning the ways of being a chief," he said, reaching a hand to gently stroke her cheek. "Then I became immersed in performing the duties of a chief when my father passed on to the other side. My young wife felt neglected. I cannot blame her for wanting to return to her parents." He paused, then added, "And her parents were not well. She cared for them until first one died, then the other."

"And still she did not return to you?" Becky asked softly.

"Had she tried, I would have not had her," Blazing Eagle ground out. "When she left, she turned her back not only on a husband, but also a *naha*—a son. She was not worthy of sharing my bed or my son's arms ever again."

Becky hugged his words to her as he framed her face between his hands and drew her lips close to his.

"I never knew what true love was until you," he said huskily. "Although we have had differences from the moment we met, I could not help but love you, as you could not help but love me. I saw it in your eyes. I felt it in your kiss. I shall feel it now as we kiss."

Becky's senses reeled, and she drew a ragged

breath when he touched her lips with his in wonder. Sweet currents of warmth swept through her as a flood of emotions were set free within her. They were both free to love! They had revealed their savage secrets to one another!

Blazing Eagle kissed her with easy sureness and cradled her close. The euphoria that filled his entire being was almost more than he could bear. He had wanted her for so long, and now she was free to be his! It mattered not to him that her brother was the dreaded outlaw. He now knew that she did not approve of such a life as that.

That was all he needed to know to release his pent-up emotions and give her a loving that her kisses cried out for as she clung to him.

"I shall always love you," Blazing Eagle whispered as he drew his lips away. He lifted her into his arms and carried her toward the stream, so shaken with desire that his knees were strangely weak.

"As I shall always love you," Becky said, laying her cheek against his powerful chest. "You do not know how much I desire you. I have never experienced such feelings before. Blazing Eagle, I am so happy, my whole body seems to be floating."

"We shall marry soon," Blazing Eagle said huskily as he laid Becky on a bed of thick, soft moss beside the stream. "But I wish to make love to you *now*. Will you allow it?"

"Do with me as you wish," Becky said, frantic with need of him. "I shall do the same for you."

Pebbles came and lay down beside them, resting his head on his paws, quizzically watching as Blazing Eagle slowly and methodically undressed Becky.

Having never been nude before in the presence of a man, Becky shyly crossed her arms over her bare breasts, her face hot with a blush.

"Do not fear what we are to share and do not be ashamed of your body *ever* in my presence," Blazing Eagle said as he gently took her wrists and eased her arms away from her breasts. His eyes became pits of passion as he gazed down at her breasts, the nipples taut and brown.

Then his gaze lowered, past the flat, creamy flesh of her belly to that place where soft, golden locks of hair covered her womanhood.

His hands trembled as he placed them at her ankles and moved them slowly up the curve of her legs to her thighs, then inward, where the secrets of her desire lay, waiting and throbbing.

"You are most lovely," Blazing Eagle said, his heart pounding as his fingers smoothed over the softness of the tendrils of hair over her warm and secret place. He delved one finger into the fronds of hair and searched until he found her bud of pleasure.

Becky inhaled a quavering breath and gasped with ecstasy as he moved his fingers over that part of her that she never knew had life before. As he stroked her, she became more and more alive, wild ripples of desire washing through her.

Blazing Eagle stretched out beside Becky. His tongue sought one of her nipples, his free hand gently kneading it as his mouth covered the nipple, his teeth nipping.

"Oh, what you are doing to me?" Becky whispered, thrashing her head from side to side. "Never—oh, never would I have believed anything could feel so sweet—so wonderful."

"You will feel so much, much more," Blazing Eagle said.

His mouth was hot and demanding as once again he kissed her. He could feel the impediment of his clothes where his manhood had grown to its full, hungry length within the confines of his buckskin breeches. He ground his hardness against her thigh, acquainting her for the first time with how a man felt when he was at the height of his desire for a woman. He gyrated against her, groaning until he could hardly stand the waiting any longer.

Pulling away from her, Blazing Eagle rose to his feet and stood over her as he removed his clothes.

When he was standing nude and she saw his full arousal, she blushed and smiled shyly up at him. When one of his hands cradled his heaviness within its palm, then circled it with his fingers and slowly moved them on himself, her eyes widened and desire swept through her as never before.

As his fingers moved, the pulsing crest of her passion leapt through her. She grew languorous at the sight of him preparing himself for the height of pleasure that awaited him.

Weakened by his stormy passion, having seen that his performance had heightened her need of him, Blazing Eagle knelt down over her and parted her thighs. He took her mouth savagely in his, his hands clasping her buttocks to mold her slender, wondrous body against his springing manhood, then probed between her thighs with his throbbing need of her.

As though practiced, as if she had done this countless times before, Becky spread her legs and welcomed the hot tip of his manhood, that pulsating hardness that pressed inward.

He groaned against her lips as he moved slowly within her, then entered her finally with one insistent thrust that made her cry out against his lips.

"I could not help but cause pain for that moment of entrance," he whispered against her lips. "Now feel what I offer you. Relax. Let it blossom within you like a rose opening to the sunlight. Let it spread. Fly with me, my woman, to the heavens. To the stars!"

"Yes, yes, the pain has passed," Becky whispered, clinging around his neck. "I feel something far better now. Oh, my darling, I never knew! I never knew!"

He moved slowly at first with careful deliberation, then faster with quick, surer movements. His hands took in the roundness of her breasts, stroking. Her lips parted and he probed. Their tongues touched as their kiss lengthened. His steel arms then enfolded her as he lifted her closer so that he could go deeper. His strokes were wild now, moving with maddening speed within her.

Becky opened more widely to him, her hips responding to him in a rhythmic movement. Her whole body quivered with sensation. Her stomach churned wildly. She felt the pulsing crest of her passion, her heat and excitement alarming her. A madness seemed to have engulfed her.

Her hands clung to his sinewed shoulders as they rode each other in rhythmic movements. Blazing Eagle cupped her swelling breasts, then kissed their nipples. He felt himself heating up like a burning flame. His mouth again seared into hers with intensity, every nerve in his body tensing as he felt himself reaching the ultimate of pleasure.

He swept his arms around her and anchored her more fiercely still, then delved even more deeply into the rose-red, slippery heat of her body. He moaned. He gasped. He clutched her near.

Then he quavered violently, spilling his seed within her.

The feeling, the intense pleasure that accompanied her climax, came at once, startling Becky. She felt as though her whole insides had burst into flames as the warmth of rapture flooded her. She clung to Blazing Eagle. She bit into his shoulder to stifle a scream of ecstasy. Then they fell apart and stretched out on their backs, panting.

Blazing Eagle turned to Becky.

She turned to him.

He crossed his wrists over his heart, sign talk for love.

She smiled at him and reached a hand to his cheek. "You are wonderful," she whispered, her body still throbbing with the aftermath of making love for the first time in her life. The momentary pain that she had experienced was long forgotten. The beautiful feelings that came afterward were worth what little pain it took to have them.

"Let us spend the night here away from the rest of the world," Blazing Eagle said, turning to place his hard body against the softness of hers. "We shall make love again and again!"

"You are your people's chief," Becky said, sucking in a wild breath of pleasure as his tongue stroked one of her nipples, then made a wet path across her belly and lower still until he reached that part of her that until today had been locked away to the world. When he flicked his tongue over her swollen bud of pleasure, she emitted a soft cry and closed her eyes as he stroked her there, making her passion come alive again.

He paused and gazed up at her. "Yes, I am chief, but I have assigned Fish Hawk to my duties until I return and resume them myself," he said huskily. "My duties tonight are to you. You are my world. My universe."

Becky wove her fingers through his thick black hair and closed her eyes as he again pleasured her in ways she would have, until tonight, thought forbidden.

After he brought her to another blissful release, he rose away from her and used a flintstone knife to cut and gather rye and slough grass.

"Why are you doing that?" she asked, moving to a sitting position.

Strange, she thought to herself, how she no longer felt awkward in her nudity in his presence. It seemed so natural that she should be sitting there, her skin fully revealed to the world.

But there was only the waning sun, the darkening sky, and the chirping birds that dove into the treetops overhead for a night's nesting to see. And Blazing Eagle.

"I will make you a soft bed for the night," he said, smiling over her. "Then I shall tend to the horses."

Pebbles climbed onto Becky's bare lap. She laughed as his fur tickled her tummy as he became cozy on her lap and closed his eyes.

"I think we shall have a bed partner tonight," Becky said, laughing up at Blazing Eagle.

"Only until I am at your side again," Blazing Eagle said, chuckling.

She watched Blazing Eagle, adoring him, as he gathered buffalo chips and made a fire within a circling of rocks. Darkness had now fallen and it was a calm, clear night. The smoke from the fire went straight up into the air. The wolves and coyotes in the hills made a great noise, howling and crying. Pebbles suddenly howled, answering them.

Blazing Eagle and Becky laughed together.

Blazing Eagle washed his hands in the stream, then sat down beside Becky and drew her next to him. "I have always taught my son patience," he said. "I have learned well how to practice it myself. Everything in its own time."

He gazed down at her and tipped her chin up with a forefinger, their eyes locked. "It was torture waiting for you, my woman," he said softly. "Was it the same for you?"

As joyous tears spilled from her eyes, she nodded. "Yes—oh, yes," she murmured. "So very, very much."

His lips bore down onto hers. She gently lifted Pebbles from her lap, then leaned her body into Blazing Eagle's. She slipped her lips from his. "Take me again," she whispered, her voice trembling with passion.

Chapter Seventeen

The next morning, as Becky and Blazing Eagle rode in the direction of her soddy, Becky could not believe the difference in herself that she felt after discovering the mysteries of lovemaking with Blazing Eagle.

It was not that she felt more adult. It was how she felt—so alive, so *needed*, so wondrously happy.

The only thing that took away from this newly found happiness was her constant worry over her brother. As far as he was concerned, she felt totally helpless.

"You will get your belongings, then you will come home with me," Blazing Eagle said, drawing Becky's eyes to him.

"But what about my brother?" she said reluctantly. "I so badly wanted the chance to turn his life around."

"You saw him, you spoke to him, and you have seen that nothing you do or say will change his life," Blazing Eagle said. "You have your life to live. Live it. Live it with me, as my wife. And do so without remorse. You are not at fault for your brother being an outlaw. Let him live his life as he would live it."

"That's easy for you to say," Becky said, stiffening her back. "He isn't your brother."

"In my lifetime I have suffered many losses," Blazing Eagle said. "I will tell you about those losses sometime."

Becky gazed at him a moment longer, then turned her eyes straight ahead again. Yes, she would go and live her life out with the man she loved.

But no, she could never, ever forget her brother. Thoughts of him would be with her day and night, as she wondered if he were alive or dead.

It truly would be no different than it was before she realized that he had survived the Civil War. She had not known then whether he was alive or dead, and she had learned to live with the not knowing.

She imagined she could again, but this time it would be much harder.

Now if he were to die, it would be a death without honor.

Becky petted Pebbles, whose patience endured the long journey on horseback. She then slapped her reins and hurried her horse into a faster lope. Blazing Eagle was soon beside her again on his mighty steed.

Becky and Blazing Eagle rode onward, past pronghorn bones drying and fading in the sun, then past a prairie dog town, where barking dogs squatted comically on the perimeter.

Blazing Eagle reached inside his parfleche at the side of his horse and took out a handful of seeds. "Perhaps you are hungry?" he said, reaching his hand toward Becky. "The seeds are nourishing."

"The baked rabbit we had for breakfast is still with me," Becky said, laughing softly. "I ate far more than usual."

"That was because you were happy," Blazing Eagle said, cupping his hand over his mouth and allowing the seeds to slide into it.

He chewed and swallowed them, then smiled at her. "Happiness encourages hungers of all kind," he said.

"Yes, I am happy—as never before," Becky said, sighing contentedly.

She became aware of a high-pitched buzzing. The incessant droning sound came closer.

Suddenly she saw what caused it when the air became blackened with mosquitoes that swarmed around her and Blazing Eagle. Even Pebbles barked as he shook his head in an effort to rid himself of the pests.

"I've never seen so many mosquitoes at once," Becky screamed, swatting furiously at the pesky things as they buzzed around her face.

"They are prairie dog mosquitoes," Blazing Eagle said, swatting at them too. "Ride in a hard gallop. You will soon leave them behind."

Becky nudged her horse's flanks with her booted heels. She slapped the reins and lay low over the horse's mane, the wind whipping her in the face as she rode at breakneck speed away from the mosquitoes. She then slowed to a normal pace when the insects were left behind.

Becky looked overhead. The wind was blowing towering thunderheads around in the sky. She winced and grew cold inside when the sky turned yellow with warning. Cracks of lightning split the horizon, and the rumble of thunder shook the earth.

She was glad that her soddy was in view now. Although it had cracks in the roof and was made partially of mud, it would give her and Blazing Eagle some shelter until the storm moved on.

Just as they rushed inside the soddy, Pebbles snuggled in her arms, the heavens seemed to open up, as if buckets of water had been overturned in the sky.

Becky placed Pebbles on the floor, then rushed around to place tin plates where the rain came through her leaky roof. She groaned as she watched her newly sewn lace curtains at the windows become wet and droopy.

In her frenzy to stop the leaks, she had not been aware that Blazing Eagle went to the fireplace mantel to study the tintype of her brother. She turned just as he set it back down on the mantel, then gripped his temples, groaning in pain.

Becky ran to him and placed a gentle hand to his cheek. "What is it?" she asked frantically, almost feeling his pain.

Blazing Eagle gritted his teeth and clenched his eyes closed as once again his memory came back to him in bits and pieces.

The shooting.

The killing.

The thunder!

The lightning!

Yes, the massacre had happened during a fierce thunderstorm!

He could feel the rumble of the land beneath his feet when it thundered. He could see the men pinning his mother down, spreading her legs. . . .

"No!" he cried, piercing the silence that now lay around him, the storm having moved quickly onward.

"Oh, Blazing Eagle, tell me what's the matter," Becky cried. She grabbed his wrists and tried to pry his hands away from his temple. "Blazing Eagle, look at me. Open your eyes. Hear me! Let me help you!"

And then it was over again for Blazing Eagle. The memory had been brief this time, but his heart thudding within his chest told him how much it had affected him.

He breathed hard as he slowly opened his eyes and gazed down at Becky. Perspiration dripped from his brow.

"Are you all right?" Becky asked. Her pulse raced from again seeing him turn into someone she did not know. As before, she had witnessed someone who seemed to have had a demon inside him.

She could not help but be afraid of that side of Blazing Eagle, wondering how often it happened and if it would ever end in violence.

"They raped her," Blazing Eagle said, his voice showing the stress of his flashback. He doubled his fists at his sides and looked wildly down at Becky. "I now know that my mother was raped!"

He shook his head and closed his eyes again. "But I did not see *who* defiled her body!" he cried softly. "My mother. My dear mother. Not only did she die that day, she was also viciously raped."

"You are remembering something of your past?" Becky asked, taking him by the hand and leading him to a chair.

He eased onto the chair. She slid another chair close to his and sat down before him, then took his hands and twined her fingers through his.

"Tell me about it, Blazing Eagle," she encouraged him. "Then perhaps it will make the memories not as painful."

Blazing Eagle's eyes wavered into hers. He knew that she had to know about his past, as he knew about hers. If they were going to be together for eternity, no secrets, no matter how ugly, should be kept between them.

"Long ago, when I was nine winters of age, there was a massacre of my people," he told her. "All were killed except for myself. I was found wandering later, my memory gone, my feelings dead. I was taken in and raised by Chief Black Thunder as though I were his own son. But in my heart, I knew that I had another father, another mother. But I could not remember who they were, or where my home had been."

"How horrible," Becky said, gasping. "Please do go on. Tell me everything. Surely you will feel much better for it."

"It is easier talking about my life with Chief Black

Thunder than what came before," Blazing Eagle said, leaving the chair and sinking onto the rug before the fireplace. Needing something to busy his hands while he talked, he slowly lifted wood onto the grate.

"Tell me about him," Becky said, sinking to the floor beside him, facing him on her knees. Pebbles snuggled next to her and drifted off into sleep.

"Often boys from ten to fifteen winters of age who are orphaned and who have no one to care for them live in a man's lodge and herd his horses and perform other small services for the lodging," Blazing Eagle softly explained. He set the flame of the match to small bits of kindling spread out beneath the larger pieces of wood. "The young brave receives his food and clothing, and after a time, when the lodge owner thinks best, he gives the young brave a pony."

The fire now fully ablaze, Blazing Eagle turned to Becky. "Chief Black Thunder did not take me in as a servant, but as a son," he said, his voice filled with pride. "Chief Black Thunder gave me a horse and all things necessary to make me a man. And because it was known then by everyone that my true father had been a powerful chief, and because Black Thunder was a powerful chief in his own right and now my adopted father, I stepped easily into chieftainship after he passed to the great beyond."

"And you had no brothers or sisters?" Becky asked softly.

"No, none," Blazing Eagle said. "Waterfall, in a sense, became my sister. She has been there since that day I was brought to Black Thunder's village. She was my same age, yet she looked after me as though she were a woman of many years' experience."

"I'm surprised that you didn't fall in love with her," Becky said, watching his reaction. "She is so very beautiful. And I have hardly ever met anyone as sweet."

"Loving one another in that way was not our destiny," Blazing Eagle murmured. "Waterfall, being a Cheyenne princess and a special woman in my village, has not yet given her heart to any special man. She is content with her life. That is all that matters."

"Moments ago, you said something about your true mother being raped," Becky said softly. "Was that a part of your remembrances of that day of your people's massacre? I truly believe it would be best to talk about it. If you are finally beginning to recall the past, and what you are remembering is so horrible, it is best to speak it aloud than to allow it to remain inside yourself to eat away at you."

"Yes, I am remembering," he said, glancing up at the tintype on the mantle. Becky followed his gaze and went cold inside. "Why are you staring at my brother's picture?" she murmured. "Was there something about it that made you remember?"

"That, and the thunder and lightning," Blazing Eagle said, shifting his gaze back to Becky.

"What about my brother brought on the remembrances?" Becky asked, her voice breaking. "Blazing Eagle, my brother couldn't have had anything to do with the massacre. He couldn't have been there. He is not much older than you. And he was with me in Saint Louis until the Civil War."

"I do not understand myself what there is about the picture that troubles me," Blazing Eagle said somberly. "But the storm brought things back to me that tear at my very soul. I recalled it storming while—while men raped my beloved mother."

"Oh, I'm so sorry," Becky said, flinging herself into his arms. She hugged him tightly. "What a horrible thing to remember. I'm so sorry."

Blazing Eagle swept his arms around Becky and took comfort in her presence. "Tell me about your life, how it was when you were small, when your brother was innocent of all wrongdoing," he said softly.

"I never knew my true mother," Becky said, swallowing hard. "Father said she died when I was born. All I have left of her is her grave. And I took flowers to it often until . . . until I came to the Wyoming Territory."

"And so you were raised without a mother?"

"No, not exactly. My father remarried. I grew to love that woman, Kathryn, as though she were my true mother."

She choked back a sob. "Then she was taken from me," she murmured. "She died from consumption. It was such a slow, painful death."

"Then you have known your share of sadness also by loss of family," Blazing Eagle said, leaning her away from him so that their eyes could hold.

"Yes, all are gone but brother," she gulped. "I buried my precious father just before boarding the train for the Wyoming Territory."

"Destiny brought us together," Blazing Eagle said, again drawing her into his embrace. "We now have each other to fill the void in our lives left by those who left us too early to walk the road of the hereafter."

"Yes, we have each other," Becky murmured.

"The storm has passed. It is time to gather your things so that we can return to my village," Blazing Eagle said. He took her by her hands and helped her from the floor.

"It won't take long," Becky said. She gave him a brief kiss before she began placing her personal belongings in her two bags.

When she lifted her brother's likeness from the mantel, she stared at it. She ran her fingers over his face where she had seen the scar on their brief meeting yesterday.

"How terribly scarred he is now," she said, glancing at Blazing Eagle. "It must be from the war—a battle scar."

Blazing Eagle said nothing. He had one more secret that he felt he should keep from his woman. He, Blazing Eagle, was responsible for the scar on her brother's face. It had happened one time when Blazing Eagle had almost gotten the best of her brother when they met along the trail.

But, as slippery as an eel, her brother had gotten away, the wound made by Blazing Eagle's knife dripping with blood.

"I'm ready," Becky said, lifting one bag as Blazing Eagle lifted the other.

Pebbles ran after them, barking and nipping playfully at their heels as they left the soddy and went to their horses.

"Our lives begin only now," Blazing Eagle said. He kissed Becky, then lifted her by the waist into her saddle. He secured her two bags at the sides of his horse, placed Pebbles in his sling, then swung himself into his saddle.

Blazing Eagle turned his horse around and rode away, Becky riding proudly at his side.

From a high butte, Edward had seen the Cheyenne chief kiss Becky, then had watched them leave together. Grim and raw-nerved, Edward wheeled his horse around and rode away into the dusk of evening. He had to find a way to get his sister to return to Saint Louis and leave this god-awful land behind.

And how could she align herself with an Indian, as though she loved him? Edward could not see a future for his sister with an Indian. He knew that she would be happier in Saint Louis with a husband who could give her the kind of life she was used to.

He would see that she was soon on a train, even if he had to carry her aboard and tie her to a seat!

His eyes narrowed angrily as he began making plans that would make things right again for his beloved sister.

Chapter Eighteen

Becky's return to Blazing Eagle's lodge was far different from her first arrival. She was there for a different purpose. She was there to be his wife, not his captive.

And there were no longer any secrets between them. The emotions that Becky now felt seemed like something out of a story book—beautiful, sweet, and serene.

As she sat beside the lodge fire on a cushion of blankets, waiting for Blazing Eagle to return after having council with his warriors, Becky looked slowly around her. She already felt as though she belonged here. Her personal belongings had been taken from her bags and lay along the floor beside Blazing Eagle's paraphernalia. Her dresses were hanging from a rope that Blazing Eagle had slung for her from pole to pole at the back of the tepee.

She had thought he would demand that she wear Indian clothing. But after seeing her pride in her dresses, he had not made such demands on her, and perhaps never would. He had said that he wanted her to become as one with his people in her own time, in her own way. If she chose to discard her clothes one day and wear buckskins, so be it. If not, so be it.

This evening she wore a soft cotton dress with a fully gathered skirt that nipped in at her tiny waist. Lace trimmed the lowcut neckline and the ends of her sleeves. Her hair glowed from a fresh washing in the river.

She turned when she heard movement behind her.

She had to learn not to be jumpy, she told herself. This was her home. Soon she would be Blazing Eagle's wife. Everyone in the village seemed to have accepted her, even if she had only been there one full day and night. Whatever their chief desired, they would approve.

"I left the council early. I have brought you and Blazing Eagle the evening meal," Waterfall said, the gentleness in her dark eyes matching her smile. "If you wish, I shall soon teach you how to cook *wasna*."

"*Wasna?*" Becky said, eyeing the platter of food as Waterfall placed it on the floor of the tepee beside her. "Why, that looks like the hash that my stepmother made when I was a child."

"It *is* hash," Waterfall said, settling on her haunches beside Becky. "Cheyenne hash. Do you know how to make white man's hash?"

"No, I was never attentive to my stepmother's teachings in the kitchen," Becky said, smiling weakly at Waterfall, whose long braids hung over her shoulders, with wildflowers woven into them. "I was more interested in being outdoors with my brother."

Becky almost choked on the mention of her brother, still finding it hard to accept that he was a criminal, when all those years as they had grown up together, he had been as gentle as a lamb.

No, it was something she would never be able to understand—or accept.

"Your brother?" Waterfall said softly. "Tell me about your brother."

Becky paled. She looked quickly away from Waterfall. How could she be expected to talk about her brother to anyone but Blazing Eagle? He understood her plight. No one else would.

If she announced to the world that her brother was the outlaw depicted on so many wanted posters across the country, their feelings about her would surely change. These gentle, peace-loving Cheyenne might not want her to stay among them. They especially wouldn't want her to be their chief's woman!

"Will you teach me how to make Cheyenne *wasna?*" she said instead, trying to avoid any more mention of Edward. "I want so badly to please Blazing Eagle in every way. I want to cook for him. Teach me, Waterfall. Please?"

Waterfall's smile faded, obviously puzzled over a sister not wanting to talk about her brother.

Then she smiled again, casting her questions

aside in her eagerness to be of some assistance to this woman who would be the wife of the clan's chief.

"*Wasna* is prepared by chopping up the bones of the buffalo or deer and boiling them until they are soft and the fat comes to the top," Waterfall said. "This is skimmed off and laid aside. Some of the dried meat is roasted and pounded fine with a stone hammer. Sometimes chokeberries are added."

She shoved the platter closer to Becky. "Take a bite and see how delicious it is," she urged. "Then I shall continue telling you about it." She took a piece herself and ate it as Becky took a bite.

"It *is* good," Becky said, nodding. "Please tell me more."

"The fat is then melted and mixed with the pounded chokeberries and meat," Waterfall said, stopping to take another bite. "This hash will keep for some time if rightly prepared."

"What is used for the storage of the hash?" Becky asked, looking suddenly at the entrance flap when she heard someone else enter the tepee.

She was flooded with all sorts of pleasurable sensations when she found Blazing Eagle standing there in only a brief breechcloth, his midnight-dark eyes devouring her.

Waterfall smiled up at Blazing Eagle and rose slowly to her feet, then gazed down at Becky again. "We women keep a skin from the tripe of the animal in which to wrap the hash," she murmured. "The *wasna* retains its flavor for a long time, yet it does harden after a while."

"My two favorite women are becoming better acquainted?" Blazing Eagle said, moving out of the shadows.

He drew Waterfall into his arms, and Becky recalled the first time she had seen Blazing Eagle and Waterfall together in such a way. She remembered the intense jealousy it had caused her then.

Now Becky felt warm and content as they embraced. She knew that it was an embrace of friends, not lovers.

She pushed herself to her feet and turned to Blazing Eagle just as Waterfall left.

"My darling," Becky whispered as he gathered her into his muscled arms. "How I have missed you."

Pleasure spread through her body as he kissed her. She sucked in a wild breath of ecstasy as he slipped a hand between them and cupped her breast through the thin material of her dress.

When he circled her nipple with his thumb, her knees became weak with passion. Her head began to spin.

"Father?"

Whistling Elk's voice made Becky wrench herself quickly away from Blazing Eagle. She felt the heat of a blush as she slowly turned and faced Blazing Eagle's son.

Becky had expected to find a keen resentment in the child's dark eyes as he turned her way. Instead, she found the same warm gentleness that she had seen in Waterfall's.

At first Whistling Elk had shown signs of resentment toward Becky. But after he knew that his father had chosen her for a wife, he had seemed suddenly happy with the idea. It was evident that he had been hungry for a mother for far too long. Especially if he would accept a white woman in his father's lodge.

Becky found it hard to believe that she could be accepted this quickly!

But Blazing Eagle's magnetism caused everyone to trust his decisions, even if it meant that a white woman would be now living as one with them.

"Whistling Elk, my *naha*," Blazing Eagle said, going to his son and placing a gentle hand on his bare shoulder. "You have come to share the evening meal with your father and the woman who will soon be your mother? I thought you were staying the night with our friend Jumping Sky."

"I am staying with Jumping Sky," Whistling Elk said, glancing occasionally at Becky as he talked with his father. "Yet I forgot my bow that I recently carved. I wish to show it to Jumping Sky and his parents. I am proud of what I have carved."

"As I am also, my son," Blazing Eagle said. "Go. Gather up your bow. Show it to your friend and his family. One day soon, my son, we shall take that bow with us on the hunt. I am sure it will perform as beautifully as my son carves."

All smiles, Whistling Elk went to the back of the lodge. He bent to his knees and reached beneath his bed and soon brought out his bow.

Becky saw the intricacies of the designs carved onto the bow when he brought it out, where the fire's glow shone upon it.

"Why, it is ever so beautiful," she said, sighing as she ran her fingers over the various depictions on the bow. "Making this must have taken a long time."

"I put many nights and days of hard work into the making of this bow," Whistling Elk said proudly. "During the winter months, when the snow is crunchy beneath one's feet, I stayed inside and carved."

"When you were not on the sled, you mean to say, don't you, my son?" Blazing Eagle said, laughing softly as once again he placed a hand on his son's shoulder.

"I also made a sled," Whistling Elk said, squaring his shoulders proudly as he gazed at Becky, obviously pleased with her attention as she listened with wide eyes that reflected the green grasses of spring.

"Tell my woman about your sled," Blazing Eagle said, glad to be able to draw Becky into the life of his son in such a way. He hoped that this would draw them together soon as mother and son.

"Do you truly wish to hear?" Whistling Elk said, his voice brimming with excitement as he awaited Becky's answer.

"Yes, please do tell me about it," Becky said, clasping her hands before her. She could see the child beaming as he talked of his sled, as he had when he showed off his bow.

She was pleased that he could be this open with her, and it made her heart sing to see him want to please her.

She now knew that they could become friends; even more than friends. They were forming a bond that would grow stronger with time.

"One day I went on the hunt with father, and we came back with a buffalo," Whistling Elk said excitedly. "The whole side of the buffalo was roasted, and after the meat was cleaned from the bones, father helped me. We took six of the ribs and placed them together. We then split a piece of cherry wood and put the ends of the bones between the pieces of wood. The whole affair was then laced together with rawhide rope on both ends of the bones. On top of those bones I fastened a buffalo head with rawhide ropes. Then I made a string of rawhide which was fastened to the front of the sled to pull it with. This was my *can-wo-slo-han*—rib sled."

"And he could even use it in the summer," Blazing Eagle said, placing an arm around his son's youthful shoulders. "I have slid down the grassy slopes in summer with him."

"Perhaps I can slide down the hills in the sled sometime soon?" Becky said, her smile fading when sadness seemed to come into the child's eyes.

"The sled is no more," Whistling Elk said, then laughed softly as his eyes lit up again. "The wolves came and dragged it away and had a feast on the buffalo bones."

There was a moment of strained silence, then Blazing Eagle broke into laughter.

"You should have seen it," he said. "We saw the wolves carry the sled away. They would get it up a hill, and then it would get away from them and slide down again into the village."

"Then you got the sled back?" Becky asked, looking from father to son.

"It was more fun watching the wolves than sliding down the hill on my sled," Whistling Elk said, wiping tears of laughter from his eyes. "So we allowed them to keep it once they got it up the hill."

"And Whistling Elk's thoughts are on more adult things now than on playing," Blazing Eagle said, ushering Whistling Elk to the door. "Sleep well, my son."

Whistling Elk gave Becky a look over his shoulder, glanced up at his father, then left, smiling.

"He is such a fine young man," Becky said, going to lock her arms around Blazing Eagle's neck. She leaned up on tiptoe and brushed a soft kiss across his lips. "But I am very glad that he left us alone for the night." Her eyes twinkled into Blazing Eagle's as she gazed up at him. "Aren't you?"

"I am glad for many things," Blazing Eagle said, framing her face between his hands. "That I abducted you; that you fell in love with me; and that my people accept you."

"What if they only pretend for your benefit, yet deep down resent and hate me?" Becky said. She swung around as Blazing Eagle placed his arm around her waist and led her toward the fire pit.

"There are some who resent you, I am sure," Blazing Eagle said, guiding her down onto the soft cushion of blankets. "How can they not? They have seen the wicked ways of so many white eyes. Those who mistrust will soon see that they have nothing to fear from you."

"Fear . . . from me?" Becky gasped, her eyes wide as Blazing Eagle sat down beside her. "Do some truly fear me?"

"Do not be alarmed to think that some might

have those feelings toward you," Blazing Eagle said, dipping his fingers into the *wasna* and placing some between his lips.

He swallowed it and dipped his fingers into the food again and placed it to her lips. "Are there not those of your kind who fear we who are red-skinned?" he asked.

"Yes, most people do fear Indians," Becky said, sucking the food from his fingers, enjoying both the taste and how it was being fed to her.

"Then you can see why it is the same among my people," Blazing Eagle said, feeding her more *wasna*.

After they had both eaten their fill, Blazing Eagle gestured toward the inside of his lodge. "You should not find it hard to accept this lodge over the one in which you made residence," he said. "My tepee is much better to live in, is it not? It is always clean. It is warm in the winter and cool in the summer. Whenever I wish to, my lodge is easy to move."

"Yes, this lodge is much better than the soddy," Becky said softly. "But I wish you could have seen my home in Saint Louis. It was so beautiful. I can still smell the lemon oil used to polish the furniture."

"You had a big house?"

"Quite."

Blazing Eagle shrugged. "Still, my lodge offers much more than the larger ones of the white man," he said. "The white man builds a big house, which costs much money. It is like a big cage. It shuts out the sun. It can never be moved."

He smiled at Becky. "Indians and animals know

better how to live than the white man," he said. "We always have close at hand fresh air, sunshine, and good water. Indians and animals always have green grass and ripe berries, sunlight to work and play, and night to sleep. We have summers for flowers to bloom and winters for them to sleep. Everything is good."

"Yes, I can see that," Becky murmured, in her mind's eye seeing her home, the flower garden flanking its sides. It had been a haven. She had hoped that Edward would claim the house as his.

But now she knew otherwise. Some day she would return to Saint Louis, but only long enough to sell her home and cut all her ties with the world she had known before being introduced into the world of the Cheyenne.

The Cheyenne world was now her world.

"The white man does not obey the Great Spirit," Blazing Eagle said, his eyes watching the flames of the fire. "That is why the Indian never could agree with him."

"Blazing Eagle, I love you," Becky said, wanting to bring the serious side of their treasured moments together to an end.

Blazing Eagle turned to her, gazed at her for a moment, then took her hands.

Together they rose from the blankets and walked slowly toward his bed.

Becky's heart thudded with anticipation of what soon would happen. The first time they made love had been a wondrous awakening of feelings she had never known before. Now she was already feeling the euphoric bliss that came from being with him.

When he pressed his hard, lean body against hers and gently shoved her onto the bed, she closed her eyes and floated on clouds as he kissed her.

They reluctantly broke away from one another long enough to undress, then Blazing Eagle knelt down over her and parted her legs with his knee. He filled his arms with her slim and sensuous body and came to her thrusting deeply.

"My woman," Blazing Eagle whispered, then seized her lips with his mouth and kissed her hungrily.

Becky's breath quickened with yearning as she was filled with delicious shivers of desire. She spread herself open to him as each of his thrusts sent a wonderful message of rapture to her heart.

His hands swept over her breasts in a soft caress, Becky's groans of pleasure firing his passions. He teased and stroked her supple body, his lips now on the slender, curving length of her throat, licking, kissing, sucking.

Becky reached her hands to his cheeks and sought his mouth with a desperation she had never known before.

They kissed.

They clung.

They rocked.

They sighed.

Then he rained kisses on her lids and on her hair, the yielding silk of her driving him almost to madness.

His fingers pressed urgently into her flesh as he lifted her closer to him. He held her fiercely, their naked flesh fusing, their bodies sucking at each other.

Giving herself over to wild ecstasy and sensual abandonment, Becky's body jolted and quivered when he pressed endlessly deeper within her.

He kissed her long and deep.

Her hips gyrated against his.

There was only the world of feeling, touching, and throbbing. Everything else had melted away into oblivion.

Unable to bear waiting any longer for that ultimate release, Blazing Eagle's body hardened and tightened.

Becky trembled with readiness as again Blazing Eagle drove in swiftly and surely. Her body arched against his as his seed filled her womb with its magical warmth and wetness.

Afterwards, Blazing Eagle rolled away from her. Becky snuggled close to him and moved her mouth over his flesh until he groaned.

He reciprocated as he knelt beside her. He lifted her closer as he bent low to suckle first one breast, then the other. Then he kissed his way down to that secret place that had been unlocked only for him. He caressed her there with his tongue, then kissed his way back to her lips and possessed them with a fiery kiss as once again he entered her.

They gave and took pleasure until they were both satiated and breathless.

"You are filled with such passion," Becky whispered later, lying beside Blazing Eagle and tracing his facial features with a finger.

"Only when I am with you," Blazing Eagle whispered back, leaning to brush a kiss across her brow.

She crawled closer and sighed. "I have never

been as content as I am now," she murmured.

She closed her eyes and drifted off.

She awakened in a sweat when she dreamed of her brother riding into a spattering of gunfire as lawmen stood on horses in a long row firing at him.

Trembling, she snuggled against Blazing Eagle. She was afraid to go to sleep again. She knew that never would she be free of her fears for her brother. She felt as though she had forsaken him.

Tears brimming in her eyes, she fell asleep again, this time dreaming only of passion-filled moments with her beloved Cheyenne chief—who would soon be her husband!

Chapter Nineteen

The next morning, after Becky returned from her morning dip in the river and Blazing Eagle had left for his morning council with his warriors, she discovered, as she had when she was held captive, that the rising sun looked down upon a village of people busy with their own chores to take care of.

A woman making a new lodge carried out the dressed skins to be used in its construction and spread them neatly on the ground in front of her tepee. The lodge cutter stood over the skins, preparing them for sewing.

Older boys scattered to the river, swimming and diving in the cool water, then ran races on the sandbars. Others were busy near a mud bank, modeling images of animals and people and lodges from the clay.

She shifted her gaze and watched other young

braves practicing at shooting their bows and arrows. Whistling Elk was among this group, showing off his new bow to the others.

She knew, though, that he would soon come home. Blazing Eagle had explained to her before he left for council that it was the usual habit of the young braves to ride out into the hills in the morning to drive in the herds of horses. From those horses certain ones would be selected to be tied in front of the lodges, to be at hand for use. The most valued ones, which during the night had been tethered there, would be turned loose and taken to the hills to graze.

Becky waved as she recognized Waterfall among a group of women who started off to get wood. It was a merry group. They were laughing and joking.

Waterfall broke away from the group and ran to Becky. "Come with us this morning," she urged. She took one of Becky's hands and gave it a yank. "I will show you. You can see how gathering wood is done. Some gather only sticks lying on the ground. Others climb trees and break off the dead branches while those below trim them."

"Whistling Elk hasn't arrived home yet from his overnight stay with Jumping Sky," Becky said, smiling at Waterfall. "I'm going to prepare him some eggs for breakfast before he leaves for his morning chores."

"That is why you asked me not to bring the morning meal?" Waterfall said, nodding. "I understand now. You wish to start learning the craft of cooking."

"Yes, I feel that it is important to learn as soon

as possible," Becky said, slipping her hand from Waterfall's. "I don't want to be a disappointment to Blazing Eagle."

"The way he looks at you?" Waterfall said, giggling behind her hand. "Never can you disappoint him in anything that you do."

The women who were waiting for Waterfall began to call for her. "I really must go," she said, turning to walk away. "I will come and see you later today."

"Please do," Becky said, waving a good-bye.

Lifting the hem of her cotton dress into her arms, Becky turned and went inside the lodge. The fire was blazing lazily over the logs in the firepit, just perfect for placing a cast-iron frying pan on them. Pebbles was asleep by the fire pit.

Whistling Elk had gathered turtle eggs yesterday. Blazing Eagle had given her fat from his store of foods that were stored in parfleches in a pit in the ground just outside the back of the tepee.

Humming, feeling very domestic today and utterly satisfied from the long night of lovemaking, Becky placed three wooden plates beside the fire. She dipped fat into the frying pan and held it over the flames.

When the fat was melted and spattering, she set the pan down and cracked the eggs into it. She then placed it on a stove near the flames and stirred the eggs with a wooden spatula.

The aroma of the eggs frying wafted from the tepee. Whistling Elk took a long whiff, then snatched up his bow and arrow and ran from the group with which he had been playing and hurried home.

Becky looked over her shoulder as Whistling Elk came into the lodge. "You are just in time," she said, smiling at him. She turned her attention back to the eggs, spooning them out of the frying pan onto the three plates. "The eggs are ready to be eaten."

After setting the frying pan aside, she went to Whistling Elk and embraced him. "It is good to be with you like this," she murmured, glad that he didn't stiffen and reject her. Her heart swam with joy when he returned her embrace.

"You make my father happy," he said softly. "That makes me happy. My father's lodge has been without a woman far too long now. I was without a mother. Waterfall was not enough. She is only a friend."

"I wish so much to be more than a friend to both you and your father," Becky said as he stepped away from her to sit down beside the fire.

She knelt beside him and handed him the platter of eggs. "I hope you like how I cooked the eggs," she murmured. "Thank you for gathering them for me."

Whistling Elk nodded. He put his fingers into the eggs and began to eat.

Becky watched for his reaction, for this was her very first time to cook anything. Back home in Missouri, she had not only had maids while her father was alive, but also a cook.

On the day of her father's funeral and the theft of her belongings, she had given them all the day off.

"Good," Whistling Elk said, smacking his lips as

he ate more of the eggs. "Father will be pleased."

"And what will please your father?" Blazing Eagle said as he came into the lodge. His hair was dripping wet from a morning swim. His chest glistened beneath the glow of the fire.

"I've prepared breakfast," Becky said anxiously, handing him a platter of eggs. "Whistling Elk has enjoyed his. I hope you enjoy yours as much."

Blazing Eagle sat down beside his son and began eating with his fingers.

Becky sat down beside him, her eyes wide as she waited for him to tell her what he thought.

But the fact that he scooped more onto his plate was answer enough for her. He was enjoying what she had prepared.

Sighing with relief, she gathered up her own plate and ate with her fingers, knowing that one of the first things she would purchase for their home would be silverware. Wooden spoons were available for soup, but that was all.

She smiled as she ate, anxious to introduce into Blazing Eagle's and his son's life her various customs that differed from theirs. She only hoped that they would welcome the changes she brought into their lives.

"Son, the horses await you," Blazing Eagle said, setting his empty plate aside.

Becky took up the plate and placed hers with his to be washed at the river as soon as Whistling Elk was through.

Whistling Elk set his bowl down and nodded, then rushed from the lodge.

"He is a dutiful son," Blazing Eagle said, reaching over to gather Becky's wrists in his fingers.

"And how do you see *me*?" she purred as she cuddled onto his lap.

"As everything to me a son cannot be," Blazing Eagle said huskily.

He wove his fingers through her long golden hair and brought her mouth to his. His tongue parted her lips and caused Becky's heart to thump with this new way of kissing her. Her tongue met his, flicking, as one of his hands swept up the skirt of her dress and found her soft and secret place.

Becky twined her arms around his neck. She moaned with pleasure against his lips as he stroked her where she throbbed with need of him.

When he thrust a finger inside her, she gasped. She became dizzy with rapture as he thrust over and over again within her.

Then he rose and swept her up into his arms. He carried her to his bed. They disrobed one another and he laid himself down against her softly pliant limbs. He molded her closer to the contours of his lean body, then shoved into her, burying himself deeply inside her pulsing cleft, then began his rhythmic thrusts, dazzling her senses.

His lips brushed her throat as he breathed her name against her soft, sweet flesh. "Becky," he whispered. "My woman, my *life*."

"I love you so," she whispered against his cheek, her arms twined around his neck, riding him.

His hands went to her breasts and squeezed them gently, rotating the stiff, resilient nipples beneath the palms of his hands.

"My love, my love," Becky gasped as the pleasure built within her.

His mouth seized hers in a fiery kiss, his hips gyrating against hers. She entwined her legs around his hips and drew him more deeply inside her, her heartbeat keeping time with the dizzying rhythm of his thrusts.

Blazing Eagle's building rapture was so intense that it shook the very core of his being. He cupped her rounded hips within the palms of his hands and lifted her even more closely to the heat of his passion.

Like lightning flashes, the tremors of ecstasy soared through Blazing Eagle. As his body shook and quavered into Becky's, his kiss became wild and frenzied.

Becky answered his needs as her own pinnacle was reached. She cried out and thrashed her head back and forth as he burrowed his face into her breasts, cushioning the sounds of his own cries of pleasure.

They lay there for a moment, clinging, then Blazing Eagle rolled away from Becky. He smiled over at her as he brushed her hair away from her eyes. "Today is the beginning of all our tomorrows," he whispered. "But each day will begin as though it were our last. We must take what we can while we can, for who knows what our tomorrows will bring."

"It is a confusing, strange world out there," Becky said, turning over to lie on her stomach. She cupped her chin within her hands and looked adoringly over at Blazing Eagle, whose body shone with a mist of perspiration. "But we have found solace here in each other's arms, haven't we?"

"I have never felt as relaxed as now," Blazing Eagle said, turning on his side to face her. "Nor as content and fulfilled."

"Blazing Eagle, come quick," Fish Hawk called from outside the tepee. "I fear something has happened to Whistling Elk. He has not come down from the hills yet with the horses."

Becky and Blazing Eagle gave each other a panicked stare, then rushed from the bed and dressed.

Slipping on her shoes, Becky stumbled after Blazing Eagle.

When they stepped outside and found Fish Hawk's face drawn into a frown, Becky knew that contentment with life had been premature.

"The other young braves have returned?" Blazing Eagle asked, looking past Fish Hawk into the far distance where the horses grazed.

"All but your son," Fish Hawk said. He turned to stare at the far stretches of the pasture beyond the village.

"Then we must go and search for him," Blazing Eagle said, not at all surprised to see that Fish Hawk had already saddled his horse, and also one for his woman.

Becky noticed that Fish Hawk had brought more than one saddled horse to Blazing Eagle's lodge. She was touched deeply to know that he had thought about her and had brought her a horse so that she could accompany Blazing Eagle on his search for his son.

They swung into their saddles, then rode from the village, Pebbles following, barking.

When they reached the grazing pastures, Blazing

Eagle's heart sank to see that not only was his son missing, but all of his valuable horses.

"The Crow," he snarled through his clenched teeth. "This must be the work of our enemy, the Crow!"

"The Crow come far from their homeland to steal horses, but never children," Fish Hawk reminded Blazing Eagle.

"There is always a first time," Blazing Eagle said, turning a dark frown to his friend. "If my son was an interference in the plans of the Crow, they would take him to silence him."

"Perhaps," Fish Hawk said, nodding.

Blazing Eagle clasped a hand to Fish Hawk's shoulder. "My friend, you are the best scout among our people," he said. "Go. Find where the Crow make camp. See if my horses are mingled with theirs. If so, we know where to find my son!"

"I shall do this for you," Fish Hawk said, squaring his shoulders.

"Hurry back to me if you discover that my son is with the Crow," Blazing Eagle said, dropping his hand to his side. "I do not wish to leave my son in the hands of the enemy for long. I fear for his life!"

Becky was listening intently to their plans, all the while wondering why they didn't suspect the outlaws as well as the Crow? From what she had seen and heard, the outlaws were capable of anything.

She swallowed a lump in her throat to think that possibly her brother might have taken the child and the horses. No, she would not think that her brother could do such a thing. She still could not accept that he had done any of the things he was accused of. She never would until she actually saw him in the act!

Her thoughts were brought back to the present when she heard Fish Hawk singing as he rode away. She gave Blazing Eagle a questioning stare.

"He sings the song of a Cheyenne scout who will soon enter enemy territory," Blazing Eagle said, looking solemnly after Fish Hawk as he rode away.

Becky listened to the song. Goosebumps traveled her flesh as his voice became softer and softer as the distance between herself and Fish Hawk grew.

"I will translate for you," Blazing Eagle said, seeing her interest. "Wolf I am. In darkness, in light, wherever I search, wherever I run, wherever I stand, everything will be good because *Maheo* protects us. *Ea-ea-ea-ho*.

"He is a good man, a skilled scout," Blazing Eagle went on, as he turned his horse back in the direction of his village.

Pebbles leapt up for Becky. She stopped long enough to reach down for him and place him in his sling. She then caught up with Blazing Eagle and rode at his side as he spoke. She sensed that he was trying to find a way not to think about the fate of his one and only son.

"Yes, Fish Hawk is a good scout," Blazing Eagle repeated. "He knows every foot of the country. He is brave and perfectly able to travel alone at night in all sorts of weather and is able to protect himself if he encounters enemies. If he needed to, he could track a swarm of bees in a snow storm."

Blazing Eagle then became silent and sank his heels into the flanks of his horse. He rode off in a hard gallop.

Becky followed his lead, glad when they arrived back at his village.

After placing their horses in the fence close to his lodge, Becky went with Blazing Eagle as he gave the news of his son's disappearance to the crier.

His head hung, his shoulders hunched, Blazing Eagle walked toward his lodge as he listened to the crier announcing the news of Whistling Elk's disappearance.

Becky followed Blazing Eagle into his tepee and sat down beside him as he sank to his haunches before the fire pit, his eyes haunted as he watched the flames caress the logs.

Becky stroked Pebbles' fur as he settled down onto her lap. She watched Blazing Eagle. She had never had children, so it was hard to understand exactly how he was feeling.

But she had been with Whistling Elk long enough to feel a deep sadness for the child. She was already learning how to love a son who would be *her* son once vows were spoken between herself and Blazing Eagle.

But for now, marriage was the last thing on their minds. All their thoughts were centered on the young brave whose life might at this very moment hang in the balance.

Chapter Twenty

Tied and held captive in a mine shaft, Whistling Elk could see past the campfire that outside twilight was lengthening the surrounding shadows. He could hear the red-winged blackbirds with their "con-cur-reee" song in the cottonwoods that ringed a pond Whistling Elk had seen before he was taken inside the mine shaft.

He knew this country well, and he had quickly recognized the pond. He had found this mine shaft one winter ago while hunting with friends. They had explored it and found nothing and had lost interest in it as soon as they left it.

The mine was alive with the sound of dripping water. It smelled of mildew and rotted, creaking timbers. A fire was burning lazily, around which stood several outlaws.

Whistling Elk glared at his abductors, singling

out one of them when he realized who he must be. His hair was the color of wheat. Surely he was the golden-haired outlaw that he had heard his father speak of often.

"Why did you bring me here?" Whistling Elk said in the perfect English his father had taught him. "Why did you take my father's horses and scatter them among those that belong to the Crow?"

Whistling Elk's father had explained that knowing the white man's language was the only way for the Cheyenne to survive among the white skins who continued to come in vast numbers to Shaiyena country. Whistling Elk knew English well, for he planned to live a long, industrious life. He would one day be a great leader like his father!

Flipping his long black coat back from his legs, Edward sat down on his haunches before Whistling Elk. "Because of Becky, my sister," he said tightly. "Your father's horses were mixed purposely with the Crow's to make it look like the Crow are guilty of the theft. It was necessary to take you captive so that you could not run to your father and tell him who the true thieves were. While your father is busy going after his horses, I'll go into your village and take my sister."

"My father will kill you," Whistling Elk hissed, his eyes two points of fire as he glared at Edward. "He is a cunning, brave man. No man tricks him. Especially not a low-down, thieving coward like yourself."

Then Whistling Elk's eyes wavered when he recalled something that Edward had said. "Becky is your sister?" he said, his voice breaking.

"Yes, my sister," Edward said. He leaned closer to Whistling Elk. "And, if need be, I'm going to carry her over my shoulder from your village. I'm going to place her on the next train to Saint Louis. That's where she belongs. Not out here where nothing makes sense."

"My father will not allow you to steal Becky away from him," Whistling Elk said, lifting his chin stubbornly. "She is my father's woman."

Edward's jaw tightened. Realizing that he had been right to think that Becky was infatuated with the Indian chief, he rose shakily to his feet.

"I've got to get her," he said. He stared down at Whistling Elk. "And I will. Soon. And you'd best pray to your Great Spirit upstairs in the heavens that your people cooperate or—or I'll be forced to do what I must to get Becky."

"No!" Whistling Elk cried. "Do not do this thing. My people will not give up their chief's woman to you without a fight! Go and explain things to Becky! She will leave peacefully without you having to harm my people. She would want what was best for my people. She is not a selfish woman who would forfeit other people's lives to better her own."

"I don't make promises I can't keep," Edward said, his voice drawn.

"If forced to, will you also kill me?" Whistling Elk asked, locking his eyes with Edward's. "My father will hunt you down and you will wish you had never been born."

Waiting for Edward to strike out at him, Whistling Elk continued staring up at him. He was

stunned when the outlaw neither said nor did anything, instead left the mine shaft, taking all but one
other man with him.

Whistling Elk turned his eyes toward the man
who was left there to guard him.

Then he looked away and closed his eyes. He did
not want to envision what might happen soon to
his people. He yanked at the ropes at his wrists. He
grunted as he scooted backwards until he found a
sharp rock behind him.

Turning slow eyes back to the whiskered man
who sat beside the fire, his back to Whistling Elk,
the young brave worked earnestly with the rope,
moving it determinedly back and forth across the
jagged rock.

His heart beat like thunder within his chest, his
eyes narrowing with victory when he felt the rope
weakening. He would stop the bloodshed before it
began! He would be a hero to his people!

He would make sure that the wicked outlaws had
no chance to enter his people's village. He wanted
not even one shot fired against his beloved Cheyenne! If he worked quickly enough, he knew a short
cut that would lead him into his village before the
marauding outlaws!

Nervous perspiration dotted Whistling Elk's
brow as he continued raking the ropes over the
rock, back and forth, up and down, back and forth.

He watched the outlaw place a plug of chewing
tobacco in the corner of his mouth, then stretch out
beside the fire, his back still to Whistling Elk.

Just a little more, Whistling Elk thought desperately to himself.

The rope had weakened!

He could tell that it was now being held together by a thin thread!

Finally, his wrists fell free.

Whistling Elk moved his hands around to the front, his eyes never leaving the outlaw.

Scarcely breathing, careful not to make a sound, he leaned down and untied the ropes at his ankles. When they fell away, and his feet were also free, he smiled ruefully.

He inhaled a deep breath, then moved stealthily to his feet. His footsteps were as soundless as the panther's as he crept closer to the outlaw.

His hand steady, Whistling Elk reached out toward the man's holstered pistol. His pulse raced as he slipped the pistol from the holster.

Before the man realized what had happened, Whistling Elk brought the butt of his gun down on the man's head, quickly rendering him unconscious.

"*Ayyy!*" Whistling Elk cried as he tossed the gun aside. "I am now free to go and save my people!"

Whistling Elk ran from the mine shaft. The setting sun was lengthening the shadows all around him. A golden eagle soared overhead, its golden-striped head and yellow talons glowing in the afternoon light.

His heart thudding, his knees weak with his hurry to get home, Whistling Elk searched through the thick brush for the man's horse. He finally found it tethered beneath a cottonwood tree beside the creek.

His fingers trembling, he untied the reins, then

swung himself into the saddle, wheeled the horse around in the direction of his village, and rode away.

"Mighty Great Spirit," he whispered, lifting his eyes heavenward. "Lead me home! Allow me to arrive before the outlaws! My people depend on me! Fill me with courage! Let me prove that I am worthy of being my father's son! Let me be in time! Please let me be in time!"

The golden eagle swept down low over Whistling Elk's head and locked his eyes with the young brave's; then his flight curved upward, and the bird disappeared into the twilight.

Knowing that his prayer had been answered, Whistling Elk smiled. He was confident now of his mission.

Chapter Twenty-one

"*Hi-ye-he!*" echoed into Blazing Eagle's village.

Becky looked quickly over at Blazing Eagle as he pushed himself up from the floor of his lodge at the sound of the warrior's cry.

"Fish Hawk returns," he said, grabbing his rifle.

"Was that Fish Hawk crying out like that?" Becky asked, scrambling to her feet.

"What you heard was the cry of a scout's return. That is Fish Hawk," Blazing Eagle said, lifting his entrance flap.

Becky stepped outside with him. Beneath a heavenly field of stars, she squinted into the darkness just as Fish Hawk rode into sight at the far edge of the village. Becky's insides were tight, wondering what Fish Hawk had found out.

She glanced up at Blazing Eagle as he stood rigid in his own anxiousness, his jaw set. She had asked him earlier why he had not ridden with Fish Hawk to look for his son and the missing horses.

He had explained to her that scouts were trained to move as silently as a bird soars overhead. He had told her that everyone knew that one man could track more successfully than many. When there were many horsemen, their horses' hooves mingled too much with those that were being tracked.

Fish Hawk drew a tight rein and gazed sternly down at Blazing Eagle. The great outdoor communal fire danced on their faces like sunbeams. Their eyes picked up the reflection, making them look even more fierce.

"Our horses *do* run with the Crow's," Fish Hawk said solemnly, dismounting and dropping his reins. "But the thieves who led them there did not ride the horses of the Crow. They left tracks of the iron-hooved white man's horse."

"That means nothing," Blazing Eagle said, his hands tightening around his rifle as his anger flowed like molten lava through his veins. "That proves the Crow now steal from the white man as well as the Cheyenne. Do you not see, Fish Hawk? It was a ploy. They rode the white man's horses purposely to fool us!"

"Perhaps. Perhaps not," Fish Hawk mumbled, daring to dispute his chief's logic. "You see, my friend, I saw no sign of Whistling Elk at the Crow camp."

"Of course the Crow would not show him to the world had they abducted him!" Blazing Eagle argued back.

"Blazing Eagle, you showed *me* to the world

when you abducted *me*," Becky said, stepping closer. "Except for a short while, you made me stay outside while I was held captive."

When both sets of eyes were directed disapprovingly at her, she looked questioningly at one and then the other.

She realized then that she had spoken out of turn. Although a part of her cried out to stand up for her rights and say what she would, another part of her did not want to make her future husband look foolish.

When Blazing Eagle saw that Becky knew not to say any more, he turned his gaze back to Fish Hawk. "We shall form a search party *and* a war party," he said. "We shall soon have our answers!"

He raised his rifle into the air. "If war is what the Crow *or* the white people are after, stealing my son is the best way to antagonize me into starting one!" he shouted.

"Blazing Eagle, may I go with you to search for your son?" Becky asked, gently touching his arm as he lowered his rifle to his side. "If you find Whistling Elk, and he is injured, perhaps I can help in some way."

Blazing Eagle turned to her. "Stay behind with the other women," he said solemnly. "In my absence, become acquainted with them. Be there if Whistling Elk returns, unharmed, while I am gone. Be there for him as though you were his true mother."

Touched that she was the one assigned to care for Whistling Elk, Becky's eyes pooled with grateful tears. "Yes, I shall stay with the other women," she murmured. "And should Whistling Elk arrive while you are gone, I will be here for him."

Their eyes held in a silent understanding, then Blazing Eagle turned away from her and proceeded to prepare for their departure.

Waterfall brought a large parfleche and gave it to Blazing Eagle. She then stepped back and stood with Becky.

"What did you give him?" Becky whispered as she leaned closer to Waterfall, her eyes never leaving Blazing Eagle as he continued placing things on his horse, most of which were various weapons.

"*Wasna*," Waterfall said matter-of-factly. "They carry hash on a war party so that it will not be necessary to light a fire which might betray the Cheyenne to their enemies."

Waterfall turned soft eyes to Becky. "You see," she murmured. "They may be gone for many days."

"Many days . . . ?" Becky gasped, paling at the thought of Blazing Eagle being placed in danger that long, and Whistling Elk too.

"If they are gone for more than tonight, then we can expect that our people's lives will no longer be peaceful," Waterfall said, her face drawn with sadness. "Once warring is begun, even if it is only between two tribes, the whites soon interfere. Then it becomes a war that spreads along the land like a raging fire gone out of control."

Becky swallowed hard as she turned her gaze back to Blazing Eagle. She had a sick feeling in the pit of her stomach to think that this might be the last time she would ever see him. She just knew that he would be riding into the face of danger.

Someone had abducted his son in order to stir up trouble for the Cheyenne!

Becky turned her head as the women of the village came together. Waterfall tugged at her arm to encourage her to join the group as the women began singing.

Waterfall leaned closer to Becky and whispered into her ear. "Sing war songs with us," she said. "A man can do many things to get power. One of the ways women reveal the power they have is through songs."

Becky suddenly felt out of place.

Everything was so alien to her!

How could she be expected to learn all of the different customs of the Cheyenne?

Even the songs that now reverberated through the air seemed mystical, especially since they were being sung in the Cheyenne tongue.

She felt foolish always asking questions, yet how could she be expected to know the answers? She felt as though she wore her ignorance on her face like some stupid person. But she had only learned so much in her studies of Indians. The rest had to be learned by doing.

And so often Waterfall seemed to anticipate Becky's questions. Now Waterfall was whispering to her.

"The women now sing a coward song," Waterfall said. "I will explain the words to you, so that you can know why it is called a coward song."

Becky nodded and listened as Waterfall began to explain the meaning of the song.

"They are singing that if you are a coward, if you

are afraid, when you charge, turn back. The Desert Woman will eat you," Waterfall said, as the men swung themselves into their saddles.

"The song means that the women will talk about the coward so badly, he would have been better off dying," she said. "A coward knows that it is worse to turn back and fight the women."

Becky began to relax. She was actually enjoying listening to the songs and learning their meanings. She looked sharply up at Blazing Eagle as he spoke suddenly to his warriors.

"My friends!" he cried, his war shield now on his left arm. It was light, but strong enough to stop an arrow or turn away a ball from an old-fashioned gun. "Use your best abilities while we search for my son. If fighting is required, remember well that only stones stay on earth forever."

He cast Becky a lingering glance, then turned and rode slowly with his men through the village in a solemn file.

When he came to the far edge of the village, he sent his horse into a hard gallop.

Tears splashing from her eyes, Becky watched him. She hoped that she would have the opportunity to sing songs for him in the future.

She prayed silently that he would return to her so that she could show him all the things she'd learned of his people. She wanted him to be proud of her and say that he was glad that he had chosen her over all the others who would have gladly crawled between the blankets with him.

She wanted him to have cause to brag about her when she became his wife!

She looked around as the women began singing again. She listened to the words as they wafted through the air, loud and clear for the men to hear as they thundered across the land.

"Whenever my friends are afraid, I will be the one to make it easy for my fighting warriors!" Waterfall translated. She took Becky's hand. "That song is a bragging war song," she softly explained.

Suddenly everyone became quiet and their eyes turned to watch the warriors returning, Whistling Elk riding proudly beside his father.

"How can that be?" Becky gasped. "They have been gone for only a few minutes, and yet they have already found Whistling Elk?"

"It is not because of some magical power," Waterfall said, her voice brimming with excitement. "Whistling Elk must have broken free of his abductors. He has returned to us on his own!"

Becky ran to meet their approach. When she reached them, Blazing Eagle reached down and swept her onto his saddle.

"Blazing Eagle, isn't it wonderful?" Becky cried. "Your son is home, unharmed. You don't have to go to war."

Blazing Eagle rode determinedly onward. Becky wondered why he didn't look happier than he did. And why did he seem even angrier than when he had left?

And why were the warriors all so silent, their horses galloping through the village instead of slowing down to move among the people?

When they reached the communal fire, the warriors wheeled their horses to a shuddering halt and dismounted.

Blazing Eagle lifted Becky from his horse as Whistling Elk came over and gave her an uncertain look. Seeing his uneasiness, Becky felt a sudden fear leap into her heart. He should be feeling triumphant! He had escaped his captors. Then why were he and the rest of the warriors behaving so strangely?

"What is it, Whistling Elk?" Becky blurted out. "Why are you looking at me like that?"

"You have a brother whose hair is golden," Whistling Elk said, his voice drawn. "He is an outlaw. He is the one responsible for my abduction."

Becky paled and she felt suddenly dizzy. "No," she whispered harshly.

"Not only that," Whistling Elk said, looking over his shoulder as the warriors ran around, ushering their women and children into their lodges while others posted themselves at strategic points throughout the village.

"My woman, what Whistling Elk is trying to tell you is that your brother abducted Whistling Elk *and* stole our horses, all as a ploy to distract me so that they could abduct *you*. They will kill anyone who gets in the way," Blazing Eagle said, his eyes glancing around him as his warriors readied themselves for the attack.

Becky's temples began to pound. She was shocked at what her brother had done. To get her, he was planning to spill Cheyenne blood.

She closed her eyes, trying to remember when Edward was sweet and caring. But now such memories would not surface. The fact was that he might even be planning to massacre the Cheyenne people to get her. It looked to her as though he was using her as an excuse to further his killings!

Wiping tears from her eyes, she slowly opened them. She found Blazing Eagle looking down at her with an iciness she had never seen before.

She took a shaky step away from Blazing Eagle, wondering if this quickly his love for her could turn to hate, to know that her very own flesh and blood might bring death to many of his people.

"No, Blazing Eagle," she murmured, eyes wide. "Please don't look at me like that. Please!"

Chapter Twenty-two

Knowing that he was making Becky uncomfortable as he stared at her, Blazing Eagle wrenched his eyes from hers. In his mind, he had been trying to compare her with her brother, to see how one could be so evil, the other so good.

As his people still scurried about, readying themselves for an attack, women grabbing up small children, older children grabbing up their precious dogs, Blazing Eagle continued to give commands to everyone.

"Prepare yourselves as never before for an attack!" he shouted at his people. "But this is only just in case the outlaws get past our warriors, who will be hiding close to the village ready to ambush the white criminals!"

Becky felt pulled in many directions as she stood there. She felt frozen to the spot from the fears that assailed her. Because of her brother, she feared having lost Blazing Eagle's love.

She feared for Blazing Eagle's safety. He could die today as he attempted to protect his people!

And she could not help but fear for her brother's life, yet in the same breath be appalled at the thought that he was responsible for such ghastly, inhumane behavior. Not only did he take the lives of white people, but now he endangered the lives of these innocent people who wished to be left alone to live as one with nature and their gods.

Now, she finally had to accept what was said about her brother being the worst kind of a man. Whistling Elk had experienced first-hand his callous behavior. Becky felt her heart sink. She had come to the Wyoming Territory hoping to discover that the rumors about her brother were false. What she had found was a truth that she could hardly stand knowing.

When a pistol was fitted into her hand, her mind had strayed so far that she stared uncomprehendingly down at the copper hand that had placed the firearm there.

She then looked slowly up at Blazing Eagle.

"My woman, you must keep yourself safe," he said, his eyes warm again for her, his face full of worry. If her brother happened to get through the Cheyenne's line of defense and stole Becky, Blazing Eagle would leave no stone unturned until he found her again.

Then pity the brother whose heart was cold toward all humanity! The outlaw would die a slow, pitiless death at the hands of Blazing Eagle!

Becky felt the weight of the pistol in her hand and shuddered at the thought of having to use it tonight, perhaps—perhaps against her very own brother!

"My woman, do you hear what I say?" Blazing Eagle said, gripping her shoulders with his fingers. "Use the firearm on your brother should the need arise."

"I'm . . . not sure if I can," Becky said, tears streaming from her eyes. "Blazing Eagle, my—very own brother?"

"Is he the same brother you knew when you were a child, or is he now someone you do not even know?" Blazing Eagle said, his eyes imploring her.

"He is . . . like a stranger," Becky gulped out.

"Then would you hesitate to kill a stranger whose soul is dark and whose every thought is of whom he will plunder and kill next?" Blazing Eagle still tried to reason.

"No, if I killed him, I know that I would be doing humanity a favor," Becky said, her voice breaking.

Blazing Eagle reached a hand to her cheek and smoothed her tears away with his thumb. "Go inside with Whistling Elk," he said. "Stay there until I return."

Swallowing hard, Becky nodded.

"I am almost certain that my warriors will stop the outlaws before they have the chance to enter the village," Blazing Eagle reassured her again. He grabbed his rifle as Fish Hawk thrust it into his hand. He gazed at Becky a moment longer, then swung around and ran with Fish Hawk to get situated at a strategic point just outside the village.

"Come," Whistling Elk said, taking Becky's hand. "In my father's absence I will comfort you."

Becky almost choked on a sob as she turned wistful eyes to the child. In him she saw a much younger Blazing Eagle. The young brave displayed the same courage, stamina, and sense of logic. Some day he would be as powerful a leader as his father.

"I will stay with you," Waterfall said as she ran up to Becky.

Whistling Elk positioned himself between the two women and ushered them inside the tepee, Pebbles at his heels. Gently he led them both down beside the lodge fire, then went to the store of weapons for a rifle and stood vigil beside the entranceway.

Becky stared at the pistol in her hand. It was ready for firing. Could she truly kill her own brother if she was forced to make that decision?

"He will be all right," Waterfall said, placing a gentle hand on Becky's arm, thinking that Becky's thoughts were on Blazing Eagle.

Becky looked quickly at Waterfall. "He will?" she said, her thoughts still on her brother. "Do you truly wish that he should live?"

"Why would I ever want Blazing Eagle to die?" Waterfall gasped out, paling. "Becky, what are you thinking about? *Who* are you thinking about? Surely you did not mean to speak in such a way about Blazing Eagle, as though you . . . might wish that he dies."

Becky's eyes widened. "No," she then said, shaking her head desperately back and forth. "I was not even thinking about Blazing Eagle. My thoughts were on my outlaw brother."

"I should have known," Waterfall said, lowering her eyes. "I know that your love for Blazing Eagle is true."

Then Waterfall's eyes met Becky's. "Yet some women would do anything to keep a brother alive," she said softly. "Next to a husband, brothers are most important to them."

"They are?" Becky said.

"You see, Becky, if a husband dies, a brother takes over the responsibility for a sister," Waterfall said, smoothing a lock of Becky's hair back with her hand. "Is that not the way it is in the white community?"

"No," Becky said solemnly. "When a husband dies among my people, the women are left to fend for themselves."

She laid her pistol aside and took Waterfall's hands in hers. "Just like *you*," she murmured. "You live alone. You fend for yourself. Why is that?"

"It is by choice that I do this," Waterfall said softly. "I am a Cheyenne princess. In time I will allow marriage to enter my life. But now I am more important to my people unwed."

"Your parents?"

"They and my brother Fish Hawk live without me and are proud of my status with my people."

Becky and Waterfall jumped and screamed when the first clap of gunfire echoed through the midnight air. Trembling, they clung to one another and listened to the screams and the war cries of their warriors.

"*Hiy, hi-i-i-ya!*" the warriors cried as the gunfire continued for a while longer. But soon everything became deadly silent.

Feeling numb inside, afraid to see the outcome of the fighting, Becky eased from Waterfall's arms. They stared at one another for a moment, then scrambled to their feet.

They all ran from the lodge. Becky's footsteps faltered and she felt faint when she found Blazing Eagle escorting her brother into the village at gunpoint. Other outlaws followed behind under the escort of other warriors.

Edward caught sight of Becky.

He moved slowly onward, his eyes now downcast.

Becky felt faint to know that her brother was, indeed, a total stranger to her now. Tears sprang from her eyes and she stifled a sob behind her hands when Blazing Eagle grabbed Edward by his arm and threw him to the ground on his stomach.

Blazing Eagle gazed at Becky, then shifted his eyes to his son as he placed a foot on Edward's back to hold him to the ground. "Whistling Elk, bring rope and tie this man's hands behind him," he said solemnly.

Whistling Elk rushed back inside his lodge, dropped his rifle, and grabbed a coil of rope to do as he was told.

Becky inched over to stand over Edward. As he was lying there, helpless, her heart bled for that little boy that he had been when they had romped and played together. They had tumbled to the ground and rolled in the grass, laughing until they cried from the thrill of being free from their parents, if only for a short while.

And how they would play jokes on one another! She would never forget the time her brother dropped a worm down the front of her blouse when he was supposed to be placing it on the hook of his fishing line.

She had run screaming from the lake, the worm cold against the flesh of her newly budded breasts. She had stepped quickly behind a tree to discard her blouse to get the worm.

Finally when the worm was tossed aside and she was dressed again, she had delighted in rushing to the embankment and shoving her brother into the water.

"Edward, how could you have changed so much?" Becky blurted out, now bending low to turn his face so that their eyes could meet. "Why, Edward? Why?"

"Sis, I wish I could explain," Edward said, swallowing hard. "But I can't. Believe me when I say it's you that I'm worried about. Get on the next train to Saint Louis. Don't stay with these Indians. Go home where you belong—where you'll be safe."

"Edward, oh, Edward," Becky wailed, crumpling into Blazing Eagle's arms as he whisked her away.

"Waste no more tears on your brother," Blazing Eagle ground out as he led Becky inside his lodge. "His days on this earth are now numbered."

"It doesn't matter when he dies now," Becky sobbed, turning to cling to Blazing Eagle as he swept her against his hard body. "He has no heart. He has no feelings."

Waterfall came into the lodge. She gazed up at Blazing Eagle and nodded toward Becky.

He understood her silent message and handed Becky over to the soft, sweet arms of Waterfall. He gazed at Becky a moment longer, then went back outside to see to the captive criminals.

"Becky, come and sit down beside the fire," Waterfall murmured. "Let me hold you. Cry until all of your pent-up feelings about your brother are washed away in the tears. Then you can start life anew with the Cheyenne. We will care for you. We are not savages. Your brother is the true savage!"

Becky eased down onto a blanket beside the fire, Waterfall at her side. She curled up on the blanket and laid her head on Waterfall's lap and gazed at the gently rolling flames of the fire.

"No Cheyenne died tonight," Waterfall said, caressing Becky's brow. She turned her gaze toward the entrance flap when Whistling Elk came inside.

"The white captives are being taken away," he boasted, settling down on his haunches beside Becky.

Becky turned quick, wary eyes to Whistling Elk. "Where are they being taken?" she asked, her voice breaking. She did not want to care about what happened to Edward! She was fighting with every ounce of her willpower not to care about him at all.

But that part of her that was still a little girl adoring a big brother could not let go so easily.

"They are being taken to Fort Laramie for the white man's law to hand down their sentences," Whistling Elk said, bending to shove another log into the fire. "The Cheyenne will not waste any more time with them."

He chuckled low. "My father allowed me to spit on each of the captives before they were bound on horses for delivery to the white pony soldiers at the fort," he said, his eyes dancing. "It pleased me so to place my brand on those heartless, savage animals."

Becky looked quickly away from Whistling Elk and clenched her eyes closed in an effort not to see her brother disgraced in such a way as that.

Yet, she reminded herself, that was not her brother. He was a total stranger to her now. He was a stranger walking in her brother's shoes, someone she loathed now with every fiber of her being.

Whistling Elk went to Becky and reached his arms out for her. "I was wrong to tell you what I did," he said, glad that she rose from the blanket and crept into his arms. "I apologize for being thoughtless. This is not a time that is easy for you."

Becky took solace in Whistling Elk's arms. They were small, but strong. Their bond became complete during those moments of comforting and sharing.

Becky then stiffened when she heard the sound of horse's hooves thudding against the packed earth outside the lodge. She tried to will herself not to go and take that last look at her brother. But nothing would keep her from it.

She ran to the entrance flap and pushed it aside. Her heart sank to her feet when she saw Edward lying across the back of Blazing Eagle's horse as though he were no more than a bag of potatoes.

When he turned his head her way, and their eyes locked, Becky was overwhelmed with a feeling of despair. She knew what her brother's fate would be in the hands of those at Fort Laramie. He would be hanged.

"Come," Waterfall said, slipping her slender hand in one of Becky's. "Do not torture yourself so. Let it go, Becky. Let *him* go."

Nodding, swallowing a sob that was lodged in her throat, Becky went back inside the lodge. When Edward cried her name, over and over again, filling the silent, midnight air with the mournful sound, Becky's whole body trembled.

"Let him go," Waterfall reiterated, clasping Becky's hand tightly.

Becky nodded and sat down beside the fire. She accepted the warmth of a blanket as Whistling Elk placed it around her shoulders. She gasped when she saw the likeness of her brother peering back at her from the flames of the fire, quickly understanding that it was only her imagination that placed the image there.

She blinked her eyes and the image was gone. Suddenly she felt somewhat less burdened.

Stretching out beside the fire, she closed her eyes and drifted off to sleep, a welcome escape from the heartache of the moment.

Chapter Twenty-three

Dawn was just breaking along the horizon when Blazing Eagle rode through the gate at Fort Laramie. He could feel eyes on him from all sides, the soldiers at the fort watching, their mouths agape at the sight of the outlaws tied to the many warriors' horses.

Blazing Eagle drew rein before Major Kent's private quarters. When Major Kent came outside and stood on his porch, his eyes wide with surprise, Blazing Eagle dismounted.

"I've never seen such a sight as this," Major Kent said, stepping from his porch to look at the outlaws. He walked down the long line of bound men, looking at each one at length.

When he came to Edward, he tilted his head so that he could look him square in the eye. "Well, if it isn't the bastard outlaw I've been after for too many years to count," he said, laughing throatily. "Good work, chief. Good work."

Smiling, Major Kent shook Blazing Eagle's hand. "I commend you, Blazing Eagle, for bringing the outlaws to me instead of taking the law into your own hands."

Blazing Eagle nodded, then turned to his warriors. "Remove the vermin from your horses," he ordered.

"How *did* you accomplish this?" Major Kent asked. He spread his legs and balanced himself on his heels, locking his hands behind him.

"They abducted my son," Blazing Eagle said, turning livid eyes toward Edward. He smiled ruefully. "But my son outsmarted the outlaw who was left to guard him. Whistling Elk escaped. He came and warned me that they were on their way to my village."

"Your son escaped?" Edward said, his eyes wide. "He's responsible for you knowing we were on our way to—"

"To massacre my people?" Blazing Eagle said, interrupting Edward. "Yes, my son is responsible for your demise, not I."

Edward winced when Fish Hawk kicked him over onto his stomach. Fish Hawk then knelt down beside Edward, grabbed a handful of his golden hair, and shoved his face into the dirt. "You do not steal Cheyenne children and horses without paying for the crime," he said, seething with hate.

Edward coughed and choked as with each breath he took he inhaled more dust into his nose and mouth. "Let me go," he managed to say in a dull whisper.

"Apologize to my chief!" Fish Hawk said, grinding Edward's face harder into the ground.

"I . . . apologize. . . . " Edward was barely able to get the words out as he fought for breath.

Fish Hawk gave Edward's hair a yank and turned him back on his side. "You deserve to die now at the hands of Fish Hawk," he said. "Not by the white man's rope. You deserve not one more sunrise on this earth. You have defiled our land. The very earth that you will soon rest in has been bloodied by your murderous ways!"

A warm hand on Fish Hawk's shoulder drew his eyes around. He gazed up at Blazing Eagle, whose eyes were soft with understanding.

"Enough, my friend," Blazing Eagle said. "Let us leave this man to the white pony soldiers. We have wasted enough time on him."

Blazing Eagle looked down at the long row of outlaws who groveled on the ground, their hands tied behind their backs. "Cowards, all of you," he hissed out as he walked slowly past them, locking eyes with one and then another. "You fed upon the innocent. If it was up to me, I would tie you to the ground and let the vultures feed upon your flesh. But I chose the easy road this time. You are at the mercy of your own people."

He smiled smugly. "They may even be more eager than I to see you die," he said, then turned and walked back toward his horse. He motioned to his warriors. "It is time to return to our people."

In his mind's eye he was thinking about Becky and her feelings at having said her final good-bye to her brother. He hoped that she would realize

270

that her true farewell had been when her brother left home to fight in the white man's Civil War. Since then she had been forced to accept that he might have died during the war. In a sense, he did. But would she see that, or mourn for him now as though it had just happened?

He would help lift the burden from her heart in all ways possible. His love for her was so intense that her hurt was *his*.

With Fish Hawk mounted at his right side, Blazing Eagle started to ride away, then stopped when Judge Newman rode through the wide gate of the fort, his blue eyes like reflections of the sky as he came and drew rein on Blazing Eagle's left side.

Judge Newman clasped a hand of friendship with Blazing Eagle, then looked past him at the outlaws who were just being helped to their feet by the soldiers. "Well, I'll be damned," he said. He shoved his wide-brimmed hat back from his brow as he then gave Blazing Eagle a wide smile. "So you finally caught up with the sonofabitch, eh?"

"The golden-haired outlaw made a false move," Blazing Eagle said, looking over his shoulder at Becky's brother as he was being led away. "He abducted my son!"

"You went after him and found him?" Judge Newman said, drawing Blazing Eagle's eyes back to him.

"No, my son escaped without the aid of his father," Blazing Eagle said, his lips tugging into a slow smile. "He arrived home before the outlaws reached my village. Because of my son, and his courage, my people were saved."

"Whistling Elk is the exact image of his father in every way," Judge Newman said, returning Blazing Eagle's smile. "And what will his rewards be for having proven himself?"

"A day of celebration in his honor," Blazing Eagle said. "You will be there? You would make my son's day complete. He looks at you with the eyes of one who idolizes."

"Well, now," Judge Newman said softly. "That is some compliment you just paid me, Blazing Eagle. Some compliment, indeed."

Judge Newman glanced over at the resident trading post, where the doors were just swinging open for the day's business.

Then he gave Blazing Eagle a mischievous grin. "You aren't in a hurry to get back, are you?" he asked, raising an eyebrow.

"My business here is over," Blazing Eagle said. "There is no reason I should not leave now and return to my people."

"What I want to do will take only a minute," Judge Newman said. His eyes danced into Blazing Eagle's. He nodded toward the trading post. "Come with me. I'd like to buy something for that son of yours—something that I brought to your village before that I know your son sees as special."

"You speak of sweets?" Blazing Eagle said. "You wish to buy him candy?"

"Something sweet, but no, not candy," Judge Newman said, laughing softly. "I think your son grew out of the candy stage long ago."

Blazing Eagle studied the trading post. In his mind's eye he remembered what he had seen there the few times he had gone to browse. There were not only things of interest for his son, but also for the woman who would soon be his wife. He recalled the ribbons of many colors. He could not help but be intrigued by the lace that had been wrapped around large bolts.

Yes, her beauty would be twofold in such lovely ribbons and lace! He burned with desire even now for this pale-skinned, golden-haired beauty!

"Yes, I shall take the time to go with you," Blazing Eagle said, then turned smiling eyes to Fish Hawk. "I shall be only a moment. Lead the warriors from the fort. Wait for me outside the gate."

Fish Hawk nodded, then shouted the command to the warriors to go with him as Blazing Eagle rode beside Judge Newman until they reached the trading post.

Swinging out of his saddle, Blazing Eagle looked toward the door of the trading post, then back at his saddle. To return home with gifts for his woman *and* son, he must have something to trade. He had not come prepared to make trade; only to give the white outlaws over to the authorities.

His gaze lingered on his saddle. It was worth a great deal.

Judge Newman dismounted. He went to Blazing Eagle and placed an arm around his bare shoulders. "I can read your thoughts," he said. "You are considering trading your saddle for gifts for your son. That isn't necessary, Blazing Eagle. I shall pay for whatever you choose to take home with you."

Blazing Eagle had heard Judge Newman's offer, yet he continued unfastening the saddle cinch.

"Gifts from the heart are not paid for by another man," he said. He gave Judge Newman a gentle smile. "And I need something valuable today for my trade, for I not only take my son a gift, but also my woman."

"Woman?" Judge Newman asked. "*What* woman? As long as I have known you, you have shied away from women. I haven't questioned you about it. I just concluded that your behavior about women had to do with your first wife."

"I will soon take a *second* wife," Blazing Eagle said. He heaved the leather saddle over his left shoulder and walked toward the door of the trading post.

"Who, Blazing Eagle?" Judge Newman said, falling into step beside him. "Waterfall? Are you going to marry Waterfall? She's a mighty fine woman, Blazing Eagle. I'd not mind having her as my own wife."

"No, it's not Waterfall," Blazing Eagle said, shaking his head slowly back and forth. "She is too much a friend ever to become my lover. And she is from my own clan. It is forbidden to marry someone of your own clan."

"Then *who*?" Judge Newman persisted. He stepped up onto the porch as Blazing Eagle swung the saddle down and carried it between his hands into the dimly lit trading post, which smelled of whiskey and leather and animal pelts that were pressed in packs for transportation.

"You have not met her," Blazing Eagle said, heaving the saddle onto a counter, behind which stood shelf after shelf that displayed housewares and bolts of cloth and lace.

Judge Newman tipped his hat to the store clerk. "Good mornin', Earl. Fine day, ain't it?"

Earl nodded, his gaze locked angrily on Blazing Eagle.

Judge Newman ignored Earl's obvious dislike of Indians, placed his hat back on his head, and turned his attention back to Blazing Eagle. "And so you're going to get married, huh?" he said. "Is she from a neighboring village?"

Judge Newman's gaze shifted and held on the jars of candy that were on display behind glass in a case beneath the counter. He smiled at the nickname the Indian children had given to him— "Many Sweets Man."

Yes, he liked that. He wore the name well and would never disappoint those who gave it to him.

"No, and her skin is not the color of the Cheyenne," Blazing Eagle said. He nodded a greeting to the clerk as the man came and fingered his saddle. "Her skin is lily white, as white as the spring clouds that float across the heavens."

"You don't say," Judge Newman said. He wrenched his eyes from the candy and gazed into Blazing Eagle's. "Come to think of it, I *did* hear about the captive that you took from the train. I also heard that she was beautiful. I heard also that you let her go. Is it she, Blazing Eagle? Is it Becky Veach?"

Blazing Eagle's bright smile and nod made Judge Newman's lips part with a slight gasp. "Truly? She is going to be your wife?" he said, shoving his hat back from his brow with a finger.

"She is," Blazing Eagle said, squaring his shoulders proudly.

"That takes the cake," Judge Newman said, chuckling. "You're ready to take another wife. She must be something special."

"Can I help you?" the clerk asked. He yanked a soiled handkerchief from the front pocket of his dark breeches and patted nervously at his mouth as he looked guardedly at Blazing Eagle. "This ain't no place for social gathering. You either buy something or get the hell outta here."

His gray eyes narrowed into Blazing Eagle's. "Especially you, Injun," he grumbled out. "Although you did us whites a service by bringin' in the outlaws, I still don't have much use for Injuns."

Blazing Eagle's temper flared like a match as he glared at the tall, thin man.

Judge Newman stepped closer to the counter. He leaned across it, grabbed the man by his scrawny neck, and sneered at him. "You pay this man some respect," he warned heatedly. "Do you hear what I say, Earl?"

"Yes, sir," Earl gulped out. "I'll do what you say. Just . . . let go. I can hardly breathe."

"You're lucky I allowed any breath to get in those stinking lungs of yours," Judge Newman growled, then yanked his hand away from Earl. "Now pay heed to what we want from you today, Earl. And make the trade fair and square for Blazing Eagle. I don't want no swindling done in my presence, or otherwise. You ought to be run back to Kansas City where you came from."

"Yes, sir, I'll do right by Blazing Eagle, sir," Earl said. He nervously ran his long, lean finger around his shirt collar. He leaned closer to Blazing Eagle.

"Mighty fine saddle you've got here, sir. Mighty fine. Pick anything out you want here in my store and I'll be satisfied with the trade for such a mighty fine saddle as this. Yes, sir. Mighty fine. Mighty fine."

Blazing Eagle walked slowly up and down before the counter, looking at everything on display behind it. His gaze settled on some pink lace and some streamers of pink satin ribbon.

Then he looked farther down the shelves and his heart skipped a beat when he saw a knife just the size that he would want for his son. As skilled as Whistling Elk was at using his hands, he could carve himself a sheath for this knife in no time. He would carry this knife proudly into adulthood.

He pointed out these things to the clerk and soon had them wrapped in paper, ready to take back to Becky and Whistling Elk.

He stood aside as Judge Newman made his choices. First he pointed out several kinds of candy and had that put in sacks.

He smiled at Blazing Eagle as he asked Earl to get a small keg of syrup for Whistling Elk.

Blazing Eagle smiled back at Judge Newman, recalling the time when Whistling Elk had stopped by Judge Newman's cabin with Blazing Eagle. Judge Newman had made what he called flapjacks and had covered a huge stack of them with sweet syrup.

Never had Blazing Eagle seen his son react so excitedly to something that he ate. He had sat down at the table and had eaten so many that Blazing Eagle had thought he might burst!

"Surely your white woman can make flapjacks, can't she?" Judge Newman said, glancing over at Blazing Eagle as he slipped his hands inside his front right pocket to get some money.

Blazing Eagle looked over at Judge Newman and cocked an eyebrow. "If you, a man, can cook flapjacks, surely my woman knows how to," he said matter-of-factly.

"Just thought I'd ask," Judge Newman said, slapping the coins on the counter.

"Will you come home with me now and share in the excitement of giving gifts and eating flapjacks?" Blazing Eagle said, hoping that Judge Newman would, for Becky needed something to help lift her spirits.

"Yes, I think I will," Judge Newman said, collecting his sacks as Blazing Eagle picked up his own.

They walked outside just in time to see the outlaws ushered into the guardhouse. "But I can't stay long," Judge Newman remarked. "I have more than one trial to see to."

Then he looked quickly over at Blazing Eagle. "You will be here for the hangings, won't you?" he said matter-of-factly. "There will be a trial for each man, but I already know what sentences I will hand down. A hanging is not good enough for these lowdown, heartless bastards."

Blazing Eagle nodded, then walked solemnly to his horse and placed his gifts inside the parfleche bag that he had tied to his horse in the absence of a saddle.

Mounting his horse, he rode off with Judge Newman at his side.

Blazing Eagle's thoughts were on Becky and how she would take the news that her brother would die soon.

"What's on your mind, Blazing Eagle?" Judge Newman asked as he sidled his horse next to Blazing Eagle's.

They rode on through the open gate, Blazing Eagle's warriors falling in behind them as they rode away from the fort.

Blazing Eagle evaded Judge Newman's question. Something made him feel that it would not be fair to Becky if he spread the word in the white community that the outlaw was her brother. He would leave it up to her to do the telling, if she felt the need to.

Chapter Twenty-four

The day had turned hot and close. Becky rolled the skirt of the tepee up so that air could circulate inside it. She had let the cook fire burn down to low embers. Her mouth was dry.

Picking up a bladder bag with which to transport water back to the lodge, she went outside into the pounding heat of the sun and walked toward the river. Sweat pearled her brow, and she was glad when she came to the shade of the cottonwoods.

Walking more slowly now since she was no longer burdened by the sun, she slung her hair back over her shoulders and looked through the break in the trees at the angle of the sun. It seemed forever since Blazing Eagle had left. Had he run into trouble at the fort? Had her brother and his outlaw friends managed to escape? Was Blazing Eagle in trouble of some kind?

She shook these thoughts from her mind and knelt down at the water. For a moment she watched the minnows at play, occasionally seeing a catfish swish past. She could hear the buzzing of bees as they gathered around a cluster of flowers beside the river.

But not wanting to be gone when Blazing Eagle returned, she dipped the bag down into the water and filled it to the top. Then she started back toward the village.

She screamed and felt faint when she heard the whiz of an arrow and saw it fly past her, lodging itself in the side of the bladder bag so that water quickly spilled from around the arrow.

Giggles came from a stand of brush, and then she saw, as though in a blur, Whistling Elk running past her toward the brush. When he yanked not one young brave from behind the bushes, but two, holding them by their arms, her eyes widened.

"Apologize to Becky!" Whistling Elk shouted. "She is soon to be my mother. She will be your chief's wife, and you treat her like this?"

"She is also sister to the outlaw!" one of the boys shouted back, trying to wrench himself free from Whistling Elk's tight grip. "She doesn't belong here!" He looked past Whistling Elk. "Leave, white woman! Leave our village!"

Seeing that the young brave did not heed his warning, Whistling Elk wrestled the one with the taunting mouth to the ground and straddled him. He held a fist threateningly over the young brave's face.

"Apologize!" he cried. "Or I shall hit you until you do."

The young brave's eyes were wild.

Becky felt bad, not for herself, but for being the cause of tension between the young braves. She dropped the bag to the ground and went to Whistling Elk. She placed a hand on his shoulder. "Let him up," she said softly. "Whistling Elk, stop this. Don't fight over me. Please."

The young brave's eyes widened even more when he saw that the white woman cared what happened to him.

"He is not being kind to you," Whistling Elk said, not budging. "How can you defend him?"

"I want no trouble between you and your friends," Becky said, gently drawing Whistling Elk away from the boy. "Especially not over me."

Whistling Elk stood at her side as the young brave scrambled to his feet.

He stared up at Becky, as though still not believing what she had done, then ran off with the other young brave.

"You should have let me hit him," Whistling Elk said, brushing dirt from his knees. "He deserved it."

"Let's go home, Whistling Elk," Becky said softly. "I must get a new bag and return to the river for more water."

"I shall do that for you," Whistling Elk said, walking beside her.

"Whistling Elk, how is it that you liked me so quickly and those two children can't seem to?" Becky asked, giving him a slight glance.

"You are kind, you are gentle, and . . ." He stopped to giggle as he looked over at her. "And you are beautiful. Who could not like you?"

Becky laughed with him, glad that she had found some camaraderie with him, for next to Blazing Eagle, this young man was fast becoming the second most important person in her life.

"And so you think I am beautiful, do you?" she teased, feeling suddenly lighthearted.

"Very," Whistling Elk said, smiling raptly up at her. "One day, I too will find someone like you to take to my blankets with me," he boasted.

"Whistling Elk!" Becky said, blushing.

"I know," Whistling Elk said, sighing. "I am too young to think such things." He smiled widely at Becky. "But I do, anyway."

Becky laughed softly. "I guess you aren't such a child anymore, are you?" she murmured.

"No," Whistling Elk said, squaring his shoulders. "I am now a man. I have proven myself enough to be called warrior."

"Yes, dear," Becky said, smiling at him. "You have. And I am very proud of you—oh, so very proud."

Yet a part of her cried out for her brother, the one with whom she could never have such innocent, wonderful conversations again.

Would she ever get used to having lost him from her life? she despaired. Would she?

Chapter Twenty-five

Night was creeping up on the Cheyenne village in its inky blackness. Becky put the last freshly washed wooden platter away just as Whistling Elk came into the lodge with an arm full of wood.

She turned to him, grateful for his presence. She felt empty inside now that she knew the full truth about her brother, but Whistling Elk was beginning to fill some of that emptiness.

"The fire will feel good," she said, as she went to him and helped unload the wood from his outstretched arms. "The Wyoming Territory is a strange land. During the day a woman could almost melt in her shoes from being so hot. At night, it's as though old man winter is breathing down one's neck."

"Is it different where you came from?" Whistling Elk asked as Becky took the last log from his arms.

He brushed bits and pieces of bark and dirt from his bare arms into the fire.

"Lordy, let me tell you, in the summer it's hot in Saint Louis, both day *and* night," Becky said, bending to shove a piece of the wood into the flames of the fire. She forced a laugh over her shoulder at Whistling Elk, trying her hardest to keep up her end of the conversation.

"And you should see how the steam rolls in from the Mississippi River after a sudden storm in the summer," she murmured. "It's like smoke from a fire."

"Did you like this place called Saint Louis?" Whistling Elk said, settling down on his haunches beside Becky. "Will you return there some day?"

Becky sat down on a blanket beside him, a forlorn look in her eyes as she watched the fire caressing the logs. "Yes, I truly loved the city of Saint Louis," she murmured, her voice thick with melancholy. She turned heavy-lidded eyes toward Whistling Elk. "And yes, I must return one day soon to finalize things, since I will no longer make my residence there."

"What things?" Whistling Elk asked, eyes wide as saucers.

"My father left me quite an inheritance," Becky said, tears suddenly pooling in her eyes when she thought of how she had hoped to take her brother home with her, to let him share the inheritance.

She swallowed hard and lowered her eyes. "Had Father known that Edward was alive, he would also have included him in the will," she said, her voice breaking. "Although, if father had known the rogue his son has turned into, I'm sure that he would not have left him a penny. My father was as honest a man as they come. He never cheated anyone."

"Your brother," Whistling Elk said, placing a gentle hand on her cheek. "You love him even now that you know the sort of man that he is?"

"When one loves a brother as deeply as I loved mine, the love never dies," Becky said, swallowing hard. She covered his hand with one of hers. "But my respect for him is gone, as are the deep, special feelings I once felt for him."

"I am sorry your brother disappointed you," Whistling Elk said, flinging himself into her arms. "If I am ever fortunate enough to have a sister, I shall never disappoint her."

"You wish to have a sister?" Becky asked, caressing his bare back as he clung to her, his thin arms hugging her to him.

"It has been lonely without a brother or sister," Whistling Elk said softly. He drew away from her and looked anxiously into her eyes. "You have given my father trust in women again. Will you also give him a child?"

"I shall give your father anything he wishes, if it is within my power to do so," Becky said, framing his small face between her hands. She leaned over and kissed his brow. "I shall also be as generous to you. You have made me so happy, Whistling Elk, by accepting me as quickly as you did into your life. I wish to give that happiness back to you, twofold."

The sound of horses arriving at the village drew them apart.

His eyes dancing, Whistling Elk ran from the

lodge. Becky followed behind him.

"It is father!" Whistling Elk said excitedly, beaming as he glanced over at Becky. "He has returned."

The mere sight of Blazing Eagle made Becky's heart beat more rapidly. She loved him so much that her knees were weak at the thought of soon being in his arms again. She needed him now as never before. She had only recently lost her father, and now, so soon after discovering that her brother was alive, he had been snatched from her life again as though he had never been a part of it at all.

As Blazing Eagle came closer, the sound of her brother crying her name was like a wound in Becky's heart.

She clenched her eyes closed at the recollection. She would always remember those torturous moments as though his desperation, his pleading, had been seared onto her heart like a brand!

"My father's saddle is missing," Whistling Elk said, drawing Becky's eyes open. "I wonder where he left it and why? That saddle was special to my father. It was a gift from a neighboring Cheyenne chief."

"Why would he part with it?" Becky asked, now noticing the buckskin bags tied to Blazing Eagle's horse, whereas usually they were tied to his saddle.

"Only if he got something valuable in trade would he part with the saddle," Whistling Elk said, then broke into a run and met Blazing Eagle.

"Father!" Whistling Elk said. He reached a hand toward Blazing Eagle and clasped his fingers around his father's hand.

"Many Sweets Man!" the children of the village

began chanting as they spied Judge Newman riding at Blazing Eagle's left side. "We love you, Many Sweets Man!"

Blazing Eagle drew a tight rein and dismounted. His eyes searched until he found Becky standing among his people as they came in a crowd to welcome him.

"I shall take your reins, father," Whistling Elk said. He gave Becky a smile over his shoulder. "I believe someone wishes a hug from you."

Blazing Eagle chuckled beneath his breath, then walked toward Becky at a dignified stride. He welcomed her into his arms as she came and melted into them.

"It is so good to have you home," Becky whispered, only loud enough for him to hear as she brought her lips close to Blazing Eagle's ear. "My darling, the hours are so long when you are not with me."

"I am with you now," Blazing Eagle whispered back, his lips brushing her ear. "Are you all right? Are you accepting your brother's fate well enough?"

"It is hard," Becky choked out. She willed herself not to cry. "But I will manage."

"He will die soon," Blazing Eagle said, knowing it was best to get the worst over by telling her now.

Becky flinched and clung to him much harder. "I know," she said, a sob lodging in the depths of her throat.

"And you are truly all right?" Blazing Eagle said, stepping back from her, his eyes wavering into hers.

"Yes, truly I will be," Becky said. She leaned into

his hand as he wiped a tear from her cheek with the flesh of his thumb.

"I have brought a guest," Blazing Eagle said. He glanced over his shoulder at Judge Newman and the children who crowded around him to accept his offering of candy.

He smiled down at Becky. "I have also brought you and my son a gift," he said. His eyes danced as he thought of Judge Newman's special gift for Whistling Elk. "Also, Judge Newman has brought what we Cheyenne call 'juice of the wood' for Whistling Elk. It is to be eaten with flapjacks. Do you know how to make flapjacks?"

"Do I know . . . ?" Becky said, eyes wide. She giggled. "Flapjacks? Of course you mean pancakes."

Embarrassed over her ignorance of the duties expected of a wife in a kitchen, she looked shyly away from him, then directed her eyes at him again. "Please forgive me when I tell you I hardly know how to boil water, much less make anything as fancy as pancakes. Sometimes even the cooks we had at our home in Saint Louis failed at mastering the art of making pancakes."

"Pancakes?" Blazing Eagle asked. "Cakes made in a pan?"

"Yes, something like that," Becky said, laughing softly. "Do I disappoint you by not knowing how to cook?"

"Waterfall will teach you," Blazing Eagle said. He gave Waterfall a smile over Becky's shoulder as she stood with the other women.

"Blazing Eagle, what on earth is 'juice of the wood'?" Becky asked as they turned and walked toward his horse.

"Syrup from a maple tree," Blazing Eagle explained. "My son ate it once at Judge Newman's cabin. He has never stopped hungering for it since."

He paused, then nodded toward Judge Newman. "I shall introduce you to my long-time friend," he said. "Come. You shall meet a white man whose heart sings the same songs as the Cheyenne."

Becky gazed at the man she walked toward. This man was a judge.

An iciness swept through her when she realized that this very man might soon be sentencing her brother. If her brother were sentenced to hang by a rope until he was dead, this man could be the one to order the hanging.

She found it hard to think about shaking this man's hand, wondering how many men he had sentenced to death in his lifetime.

Yet she knew that this man worked for the betterment of mankind. This land was brimming with murdering thieves who did not think twice about taking the life of an innocent victim. This judge helped clean the land of such vermin.

She would not allow herself to feel anything but kindness toward him, even though her brother's fate lay in his hands.

"My friend, I would like you to know the woman who is soon to be my wife," Blazing Eagle said as they stepped up to Judge Newman. Blazing Eagle glanced down at Becky. "Becky, I would like you to meet a friend not only of the Cheyenne, but of all people whose hearts are pure."

Judge Newman handed the last piece of candy to

a child, slipped his empty sack into the right pocket of his jacket, and put out his hand to Becky. "Pleased to make your acquaintance, ma'am," he said amiably, his eyes slowly raking over her. "You're gettin' one mighty fine husband when you marry Blazing Eagle."

"No one knows more than I the goodness of this man I will soon marry," Becky said, shaking the judge's big hand. "And, sir, do you have a wife?"

"No, thus far none will have me," he said, laughing.

Becky was mesmerized by his blue eyes and his warm smile. "I am sure that mistake will soon be corrected," she said, laughing softly as she eased her hand from his.

"Do you know something I don't?" Judge Newman teased back.

Blazing Eagle went to his horse and untied the ropes that held his buckskin bags in place. Whistling Elk took one of the bags as Blazing Eagle handed it to him, then watched his father take the other wrapped package over to Becky.

"There are two special gifts inside this bag for you," Blazing Eagle said to Becky, enjoying how his words made her eyes widen with surprise.

He turned to Whistling Elk and nodded toward the bag in his arms. "My son, be careful as you reach inside that bag for *your* gift," he said. "What I bought you was wrapped in paper, yet still be careful."

Becky and Whistling Elk thrust their hands inside their separate bags at the same time.

Her heart beating excitedly, Becky brought out the wrapped gifts.

Blazing Eagle took the bag from her and watched as she opened the first gift. He squared his shoulders proudly when he saw her reaction to the ribbons.

"How beautiful!" she gasped. "So soft. So colorful and pretty!"

"Open the other one," Blazing Eagle said, holding the ribbons for her in his free hand.

Becky tore apart the paper and slid the lace from inside it. She sighed at the daintiness and prettiness of it.

"Thank you," she said. She smiled radiantly up at Blazing Eagle. "Oh, thank you so much for the gifts."

She leaned close and stood on her tiptoes to kiss him on the cheek. "You knew these would help lighten the load I am carrying within my heart today," she whispered into his ear. "Thank you, my darling. Oh, how I love you."

She turned to Whistling Elk when she heard his gasp of pleasure.

"A knife!" he cried. "My very own store-bought knife!"

"It is a gift to you for the courage you have recently displayed to your people," Blazing Eagle said, placing a hand on Whistling Elk's shoulder.

Whistling Elk beamed up at him, but then the smile waned. He glanced over at his father's horse, then up at his father again. "You traded your saddle for these gifts. That makes what you gave both me and Becky today worth even more. For it is known by all what you felt for that saddle."

"The trade was worth the smiles I brought to

your faces," Blazing Eagle said, gazing from Becky to Whistling Elk.

Judge Newman came to Whistling Elk with a small jug held between his hands. "Whistling Elk, your father told me what you did," he said. "For your courage, for your loyalty to your people, I have brought you some 'juice of the wood'."

Whistling Elk's eyes widened again as he took the jug in his free hand. "For me?" he said, awestruck at the judge's generosity. This syrup meant more to him than all the candy in the world!

"Your very own," Judge Newman said, laughing softly.

Then Judge Newman turned to Blazing Eagle. "I must return to Fort Laramie now, to tend to duties that await me there," he said. He smiled at Blazing Eagle and clasped a hand on his shoulder. "Thanks to you, I have outlaws to sentence. I will hand down the sentencing tomorrow. The outlaws will hang at sunup the next day if you wish to come and be witness."

At those words, Becky's heart sank.

"No, I wish not to be there," Blazing Eagle said, giving Becky an uneasy glance. Then he looked at Judge Newman again. "I've duties of my own to tend to."

"I understand," Judge Newman said, then went to his horse and mounted it. He tilted his hat toward Blazing Eagle, motioned with it toward Becky and Whistling Elk, and rode away.

Suddenly Whistling Elk became surrounded by the children of the village. They were all eyes as Whistling Elk first showed them his knife, then the jug of syrup.

"I shall bring out a goat-horn spoon and share the syrup with everyone!" Whistling Elk said, then turned to his father. "Can I stay the night with Jumping Sky? We have so much to talk about. And can I take my knife with me to look at before I sleep?"

"Yes, you can stay the night, and yes, you can take the knife," Blazing Eagle said. "If I did not trust you with a knife, I would have not traded for it as a gift to you."

"Let us all go to my lodge!" Jumping Sky shouted. "Mother will let us use her spoon for tastes of the syrup!"

"I must first see to my father's horse," Whistling Elk said, handing his gifts to Jumping Sky to hold for him.

Soon Whistling Elk returned, his chore done.

Becky held her gifts close to her heart as she watched Whistling Elk run away with the other children.

She then gazed up at Blazing Eagle. "He is such a happy child," she murmured. "Has he ever lodged a complaint about anything in his entire life?"

Blazing Eagle's eyes wavered. "Yes, but only about one thing," he said, his voice drawn.

"And what is that?"

"Not what. *Who*."

"Who then?"

"His mother."

Becky swallowed hard and looked again at Whistling Elk as he sat down among the children as the goat-horn spoon began its way around the circle, each one having his or her taste.

"Come," Blazing Eagle said, slipping an arm around Becky's waist. "Let us go to my lodge and talk of marriage. The women of the village will teach you the ways of a Cheyenne marriage."

"That would be wonderful," Becky said, yet felt guilty to be talking of marriage at such a time as this, when her brother, who was once so beloved to her, would soon die.

But she had learned before how to accept losses in her life.

Life had a way of going on.

Chapter Twenty-six

Blazing Eagle led Becky inside the lodge, then turned her to face him. First he took the gifts from her arms and laid them aside, then he slowly undressed her.

She trembled with ecstasy beneath Blazing Eagle's eyes as they grew black with passion. Her heart beat wildly as she welcomed this way to help her forget what troubled her. She lifted her arms so that he could draw her dress over her head.

Blazing Eagle tossed the dress aside, then her undergarments. He knelt before her and lifted first one foot and then the other as he removed her shoes, then set them aside.

His pulse racing, Blazing Eagle looked up at Becky and trailed his eyes over her liquid curves. He slowly ran his hands up her slender legs to her slim, white thighs, her flesh like satin against his fingers.

The scent of her reminded him of wild roses that climbed the trunks of the trees in early spring.

Their eyes were locked in a silent, mutual understanding. The tepee almost pulsed with the inevitability of pleasure as his hands moved higher, across the gentle curve of her hips. He teased circles around her belly, then higher to her breasts, just missing the nipples each time so that they strained with added anticipation.

The sureness of his caresses inflamed Becky with desire. She sucked in a wild breath of pleasure when he finally cupped her ripe breasts within the palms of his hands, his thumbs caressing her taut nipples.

Then Blazing Eagle rose to his feet and lifted Becky fully into his arms and carried her to his bed, their eyes holding, silently promising ecstasy.

Becky stretched out on the bed and watched him undress slowly, shivering with rapture when she gazed at his lithe and well-aroused body. The sinews of his shoulders corded as he tossed his clothes aside.

Their eyes still locked, he bent over and removed his moccasins.

Becky held her arms out for him, trembling. "Come to me," she whispered, the huskiness of her voice foreign to her. "Oh, how I need you."

His eyes charged with dark emotion, Blazing Eagle crawled onto the bed and moved over her and surrounded her with his hard, strong arms. Pressing her up against him so that she could feel the strength of his desire as he rested his heavy manhood against her stomach, his mouth explored her passion-moist lips in slow, teasing kisses.

Then his mouth seized hers in a fiery kiss. In one swift movement, in a silent rush of power, he parted her legs with his knee, then thrust himself into her. His lean, sinewy buttocks moved rhythmically as he slid himself more deeply within her.

She wrapped her legs around his waist and offered herself to him when she felt his shaft reach beyond that point that he had reached before within her. It seemed to be a secret place. His exploring there with his warm and throbbing manhood made her go wild with pleasure. Tight and hot he filled her, so wonderfully that it drew her breath away with ecstasy.

A surge of tingling heat flooded Blazing Eagle's senses. His lips found her nipples, his tongue flicking over them. His hands went beneath her and lifted her closer, drawing her into the warmth of his body. He felt her breath catch and hold when he kissed her again, his hands filled with her breasts, his body thrusting, ever thrusting.

Filled now with a hungry need to reach that place where they would float on wings of rapture together, Becky moved her body sinuously against his. Her hands went to his buttocks and pulled him even more tightly against her. She was overwhelmed with longing, with a sweet, painful longing!

And then she felt the beginning of ecstasy as their bodies strained together. Their groans of pleasure mingled as they continued to kiss. Becky could feel the ecstasy grow, now almost to the bursting point.

Blazing Eagle ran his hands up and down her body. Becky reached down and touched the very heat of him as he withdrew, then thrust himself within her again, each time more vigorously, more demanding.

Their bodies quivered and quaked. They clung to one another. Blazing Eagle drew his mouth from her lips and laid his face on her breasts, his groans mingling with her sighs of pleasure as they reached the peak they sought, their bodies then subsiding into slow, quivering shimmers.

Blazing Eagle rolled away from her and lay at her side, his eyes closed.

Becky turned to him and watched his heavy breathing, then roamed her fingers over his perspiration-laced body. "You make it all so magical," she murmured. "Before you, I was never with a man. I had no idea what mysteries waited to be unfolded to me."

"And so you now know," Blazing Eagle said, laughing softly as he turned to face her. "I can tell that you are not disappointed in your findings."

"Never," Becky said. Her sigh was heavy with pleasure as she moved closer to him and shaped her body against his. "I only wish it could last longer."

"That would only spoil you to the point that you would not ever want it again," Blazing Eagle said. He traced the shape of her lips with a forefinger. "If rationed out, then the need for it becomes more powerful."

"I could make love all night and never grow tired of it," Becky said. She trembled when he lowered the trail of his finger and now circled a nipple.

"Shall we test your theory?" Blazing Eagle teased.

"Do you have all night?" she teased back.

"Not tonight, but perhaps tomorrow night?" he said, his eyes gleaming into hers.

"Why not tonight?" Becky asked, her lips curving into a pout.

"I must leave now," Blazing Eagle said. When he started to rise from the bed, Becky reached a hand out and grabbed his wrist, causing him to turn quizzical eyes down at her.

"Please don't leave," she murmured, truly not wanting to be alone with thoughts about her brother that she knew would return to haunt her.

"I must," Blazing Eagle said, easing his wrist from her grip. He turned to her and framed her face between his hands and gently kissed her on the cheek. "I must not wait any longer before going to take back the horses that were stolen from me."

Becky abruptly sat up, and his hands fell away from her. "That means that you will have to travel to the Crow camp to *steal* the horses," she said, her voice breaking. "I'm afraid, Blazing Eagle. Should anything happen to you . . ."

He placed a finger to her lips, sealing her words behind them. "Do not waste time worrying over Blazing Eagle," he said. "You must learn to accept what fate hands you before worrying it *into* happening."

"My father always scolded me for worrying too much," Becky said as she gently smoothed his finger away from her lips. She smiled sheepishly up at him.

"Your father was a wise man," Blazing Eagle said, leaving the bed. He reached down and slipped on his breech cloth, stepped into his moccasins, then stroked his fingers through his long black hair and straightened it back over his shoulder.

"How long will you be gone?" Becky asked, slipping from the bed and quickly dressing.

"As long as it takes," Blazing Eagle said solemnly. He went to his store of weapons and picked up a pistol. He checked the firearm and made sure that he had a cap and cartridge in the loading gate.

"Now what kind of an answer is that?" Becky said, frustrated.

He laid his pistol aside and drew Becky into his arms. "You must learn not to question so much, but to accept that what I do is right," he said somberly. "My woman, I am a powerful leader, a chief of many valiant warriors. Trust that everything we do is done at the best of our ability. You will relax more during the long hours of my absence."

"Should I ask, I doubt that you would allow me to go with you tonight," Becky said, giving him a sidewise, wishful glance.

"What we are about to do is done only by warriors," Blazing Eagle said. He picked up his pistol again and thrust it inside his waistband. He reached for a Colt Model 1855 percussion rifle, then turned and left the lodge.

Becky followed him outside and stood back with the other women as the warriors prepared to leave on an expedition of daring and danger.

Waterfall came and stood beside her. Their hands met and their fingers intertwined as the warriors used lumps of soft charcoal to draw magical symbols on their horses' flanks. Then they hung medicine bundles from the hair bridle of each of their horses.

Never taking her eyes off the man she loved, Becky watched Blazing Eagle dangle a pouch from the buckskin thong on his breechclout.

"What is that bag that Blazing Eagle has hung from his breechclout?" Becky whispered to Waterfall.

"That is his medicine bag which contains the special totem for his clan," Waterfall whispered back. "The bag for each man contains many things—feathers, claws, beaks, or precious stones. Blazing Eagle's medicine is the rattlesnake."

Becky's eyes widened as she gave Waterfall a wide-eyed stare. "A rattlesnake?" she gasped.

Waterfall laughed softly. "The rattles of the snake," she corrected. "Not the snake itself."

"Oh, I see," Becky said, laughing awkwardly.

They clung to one another as the warriors then circled the blazing council fire, chanting. Becky was not at all surprised to see Whistling Elk and his friends join the dancers, themselves looking as fierce as those who would actually go on the search for the horses tonight.

"With great skill and cunning we will bring home our horses tonight!" Blazing Eagle cried out, drawing the dancing to a close. "Mount your horses. Let us go and get back what was wrongly taken from us!"

Just as they reached for their reins, they turned abruptly to the sound of many approaching horsemen. Several warriors ran to the outskirts of the village, their rifles readied in case an enemy was arriving.

But their rifles were soon lowered when they recognized the horses that were not saddled being led into the corrals by several Crow warriors. Blazing Eagle and Fish Hawk stood side by side as the powerful Crow chief, flanked on each side by an armed warrior, came into the village and drew rein before Blazing Eagle.

"You have brought our horses to us?" Blazing Eagle said, gazing up at Chief Laughing Deer.

"That is so," Chief Laughing Deer said in a low, gruff voice. "We found them mingled with ours. We know yours from ours. We brought them back to you."

"That is good of you," Blazing Eagle said warily, never trusting the motives of this Crow chief who had more than once stolen from Blazing Eagle.

"I must know how they became mixed with ours," Chief Laughing Deer said. "First they are not there, and then, as if by magic, they are."

"It was the work of outlaws who tried to direct our attention elsewhere by stealing our horses and mixing them with yours," Blazing Eagle said, folding his arms across his muscled chest. "I must know what prompted you to return them when you and your warriors have gone to such lengths in the past to steal from us."

"The victory is in the stealing, not in possessing what someone else has stolen for us," Chief Laughing Deer said. "Who is to say now that we might or might not come again tomorrow night, when the sky is the color of the crow, and steal these horses back again?"

Blazing Eagle's jaw became tight. His eyes narrowed angrily. "You make careless conversation now," he said tersely. "Should you come again, you will regret it. We will come and steal twice what you steal from us!"

"This is the true talk of those who are still enemies," Chief Laughing Deer said. He glared at Blazing Eagle a moment longer, then wheeled his horse around and rode away in a lope. He looked over his shoulder at Blazing Eagle. "Tonight we were generous. Never shall we be again!"

"Tonight you were foolish!" Blazing Eagle said, shaking a fist in the air at the Crow chief.

Becky paled at the show of hate between these two powerful chiefs. She feared that eventually it would lead to an outbreak of war. She was quickly learning that living in this wilderness was nothing at all like living the peaceful life back in Saint Louis.

Yet now that she had found sweet love in a Cheyenne chief's arms, she would risk anything to stay with him. Life as she had known it had ended the moment her father had taken his last breath.

Her heart sank at the memory of her father, for that brought Edward to mind. He would soon die for his sins against mankind! She would never see him again. Never.

Blazing Eagle watched until the Crow had left his village and ridden out of sight. Then he turned back to Becky. "That is done," he said matter-of-factly. "Now we think of tomorrow."

"What's happening tomorrow?" Becky asked, anxious to see if tomorrow would be hers and Blazing Eagle's wedding day.

"Tomorrow we must honor my son with a victory dance," he said. "The victory dance will be in honor of his deeds of valor!"

"Oh, I think that's wonderful," Becky said, glancing over at Whistling Elk as he stood in a circle of young boys, laughing and talking.

She was not disappointed that Blazing Eagle was placing his son before her. That was how it should be. His son had been a part of his life much longer than Becky had.

And his son deserved his special day! Because of him, everyone could still dance and laugh and look forward to all their tomorrows.

"*Then* we shall focus on our plans of marriage," Blazing Eagle said, placing a gentle hand to her cheek.

She smiled up at him, then watched him walk away to talk to the village crier.

She stood back with Waterfall and listened as the crier then rode around the village on his horse and made the announcement through the village of the victory dance tomorrow. She discovered that, since she knew the subject of the crier's announcement, she was able to understand a few words also.

Becky welcomed Whistling Elk as he came and hugged her fiercely. "Tomorrow is my special day!" he cried, his eyes anxiously wide. "Are you happy for me?"

"I am both happy and proud for you," Becky said softly. She smiled at Blazing Eagle over Whistling Elk's shoulders. She felt as though she belonged, as though she was already a part of this wonderful family of Cheyenne!

Chapter Twenty-seven

Becky was impressed with the way the Cheyenne celebrated things with much singing and dancing. And she was so full from having eaten so much at the feast that she felt as though she might burst.

She now sat on a platform that was covered with rich pelts. Blazing Eagle sat at her right side. Pebbles was snuggled on her lap, snoozing.

Being the princess of this clan of Cheyenne, Waterfall sat on the chief's left side, a place of honor. She leaned behind Blazing Eagle often and whispered to Becky as she explained the different dances and the clothes worn for each dance.

Fish Hawk sat close by, best friends sharing the moment of glory for Whistling Elk.

Along with many warriors, Whistling Elk was now dancing the Victory Dance performed in his honor. Once the dance was over, he would enter the ranks of warrior himself.

Those dancing with him had been in one battle or another during their lifetime. Each man was dressed in clothes he had worn in the fight. Those who had been wounded had painted the spot where he had been wounded with bright red paint, to represent blood.

Also among those who were dancing were scouts who had gone out first during times of skirmishes with various warring tribes those long years ago. These scouts wore eagle feathers today which had been trimmed down. Those who had killed an enemy wore an eagle feather straight up at the back of the head. If he had been wounded, his feather was painted red.

Whistling Elk wore the clothes that he had worn when he was abducted, the same that he had been wearing when he had knocked the outlaw out in order to set himself free, enabling him to return home to warn his people that the outlaws were on their way.

Because he had valiantly overpowered the outlaw, his enemy, Whistling Elk wore his eagle feather proudly straight up at the back of his head.

While the drums beat out a steady rhythm and the rattles shook in time to the beat of the drum, Whistling Elk swirled, stamped his feet, whirled around again, then bent low, his head bobbing in time with the music.

The rattle was an important musical instrument of the Cheyenne, which was used in doctoring, dancing, gambling, and religious ceremonies.

"Is Whistling Elk not a handsome young man?"

Waterfall whispered as she leaned closer to Becky. "It is good that he will soon be called warrior. Little boys are always ambitious for glory. Years ago they went with war parties at a tender age. Little boys who did this received much consideration from the older members of the tribe. They were carefully looked after."

"But there is no warring now between tribes," Becky whispered back. "There can't be much chance for the young men to win the title of warrior. Whistling Elk was forced into this sort of situation when he was abducted. But these sort of things surely don't happen often enough for the young braves to be able to prove their bravery."

"Yes, things *are* different now," Waterfall whispered back. "Now it is the highest ambition to be brave, not to fight. Whistling Elk proved himself worthy of both honors when he went up against the outlaw."

"And he is worthy of such honors," Becky said. "Because of his courage, we are able to sit here today and enjoy the festivities. If he had not been able to return to this village with the news that my brother and his outlaws were on their way here, I hate to think what might have happened."

Waterfall saw the look of pain in Becky's eyes that speaking about her brother caused. She quickly changed the subject. "Becky, soon you will marry our beloved chief," she whispered to her. "Not so long ago a maiden would not become engaged to a young man who had not been to war because it was felt that a man who had not been to war was not yet grown up."

Becky started to reply, but the activities had quickly changed. Horses had been brought to Whistling Elk and one of the warriors. Both swung themselves into the saddle, and then were handed axes.

"Come with me," Blazing Eagle said, reaching for one of Becky's hands.

"Where are we going?" Becky asked, following him from the platform. She threaded her arm through his as she looked over her shoulder and smiled at Waterfall, who scampered after her and Blazing Eagle, Fish Hawk assisting her.

"My son is going to participate in an axe-throwing contest," Blazing Eagle said, guiding Becky through the crowd of Cheyenne.

Soon everyone stood in two long rows opposite each other as Whistling Elk and the warrior positioned themselves at one end on horses, facing a huge tree trunk at the other end. Becky's eyes widened when Whistling Elk dug his heels into the flanks of his horse and rode toward the trunk at the far end. His left arm gripping the horse's neck, his right arm was raised high over his head. A double-bladed, spiked throwing axe was clutched tight in his fist.

His black hair streamed behind him as his horse finally reached a full gallop.

Becky's heart pounded as she watched Whistling Elk draw near to the tree trunk. She flinched and covered a gasp behind her hand when he released the axe. She sucked in a breath of excitement as she watched the flight of the axe. It twirled end over end, then sliced into the tree trunk with a solid thump.

The crowd applauded, then grew silent as the other warrior repeated Whistling Elk's ride toward the tree trunk. When his axe sliced into the tree trunk right next to Whistling Elk's, cheers rose into the air.

"Who is the winner?" Becky asked.

"Both," Blazing Eagle said, his eyes proud as Whistling Elk and the warrior's horses sidled up against each other and rode in a soft lope toward him.

Blazing Eagle stepped forth and greeted them with a smile and handshake. The warrior rode away and got lost among the crowd. Whistling Elk stayed and dismounted. He stood proudly before his father, awaiting the moment he would be declared warrior.

"Bring the many ponies forth!" Blazing Eagle said, as a young brave appeared at the far end of the long row of people with ten ponies. "Come. Bring the ponies to me!"

The young brave's hands were filled with the ropes that led the ponies behind him. He walked them hurriedly toward Blazing Eagle and handed him the ropes, then lost himself quickly in the crowd.

"Today I give away these ponies in honor of my son's deeds!" Blazing Eagle shouted, loosing first one rope from his hand. He watched the pony trot away, then he loosed a second one. "The ponies belong to those who catch them."

As all ten ponies were released, there was a scramble for them, but soon they were all captured and led away.

Whistling Elk stood proudly still before his father. His eyes brimmed with excitement when Blazing Eagle stepped toward him. His eager eyes watched his father take an object from a buckskin pouch at his right side, his heart thundering when he recognized what it was. He held his chin high as his father reached out for him to place the prized object around his neck.

"My son, I present you today with the war whistle that my adopted father gave to me on the day I earned the title of warrior," Blazing Eagle said proudly. "Such a whistle is blown only when men go into battle. It will hang silently around your neck by a deerskin, not to be used during warring, but instead to represent to others that your courage saved your people from death and destruction."

"I wear it proudly," Whistling Elk said, his voice breaking in his excitement as his father slipped the whistle over his head, a down feather of an eagle tied at the end.

"This war whistle that is now yours was made from the wing-bone of the sandhill crane," Blazing Eagle said as he stepped away from his son and stared proudly at the whistle hanging from his neck.

He then looked into his son's eyes. "The sandhill crane is a bird of great courage. If wounded and unable to fly away, it fights hard and will attack a man if he comes near it," he said. "Like *you* my son, the crane does not fear anything. Courage like this is greatly desired by every warrior. You are like the crane. Your courage is greatly admired and appreciated by this father and your people who honor you today. You can now call yourself a warrior."

The crowd cheered. Chants filled the air as father and son embraced.

When Blazing Eagle stepped away from Whistling Elk, he made room for the young braves to surround his son to admire and look at his war whistle.

Becky was touched deeply by the ceremony. Tears pooled in her eyes. It was wonderful to see Whistling Elk honored in such a way.

Her thoughts became bitter when she thought of someone else who had lost all of his dignity because of this young warrior, and who would soon lose his life. She felt that her brother was as deserving of his fate as this young warrior was deserving of his.

And she no longer felt anything for Edward, except for a deep feeling of sadness and loss. She knew that, in time, this too would pass.

Until it did, she would fill up her days and nights with the wonders of this life that she had discovered with the Cheyenne.

Everything became quiet when the sound of many horsemen resounded through the air, surrounding the people like claps of thunder. Becky moved quickly to Blazing Eagle's side as she watched many soldiers from Fort Laramie move into sight. The barrels of the firearms in their hands picked up the shine of the sun, flashing like spokes of lightning.

The Cheyenne moved together in a cluster and huddled there as they waited to see what brought the soldiers to them today to interfere once again in their lives.

Blazing Eagle gave quick commands to his warriors to take their positions with their firearms. The way the soldiers were arriving, their firearms clasped in their hands, was a threat Blazing Eagle could not ignore.

And he could not fathom what brought them there in such numbers. Except for having derailed the train, the Cheyenne had not been involved in any wrongdoing. And that had been overlooked.

They had been favored by the pony soldiers when they had taken the outlaws to the fort for incarceration.

What then could they want here today, a day set aside for the honoring of a powerful Cheyenne chief's son? Blazing Eagle wondered. He reached one arm out to move Becky behind him, to protect her if need be with his body; with the other he reached for Whistling Elk, to position him at his side as one who now stood proudly tall as a warrior.

Becky trembled as she stood in her husband's shadow. Yet she did not wish to stand behind him like a coward!

As the soldiers came closer, Becky stepped up beside Blazing Eagle just in time to see who was at the head of the thundering horsemen.

Judge Newman!

And his weapon was not drawn.

It was obvious to her now that these soldiers were not coming as a threat to the Cheyenne. But why then, she wondered, would they be arriving in such number with their weapons drawn?

Judge Newman wheeled his horse to a halt just

at the edge of the village. Only he proceeded forward. The children broke free of their parents and ran beside him, their eyes wide as they expected the usual offerings of candy.

When Judge Newman didn't reach inside his pocket for the candy, instead looked solemnly past the children as he rode onward toward Blazing Eagle, the children fell away from him and stared in silence at him.

Blazing Eagle took a step forward when Judge Newman drew a tight rein before him, then dismounted.

"What has happened to bring you and these soldiers to my village?" Blazing Eagle said, not offering a handshake of friendship this time. He was too puzzled by the judge's solemn attitude, and by his being accompanied by soldiers, whereas usually he came alone.

"The outlaws escaped," Judge Newman said, his voice drawn. "Every damn man escaped."

Becky felt faint at the news. She clutched Blazing Eagle's arm to steady herself.

"How?" Blazing Eagle said tightly. "How did they manage to escape?"

"It seems that not all of the gang were imprisoned," Judge Newman said, frowning. "The rest stormed the fort while most soldiers were sleeping. The soldiers were caught off guard. But only one man was killed."

Judge Newman paused, then said with wavering eyes to Blazing Eagle, "It is with heavy heart that I bring news to you of Major Kent's death."

Blazing Eagle's stomach felt as though someone

had hit him, his breath was so suddenly taken by the news. He was filled with anguish, and then anger ruled his heart.

Becky felt faint.

"We have formed a search party to look for the outlaws," Judge Newman said, looking over his shoulder at the many solemn-faced soldiers who waited for him to finish with the duty at hand. "We only stopped long enough at your village to share the news with you."

Becky turned and ran to Blazing Eagle's tepee. Sobbing, she threw herself onto the bed. She pounded her fists against the mattress as she cried Edward's name. "How could you continue to be so heartless?" she cried. "Edward, oh, Edward, when will it stop?"

Strong arms soon enfolded her. Becky clung to Blazing Eagle as he comforted her. She closed her eyes and sobbed against his bare chest as she listened to the distant sound of the horses riding away from the Cheyenne village.

She prayed that Edward would soon be caught, his reign of terror stopped.

"You did not go with them to search for my brother?" Becky murmured, turning her eyes up to Blazing Eagle.

"My place is with you. My place is with my people," he said, brushing a kiss across her lips, tasting her tears that had wetted them. "The pony soldiers became careless, not the Cheyenne. The outlaws are their responsibility, not the Cheyenne's."

"I'm so sorry about Major Kent," Becky said, almost choking on a sob. "I'm so sorry my brother is responsible for his death!"

"Yes, I am saddened over the death of my friend as I am saddened over your having to suffer the humiliation of having such a brother who would be a part of such a crime as this," Blazing Eagle said. "But I will not let these ugly circumstances stand in the way of our approaching marriage."

He eased her from his arms and went to the back of the tepee. Kneeling, he reached inside a parfleche and took a necklace from inside it.

Becky's eyes were wide as he came back to her, the lovely necklace stretched out between his hands, giving her a better look at it. She gazed at it, awed by its loveliness. It was silver with many turquoise stones imbedded in the silver. The necklace seemed to be in the design of some sort of flower.

"This is called a squash blossom necklace. It belonged to my adopted father's wife and to the women of her family through generations," Blazing Eagle said. "It was handed down to each woman of the family. It would have been my sister's, had I been blessed with one. Since I was not, it is yours to wear."

He stepped behind her. "Lift your hair so that I can place the necklace around your neck and fasten it," he said softly.

Her fingers trembling, Becky gathered her hair in her hands and lifted it. "Did your first wife wear the necklace?" she could not help but ask.

"Yes. Until she chose not to be my wife," Blazing Eagle said. "She gave up our son when she left, as well as her right to wear this special necklace."

Not wanting to talk anymore about his first wife,

too happy to ruin the moment for her and Blazing Eagle, she became quiet again as he spoke to her in a soft, loving voice.

"The squash blossom necklace is only the first of many wedding gifts I shall give to you," he said, snapping the necklace in place.

He turned her to face him as she let her hair flutter back around her shoulders. His hands framed her face as he drew her closer. "The squash blossom necklace represents fertility," he murmured. "Whoever wears it will bear many healthy children. The reason my adopted mother was not blessed in such a way was because she died long before her time. She had not been married long to my adopted father before a mysterious illness took her away."

"And your adopted father never married again?"

"He loved only once, as I will never love anyone but you."

"I wear this necklace proudly for you," Becky said, moving her fingers over the necklace, adoring it. "And I promise you as many children as you wish, my darling."

He drew her within his arms and held her close. "I hope that receiving the necklace at this time helps somewhat to lift the sorrow over your brother's behavior from your heart," he said, trying to shut out of his memory the fact that Major Kent was dead.

"All I am feeling at this moment is gratitude," Becky said, clinging. "I am so grateful for having found you, for having your love. Without you, I would now be nothing."

"Never think so little of yourself," Blazing Eagle

said, leaning her away from him so that their eyes could lock. "You are everything good on this earth. *I* am grateful for having found *you*. You are my everything."

They kissed.

The kiss was not as passionate as it was sweet.

Chapter Twenty-eight

In the gray half-light of dawn, the dew still clung to the grass. A low mist hung over the river like a pale ghost.

Becky was in Waterfall's lodge. Her shoulders were proudly squared as she sat on a blanket beside the fire, while Waterfall combed her hair for the upcoming marriage ceremony that morning.

When Becky had awakened a short while ago, Blazing Eagle had gone for his morning swim in the river.

Giggling, her eyes dancing, Waterfall had come and taken Becky away, saying that when the sun rose in its brilliance, Becky would be Blazing Eagle's wife.

"The comb you use is much different than mine," Becky said, glancing at the comb in the hand mirror that Becky held as Waterfall took another long stroke through Becky's golden hair.

"The comb I use today was made from the rough skin of the end of a buffalo tongue, scorched to harden it," Waterfall said, admiring how well the buckskin dress that she had made for Becky fit her.

Waterfall had made the dress from the skin of a deer. She had ornamented it with elk tusks and stained porcupine quills. The sleeves were like a cape, and hung down to the elbows.

Becky's leggings were pulled over her moccasins. They were tied under the sole of the foot and reached up to the knee. The moccasins were decorated with beads, fringes, and porcupine quills.

"Buffalo tongue?" Becky said, gasping at the thought.

"Would you rather I use a comb made from the tail of the porcupine?" Waterfall said, her eyes innocently wide at Becky's obvious shock over what the comb had been made from. "To make a porcupine comb, the fresh skin is stretched over a stick, sewed tight, and dried, the quills trimmed off evenly."

Waterfall laid the buffalo tongue comb aside and lifted the one she had made from the porcupine. "I shall use this one," she said, showing it to Becky. "I should have, anyway. It is much nicer to look at."

Becky smiled wanly at Waterfall, then gazed at the porcupine comb. "It *is* prettier," she said, looking at the long seam, which was beaded and ornamented with quills.

"I spend much spare time sewing and beading different things for my use, and that of others," Waterfall said, laying the comb aside.

"You are so kind to everyone. Do you ever think of yourself? What do you do for your own pleasure?" Becky asked, watching in her hand mirror as Waterfall began braiding white columbine petals into Becky's long golden hair. The sweet smell of the flowers was overpowered by the smell of many elk steaks cooking over the tripods of the huge communal fire.

Today everyone had risen before the moon had escaped from the heavens.

Today was a special day—the day their chief would take a bride!

"Everything I do for everyone else is how I take pleasure from living," Waterfall said, smiling into the mirror at Becky. "One day, though, I do wish to have a warrior treat me as I have witnessed Blazing Eagle treat you. Even from the moment he brought you here, even when you were a captive, I saw in his eyes that you were special to him. He even then treated you grandly enough, did he not?"

"I am sure he would have treated me better had I not been so stubborn when he asked me questions that I refused to answer," Becky said, thinking back to when she had scarcely spoken to him.

Oh, but how she had watched him, clinging to his every word when he spoke to her.

She had loved him even then, but had been too bullheaded to allow herself such wonderful feelings for a man who had taken her as captive.

"You loved him from the start, did you not?" Waterfall asked, tying a strip of leather around the tip of Becky's second braid.

"Yes, I imagine I loved him even before we ever

321

met," Becky said, sighing. "In my heart he was there from the moment I was born. It was our destiny to meet. And I shall love him even after I have taken my last breath."

"Then you also believe, as I believe, that our destiny is planned the moment we are but a seed planted in our mother's womb?" Waterfall said, stepping around to stand before Becky. She reached a gentle hand out for Becky's face, running her fingers over her frail cheekbones and finely sculpted features.

"Yes, that is my belief," Becky said, inhaling a quavering breath to know that she was almost ready to speak words of forever with her beloved.

"I have not yet discovered whose seed was planted just for me," Waterfall said, blushing.

"When you do, *he* will be the truly lucky one," Becky said, gathering the skirt of the dress into her arms. She rose softly to her feet and embraced Waterfall. "And you will be such a lovely bride."

"You will comb my hair and place flowers in my braids on the day of my marriage, as I have done for you?" Waterfall asked, stepping lightly away from Becky so that their eyes could meet and hold.

"Yes, I would feel badly if you asked someone else to do it," Becky said softly. "I want to think that, even though we have not known each other for long, you are my best friend."

"I have many friends, but I feel as though you and I have known each other in another world, in another time, and yes, I wish to be your best friend as well," Waterfall said, lifting the mirror up in front of Becky. "Look at yourself. See how lovely you are. Blazing Eagle's eyes will sparkle when he sees you."

Becky gazed at her reflection. She reached back and touched a braid, then moved her fingers to her lips. Waterfall had colored them with bloodroot. She had also placed a dot of the bloodroot coloring on each cheek.

She smiled over the mirror at Waterfall. "I *feel* beautiful," she said, laughing softly.

"You are not bold enough to say that you also *see* yourself as beautiful," Waterfall said softly. "But you are, Becky. You are even prettier than those flowers I have placed in your hair."

Pebbles came running into the lodge, yapping, his tail wagging. "Oh, Pebbles, have you been neglected of late?" Becky said as she swept her pup into her arms. She cuddled him close. "You are going to have to grow up so that *you* can find your soul mate. It's wonderful to be in love, Pebbles."

Pebbles barked, then jumped from Becky's arms and ran from the lodge again.

"He has found friends among our people's dog population," Waterfall said, laying the mirror aside. "You can be certain that one day he will mate."

"It is only moments now before you will become the wife of our powerful chief," Waterfall then said, clasping her hands before her. "Then you will spend much time in the lodge where the tribe's unmarried women learn the domestic arts from the older women, since you were not here in your early teen years to have these teachings."

"But I shall feel somewhat out of place, won't I?"

Becky murmured. "I will already be married. Surely I can teach myself things that you have not yet taught me. I do not want to look like a child in my husband's eyes by attending lessons meant for children."

"If you wish it," Waterfall said, "I will explain things to you in the privacy of your lodge."

"I would truly appreciate it," Becky said softly. She glanced toward the entranceway. "Where is the ceremony going to be held? When will I see Blazing Eagle?"

"Where? I shall not yet say. But when will you see your intended? Soon," Waterfall said, sighing with obvious relief when Whistling Elk stepped inside Waterfall's lodge and nodded to her. His eyes turned Becky's way and they showed a keen admiration when he raked them slowly over her. Then he left as suddenly as he had arrived.

"Why did Whistling Elk come and leave so quickly?" Becky asked, puzzled.

"There is a part of today's ceremony when eight young braves will assist Blazing Eagle," Waterfall said. "Whistling Elk has just given me notice that the young men are ready."

"What will they be doing?" Becky asked, her pulse racing at the thought of this day's activities finally unfolding around her, the happiest day of her life.

"You shall soon see," Waterfall said. She gave Becky a hug, then walked away from her. "I will go now for one of Blazing Eagle's finest horses."

Waterfall left the lodge, leaving Becky alone with a pounding, anxious heart.

Waterfall came back inside the lodge and took Becky by the hand. "Come," she said. "You must go outside and mount the horse. I shall lead it to Blazing Eagle's lodge."

"We will be married there?" Becky asked, following Waterfall outside.

"There is much for you to learn of Cheyenne ways," Waterfall said, helping Becky into the saddle that was draped with wildflowers. "You shall learn by doing."

Becky inhaled a nervous breath. Then she stared straight ahead, her chin held proudly high, her pulse racing, as everyone came from their lodges and silently watched her being led toward Blazing Eagle's lodge.

Once there, Becky started to dismount, but Waterfall whispered to her to stay in the saddle. Blazing Eagle would soon lift her down.

When Blazing Eagle stepped from his lodge, Becky's heart filled with ecstasy when she saw how handsome he was in his fine new clothes. His leggings were decorated with feathers. His moccasins were adorned with porcupine quills.

But it was the white-tailed deer's tail on a belt that passed over his shoulder that caught her full attention. She had read that to the Cheyenne, the white-tailed deer are powerful in love affairs and are to be asked for help. Those who have these deer for their helpers wear on the shoulder belt the tail of a deer, with some medicine tied to it.

She had also read that in approaching the woman of his desire, the Cheyenne warrior would always walk up to the woman on the windward side, so that she might get the scent of the medicine.

With a thudding heart, she watched Blazing Eagle spread a blanket on the left side of the horse, which today was the windward side. She melted inside when he placed his hands at her waist and lifted her from the horse.

She looked at him questioningly when he set her in the middle of the blanket, then stepped away from her as eight young braves, Whistling Elk among them, appeared at the four corners of the blanket.

Although Whistling Elk had outgrown the title of brave, he proudly assisted those young braves, who lifted the blanket up from the ground by the corners and edges, balancing Becky in the middle.

Becky grabbed for the edges of the blanket as she was carried into Blazing Eagle's lodge.

After Becky was placed on the floor of the lodge on the blanket, the young braves left. She turned and watched for Blazing Eagle's entrance.

Instead, Waterfall came inside and made sure that Becky's hair and clothes had not been mussed.

"I'm so nervous," Becky said, smiling weakly at Waterfall.

"It is only natural that you would be," Waterfall said, then sat down beside the fire and lifted a small platter to Becky's lap. "Through the night I prepared food for you. It is for only you to eat."

"Why?" Becky asked, gazing down at the assortment of meats and vegetables that Waterfall was so diligently cutting into small pieces.

"It is the custom that the woman is fed before the

ceremony," Waterfall said matter-of-factly. "And notice how small I cut up your food. That is so there will be no real effort needed to eat."

Becky picked up a small piece of meat with her fingers and nibbled on it, yet found even those small pieces hard to swallow. She was too excited, too nervous to eat!

But she did as she was expected. She ate every last bite, then watched Waterfall carry the empty plate away as she left.

Becky rose gingerly to her feet. She gazed raptly at the entrance flap, awaiting the arrival of her beloved. She only hoped that no one else came and involved her in any other rituals. She could hardly stand much more of this pampering. She wanted to be with Blazing Eagle!

Blazing Eagle came into the lodge. He carried two rings made from the horn of a mountain goat. His eyes were smoldering with passion as he stepped up to Becky.

She was mesmerized by him, by his handsomeness, by his mere presence. Her love for him was so intense, so moving, that her shoulders swayed.

"My woman, I carry two rings into our ceremony," he said solemnly, holding out his palms, a ring in each. "One is for you. One is for me. With these rings we plight our troth. Should you not wish to marry me, you can throw the ring away. That would mean that you throw away both the ring and the man. Should you wish to marry me, allow me to place it on your finger. You shall then be my wife. You shall be mine forevermore."

"I wish to wear the ring," Becky said, her eyes

locked with his as he slipped the ring on her finger. "I wish to be yours forevermore. I shall bear you many children. I shall fill your lodge with much laughter. I shall care for you till the end of time."

The ring on her finger made her thrill inside to know that finally she was his wife!

Her heart pounding, she took the other ring and slipped it on his finger, her hands trembling as she gazed first at his ring, then at hers.

"I shall be there for you always," Blazing Eagle said, sweeping her into his arms. "I shall house you. I shall feed you. I shall clothe you. I shall give you many sons and daughters. I shall share in all tomorrow's laughter with you, my wife."

Dizzy from her joyous bliss, Becky moved into Blazing Eagle's arms. Their lips came together in a frenzy of kisses. Then he lifted her into his arms and carried her to his bed. "This time we make love as man and wife," he said huskily, bending to kiss her pale upturned cheek.

Becky blinked back tears of happiness. She was soaring on clouds of bliss. She was giddy with excitement, for she had finally married her Prairie Knight!

Blazing Eagle laid her down across the bed, then knelt over her and slowly undressed her, the touch of his hands grazing her flesh making her tremble.

"I want you so badly," she whispered, her eyes touching him gently with their promise.

"I will always want you," Blazing Eagle said, tossing her dress away. He filled his hands with her breasts. His blood hot, he leaned over her and flicked his tongue over her nipples.

She moaned as his mouth explored her secret places, and then they came together, caressing, kissing.

They climbed to the sky, touched the stars, and rode the clouds. Theirs was a love all consuming, their tongues touching, their bodies moving rhythmically together as his thrusts reached deeply inside her.

"My husband," Becky whispered as his lips moved to kiss the hollow of her throat.

She ran her fingers through his thick black hair.

She closed her eyes in ecstasy as she felt the intense wonder of release in his arms, his body quivering into hers.

Chapter Twenty-nine

Becky awakened the next morning as the pure luminous color of dawn was overcoming the silent shadows. Wisps of last night's fire hung like a ghost overhead in the lodge. A warm wetness between her legs made her eyes widen. She was startled to realize that her monthly flow had begun. She was glad that Blazing Eagle had left already for his early morning swim, for that would give her time to decide what to say to him. This was a dilemma that she had never even thought about.

She panicked at the thought of his return. How *was* she to tell him about this personal problem? She was embarrassed at the very idea of having to explain to him.

Even her father had never been aware of her monthly flow. He had never questioned why once a month she had been more ladylike in what she did, declining to ride a horse or participate in strenuous activities.

"How can I even *tell* Blazing Eagle?" Becky whispered, slipping gently from the bed. "Oh, this is so embarrassing!"

She went to her travel bags and reached inside for a smaller bag. Within it she kept the gauze pads that her stepmother had taught her to wear during this dreaded time of month.

After she was protected enough to move around and was dressed in one of her less fancy cotton dresses, she stood over the fire and slowly brushed her hair.

When Pebbles came into the lodge in a breathless rush, she knew to expect to find Blazing Eagle behind him.

Becky's eyes wavered when Blazing Eagle came into the lodge. He looked so tempting to her in his brief breechcloth, his hair dripping across his bronzed shoulders, his body sleek from the wetness.

"I had hoped you would still be in bed," Blazing Eagle said huskily. He pulled Becky into his muscled arms. His eyes gleamed mischievously into hers. "You have wasted time getting into a dress. You will only have to take it off again."

"Blazing Eagle, I . . ." Becky began. But her words were stopped by his fiery kiss and his hands at her buttocks, yanking her even more closely to him.

Becky dropped the hairbrush. She was breathless from his kiss and from the need eating away at her insides, a need that she for now must be denied, as she must deny her husband!

When she felt the strength, the full, hot length of Blazing Eagle's manhood pressed against her stomach through her thin dress, her senses returned.

Wrenching herself free, Becky inched away from Blazing Eagle. "We can't this morning," she murmured, her heart pounding. "We just . . . can't."

"You deny me?" Blazing Eagle said, his eyebrows rising. "You deny yourself? My wife, that is not the way it is between husband and wife, especially the morning after vows have been spoken."

He came to her and reached for her wrists, his eyes dark with passion.

"Of course you are jesting," he said, chuckling. "You are playing a game with your husband?"

His mouth came down upon hers in an explosive kiss. Becky moaned as pleasure swept through her like wildfire. His passion, her own, made her momentarily forget why she had denied him. She twined her arms around his neck and abandoned herself to him, sucking in a wild breath of rapture when he bunched up the hem of her skirt in one hand while his other hand crept up her leg.

Mindless with need of him, her head spinning, Becky parted her legs. She trembled as his hand crept farther up, to the sensitive skin of her thighs, causing her to gasp.

Then when he started to reach his fingers inside her undergarment and he felt the layers of gauze nestled there, his breath slowed and his fingers lightly explored this strange encumbrance.

Then he stepped away from her as quickly as a

thunderclap and stared down at her, his lips open.

Becky stood there for a moment, staring up at him. Her heart felt as though it had leapt from inside her at the abrupt halt of their passion.

Then, as he still stood there, speechless, Becky reached a hand out toward him. "I tried to tell you," she said, her voice breaking. "I . . . I am having my monthly flow. That is something I have no control over."

She swallowed hard. "Don't stand there like that. Don't stare at me as though I have committed some sort of sin!" she cried. "I hate my monthly flow! Now that I am married, I hate it more than ever! But I can't wave a magic wand and make it stop!"

She fell silent as her heart sank. There seemed to be no rage in how he looked at her. Yet there seemed to be no understanding, either!

Suddenly he grabbed her by her wrist and ushered her outside his lodge without yet having said anything to her about this unavoidable circumstance.

While everyone stared and ceased working at their morning chores, Blazing Eagle led Becky away from his lodge, his hand tight on her wrist, his steps determined.

Panic seized Becky. The way he was behaving was as though he was going to discard her.

"What are you doing?" Becky cried, tears flooding her eyes. "Where are you taking me?"

Still he gave her no explanation. He just kept leading her through the village, with Pebbles barking and snarling at his heels.

When Blazing Eagle reached a grass-roofed hut

at the far outer edge of the village, he took Becky inside.

He released his grip on her arm, turned, and left again, leaving her standing in the darkness, now fearing her fate.

Sobbing, Becky stood in the darkness. She hugged herself with her arms, her eyes searching around her for some explanation as to why she had been brought here and abandoned.

Pebbles jumped up on Becky's legs, whimpering.

Finding comfort in his presence, thinking that he might now be her only true friend on this earth, Becky reached down and picked him up.

Cramping from the monthly flow, Becky groaned. Hardly able to stand, the cramps now so intense, she crumpled to the grassy floor of the hut and hung her head, her face burrowed in the soft fur of her pup.

"Why?" she sobbed. "Blazing Eagle, why did you do this to me? I didn't want to reject you this morning. I had no choice."

Soft footsteps entering the lodge caused Becky to look up. When she found Waterfall shadowed in the doorway, she did not know how to react. How was Becky to trust anyone now that Blazing Eagle had shoved her inside a hut without any explanation?

She guardedly watched Waterfall come into the lodge. She said nothing as Waterfall got a fire started in the fire pit in the center of the earthen floor.

Then, when Waterfall turned to her and smiled, everything within Becky seemed to fall apart and tears fell in torrents across her cheeks. "I don't understand what's happening," she said, the sobs wracking her body. "Waterfall, Blazing Eagle brought me to this place. He didn't tell me *why*. Can you? Will you tell me why I'm here, instead of back home with Blazing Eagle?"

"He did not bring you here because he is angry," Waterfall said softly. She sat down beside Becky and took her hands within her own. "It is because of your 'weeps' that he has brought you here—because of the blood that comes with the moon. It is tradition, Becky, nothing more. It is another of our customs that you will have to accept."

"Then all of this is because I am having my monthly flow?" Becky said, her eyes imploring Waterfall. "I don't understand why this has anything to do with anything. I have never been treated as though I have the plague because of my monthly flow."

"The plague?" Waterfall said. "What is this thing you call plague?"

"A terrible disease, a disastrous evil," Becky blurted out.

"No," Waterfall gasped. "You are none of those things to the Cheyenne. You are our chief's woman. You are revered. Please understand, Becky. *All* women must spend their time of weeps in a menstrual hut. This one that you are in is mine. I will help you build one for yourself after you are well again and able."

"Menstrual hut?" Becky whispered, hope springing forth within her.

"Yes, Becky," Waterfall said softly. "During a

woman's time, she must sleep in her menstrual lodge. The Cheyenne men believe that if they lie beside their wives at this time, or if they come in contact with a woman who is not yet married and is being troubled by the flow, the warriors might be wounded in their next battle or while on the hunt."

"Oh, I see," Becky said, wincing to know that she had so much more to learn than she had ever imagined. She had learned only so much from the books she had studied in school.

There were so many customs that had not been written about, perhaps because no one had been knowledgeable enough to explain them.

"And several warriors are guarding you," Waterfall said matter-of-factly.

"I am . . . guarded?" Becky gasped, paling. "Blazing Eagle is guarding me as though I am a criminal? As though I have done something wrong?"

Waterfall giggled behind her hand at Becky's reaction, then reached out and affectionately touched Becky's cheek. "No, it is not for that reason at all," she said softly. "It is to guard you against your brother. If he is near, and he realizes that you are staying separately from your husband's lodge—don't you see? This would give him the opportunity to steal you away. But with warriors everywhere, he would not dare to attempt getting anywhere near this hut."

"My brother," Becky said, her eyes taking on a forlorn gaze. "Edward. How could I have forgotten about Edward?"

"Blazing Eagle's mind never strays far from the golden-haired white man who has brought destruction and death to this beautiful land of the Cheyenne," Waterfall said, her jaw tightening. "Only until the golden-haired man is dead will Blazing Eagle be able to place him from his mind, from his very soul."

"I want to blame the Civil War for my brother's affliction," Becky said, sighing remorsefully. "But that would be the easy way out. There had to be a weakness in his character even before the war that I never saw. Someone doesn't turn into a murdering fiend overnight. There had to be something long before the war that no one could see when they looked at my brother."

She paused and drew Pebbles into her arms. She cuddled him close. "I can't remember a time when Edward wasn't sweet and gentle to everyone," she said, her voice breaking.

She turned quick eyes to Waterfall. "It's as though my brother had two separate personalities, and the ugly one did not surface until he experienced the ravages of war," she said, her voice breaking. "Then the evil side of him overpowered the good."

Becky lowered her eyes. "I doubt the good side will ever surface again," she said, swallowing hard.

"I am leaving now," Waterfall said, rising to her feet.

Becky looked quickly up at her. "Why?" she gasped. "Did I say something that offended you? Please, Waterfall. Don't leave me here alone." She looked guardedly around her, finding no comforts. There wasn't even a bed.

"I will be gone for only a short while," Waterfall said. She fell to her knees again and gently framed Becky's face between her soft, small hands. "I am going for food. Later I shall go and gather up several pelts and blankets so that you can sit and sleep comfortably during your stay here away from the comforts of your lodge."

"Thank you," Becky said, almost choking on a grateful sob. "This is something so new to me. I . . . I feel quite alone."

"Please understand that Blazing Eagle had no choice but to bring you here," Waterfall murmured.

"But he was so cold, so . . ."

"Yes, and that is because he felt the need to get you to the hut as quickly as possible. Since you awakened this morning with the weeps, that had to mean that sometime during the night it started," Waterfall was quick to explain. "You see, Becky? You had already slept for a short while with Blazing Eagle after your weeps started. It was imperative that he get you quickly from his lodge, especially his bed. If not, his life might be endangered during the next hunt or while out gathering up his horses."

"But without even an explanation?"

"That is why *I* am here," Waterfall softly explained. "Until your weeps are over, I will be Blazing Eagle's voice. I shall see to your every need while you are away from your lodge. You won't want for a thing, except . . ." She blushed and giggled. "Except for your husband and what you now share with him between his blankets."

Becky lowered her eyes, then smiled up at Waterfall. "It is something magical that we share," she said, her eyes taking on a faraway, wondrous gaze. "I never knew what it could be like to be with a man in . . . in that way."

"Does it make your heart flutter like a baby bird's wing in a nest as it anticipates feeding from its mother?" Waterfall asked, eyes wide.

"It makes me melt inside," Becky said, giggling at the very thought of sharing such private moments with someone else besides Blazing Eagle. Sometimes it was even hard to believe that she had so openly shared everything with *him*, a *man*.

But that was the magic of it. All inhibitions had been swept aside the first time she had been held by him. From that point on, her body reacted to every nuance of his lovemaking.

"You make me want to have my very own man," Waterfall said, sighing. "Do you think I shall feel the same as you when I climb between blankets with a man? Will I experience the same joyous bliss that I see in your eyes when you speak of Blazing Eagle?"

"Yes, if you love the man, and he loves you as passionately," Becky said. She watched Pebbles run from the lodge to romp and play with his newly found dog friends.

"I think I may love a man like that," Waterfall whispered as she glanced guardedly toward the door. She then took both of Becky's hands and squeezed them excitedly. "I truly feel something when I see him. I have for so long, yet I have not said anything to anybody about it. Now, as I live among my people in the status of soldier girl, I must look past those sorts of feelings and see only into the future when I am no longer a revered princess of my people."

"Who is he?" Becky asked, her eyes wide. "Do I know him?"

"Yes, you have met him," Waterfall said dreamily.

"Who, Waterfall? Who?"

Waterfall softly stroked Becky's cheek. "His face is as white as yours," she murmured.

"You are in love with a white man?" Becky said incredulously.

"Yes, I truly believe that what I feel is love," Waterfall said, blushing excitedly.

"Waterfall, I am dying to know who," Becky insisted.

"Judge Newman," Waterfall said. Her eyes filled with a silent rapture at the very idea of allowing herself to let the man's name pass across her ruby lips.

"Judge Newman?" Becky said, eyes widening. She recalled how his blue eyes had mesmerized even her.

"Yes, Many Sweets Man," Waterfall said, sighing.

"Why, he is perhaps the most handsome man I have ever seen," Becky blurted out, then smiled widely. "Besides my husband, that is."

"Then you have also been captured by Judge Roy Newman's eyes that are the color of the sky?" Waterfall said, again sighing.

"You are absolutely in love with him," Becky said, laughing softly. "Just listen at how you say his name. It is as though it is honey pressed against your lips."

"Yes, I know the sweetness of how it feels to speak his name," Waterfall said, then pushed herself up from the floor. "But it is best not to talk so openly of my feelings about him just yet. I am not certain how he feels about me."

"Has he given any indication that he feels something for you, Waterfall?"

"Yes, I have caught him looking my way many times. I see something in the way he looks at me. It makes me feel strangely giddy."

"Then it is only a matter of time before he will approach you about his feelings for you."

"I think I shall die if he touches me," Waterfall said, giggling. Blushing, she ran from the lodge.

"She is so much in love!" Becky said, then groaned when the cramps began again in her lower abdomen.

She felt so relieved, now that she knew the reason for Blazing Eagle's strange behavior, that she scarcely felt the pain that normally would double her over.

Instead, she drew her legs up before her and hugged them, allowing herself only to relive those tingling feelings that Blazing Eagle's nearness caused.

Waterfall came back into the lodge with a tray of food, a jug of fresh river water, and a small buckskin bag.

She laid the small bag aside, then laughed and talked as she shared the morning meal with Becky.

Afterwards, Becky's smile faded when Waterfall

became somber as she placed the small buckskin bag on her lap.

"Waterfall, what's in the bag?" Becky finally asked. "Why are you suddenly so quiet and somber?"

"There is another practice of the Cheyenne that I am sure is new to you and your white world," Waterfall said, removing a rope from the bag. "It is something that I am sure you may not find pleasant at first. You will grow used to it and soon not even realize that you are wearing it."

"Wear it?" Becky gasped out, staring at the rope. "Why must I wear that thing?"

"It is a protective rope that you will wear as soon as your time is past and you leave the hut to again mingle among our people," Waterfall said, holding the rope out toward Becky. "Take it. I shall explain how it is worn, but do not wear it during your time."

"Waterfall, I still don't understand," Becky said, slowly reaching a hand out for the rope, then suddenly taking it and dropping it in her lap.

"A protective rope is worn by wives all the time, except during their monthly weeps and at night, when they are in the blankets with their husbands," Waterfall explained. "It is a complete protection to the women who wear it. All men respect the rope. Anyone violating it will be killed immediately."

Becky sighed, finding this latest custom even more strange and hard to accept than the menstrual hut.

"If I must, I must," she then said, holding the rope up to study it. She stretched it out between her fingers. "How is it worn?"

"The rope passes about the waist, is knotted in front, passes down and backward between the thighs, and each end is wound around the thigh, down nearly to the knee," Waterfall softly explained. "The wearing of this rope is somewhat confining, yet those who wear it can walk freely."

There was a strained silence as the knowledge that she would be subjected to this strange ordeal sank into Becky's consciousness.

Waterfall then rose quickly to her feet. "I will go and get my sewing basket," she said, her eyes meeting Becky's as Becky gave her a forlorn stare. "I shall teach you the more pleasant habits of the women. I shall teach you the art of beading."

Waterfall left the lodge. Becky studied the rope at length, then shuddered at the thought of having to wear it and tossed it aside.

"Lord, what else?" she whispered to herself.

But she knew that it was worth any sacrifice she would be forced to make to be Blazing Eagle's wife.

When Pebbles came into the lodge and leapt onto her lap and snuggled, she stroked his soft fur. Her pup seemed to be content enough to be Becky's companion in the absence of her husband.

But Becky knew that she would be counting the days off, one by one, until she could be with him again.

Her thoughts strayed to Edward. She hoped that after coming so close to seeing his maker, he might give up his life of crime.

"Wouldn't it be wonderful if he returned to Saint Louis and became a law-abiding citizen again?" she asked herself.

Then she frowned, remembering the sheriff and the poster that hung on the wall of his office. Edward could never again be a normal citizen of any community. What he had done could not be undone. He was doomed.

Waterfall came with her beading, then left. The hours passed. Becky stared at the dull red glow of the dying coals in the fireplace.

The minutes, the hours, the days! She would have to be here for so long in this drab place of isolation! She would not be with Blazing Eagle for days, to be held by him, to be caressed, to be kissed.

She hung her head in her hands and sighed heavily.

Chapter Thirty

After two days without his wife, Blazing Eagle was restless. He knew that he had energy to burn off and had decided to do that while hunting. His horse was ready outside his lodge. Fish Hawk was on his own steed, patiently waiting to join Blazing Eagle on the hunt.

Waterfall gave Blazing Eagle a glance over her shoulder as she gathered his morning dishes to wash them in the river. "Your wife wishes you well," she murmured.

"Has she adapted to being isolated in the menstrual hut?" Blazing Eagle said. He took up his bow and slung his arrow quiver over his left shoulder.

"She misses you, but yes, she has adapted well enough," Waterfall said. She moved to her feet, her arms laden with the dishes. "While she is there I am teaching her beading and cooking."

She giggled as her eyes danced into Blazing Eagle's. "Her clumsiness in cooking proves that before she came to our village, she was a woman of the outdoors instead of the kitchen," she said.

"And so you think I should plan on being a thin, gaunt chief?" Blazing Eagle teased, chuckling beneath his breath.

"No, Blazing Eagle," Waterfall was quick to say. "She is an intelligent woman. She learns quickly. She will surprise you when she returns to your lodge and prepares many tasty meals for you."

"That is good," Blazing Eagle said, laying his bow aside long enough to tie a pouch of tobacco onto the belt of his breechclout.

He lifted his bow again and walked toward the entrance flap. "I will busy my hands and mind today on the hunt," he said. He stopped and turned to Waterfall. "How many more sunrises before I can fill my arms with my wife?"

"Two sunrises have passed, and I believe there will be only a few more before she can leave the menstrual hut," Waterfall said softly.

"My woman is special in many ways," Blazing Eagle said, lifting the entrance flap so that Waterfall could leave the lodge ahead of him. "I see her willing the weeps to stop soon so that she may come home to me."

Waterfall smiled at him as she stepped from the tepee. She nodded a hello to her brother Fish Hawk, then fell into step with several other women who were headed for the river.

"My friend Fish Hawk, are you ready to hunt until the sun loses its luster in the sky?" Blazing Eagle said, swinging himself into his saddle.

"It has been too long since our last hunt," Fish Hawk said. He snapped his reins and rode at a slow lope beside Blazing Eagle.

"Many things have been on my mind," Blazing Eagle said, casting a lingering stare at the menstrual hut as he passed it.

He shifted his gaze and counted mentally the warriors who stood guard in strategic places around the hut. He was glad to see that there were enough to stop the outlaws.

"Your wife is kept from you too soon after your vows were spoken," Fish Hawk said, following the path of Blazing Eagle's eyes.

"That is so, but it is best that she is away from me at this time," Blazing Eagle said. He sank his moccasined heels into the flanks of his horse and sent it into a gallop away from his village.

"When she was free of her flow, and she shared your blankets, was she as you expected her to be in bed, my friend?" Fish Hawk asked, smiling devilishly over at Blazing Eagle.

"Even more," Blazing Eagle said, squaring his shoulders proudly as he recalled how she answered his needs with her own.

"That is good," Fish Hawk said, nodding.

"And when will you select the perfect woman for your lodge?" Blazing Eagle asked, his waist-length hair fluttering in the breeze as he still rode at a hard gallop across the land of tall, weaving grasses.

"My eyes have been on one woman but she does not give me back the look of a woman who appreciates being admired by me," Fish Hawk said glumly.

"And who are you speaking of?" Blazing Eagle asked. His spine stiffened as he caught sight of a deer that was fleeing from the sound of the horses' hoofbeats. His heart, the heart of a hunter today, leapt as he watched the deer take its flight.

"I speak of White Water of our neighbor Cheyenne tribe," Fish Hawk said. "Princess White Water."

"She is a soldier girl for her clan. She is not free yet to choose a husband," Blazing Eagle said. He gave Fish Hawk a questioning stare. "Like your sister, Waterfall, White Water's duties are still to her chief and people."

"Then you think that is why she ignored my glances?" Fish Hawk asked.

"She is not free to appreciate glances from any man," Blazing Eagle said flatly. "Turn your eyes in different directions, my friend. You will find appreciative women if you will look for them beyond the sweet, innocent beauty of White Water."

"I have seen her lower her eyes bashfully when another man looks her way," Fish Hawk spat out venomously.

"Who is this man?" Blazing Eagle demanded.

"Judge Newman," Fish Hawk replied.

"Many Sweets Man?" Blazing Eagle said, his eyes widening. "Surely you imagine things. He looks at Waterfall with favor. How could he also be intrigued with White Water? No. You are wrong. He is a man who would not toy with the affections of two women."

"When a man's heart sings a woman's name day and night, and that woman gives another man certain attentions, it is not imagination that makes the injured man's heart sing out of tune!" Fish Hawk said, his eyes filled with jealous fire.

"Again I tell you that you are wrong," Blazing Eagle said flatly. "Now let us speak of other things or speak not at all."

They rode onward in silence, and not so much because their conversation had placed a strain between them, but because hunters always went forth solemnly, aware that killing any creature disturbed the harmony of the world.

When they reached a pond that was bathed with the shade of many cottonwood trees, they drew tight rein and dismounted. They knew to expect deer at the water sometime today. They would hide and wait.

They passed through many cottonwoods and led their horses through the thicket. They found a cool hiding place beneath a small overhang of rock. They tethered their horses, then shared some beef jerky, their eyes never leaving the pond, their voices stilled by their eagerness to return home with meat and pelts.

Suddenly four deer emerged from the thicket and cautiously approached the pond. Blazing Eagle and Fish Hawk rose slowly, silently, to their feet.

"Brother deer, give up your life," Blazing Eagle prayed quietly as he notched a stone-tipped arrow to his bow.

He glanced at Fish Hawk, seeing if he was ready to shoot. When he saw that he was, he once again looked at the deer, raised his bow, and stretched the arrow tightly as he drew back his arm in a steady aim.

He held his aim a moment, then loosed his arrow.

Fish Hawk loosed his.

Blazing Eagle's struck a deer's chest, the flint point driving deep into the vitals, tearing into the animal's heart.

Fish Hawk's struck another deer's chest.

When the two deer fell, the other two leapt away, their dark eyes wide with fear.

"We did well, my friend," Blazing Eagle said, placing his bow on the ground.

He and Fish Hawk approached the slain creatures with awe and respect. They knelt down beside them and each made tobacco offerings to the earth, the sky, and the four directions.

Only Fish Hawk busied himself readying his deer for their return home to the village. He made the throat cut, then hung the carcass on bare branches of the cottonwoods so that the blood would drain.

As Fish Hawk cut away the hide and butchered the meat of his kill, cutting off slices of venison roasts, Blazing Eagle only watched. He wished to return home with a full, uncut carcass. He had plans for the slain animal. He had someone to offer it to.

As evening advanced, they returned from the hunt. Fish Hawk's horse was laden with meat. Tied to the back of Blazing Eagle's horse was the carcass of his kill.

Once inside their village, Fish Hawk and Blazing Eagle went their separate ways. Fish Hawk went to his lodge. Blazing Eagle rode onward, passing his own lodge, his eyes on someone else's. Occasionally when he killed a good, fat deer, he offered the meat to his friend who possessed spiritual power, to secure the benefit of his prayers.

Today he sought prayers again from Young Bear, for Blazing Eagle could not feel at ease with things around him. His wife's brother, who killed for profit, was always on his mind!

And he never relaxed with the white pony soldiers being always so near at hand. Should they ever decide to go against the Cheyenne, the slaughter of his people would be swift. The pony soldiers had large cannon guns that could wipe out half his village in one firing.

Yes, he never trusted completely, even though treaty papers had been signed between himself and the soldiers.

Prayers were always needed to give him comfort.

Today his payment was adequate for such prayers, for the meat was fat, and there was plenty of it.

Blazing Eagle drew a tight rein before Young Bear's lodge. After untying the carcass, he hoisted it over his right shoulder and went and laid it down just outside Young Bear's entrance flap. He waited with folded arms across his chest for Young Bear to emerge from his lodge. Blazing Eagle knew that Young Bear had heard his approach and had seen his shadow through the fabric of his lodge as he took the carcass from his horse.

Young Bear lifted his entrance flap and gazed down at the carcass, then gave Blazing Eagle a warm smile. "You have brought a gift for this old man?" he said. His voice was feeble. His face was gaunt and pale, like the color of his graying hair.

"It would please me if you would accept my gift," Blazing Eagle said. Scarcely breathing, he watched as Young Bear bent over and placed his hands around the throat of the deer and pulled the carcass around on its belly until the head faced east.

Blazing Eagle's heart thumped as if drums were beating within his chest, knowing by the way Young Bear had turned the carcass that the old man had accepted the present.

Blazing Eagle didn't make a sound as he watched Young Bear take his knife from a sheath at his right side and slit the animal down its back, reaching inside to take out the right kidney.

His eyes filled with warmth and kindness, Young Bear handed the kidney to Blazing Eagle, who then pointed it toward the east, south, west, and north, then up to the sky and down to the ground.

"My son, may you live to be as old as I am and always have good luck in your hunting," Young Bear said. "May you and your family live long and always have abundance."

Those were the words most sought by those who came to seek this old man's goodness and prayers. Blazing Eagle smiled at him, gave him the kidney, then turned and mounted his horse and rode away.

Filled with peace, Young Bear's goodness having momentarily cleansed Blazing Eagle of his worries and his loneliness for his wife, Blazing Eagle went to the river and walked his horse into the water. As he splashed the water over his horse to wash the blood and dirt from it, he smiled when he heard the village crier riding through the village, telling of Blazing Eagle's good deed.

He looked toward the menstrual hut, knowing that Becky surely also heard what he had done today to kill time until he could once again spend it with her.

A long-winged silhouette moved silently across the grass tops, and an eagle settled down amidst the cottonwood trees. A chorus of coyotes howled low in the distance.

After bathing his horse and himself in the river, Blazing Eagle retired to his lodge and burrowed himself into the nest of buffalo hides that made up his bed, while others sat outside by open fires smoking and singing ancient chants.

He ran his hand over the soft pelts where Becky had lain beside him. "Soon you will join me again, my woman," he whispered huskily to himself. "Ah, and when you do, how I will make love to you!"

Chapter Thirty-one

The flaming glory of the sun had risen and fallen four times. On the fifth day, Becky awakened free of her monthly flow. She was radiant. Her heart pounded at the thought of being reunited with Blazing Eagle. She had only seen him from a distance as she stood at the door of the menstrual hut.

She wondered if he had missed her as much as she had missed him.

Did he anticipate her arrival back at their lodge as much as she wished to be there?

Scrambling to her feet, Becky found a basin of water that Waterfall had brought to her from the river. This had become a morning ritual. Sponge bathing. Slipping into a clean dress that Waterfall had taken from Becky's wardrobe for her, taking much time brushing her hair, and eating.

All of these things had helped pass the day, yet

there had been still so much time left. Waterfall had helped her pass those hours with beading, cooking, and lessons in the Cheyenne language, all of which had brought them closer together.

Anxious to leave the hut, Becky hurried through her chores, yet she knew that she could not leave just yet. Waterfall had explained to her that she must participate in a ceremony of purification before she could leave the lodge.

"I wonder what I must do?" Becky whispered to herself. Waterfall had refused to explain the custom to her. She had said that it was taboo to speak of something so ritualistic. She would learn by doing.

Pulling the brush through her hair one more time, Becky thought about just how much Waterfall had done for her. She had even sneaked in early this morning to start the fire, which was very welcome, since the cooler mornings of September had arrived with an early frost. Yet the chill in the air was invigorating after the blistering hot days of summer.

"I wonder if my flowers back home were killed by an early frost also?" she whispered to herself. She closed her eyes and envisioned her garden of snapdragons, petunias, and geraniums. She tried not to picture them smothered by weeds or shriveled up and dead, since she had been forced to neglect them by leaving for the Wyoming Territory.

"My mums should be in bloom soon," she said, brushing tears from her eyes. She would not be there to enjoy them ever again.

But she truly didn't mind. This new life that she

had found in the arms of a wonderful Cheyenne chief was worth any sacrifices that she had to make to be with him.

After she sold her home, only then would the ties of her past be truly severed.

"Becky, soon you will be with Blazing Eagle again," Waterfall said excitedly as she entered the lodge with a tray of breakfast foods, a delicious smell wafting from them.

Becky rushed to her feet. "I can hardly wait," she said, taking the tray as Waterfall handed it to her. "Have you seen Blazing Eagle this morning? Do you think he is as anxious as I am?"

"*Ne-hyo*, he is," Waterfall said, giggling. "As I retrieved my morning water from the river, I saw him upriver. He was draping elk hides over a willow-branch frame to form a sweat lodge."

"I read about sweat lodges in my studies of Indians," Becky said, sitting down beside the fire with Waterfall. She chose fruit this morning over meat and ate heartily. "I don't think I could tolerate such heat as one must endure in a sweat lodge."

"If I should ask you to join me and other women in a sweat lodge only for women, would you not enter one with me then?" Waterfall said, handing Pebbles a piece of cooked venison as he came into the hut in a rush. His fur was wet from having taken a morning swim. He smelled as fresh and clean as the river.

"Women also enter sweat lodges?" Becky asked. She handed Pebbles another piece of meat from the tray as he approached it, sniffing.

"Not often, but *ne-hyo*, we do have our own times

in such lodges," Waterfall said, nodding.

Becky gazed at a small buckskin pouch that Waterfall had tied to the belt of her dress. "You have in that pouch what is required for the ceremony of purification this morning?" she asked.

"*Ne-hyo*—yes, everything," she said, her eyes dancing as her lips tugged into a smile.

"But the pouch is so small," Becky said. She welcomed Pebbles on her lap as he stretched out on it, his tail wagging.

"It is large enough for what is needed," Waterfall said. She picked up the platter, on which only a few pieces of meat and fruit were left. "I shall take this from the lodge, and when I return, we shall begin the ceremony."

Becky's heart pounded as she nodded. She wished that she could blink her eyes and the ceremony would be over. Then she would rush into the arms of her beloved!

Blazing Eagle stripped himself naked, slipped inside his small sweat lodge, and started a fire to heat the circle of rocks that he had placed in the center of the small-framed lodge.

When the rocks were finally glowing red hot, he lifted a basin of water that he had placed in the lodge before entering and poured the cold water over the rocks.

A quick, blinding steam rose from the rocks. It was so hot at first that he could barely breathe. But he could feel his muscles relaxing, like a bowstring being slowly released.

He sat there for a while, closed his eyes, and enjoyed these moments of being alone with his thoughts before returning home, where soon his wife would return to him.

His loins ached with need of her. His heart soared at the very thought of her in his arms, clinging, kissing, touching.

His heart swelled with pride to know that she had been strong-willed enough to stay in the menstrual hut without complaining. Each day, as Waterfall had reported his wife's progress to him, he had known even more surely that he had chosen right when he had taken her into his lodge and his life.

Their lifetime together would be one of understanding, of growing together as though they were one in spirit, in all thoughts and deeds.

No, he could not have chosen more wisely when he singled her out from all the other women he had known to be his wife. She was nothing like his first wife, whose name he did not even care to breathe across his lips! He never again wanted to taste the bitterness that her name would cause!

The fire lowering, the steam evaporating, Blazing Eagle stepped outside and rubbed the glistening sweat off his body with clumps of sage.

Then he plunged into the river, invigorated anew by the cold water rushing against his hot flesh. He swam in masterful strokes through the water for a while longer, then left the river and dressed again.

He paused only long enough to watch the antics of a little grey bird perched tentatively on a rock a short distance away. It walked down the rock's slick side, slipped its head in the water, and drifted to the next rock. In an erratic bobbing and zigzagging manner, it moved upstream and out of sight.

Blazing Eagle's heart thudded like a hammer within his chest as he started for home. He doubted that his wife would be there yet, but knew that she soon would be.

His lips curved into a smug smile when he thought of how cleverly he had encouraged his son to spend the day with his friends. When Becky returned to their lodge, they would have the long day to reacquaint themselves with how their bodies could please each other.

Ne-hyo, he thought to himself. They would make up for the four nights lost to them!

"Let us now begin the purification ceremony," Waterfall said, smoothing the dried grass aside on the earthen floor, leaving a circle of clean earth. "I shall make a place for hot coals from the fire."

She reached outside the door, where she had left some crude tongs. She got them and turned back around and faced the fire.

As though she were silently meditating, she solemnly plucked first one hot coal from the fire, and then a few more, until a small pile of them glowed red in the circle.

Becky's pulse raced, fearing this strange ritual, yet anticipating getting it behind her.

Waterfall leaned outside the hut and grabbed something else that she had purposely left there before she had entered the lodge earlier in the morning while Becky was still sleeping. Becky stared at the beautiful white robe made of rabbit fur as Waterfall draped it around her shoulders.

"Wrap the robe snugly around you," Waterfall said, stepping back from Becky.

Becky did as she was told. She snuggled into the robe, then gazed at Waterfall, awaiting further instructions. Her gaze shifted when Waterfall untied the small buckskin pouch at her waist.

Scarcely breathing, wondering what was inside the pouch, Becky watched Waterfall draw it open with her slim, beautiful fingers. Then, she watched Waterfall sprinkle various things onto the hot coals. "What is that?" she finally blurted out.

"It is a mixture of sweet grass, juniper needles, and white sage," Waterfall said, still spreading the mixture over the hot coals, causing them to sizzle. Thick, gray smoke lifted from them, the aroma spicy yet also somewhat sweet.

"Now, Becky," Waterfall said, looking over at her. "Lift the robe only high enough so that you can stand over the hot coals, so that you will be standing over the smoke with your feet on either side as the smoke purifies you."

Becky turned her eyes down to look guardedly at the hot coals, finding that she was unable to see them through the thick fog of the smoke.

"I'm afraid I will step on the rocks," she said, giving Waterfall an anxious look.

"The Good Spirit will guide your feet," Waterfall said, gently taking Becky by the arm. "You must do as I say now, while the smoke carries the scent of the herbal mixture into the air."

Becky smiled weakly, stared at the smoke again, then swallowed hard as she placed first one foot beside the circle, and then the other, Waterfall holding her by the elbow to steady her.

Relieved that her feet had not come in contact with the hot coals, she sighed. The smoke burned her eyes and throat. She closed her eyes and mouth, her nostrils flaring now with the stinging aroma of the smoke as it wafted up to them.

Then, she knew not how it happened, but suddenly she didn't mind the smoke at all. She felt lifted above it, as though she was soaring. A keen euphoria swept through her. She felt dizzied by it.

Only when Waterfall led her away from the smoke by her elbow, did she come out of the trance. She looked wide-eyed at Waterfall. "What happened?" she murmured, her face hot, her heart beating soundly.

"You have been purified," was all that Waterfall offered in response.

When a man's voice arose from somewhere outside, loud and demanding, Becky's surprise at what had just happened changed to another sort of wonder when the man shouted, "There goes my wife! I throw her away!"

A strained silence ensued. Becky silently questioned Waterfall with her eyes, then looked toward the door again when the man's voice boomed out so loud that she knew the whole village must have heard him.

"A horse goes with the woman who is now no longer my wife!" he shouted.

Becky swallowed hard as she again stared at Waterfall. "I don't understand," she murmured. "What does the man mean by saying that he throws his wife away?"

"He has divorced her," Waterfall said matter-of-factly as she slipped the robe away from Becky.

Becky paled. "It can be done that easily?" she gasped. "He just says he is going to throw her away, and he *does*?"

"Not entirely," Waterfall said, slowly folding the robe. "While you were going through the ceremony of purification, there was another ceremony being held in another lodge. Whoever of our village wished to witness the divorcing went into the man's lodge. They sang a song of the man's choosing as the man held a stick in his hand. With that stick he struck a drum. Then he rushed outside and threw the stick up into the air. As he threw it, he shouted that he gave his wife away. Whoever got the stick he threw away could then have the woman. But if the man said that a horse also went with the woman, the man who picked up the stick only got the horse, not the woman."

"How strange," Becky murmured; she was troubled deeply by the Cheyenne practice of divorce.

"How is divorce done in your culture?" Waterfall asked.

"It is not done with such public embarrassment," Becky said. "And a man cannot cast aside a wife all that easily. The woman is treated with more respect." She cleared her throat. "Sometimes women even divorce their husbands. Can that be done in your culture?" The question had hardly passed her lips when she recalled what Blazing Eagle had said about his wife. She had divorced *him*.

"*Ne-hyo*, a man *or* woman can throw their spouse away," Waterfall said, then smiled sweetly at

Becky. "Do not look so concerned. Blazing Eagle would never throw you away, nor would you *he*. Your love for one another was written in the heavens."

"I do love him so," Becky said softly. "I do hope he loves me as much."

"He waits for you now," Waterfall said, ushering Becky outside. "Go to him. Be with him as man and wife. Then see whether or not you have cause to question his love for you."

The wind felt good on Becky's flesh. The air was cool and pure, smelling of rain. She gazed toward the trees. While she had been stored away, like someone who was contaminated, the leaves had begun to change.

Autumn.

She loved autumn.

She even looked forward to the long, cold days of winter. She would never be cold, not with Blazing Eagle there to warm her very soul!

"Thank you for everything," Becky cried to Waterfall over her shoulder as she broke into a run from the menstrual hut. "I shall repay you twofold for your kindness!"

Waterfall nodded and watched with an envious heart as Becky ran into her lodge, where her man awaited her with the magic of his kisses.

"One day I shall know the same sort of love as she," she whispered, then walked with a lifted chin toward her own lodge, Pebbles scurrying after her since he now spent as much time with her as with Becky.

Chapter Thirty-two

Thunder rolled overhead. The sky was darkening as Becky stepped into her and Blazing Eagle's lodge.

All sounds, all thoughts of an impending storm, were lost to her when she saw Blazing Eagle sitting there beside the fire on a pallet of furs, nude, his arms outstretched for her.

Overwhelmed by passion, Becky went to him and melted into his arms. "My husband," she whispered, her fingers trembling over his bronze, handsome face that revealed his naked desire.

Their lips came together in frenzied, hungry kisses.

Then, driven by needs building in him these past nights, Blazing Eagle stood up and reached a hand out for her. "Come to bed with me," he said huskily.

"My wife, feed my needs . . . my hungers. I shall feed yours."

Her eyes locked with his in silent, urgent understanding, she reached her hand out for him as she rose to her feet. Becky then drifted toward him and was soon again in his embrace, their lips on fire as they kissed.

Then he swept her up into his arms and carried her to the bed. Before laying her down across it, he quickly disrobed her.

When she was standing silkenly nude before him, he greedily raked his eyes slowly over her, each place he looked firing his desire even more.

He ran his fingers over her curves, causing her to suck in a wild breath of pleasure when first he cupped her breasts within his palms, then slid his hands lower, over the curve of her slim, white thighs, then around to the place where she ached for him—to the very core of her desire.

As he stroked her, moving purposely slow, taunting her, Becky threw her head back. Her golden hair spilled over her shoulders. It tumbled down her back as she breathed raggedly, sighing and moaning.

Then when he lifted her and laid her across the bed, her pulse raced at knowing what the next moments would bring her—that release she had only been able to dream of these past nights.

With trembling fingers, her hands sought and found his manhood. She delicately circled her fingers around him, thrilling anew at how large he could become, how thick and throbbing.

"Come to me, darling," she whispered, hardly

recognizing her own voice in its huskiness as she guided him inside her.

He wove his fingers through her hair and brought her lips to his as he began his deep, eager thrusts. He kissed her long and deep, his lips drugging her. The sensations searing, their bodies strained together.

Becky wrapped her legs around his back, her soft, full thighs opening wide, enabling him to thrust even more deeply within her.

They moved together in a wild, dizzying rhythm. They rocked and swayed. They moaned spasmodically. Their lips parted, tongues touching.

Blazing Eagle slipped his hands from her hair and wrapped them around her breasts, her resilient nipples growing hard against his palms.

She whimpered tiny cries of ecstasy when his mouth moved over her nipples, teasing first one with his flicking tongue, and then the other.

The air was charged with excitement. And as the storm brewed outside their lodge, the thunder shaking the ground beneath their bed, they took flight together and found the pinnacle of passion once again as their bodies quaked and shimmered in their shared, joyous release.

As they rolled away from one another, Blazing Eagle became aware of the true violence of the storm.

It was earth-shaking. Rain was falling in sheets against the lodge. The wind was like demons set free from hell.

Through the fabric of his lodge he could see that the lightning was vivid and constant, the thunder like a million drum rolls.

The poles that held the lodge up shimmered and squeaked. The buckskin covering rattled, the howling wind sounding as though it might rip it from the poles.

"I must go and make sure the stakes are secure in the ground," Blazing Eagle said, scurrying into his breechclout.

"I'll come with you and help you," Becky said, bolting from the bed, slipping her dress over her head.

Together they stepped out into the cold, driving rain. The wind was so strong that Becky lost her balance and fell to the ground into a pool of mud.

Blazing Eagle reached down and lifted her from the ground, his mighty hands brushing streamers of her wet hair back from her face.

"Go back inside!" he shouted through the howl of the wind.

"No!" Becky cried, shivering from the coldness of the rain, her dress clinging. "Together we can get it done more quickly. Then you can also come inside."

Blazing Eagle nodded. He checked the stakes on the left side of the entrance flap.

Becky checked those on the right.

When Blazing Eagle found some that had loosened, he grabbed a stone hammer and pounded them even more deeply into the ground.

The lightning was incessant overhead.

The thunder was deafening.

The sky had blackened so, it looked as though day had turned into night.

Blazing Eagle turned and watched the play of the

lightning, then something else came into his mind's eye. He groaned and held his temples as that day so many years ago unfolded before him. It was so vivid, it was as though he was there, a boy of nine winters again!

On that day, in that early dawn, there was a storm. It had been as fierce as today's. But the larger threat came to his people on horses!

He remembered it well now. He clenched his teeth and shivered as he recalled how guns flamed as red as blood against the inky black, stormy sky that day.

He could even now hear the deadly hail of the bullets, how they hissed and screeched.

Then the arrows joined the bullets. In sheets they flew through the air, killing and maiming the white men on horses and the red-skinned enemies on foot.

There was an instant panic among Blazing Eagle's people.

How could he ever have forgotten how the Cheyenne warriors had tumbled out of their lodges, some naked as they had slept, some carrying guns, others bow and arrows.

Children wailed in terror. There was a chaos of screaming, milling confusion.

As the rains ceased on that day, a pall soon rose from the burning lodges. The air was thick with the acrid stench of black powder, of burning hair and hides, and of blood.

"Mother!" Blazing Eagle gasped out now as his memories became even more vivid, even more real, as though it was happening now, not then.

His lungs ached as he panted. He could not blank from his mind anymore what had happened to his mother that day.

A bullet in the stomach had downed her. As she lay there reaching for Blazing Eagle, several bearded white men had jumped from their horses and held her down. Her legs were spread. Her skirt was lifted.

As she breathed her last, she was unmercifully raped—not by one man but by several.

When they were finally done with her, a man leaned low over her and scalped her!

As Blazing Eagle had stood there screaming, someone else on horseback had ridden up and reined in before him, blocking his view of his mother.

Wild-eyed, he had looked up and teetered backward when he saw not a white man staring down at him, but instead a woman! A beautiful, golden-haired woman, whose bandanna had slipped off, revealing her face!

She had been dressed as a man, a black cape worn over her shirt and breeches. And she had worn a wide-brimmed hat that had not hidden well enough her feminine facial features or the long locks of golden hair flowing freely from beneath it.

When the woman's eyes locked with Blazing Eagle's, he had seen how green they were, as green as grass in the spring.

But also in them he had seen a silent pity, a look of sorrow.

In an instant she had swept him up onto her saddle and ridden away from the village with him. She took him far enough away so that no one could see her release him to safety.

She had lingered a moment longer as she stared down at him, then wheeled her horse around and rode away.

"No!" he screamed now, his temples pounding, his heart feeling as though it had been wrenched from inside his chest. "It can't be. It can't be!"

His screams made Becky flinch. Slipping and sliding in the mud, holding her wet hair back from her eyes, she ran around to the front of the lodge and found Blazing Eagle crumpled to the ground, his face held within his hands.

"What happened?" she cried, falling to her knees in the mud beside him. She tried to wrench his hands from his face, but they seemed locked there.

"Blazing Eagle—oh, darling, what's wrong?" she cried. "What happened?" She yanked at his hands, again to no avail. "Please look at me. Tell me what's wrong. Come inside with me. Let me dry you by the fire!"

Suddenly he turned angry, accusing eyes at her. The look he gave her was so filled with contempt, so filled with seething rage, she felt as though she'd been struck. His dark eyes burned with disgust!

"Lord," Becky gasped, moving shakily to her feet. "Don't look at me like that. Why would you? I haven't done anything."

Blazing Eagle rose stiffly to his feet and glared down at Becky as the rain ceased. In his mind's eye he was reliving everything again. *All* of it. After all those years, he finally had total recall, and what he had discovered pained him to the very core of his being.

The woman who had saved him that day was the exact image of his wife! The woman who had saved him that day was part of an outlaw gang! She had stood by and watched his people die! Perhaps she had even fired on them herself. He would not think kindly of her because she had singled him out for pity, not when everyone else had died.

It made no sense to him that the woman had looked like Becky. What had happened had occurred twenty winters ago!

But because the woman had looked so like her, he would always associate Becky with that day. He now knew that he could not live with her.

He could not look into those green eyes every day, nor touch that golden hair every day, without recalling the woman outlaw who had ridden with those who had taken his birthright away!

No, as much as he loved Becky, he could no longer bear to live with her.

"Blazing Eagle, you are looking at me as though you hate me," Becky cried, covering her mouth with her hand. "Lord, Blazing Eagle, what has happened to make you look as though you despise me?"

He could not find the strength, the courage, to explain why he had to send her away. The fact was that it had to be done. He did not want to look at her ever again! Seeing her was the same as seeing death!

He grabbed her by the wrists and yanked her into his lodge. He threw her to the floor beside her travel bags. "Fill the bags with your clothes, then leave!" he said, turning his back to her.

He vowed to himself that he would never look at her again. Although he would always love her, he could no longer bear the sight of her.

"Blazing Eagle, you can't mean it," Becky sobbed, crawling to him and clinging to his legs.

When he jerked himself away, causing her to fall to the floor, she lay there for a moment and cried, her heart breaking.

Pebbles came to her and whined. Becky ignored the pup.

"Fill your bags and leave," Blazing Eagle said icily, folding his arms across his bare wet chest.

Becky crawled back to her bags. Tears blinded her as she swept her clothes inside.

Stumbling, feeling dead inside, she lifted her bags and walked past Blazing Eagle.

When she reached the entrance flap, she turned and stared up at him. "Won't you ever explain what caused you to do this to me?" she asked, her voice breaking.

When he refused to answer her, but only stood there looking somewhere blankly over her head, she sighed heavily and left the lodge.

Pebbles barked as he followed her to the horses. He jumped up at her, over and over again, as she placed the saddle on her horse.

When he nipped her ankle with his teeth, that drew her instant attention.

She flinched and cried out, then gazed down at her pup who stood there looking up at her pitifully.

"All right, I'm sorry I ignored you," she said, lifting him into her arms. She snuggled him close to her heart. "You are all I have left on this earth."

After securing her bags, slipping Pebbles into one so that his head was free, she swung herself into the saddle and rode the horse from the corral.

Before riding from the village, she stared at Blazing Eagle's lodge. "You can divorce me this easily?" she whispered.

She turned her eyes heavenward, where the black clouds were floating away, the blue sky peeking through. "Why, Lord? Why?"

Then, with her head hung, she rode away.

Blazing Eagle died a slow death inside when he heard Becky's horse leave the village. He buried his face in his hands and wept. "What have I done?" he cried. "What have I done?"

Chapter Thirty-three

Downhearted and feeling abandoned, Becky entered her small soddy. Shivers ran up and down her spine as she looked around at the drabness and felt how alone she was. The silence was strange after living at the Cheyenne village long enough to get used to their chants, their songs, and the laughter of the children.

Now it was only her and her pup.

Well, she told herself angrily, she would soon change that. She would return to Saint Louis and become involved in the social life of the city and find a man who would be loyal to her, who would love and trust her!

"Loyal," she whispered, remembering the rope that she was supposed to wear that proved her loyalty to one man—to the man she would never again call her husband!

She searched through her travel bags until she found the dreaded rope. With trembling fingers, she removed it from the bag. She stamped to the fireplace and threw the rope into the cold ashes.

"That's not enough," she whispered to herself. "I'm going to burn that damn thing. I don't want any more reminders of why I was ever going to wear it. I was so foolish to have thought that Blazing Eagle truly loved me. He used me, then sent me away as though I was no more to him than an animal he grew tired of."

Feeling the cold seeping through the roof of her soddy as the wind blew in, Becky bent to her knees and stacked wood on the fireplace grate.

After a comfortable, warm fire was burning, she turned and once again gazed around her. She would have to tolerate living here until she arranged passage on the train and the riverboat that would carry her back to Saint Louis. She would live in her father's house after all.

And now she would welcome the memories. They would comfort her when she allowed her thoughts to stray to these few weeks with Blazing Eagle.

Never would she think of him in a pleasant way! She hated him!

Pebbles ran to the door and barked and snarled.

Becky's insides turned cold. Her spine stiffened when she heard someone outside, approaching the soddy.

Pebbles barked incessantly. Becky picked him up and patted him, glad when he finally calmed down.

She eyed the door with a pounding heart. She

had not heard the arrival of a horse. Whoever was there had left his steed tethered elsewhere.

She recalled the time that Blazing Eagle had arrived in such a way. Her heart leapt to think that it might be him again.

"I can't allow myself to feel anything for him again!" she whispered. "What he did is unforgivable. No explanations can ease the pain he's caused me."

The sound of the footsteps now closer, Becky looked anxiously around for something with which to protect herself. Even if Blazing Eagle had come to talk to her, she wished to have a firearm to aim at him, so that he would be convinced that she did not wish ever to see him again.

But in her haste to leave the Cheyenne village, she had left without taking up a weapon.

Hugging Pebbles to her chest, Becky took slow steps away from the door and hid herself in the dark shadows. She scarcely breathed as the door swung open and the figure of a man was shadowed in the doorway.

It was dark outside now. The only light that she had in her cabin was the soft glow of the fire, and it did not reach the door. She still had no idea who was there, or what he might want of her.

"Becky, don't be afraid," Edward said, his voice drawn. "It's me. Edward. I've come to show you something."

"Edward," Becky gasped, placing a hand to her throat. "Lord, Edward, why did you have to come here? Please leave. I've had enough heartache for one day."

"Why are *you* here instead of with Blazing Eagle?" Edward said, stepping out of the shadows.

"How did you even know that I *was*?" Becky said, meeting him halfway across the room.

"I saw you leave the village," he said. "I was nearby. I was watching for you to go to the river alone so that I could explain everything to you. When you left on horseback, crying, I chose to follow you instead of confront you, to see where you would go."

"You followed me?" Becky gasped out. "You were with me all the time?"

"Yes," Edward said, stepping closer. "I saw that you were distraught enough without knowing your escaped outlaw brother was there to add to your torment. Why did you leave? It looked as though you were forced to."

Tears pooled in Becky's eyes. "He sent me away," she blurted out. "And I have no idea *why*."

"I tried to get you to return to Saint Louis," Edward said, reaching inside his coat pocket and bringing out a diary. "I guess you had to find out in your own way why it would be impossible to live with Indians. Their views on everything are much different than ours. Who is to say why the chief decided to send you away?"

He paused, then added, "You probably did something that was taboo that had to do with their religion," he said. "Don't try to figure it out, Sis. Just go home where you belong. I'm going to clear my name, then go home myself. We can begin anew, you and I. Would you like that?"

Becky's heart skipped a beat. "You are going to

clear your name?" she said, her voice breaking. "How, Edward? How on earth do you expect to do that? You are wanted all over the country for your train robberies, for your killings. If you even get near the fort now, I'm sure you'd be gunned down first and questioned later."

"Not if you are with me," Edward said, holding the diary up to the firelight so that she could see it. "Read this, Becky. But let me warn you that you are soon to get the shock of your life. I did the day I found it among father's things after I became partners with him before I left to come to the Wyoming Territory."

"Before you left for the war, don't you mean, Edward?" Becky said, her eyes locked on the diary, not yet taking it. "When you left, it was to join the war."

"No, Sis," Edward said. "I never saw one day of fighting during the Civil War. I've been here in the Wyoming Territory all along."

Becky's eyes shot upward. She stared blankly at her brother. "You lied to me and father even then?" she gasped, placing Pebbles on the floor. She was glad when he cowered next to her instead of going into another bout of barking. "You had no intention of fighting for your beliefs? You came out here and became an outlaw instead?"

"I've never been an outlaw," Edward said, stepping up to her. He took her hand and shoved the diary into it. "I came out here, Becky—"

"You came out here for only one reason, Edward," Becky said, giving him a stubborn stare. "To kill. To rob. To maim. But I'll never understand why. If I knew that you had been lured here by the gold and silver that lined the streams, I could accept that. But you didn't. You came out to get what you could, at any expense, even at the cost of your family's reputation."

"Becky, that's not the way it was at all," Edward said, raking his fingers through his long golden hair. "I lied to you because I had to. Because of our mother, Becky. All because of our *mother*."

Becky paled. "Our stepmother?" she said softly. "Why, Edward? She was always so kind to you. You loved her. I know you loved her."

"I'm not speaking of Kathryn," Edward said, sighing heavily. "I'm speaking of our *real* mother. The one whose grave you and I both took flowers to every Sunday of our childhood."

"Yes, and I wished that I could have known her," Becky said, her voice hollow with emotion.

"Becky, all those times we went there, the grave was empty," Edward told her. "There was nothing there. No casket. No body. *Nothing*."

Becky took a shaky step away from him. "What . . . do you mean?" she said, her voice scarcely a whisper, stunned by everything that was being disclosed to her. It all seemed so unreal, as though she were someone else. How could Edward be telling the truth? How?

"Mother never died," Edward said in a rush of words. "She left us, Becky. She disappeared one night shortly after you were born. Father couldn't stand the disgrace of people knowing. He told everyone she was dead. He paid a mortician from another county to falsify her death certificate. He had a closed casket funeral. No one suspected that there was no one in the casket."

"No," Becky said, growing dizzy from the shock of hearing all of this.

"Mother came to the Wyoming Territory to be with her lover," Edward further explained. "She met him one day while shopping in Saint Louis. Even when she was pregnant with you, Becky, she slept with the man. Then she went to him as soon as you were born. She waited until you were born because she didn't want to be saddled with *any* child. She left to join her outlaw husband in the Wyoming Territory. She's been here ever since."

Becky held her temples with her hands. They throbbed. She felt sick to her stomach. All of this was too far-fetched to be real. "You are lying!" she cried. "Oh, Edward, please tell me you are lying!"

"I'm *not* lying," Edward said, going to gather her into his arms. As she clutched the diary, he held her in a comforting embrace. "Becky, I've been here all of this time trying to find mother—trying to find the answers as to how she could do this to us. But she and her outlaw husband and their gang have managed to keep one step ahead of me and my men. I don't see how, but they seem always to disappear into thin air."

"No," Becky cried.

"I hired several men to help me find our mother, to bring her back, to try and get her life changed back to what it should have been," Edward said. "We only got accused of what mother and her lover were guilty of. When there was a crime, our mother was always at the crime scene. No one ever saw her face. It was hidden well behind a bandanna. But they saw her hair. That is why I was accused of the crimes. It's understandable. I was always nearby. My hair was the color of the outlaw's. It is the color of our mother's. And to disguise herself, she wore men's clothes. She wore bandannas. She's toughened while living the life of an outlaw. Her build is like that of a man."

"No," Becky said, eyes wide. "It's all too much to believe. You've made it all up. And there is proof of you being the liar that you are. The wanted posters. They have your likeness on them. Only yours!"

"No, not quite," Edward said, his eyes taking on a wounded look. "I was caught once after our mother and her friends had robbed a bank. I and my men were so close to catching up with mother that day. But I was too close. The sheriff accused *me* of the crime."

"You were arrested?"

"Yes, but only me, thank God," Edward said. "I had ridden ahead of the men, so damn close to mother I could almost reach out and touch her, when the sheriff and his posse suddenly surrounded me. My men stayed behind, hidden. My mother and her gang rode onward. All the sheriff was interested in that day was arresting the low-down, murdering golden-haired outlaw. They thought they *had*."

"How long were you incarcerated?" Becky asked, slowly beginning to believe. Surely no one could be skilled enough to make up such a tall tale as this.

"Two nights," Edward said, then smiled slowly. "But the jail break came swift and clean. No one was killed. But it was then that the wanted posters began showing up all over the place. Apparently they never caught up with Mother to arrest her, to get *her* likeness on a wanted poster. She and her gang are as slippery as eels, Becky. I doubt anyone will ever catch them."

"Your men?" Becky said. "Where are they now?"

"We went our separate ways," Edward said solemnly. "None of their likenesses ever appeared on wanted posters. They are as free as the wind. I am the only one who has a problem on his hands."

He nodded toward the diary. "But after I show that to Judge Newman, he'll see the truth for what it is," he said, then gazed up at Becky again. "You will accompany me to the fort, won't you? When they see you with me, they will listen to what I have to say. After they read the diary, my name will be cleared. We can then return to Saint Louis together. Becky, will you help your brother? Will you go with me to the fort?"

Becky didn't answer him, only stared.

Then she dropped the diary to the floor and flung herself into his arms. "Edward, my sweet Edward," she said, sobbing. "I knew you couldn't do those horrible things you were accused of doing. I could never truly accept that you had. Thank the Lord it was all untrue. I've got you back with me, Edward. Oh, how I love you."

"Honey, I'm so sorry for having lied to you all these years," he said softly, gently stroking her back. "But I had no choice. If I had ever told anyone my plan, I'd never have been given the opportunity to see my plan to the end."

He laughed throatily. "Seems my plan is shot to hell, anyway, isn't it?" he said. "And I confess, it's time to finally throw in the towel. If I haven't caught up with Mother yet, I never will."

"Does she know about you?" Becky asked, easing from his arms. She bent over and picked up the diary, gazing at it as Pebbles stretched out on her feet and went to sleep, content enough now that Edward was a friend.

"I'm sure she heard about someone being caught for her crimes that one time, but she never had cause to associate me with the young boy who was her son those many years ago," Edward said.

Then he gripped her shoulders. "You are my one and only chance, Becky," he said, his eyes imploring her. "With you at my side, I can hand over the diary and not get my head blown off while doing it."

He stepped away from her and gazed down at her as she slowly opened the diary.

"The diary will clear your name?" she said, gazing down at it.

"Just read a few pages, Becky, and you will see," Edward said, his voice drawn. "All those years, before you were conceived, when I was her only child—even then, Becky, she resented having me. All of her motherly affection to me was pretense. She regretted every day of being married to our father and of having to be a mother."

Becky's eyes filled with tears when she began reading the life of an unhappy, tormented woman. As she turned each page, the rage and madness that her mother suffered was plain in her writing.

Becky swallowed hard when she flipped the pages and started reading the passages in her mother's handwriting about how she resented being pregnant the second time, and how she would gladly turn her back on her child to be with the man she loved.

Her mother had written of her love for this man in detail and of the sexual feelings she had for him. And she had written about how she looked forward to the excitement of riding with him as he led his outlaw friends into more mischief in the Wyoming Territory. Her life in Saint Louis had been boring. The life of crime would be welcomed over the life that she had had with her first husband.

"I can read no further," Becky said, slamming the small diary shut. "She wrote enough here to condemn herself and to free you. I wonder why she didn't take this with her?"

"I imagine it is because Father found it before she left and kept it as he ordered her from his home," Edward said, taking the diary and stuffing it into his pocket again.

"Father ran her off?" Becky gasped out. "How do you know?"

"He told me so," Edward said, his eyes gazing into his sister's.

"When?" Becky said guardedly. "Oh, Edward, don't tell me that he knew all along where you were. Did he know that you had gone to the Wyoming Territory instead of to fight for the war?"

"Yes, he knew," Edward said softly.

"Then all the while he was mourning for you, saying he thought you were dead, he knew that you hadn't gone to war?"

"He knew," Edward said. "If he mourned for me, it was only because he thought that I might have died while trying to find Mother."

"You didn't contact him? Not once?"

"How could I have sent a wire? Then everyone would have known."

"You should have found a way," Becky said accusingly. "He mourned for you until he died."

"Becky, don't you see?" Edward said. "His sadness wasn't for me. It was for what our mother had turned into. And also it was for my not having succeeded at finding her to bring her back to him."

"But he always acted as though he truly loved Kathryn," Becky said, her voice breaking.

"He did. But he also loved our mother, I am sure, until he took his last breath."

Becky turned her eyes from him. "How could he?" she said, covering her mouth with her hand.

"Once you love as deeply as he loved our mother, that sort of love is never forgotten," Edward said. He placed a finger to Becky's chin and turned her eyes up to his. "Becky, can you forget Blazing Eagle?"

Becky stared up at him, then slowly shook her head back and forth. "I shall never forget him," she said. "I loved him so, Edward. With all of my heart."

"Why did he send you away?" Edward asked softly. "Surely you have some idea."

"It had something to do with his past," Becky said, recalling his moments of torment. "But I don't know what. And now I never shall."

"You are better off without him," Edward said,

again drawing her into his arms.

Becky closed her eyes tightly, so much wanting to believe what her brother said, yet knowing that never would she believe that she was better off without Blazing Eagle. He was her every heartbeat!

Then Becky recalled something. She looked anxiously up at Edward and ran her finger across the deep slash of a scar on his face. "Tell me about the scar," she said, her voice breaking. "If you didn't get it while fighting the war, then *how*?"

"I'm not sure if you truly want to know," Edward said warningly.

"Please tell me," she said, searching his eyes for answers.

"Blazing Eagle did it," he said warily. "One day he and his warriors caught up with me and my men. They also thought we were the outlaws, and we had a scrape. It ended up with me being slashed by his knife. I was lucky to get away that day with my life."

"Lord," Becky said, paling.

Then she thought of something else. "Edward, Major Kent was killed on the day of your recent escape from the guardhouse," she reminded him. "Surely one of your men, or even *you*, are responsible."

"No, that's not the way it happened at all," Edward said, his eyes filled with sorrow. "You see, one of Major Kent's own men killed him. It was an accident. Lieutenant Dowling was guarding me in the guardhouse. He was sitting there, lost in thought, as he was cleaning his firearm. When Major Kent came to report to the lieutenant that my men had arrived, the Lieutenant's firearm discharged by accident as he rose to his feet. It hit the major square in the chest. The stupid lieutenant had forgotten to remove the ammunition."

"How horrible," Becky said. "I truly liked Major Kent. He was a kind and caring man."

"It was convenient for the lieutenant to place the blame for his death on me and my men," Edward growled out. "The coward."

"But the soldiers said that your men were responsible for the major's death," Becky said.

"Yes, and so they would, wouldn't they?" Edward said, laughing sarcastically. "To save face for one of their own, they cast the blame elsewhere."

"Then we also have *that* mistake to clear up, don't we, big brother?" Becky said, firming her chin. "Let's go, Edward. Let's reveal a few truths to the authorities."

Edward drew her into his arms. "Sis, it seems you are my salvation," he said, nestling his nose into the sweet scent of her hair.

"I only hope they will believe us," Becky said. But for this moment she reveled in the closeness of her brother, in knowing the truth, and realizing that he was still as sweet and innocent as he had been those years ago when they had been best friends as children!

Chapter Thirty-four

Becky and Edward rode out the next morning when the sun was only a splash of orange along the horizon. As Becky rode beside her brother on their way to Fort Laramie, she closed her eyes and imagined that it was ten years ago, when she and her brother had gone on their outings in Saint Louis, enjoying their private times together away from the chores of the day.

"Don't you feel it, Edward?" Becky asked, opening her eyes and looking quickly over at him.

"Feel what?" he asked.

"How wonderful it is to be together again," she murmured. She patted Pebbles as he whined from the sling at the side of her horse. "I only wish it were the same—that you didn't have to face the accusing looks; the threat at Fort Laramie."

"While eluding the authorities these past years,

thinking of you and home was all that got me through the long nights of hiding out," Edward said hoarsely. "I should've given up long ago. But I had to try and find Mother, to face her with the truth. Although I never had the sort of love a mother gives a child, I still bonded to her. If she could have only been like Kathryn. . . ."

"Kathryn was such a compassionate, caring woman," Becky said. She shielded her eyes from the bright rays of the sun as she peered ahead, to see if she could get a glimpse of the fort.

She truly dreaded approaching the fort. If the guards got trigger happy after seeing Edward, all could be lost to both of them in a flash of gunfire.

A thought came to Becky that made her go suddenly cold inside. She looked over at her brother. "Edward, father was a bigamist," she said in a rush of words. "He *knew* mother was still alive, yet he married Kathryn."

"Sis, remember that there was a signed death certificate," Edward said. "To the world our true mother was dead. That made father's marriage to Kathryn legitimate at least in the eyes of the community."

"But if you had found Mother and taken her back to Saint Louis, then everyone would have known," Becky said, her voice breaking. "Lord, Edward, our family would never live down the scandal."

"Becky, Father is dead, and our mother will never return to Saint Louis," Edward said.

"But if you had found her and brought her back with you . . ." Becky said, but Edward quickly interrupted.

"Becky, I knew the very moment that I understood the sort of life she led that she would never return to Saint Louis," he said thickly. "I just wanted to find her to make her face up to what she was doing. I wanted to make her stare me straight in the eye and tell me she was sorry."

"Edward, you were wasting your time," Becky said, her voice breaking. "And while you were wasting your time seeking out a mother who cared nothing for you or me, I was sick with worry about you. Why couldn't you have confided in me? I would have understood what drove you to the Wyoming Territory."

"This was something I had to do by myself," Edward said, turning his eyes from her. Then he looked at her again, his eyes filled with pain. "Don't you see? I was ashamed. All along I thought mother was dead and—and—"

"Edward, we don't have to talk about it anymore," Becky interrupted. "It's enough for me to know now that you are alive. And now that I know that Father knew all along that you weren't dead, and he carried the secret to the grave with him, his mind at peace with how you chose to live these last several years of your life, I can learn to live with the knowledge also."

"I never meant to hurt you, Becky," Edward said, swallowing hard. "I was a damned heartless fool for having allowed you to believe that I might have died during the war. Forgive me?"

Becky sidled her horse close to his. She reached over and placed a gentle hand on his cheek. "I love you," she murmured. "And you know that I have forgiven you. I'm so glad that we are together again."

"Perhaps not for long," Edward said, glancing up, staring at the fort as it came into view. "If the authorities don't believe me, I may be swinging from the end of a rope by sunup tomorrow."

"Don't think such a thing," Becky said, shuddering at the thought. "You have the diary. Surely that is enough proof of who the true outlaws are."

"Remember, Sis, that I was incarcerated twice," he said, clearing his throat nervously. "And that my men broke me free. In a sense, even though I am innocent of other crimes, the fact that I am considered an escaped felon might be enough to put me behind bars the minute they see me."

"But you were wrongly imprisoned," Becky said softly.

"Yeah, but tell that to the judge," Edward said, laughing sarcastically.

"The judge!" Becky blurted, eyes wide. "I *know* the judge personally. Judge Roy Newman. I met him while I was at the Cheyenne village. He's a decent man. Surely he will believe you and know that you are innocent. Surely he will set you free."

"We shall soon see, won't we?" Edward said, gesturing toward the fort as it now loomed closer and closer.

Becky paled and gripped the reins more tightly as she rode onward beside Edward.

She held her chin high when they rode into the shadows of the fort, where sentries in strategic places along the wall stared down at them.

"Halt!" one of the sentries shouted. "Who goes there?"

"Becky and Edward Veach," Becky shouted back.

"It's the golden-haired outlaw!" another sentry shouted, quickly recognizing Edward.

A scramble of activity ensued as the gate opened, and several soldiers came running toward Becky and Edward, their rifles poised for firing.

"Get down from that horse!" one of the soldiers shouted at Edward, his aim steady on him. "Hands up in the air. You make one false move and you're dead."

"Stop!" Becky cried as Edward slowly dismounted, then stood before the soldier, his arms raised. "You are making a bad mistake. This isn't the outlaw. He's my brother."

"Brothers can't be outlaws?" the soldier said sarcastically. He nodded toward Edward. "Get a move on. Walk through that gate. Don't try anything."

Another soldier came to Becky and grabbed her by her wrist, forcing her from her horse.

Pebbles barked and jumped from the sling, soon nipping at the soldier's heels as he ushered Becky through the gate.

"Kill that damned dog!" the soldier shouted at another soldier.

"No!" Becky screamed. "Don't hurt him. He—he is only defending me."

Becky wrenched herself free of the soldier's grip. She leaned down and swept Pebbles into her arms and held him protectively close. "You'll have to kill me first to get to my dog," she said, her chin held high. She glanced ahead, dying a slow death inside when she saw Edward shoved into the major's office.

"You can have the dog," the soldier growled out. "But keep him quiet, do you hear?"

"Yes, I'll do as you say," Becky said, then pleaded up at him with her eyes. "Please take me to the major's office. I want to be with my brother."

"Do you also want to join him behind bars?" the soldier said. "I can sure arrange that, you know."

"No, I just want to be there to speak in my brother's behalf," Becky said, wincing when the soldier gripped her wrist again, forcing her onward.

"Nothing no one says is going to save that stinkin' outlaw," the soldier hissed through yellowed teeth.

"He isn't an outlaw," Becky cried. "It's all a mistake. The true outlaws are out there even now wreaking havoc on the countryside. My brother is innocent. He has a diary to prove who the true culprits are."

"Just shut up," the soldier said, releasing her wrist. He gave her a shove. "And you'd best not annoy the major. He's new here. And he don't take no guff off anyone."

Becky's spine was stiff as she entered the major's office. She looked quickly over at Edward, whose arms were tied behind him as he stood before the large, paper-cluttered desk. A large, heavy-set man sat behind it, dressed in full uniform. His face was as round as a full moon. His eyes were mostly buried in the fat of his face; thick, gray brows furrowed above them. Over and over again he ran the pink tip of his tongue across his lips.

The more she listened to the major, the more her heart sank.

"Do you think I'm going to sit here and listen to

a pack of lies about you not being who I say you are?" Major Braddock said, his voice deep and gravelly. He gestured toward a lieutenant. "Take him away. Lock him up. Judge Newman will come tomorrow and hand down the sentence."

"No!" Becky cried, rushing forth. She gave Edward a quick glance, then put the palms of her hands on the desk and leaned closer to the major. "After reading the diary, how can you still accuse my brother of being the outlaw?"

"He didn't let me show it to him," Edward said, drawing Becky's eyes quickly around to him.

"What?" she gasped.

Then she glared at the major. "You are ignoring evidence that can prove my brother is not the outlaw everyone is after?" she said. "Give him a chance. Read the diary. All that you need to read are a few pages, and you will understand why my brother came to the Wyoming Territory."

"Take him away!" Major Braddock shouted, flinging an agitated hand in the air. "Take him to the guardhouse!" The muscles in his jaw were clenched. His lips were pursed in a hard, thin line.

The soldiers snapped to attention.

"No!" Becky cried as Edward was led toward the door. She felt a sick hopelessness assailing her. "You can't." She leaned down into the major's face. "If you don't look over the evidence, I'll be forced to go to the newspapers in St. Louis with the diary. I'll make sure everyone learns of what really happened and the miscarriage of justice you are perpetrating."

"All right," Major Braddock said, slouching down

into his chair. Slowly his breath whistled past his lips. He gestured toward the lieutenant. "Don't take the man away just yet. He says the diary is in his pocket. Get it. Give it to me. I'll give it a glance."

Becky sighed heavily and straightened her back as she edged closer to Edward while the lieutenant fished the diary from his pocket. She sneaked a hand over and placed it affectionately over his bound hands. She scarcely breathed as the major opened the diary and flipped the pages, taking hardly any time to read the passages.

Then he flung the diary onto his desk. "I see here the scribblings of a woman tired of her husband and family," he said, giving Becky a slow smile. "And just because she writes of having decided to join her outlaw husband in the Wyoming Territory doesn't point to who the outlaw is, or if he is the one we're after." He folded his arms across his massive chest. "I've got the only outlaw I need for a hanging." He nodded to the lieutenant. "Take him away. Lock him up."

Becky felt faint to know that the major had blatantly refused to see the truth in what was written in the diary.

She watched as Edward was taken from the office; then she glared down at the major. "You'll be sorry," she said, then turned to leave, but stopped when several soldiers came into the office in a huff.

She felt weak in the knees as she listened to another man being accused of vicious crimes.

Blazing Eagle!

Everyone had forgotten about her, so Becky stood back and listened.

"And so settlers close to our fort were attacked and killed by arrows last night, eh?" Major Braddock growled out, placing his fingertips together before him.

"Yes sir," Lieutenant Frye said, standing at attention and saluting the major. "The blame falls on either the Crow or the Cheyenne. I'd say Blazing Eagle is at fault. Rumor has it that he has had some sort of recollection about what happened to him as a child, something about a massacre. That's why I think he's responsible for these deaths. He surely went on the war path with a vengeance."

"Who can tell one Injun apart from another?" Major Braddock said, shrugging. "Let's first concentrate on the Cheyenne. Take a cavalry detail out to Blazing Eagle's village. Subdue the hostile savages. If necessary, kill everyone. Now that I'm in charge of what goes on around here, I mean to show the heathens a thing or two."

"Blazing Eagle is innocent of any crime except having been born an Indian!" Becky cried. "For this you would annihilate his people?"

Her knees shaking, fear gripping her insides, Becky ran from the office. She knew now that this Major Braddock was the sort of soldier who wished for the total extermination of the "treacherous savages". Where Indians were concerned, he was a man caught up in a raging passion that replaced reason.

Holding Pebbles in her arms, she ran across the courtyard. Although torn now between the welfare of her brother and the man she still loved with every fiber of her being, she knew that for now no one could do anything to help Edward. Not until Judge Newman came.

She would take this time to go to Blazing Eagle, to warn him of the major's orders. She knew enough of this land now to know a short cut to his village.

She would do everything within her power to head off the cavalry and warn Blazing Eagle that they were coming!

After placing her dog in his sling, Becky swung herself into the saddle.

Breathless, afraid for both men in her life, Becky swung the horse around and kicked her steed into a gallop.

She rode hard, then looked over her shoulder. She was far enough away from the fort now that she could only barely make out the soldiers as they rode through the wide gate. It was horrible to know that Fort Laramie was now in the hands of a major who was truculent and loud-mouthed and who had a raging thirst for blood and glory, with a bigot's hatred of all Indians. She had always heard that to some, killing Indians was a soldier's road to glory.

The thought sickened her.

Yanking her reins, she turned her horse right and took off through the tall grass. "Lord, let me be in time," she whispered. Her heart ached to think that Blazing Eagle might be responsible for the slayings.

Then she felt guilty, for she knew that he was not the sort to kill innocent people.

A thought came to her as fast as a whip crack, making her heart skip a beat. "Mother!" she gasped out. "Was it you? Did you and your husband's outlaw gang use bows and arrows to mislead the authorities into thinking it was Indians?"

She inhaled a quavering breath. "Surely it was," she murmured, wishing she had never found out the truth about her mother.

"Edward," she then whispered, pain circling her heart at the thought of him back at the fort, incarcerated. She felt as though she had abandoned him. He might even believe that she had!

But she couldn't abandon Blazing Eagle at the worst moment in *his* life. She had to get to him in time, then return to Edward and do everything within her power to make things right for him as well.

"Oh, if only there were two of me!" she cried to the heavens, yet knew that even under those circumstances, it was unlikely she could save either one of the two beloved men in her life!

Chapter Thirty-five

Knowing that she shouldn't be far from Blazing Eagle's village, Becky snapped her reins and sank her heels into the flanks of her horse and rode even faster.

She suddenly became aware of a horse gaining on her from behind. Knowing that it was only one horse, instead of many, made her wonder who it might be. It couldn't be the soldiers.

Then who . . . ?

She glanced over her shoulder, then took a second quick look when she recognized Judge Newman trying to catch up with her. Surely he was there for all the right reasons. He was Blazing Eagle's friend. He wouldn't want harm to come to him and his people.

Glad to have an ally on this mission of the heart, Becky reined her horse to a stop and waited for

Judge Newman. Knowing that this man would be judging her brother, she wished she had time to speak with him now about Edward. But time did not allow it.

Her heart sank when she remembered that in her haste to leave the fort she had not thought to take the diary with her. That was the evidence that could clear her brother, and now it might be lost! Surely the conniving, evil major would burn it, to keep the truth from being known by anyone else. He seemed determined to see Edward dead, no matter that he might be innocent. The major seemed hell-bent on a hanging. She wished it could be *his*!

Judge Newman reined in beside Becky. "I was summoned to the fort to prepare for a sentencing," he said, tipping his hat so that he could wipe a bead of perspiration from his brow. "When I arrived there, I discovered that Major Braddock had sent soldiers to Blazing Eagle's village. I'm on my way to stop their planned massacre." He placed his hat back on his head, his blue eyes intent on Becky. "That's where you're headed? To Blazing Eagle's village? To warn him?"

"We *must* get there before the soldiers," Becky exclaimed.

"But I don't understand what you are doing away from Blazing Eagle's village in the first place," Judge Newman said. "You're his wife. Why aren't you with him?"

"It's a long story," Becky said, nervously looking over her shoulder in the direction of Blazing Eagle's village. "I'll explain later. We must hurry onward. We don't have much time."

Judge Newman nodded, slapped his reins, and rode off with Becky. He gazed over at her. "They caught the lunatic outlaw!" he shouted. "I won't waste a minute laying down the law with him. He'll hang at sunup tomorrow."

Becky went cold inside. "No, you *can't*!" she shouted back at him over the thundering beat of the hooves. "Judge Newman, that's my brother they have incarcerated. He's innocent. Do you hear? Innocent!"

"Your brother . . . ?" Judge Newman stammered out. "Good Lord, woman, your *brother*?"

"Yes, and I've much to explain to you about why he isn't the outlaw," she said. "You've got to believe me when I say that he isn't the outlaw everyone thought he was. It was someone else!"

Damn it, *who*?" Judge Newman said back to her. "It's his likeness that's on the wanted posters. He was even recently locked up for one night at the fort, to be sentenced the next day. He escaped. Now would an innocent man escape?"

"Yes, he would if no one believed he was innocent," Becky said, her voice breaking. "Please spare me the time later to explain everything to you. I wish to prove my brother's innocence. I shall explain later who *is* the golden-haired outlaw that everyone wishes to see hang."

"I'm a fair man," Judge Newman said, nodding. "I'll listen. If you can prove his innocence, I'll set him free. If not, by damn, he'll hang faster'n a rattlesnake strikes its victims."

Becky swallowed hard. She stared at him for a

moment, then looked away. If he only knew that if he were to sentence the true outlaw to death, it would be her very own mother!

She still found that hard to believe.

But surely it was true. Edward had not wasted these past years chasing a ghost. He had been after the real thing.

"She wore a bandanna most times, to hide her identity," Becky said, not even aware that she was speaking instead of thinking. "And that day I thought I saw Edward in Cheyenne, it . . . must have been my mother."

"What's that you say?" Judge Newman said, leaning closer to her.

Becky paled. She gave him a half glance. "Nothing," she said. "I was thinking out loud. That's all."

He questioned her with his eyes, then turned his attention back to the reason he was there. His heart pounded out the miles, hoping that he would be in time.

He glanced over at Becky again. He hoped *they* would be in time. He admired this woman's courage. Her fire.

And he now knew what had drawn her from Blazing Eagle's village.

Her brother.

She had gone to the fort to defend her brother.

But he was puzzled as to why Blazing Eagle had not accompanied her there, if her brother, in truth, was innocent. Blazing Eagle wanted justice done. And if this man who was behind bars was not the criminal, he would have been at Becky's side, fighting for the freedom of the wrongly accused man.

Then his thoughts went to another man accused wrongly. Blazing Eagle! His people! Even the Crow. The most recent killing was the work of white criminals trying to make it look like the work of Indians. He had seen it countless times before. He just couldn't understand why the major was so hell-bent on killing Indians for the crime.

Unless he had a deep-seated hate for Indians.

If so, he had no place in Wyoming, where white men and red men were struggling to learn to live together. Of course, there were renegades who still fought the system. But not Blazing Eagle. He was a peace-loving man. He would never slaughter innocent white people. He saw no gain in such actions.

When the village came in sight, Becky's heart raced and her throat went dry. She had been sent away. Would she be welcomed back? After Blazing Eagle knew why she was there, surely he would accept her back into his life. She had come to help save him and his people! She was proving her loyalty to them.

She hoped she would soon discover why he had seen the need to send her away, to push her from his life.

Several warriors on horseback suddenly appeared from the thick brush. They flanked Becky and Judge Newman and rode with them.

"Why are you here?" Fish Hawk asked, looking from Judge Newman to Becky. The other warriors said nothing with their tongues, but their eyes spoke their disdain. "Why do you two ride together? I saw a desperation in the way you were riding, and in your eyes."

Neither Judge Newman nor Becky slowed their pace. "Fish Hawk, hurry to your village and warn Blazing Eagle that the white pony soldiers from Fort Laramie are on their way to attack his village," Judge Newman shouted over the thundering hooves of the horses. "The Cheyenne are being blamed for a recent raid on settlers where many deaths occurred. The soldiers are wrong! I am here to speak in your behalf!"

He glanced over at Becky, who seemed strangely quiet in the company of the Cheyenne, then looked back at Fish Hawk again.

"This woman, your chief's wife, is also here to help do what she can," he quickly added.

Fish Hawk glowered at Becky, gave Judge Newman a nod, then rode off with his other warriors toward the village.

Judge Newman sighed. "We are in time," he said, relieved. "The Cheyenne have time now to ward off the attack in their own way."

He peered with a raised eyebrow at Becky. "I saw something in the way Fish Hawk looked at you. Something is not right between you and the Cheyenne," he said. "Do you wish to tell me about it?"

"Later," Becky said solemnly. "When I speak to you about my brother, I shall also tell you how I was sent away from my husband's village. By then I hope to have answers myself as to why. I still hope that he will ask me back."

"He sent you away?" Judge Newman gasped. "There must be a reason, for I know how much the man loves you."

"I hope he still loves me," Becky said, her eyes

wavering into his. "But right now, my concerns are only for my husband and his people. Many soldiers must have been sent from the fort."

"But they can't outnumber the Cheyenne," Judge Newman said, smiling. "Of late, the numbers have lessened at the fort. Under Major Kent's supervision, a huge number of soldiers were not needed at the fort. They were dispersed elsewhere. Major Braddock mistakenly did not increase that number, which he should have since he has chosen the path of war instead of peace."

"And now that Blazing Eagle knows of the attack, he can ready himself for it," Becky said, sighing heavily. "Thank God we are in time."

Becky's heart skipped a beat when she recognized Blazing Eagle on a horse, riding toward her and Judge Newman. When he drew up next to them and rode beside Becky, his eyes were heavy with emotions she wished she understood.

Her thoughts were scrambled. Was he glad to see her? Did he regret sending her away? Would he ask her to return? Or had he already divorced her?

She knew that she wasn't going to learn the answers to any of her questions just yet. He had come only to usher her and Judge Newman safely into his village. She hoped that he would speak his heart to her later. He did not even have to apologize for sending her away. She would be so happy just to know that he wanted her again.

"Follow me!" Blazing Eagle said, raising a fist in the air.

Becky followed alongside Judge Newman as Blazing Eagle broke away from them and rode on ahead. When they entered the village, Becky scarcely breathed as she looked guardedly around her. She was not sure how the people would accept her since they had seen their chief send her away.

But she soon realized that she didn't have that to worry about. The women and children were in the safe confines of their lodges. The warriors were hiding somewhere, awaiting the arrival of the soldiers.

Judge Newman reined in his horse and slid quickly from his saddle. He went to Becky and helped her from her horse.

She grabbed Pebbles, then stood stiffly when Judge Newman tried to usher her away, toward Waterfall's lodge, as Blazing Eagle dismounted, silently watching.

She turned to Blazing Eagle and gazed up at him. "I mean to stay with you," she said, lifting her chin stubbornly. "I have come to help you. I mean to be at your side and do what I can to help."

She placed Pebbles on the ground. Familiar with everything, he ran off toward Waterfall's lodge, barking and wagging his tail.

"You will only be in the way," Blazing Eagle said flatly as he stared down at Becky. "Go. Stay with the other women."

"But, Blazing Eagle—" she said, her voice quavering.

"I do not want you to get hurt in a possible crossfire," Blazing Eagle said, placing a gentle hand on her cheek. "My woman, my *wife*, you are my life."

"Do you mean that?" Becky said, but was interrupted by Blazing Eagle.

"I was wrong to send you away," he said thickly. "I cannot blame you for what others have done in the past to the Cheyenne. I was wrong to place you with those who came and massacred my people those many winters ago. Although the woman had hair as golden as yours, and a face that seemed made by the angels, you are nothing to her, no kin, so I cannot blame you for the part she had in the murder of my family."

Becky paled. When she eventually told him that the woman was her mother, would he then send her away again?

But she must tell him. Soon everyone would know. When it came out at her brother's trial, the word would spread like wildfire.

And she would not let the fact that everyone knew cause her to lower her eyes with shame. Her mother was nothing to her. She had never even known her!

The sound of thundering hoofbeats rumbling across the land as the column of soldiers swept into sight in the distance made Becky and Blazing Eagle turn and stare at their approach.

Blazing Eagle's eyes shone with intense hatred when he saw that the troops rode with their carbines at their hips, not holstered as they would be on a peaceful mission.

Blazing Eagle then turned to Becky. "You *must* join the women!" he said, his voice a deep command.

Becky nodded and ran toward Waterfall's lodge. Waterfall met her approach and grabbed her hand. They ran inside Waterfall's lodge, clinging.

"It is so good to be with you again," Waterfall murmured.

Becky swept Pebbles up into her arms to keep him from running from the lodge to bark and snarl at the soldiers. She then stood beside Waterfall and watched history being made as Judge Newman walked toward the approaching soldiers, appearing as though he was weaponless.

Blazing Eagle and Fish Hawk went with Judge Newman, bold and courageous in the face of the approaching enemy as they blocked the soldiers' entrance into the village.

The soldiers drew a tight rein a few feet away from Judge Newman, Blazing Eagle, and Fish Hawk.

"What the hell do you think you're doing?" Lieutenant Frye said. He glowered down at the judge, then turned slow eyes to the two Indians, lingering longer on the chief.

"Step aside or get trampled!" Lieutenant Frye ground out.

"I don't think you want to do that," Judge Newman said flatly. He balled his fists and planted them on his hips. "I am personal friends with the president, or have you forgotten? If anything happens to me today while you have come to wrongly attack the Cheyenne, you will be the one to pay. You won't only be court-martialed, you'll hang."

"We are here at the orders of Major Braddock," Lieutenant Frye said, gripping the handle of his sabre more tightly. "You don't have any authority to stop us."

Judge Newman yanked a pistol from beneath his

coat. He aimed it at the lieutenant. No one offered to stop him, for he already had his pistol cocked and ready for firing. "Don't dare come any closer to the Cheyenne village, or by damn, you'll be the first one to die," he said to the lieutenant. "Just turn around and return to the fort. I'll make things right for you when I wire the president."

"I don't give a hang what you say. Step *aside*," the lieutenant said, his eyes glittering recklessly.

"Do you want to die?" Judge Newman said, his lips set in a smug smile. "If so, proceed. But you'd best first listen to what I have to say."

"Speak your mind, *then* step aside," the lieutenant snarled. "I've come to follow orders. I intend to do as I was told."

"The white man has again unjustly, *wrongly*, accused the Cheyenne *and* the Crow of acts which outlaws are responsible for," Judge Newman said, his voice tight. "Your presence here is illegal. You arc in violation of the treaty signed with the Indians!"

"To hell with treaties," Lieutenant Frye said, waving his saber in the air. He swung it threateningly close to Judge Newman, just missing his face. "Treaties are made to be broken. Especially with Injuns." He leaned closer to Judge Newman. "Now step aside, or the next time I won't miss with my saber."

"You swing that damn thing near me again and I'll blow your head off," Judge Newman said, taking a daring step closer to the lieutenant's horse.

"You stupid idiot," Lieutenant Frye growled out, then paled and went wide-eyed when all of Blazing

Eagle's warriors stepped out into the open, their firearms aimed at the soldiers.

Blazing Eagle moved to Judge Newman's side again. He glared up at Lieutenant Frye. "White men, I have made good on my oath to the white chief in Washington. Now *leave*," he said, his rifle aimed at the heart of the lieutenant. "If you do not leave, your white scalps will be taken and thrown away like so much horse skin!"

There was a silence, then Lieutenant Frye slid his saber into its sheath. Trapped and at the Indians' mercy, he pried his index finger between his tight collar and thin neck. He then turned to his men and shouted the command to retreat.

Becky ran from Waterfall's lodge as the soldiers rode away. She ran into Blazing Eagle's arms.

Blazing Eagle held his rifle away from her as he swept one arm around her waist. Their lips met in a frenzied kiss.

Judge Newman slipped his pistol inside his holster. His gaze went to Waterfall when he felt her eyes on him. Their eyes met and held; then, slowly, they smiled.

Blazing Eagle eased from Becky's arms, touched her face gently, and turned to Judge Newman.

"Many thanks, my friend," he said, reaching his free hand out for the judge. "What you did today, as you spoke in my people's behalf, will always be remembered. Stay for a smoke and council. Later we will have a feast in your honor." He turned warm eyes to Becky. "And also my woman's. She, too, came with a warning of the planned attack."

"Yes, she is a fine, brave lady," Judge Newman

said, smiling at Becky. Then his smile faded as he looked over at Blazing Eagle. "But I can't stay, Blazing Eagle. I must wire the President of this planned atrocity. Major Braddock must be replaced by someone who is more level-headed. I must be there to receive the reply and see that his orders are carried out."

Becky paled when she suddenly recalled something else that Judge Newman had to do. Hand down a sentence on her brother! She had to be there to make sure her brother's rights were protected!

She looked quickly at Blazing Eagle. What if he wouldn't understand why she had to leave again, this time by her own choosing?

Judge Newman embraced Blazing Eagle, gave Waterfall a smile, and walked toward his horse.

Becky stiffened, not sure how she could handle this with Blazing Eagle, but she knew she had no choice but to tell him that she had to leave.

"Judge Newman," she shouted, drawing his attention. He turned to her with a questioning in his eyes. "Wait. I'll ride back with you to the fort."

Blazing Eagle's lips parted in a slight gasp as he stared at Becky.

"Blazing Eagle, I have no choice but to return to the fort with Judge Newman," she murmured. She swallowed hard, knowing how he felt about her brother. "My brother is incarcerated at the fort. He will stand trial soon, perhaps even tomorrow. I must be there for him. Please understand."

Wooden-faced, Blazing Eagle listened.

"You will speak in a ruthless outlaw's behalf?" he

gasped. "He does not deserve such loyalty. Not even from a sister."

"He is innocent," Becky said, looking up at him with pleading eyes. "I have proof that my brother isn't the outlaw. Please trust me. I shall return, if you want me, once the trial is over and my brother is set free."

Blazing Eagle set his jaw and clenched his lips together as he glowered at Becky.

When he said nothing to her, Becky shuffled her feet nervously. She knew the importance of getting back to the fort as soon as possible. Especially since the soldiers had been turned away. If they arrived at the fort and stirred up the major's wrath, then all hell could break loose.

"I must leave," Becky said, her voice quavering. "But I'll return as soon as I can."

Still Blazing Eagle said nothing. He stood mute as he stared down at her.

"I *will* return," Becky said softly. "That is, if you haven't divorced me."

Still he said nothing to her.

Becky stared up at him a moment longer, then bent over and grabbed Pebbles into her arms. When Waterfall brought her horse to her, Becky placed Pebbles in his sling, then swung herself into the saddle.

She took one last look at Blazing Eagle, then rode away with Judge Newman, feeling as though she had just severed her ties with Blazing Eagle.

Tears pooled in her eyes as she rode in a hard gallop alongside Judge Newman. She just hoped that she could save her brother.

She just hoped that she could return to Blazing Eagle again, and all would be forgiven!

Chapter Thirty-six

In the early dawn hours, when the world seemed coated in grey and the sky lacked definition, Becky sat in the courtroom at Fort Laramie.

Shadows pooled in the corners of the room; a lone lamp shone its faint light upon the face of her brother as he sat with his back to the room. Judge Newman paced the floor, his lips drawn tight.

With his right hand, Judge Newman pulled his gold watch from his vest pocket. He noted the time, then gazed toward the door.

He sighed with relief when the replacement for Major Braddock sauntered into the room in full uniform. His neatly groomed brown hair fell over the glittering gold epaulets that decorated his blue tunic.

More gold braid and tassels spilled down his chest, while broad gold stripes gleamed at his cuffs.

A young man direct from West Point, his face was youthful, his eyes warm and friendly.

Luckily, it had not taken the President long to order Major Braddock from the premises. In fact, he had passed down the order only 24 hours after receiving Judge Newman's wire.

The President had sided with judge Newman in feeling that there had been enough bloodshed in the Wyoming Territory. They most certainly didn't need a hot-headed, bigoted major at Fort Laramie.

Becky watched the new young major take his place in a chair across the aisle from her brother. She clenched and unclenched her hands, concerned that there was no attorney there to speak in behalf of Edward.

As she had feared, Major Braddock had destroyed the diary in which lay the solid proof of why her brother had been in the Wyoming Territory.

Her thoughts momentarily strayed to Blazing Eagle. She felt a searing pain to think that she might have lost him forever now. Would he ever understand that for these few hours, her brother had to come first in her life?

Although Edward had abandoned her these past several years, there was no way she would abandon him. He had disappeared for a purpose. And she would fight today, tooth and nail, to keep him from being hanged.

She glanced up at Judge Newman as he shoved his watch back inside his vest pocket. Her eyes followed him as he stepped behind a desk and laid his law book down beside the kerosene lamp, now slowly turning the pages.

Becky nervously bit her lower lip. Had she wasted her time pleading her brother's case after she had returned to the fort with Judge Newman? She thought that he had believed her at the time.

But now? As the large chime clock on the wall ticked the time away, she wasn't sure about anything.

She looked over her shoulder. Only a few settlers were in attendance. There were also a few soldiers, among them those who had witnessed the atrocities left behind by the golden-haired outlaw.

None had actually seen the outlaw face to face.

But several dying settlers had described the one who had led the massacre. It was the golden-haired outlaw who had been described.

But there was one positive thing in her brother's favor. The outlaw had always worn a bandanna to hide his identity. It was the hair that everyone remembered. The long, golden, flowing hair as he rode away, his firearms smoking.

And also *she* was in Edward's favor. She would talk until hell froze over to finally convince everyone of her brother's innocence.

If only she had the diary, she thought bitterly to herself. If only . . .

Judge Newman cleared his throat and banged his gavel against the top of the desk, not only interrupting Becky's thoughts, but causing her to jump. Wild-eyed, she looked up at the judge, then at her brother, whose back was to her.

"Edward, stand and turn so that everyone can take a good look at you as I speak," Judge Newman said, his eyes momentarily locking with Becky's.

Edward turned around and looked slowly from person to person, then held his gaze on Becky, who smiled sweetly up at him. He squared his shoulders and returned the smile.

Stroking his jaw, Judge Newman slowly scanned the faces of those who were there to hear the sentencing. "Take a good look at this man," he said flatly. "After a short investigation, I now know for certain that this man isn't responsible for Major Kent's death. Is there anyone among you who can say you actually saw him doing the other deeds of which he is accused? Did you see his face? Was it as plain as day to you so that you can truly say he is guilty of the crimes accused?"

Becky still watched Edward, her heart warming through and through when he smiled at her again. She felt that his goodness would show through in such a smile. How could anyone lie and say that they had seen his face clearly, when they had not?

"Now listen carefully to what I have to say," Judge Newman said, slipping his hands into the front pockets of his dark breeches. "Would you say it was possible that the golden-haired outlaw could have been a woman?"

He placed a hand out before him when he heard gasping sounds. "Now don't be hasty in your reply," he said, smiling slowly. "Just imagine it now; the long and flowing golden hair worn beneath a wide-brimmed hat. The bandanna hiding the facial features. The stocky build."

He looked from person to person, and Becky's heart thumped to know where he was going with this, and that he surely *did* believe that a woman could have done these crimes. Why else would he be trying to place that picture in the minds of those who were listening?

She smiled at Judge Newman when he glanced her way, then twined her fingers together and placed them comfortably on her lap. She was relaxed now. She felt that things were going to be all right.

"I am imagining a woman who has grown muscled from a hard living so that she might have the build of a man," Judge Newman said, settling down on the edge of the desk. "I can believe it is a woman *if* she happened to marry an outlaw, then became drawn into the criminal life out of the need to be with her husband. I see a woman who was restless and whose children meant nothing to her when she fell out of love with the children's father, lured into the arms of a bragging, lying outlaw."

Judge Newman paused, then went and stood in front of Edward. "Isn't that how it happened, young man?" he asked. "Your mother left your father? She came to the Wyoming Territory to be with her outlaw lover? She became an outlaw in her own right? She is even now the head of an outlaw gang? Isn't it so that the golden-haired outlaw *is* your mother?"

Edward paled. He swallowed hard, then looked the judge directly in the eye. "Yes, that's how it happened," he said, his voice breaking. "That's how it *is*."

"And why are *you* in the Wyoming Territory, Edward?" Judge Newman went on. "Isn't it to hunt down this woman who abandoned you as a child?"

"Yes, exactly," Edward said, then looked past

Judge Newman with a start when one of the settlers, a woman whose face was gaunt and whose
breasts hung long and flaccid beneath her soiled
cotton dress, began shouting.

"He's lying!" she screamed, waving a fist in the
air. "How could you believe such hogwash as that?
That man. I saw him! I know he's the outlaw that
came and killed my children and husband. He stole
my cattle. He's that very same damned outlaw!
Don't waste no more time on him. Hang him!"

Edward stepped around the judge and stared at
the woman. "Ma'am, you couldn't have seen me,
'cause I wasn't there," he said, his voice drawn. "I've
never committed any crime in my lifetime. Think
about it. You *know* you didn't see me."

"It was you!" she screamed. When she lunged out
of her chair, it took two soldiers to keep her from
attacking Edward.

"Order!" Judge Newman said, banging his gavel
against the top of the desk. "Let's have order in this
courtroom!"

Tears streamed down Becky's cheeks as she
gazed up at Edward and saw the defeat in his eyes
just before he hung his head. She was grateful to
the judge when he went to Edward and patted him
on the back, then led him down onto his chair.

Judge Newman stood before the crowd again; a
strained hush now enveloped the room.

"Usually I find it easy to hand down the sentence
of hanging to heartless criminals," Judge Newman
said, now pacing slowly back and forth before the
people, his hands clasped behind him. "But this
time is different. *I* see this man as innocent. No one

has absolute proof that he is a criminal. Yet I don't have any absolute proof that he *isn't*, except that when both he and his sister told me about their mother, who is the criminal that everyone wishes to see hang, I found I believed them."

He stopped pacing and gazed at Edward with warm, friendly, and trusting eyes. "Do you have anything else to say before the decree of this court is carried out?"

"I would like to speak my mind in my son's defense," a throaty, tired voice said as the door opened at the back of the room, spilling a rectangle of light onto the floor.

Everyone turned and stared toward the doorway.

Judge Newman squinted his eyes, then took a step forward when out of the doorway stepped a tall, muscled, stiff-lipped woman, dressed in man's clothing. Her hair was as golden as wheat. When she stepped fully into the light so that everyone could see her, gasps rippled around the room.

Becky rose quickly from the chair. She grabbed for it when she felt suddenly faint at seeing the woman she knew was her mother. This woman was larger and more muscular than she was, but the hair, the green eyes, and the facial features, which had once been soft and beautiful, were a mirror of Becky's.

Edward's creaky, straight-backed chair clattered to the floor as his mother slowly made her way down the aisle, alone. When their eyes met, and he saw no emotion in hers, he felt dizzy. Finally he had come face to face with the woman who had abandoned him and his sister all those years ago.

"Mother?" Edward said, taking slow steps toward her. Becky moved to his side and clutched his hand.

Claire Veach Myers crudely, unfeelingly, stepped around them and went to stand before the judge. "I hear there's soon to be a hanging," she said, holding her chin high.

"Well, not exactly," Judge Newman said dryly. "I was about to exonerate this young man and set him free." His eyes slowly raked over her, finding it hard to believe that she was truly there in the flesh.

And by God, he thought to himself, it was true. This woman, who had the build of a man, had to be the outlaw everyone hated with a passion.

Claire glanced over her shoulder at Edward, then faced the judge again. "Word spread that my son was going to hang," she said, her voice drawn. "I had no idea he was in these parts until yesterday." She looked at Edward again, then slid a slow look Becky's way. "Nor my daughter, whom I have not seen since the very day of her birth.

"I've come today to set things right in my life," Claire said. "My husband, George, died a few months ago. Him not ridin' with me and our gang makes it no longer exciting. It's become humdrum. So I came today not only to save my son's life, but to give my life up for him. It's about time I did somethin' decent for someone."

"After how many killings, ma'am, did you decide to do this?" Judge Newman said sarcastically. "Or did you give yourself up because you thought just possibly the sentencing might go lighter on you?"

"Think what you want to think," Claire said, shrugging. "I'm here. That should be all that matters. I'm ready to die. Life without my George ain't no life at all. Hang me."

Judge Newman kneaded his chin. "Now maybe that just might be too easy," he said, chuckling. "Maybe I'll sentence you to life in prison. Prison life is sometimes a worse punishment than dying by hanging."

"Hang her!" the crowd began chanting. "Hang her! Hang her!"

Judge Newman pounded his gavel on the desk to silence everyone. "I do the sentencing here!" he shouted. "And I *do* sentence this lady to life imprisonment. She'll be taken away to California tomorrow!"

He glowered at the woman. "Where's the rest of your men?" he grumbled out.

"They ran off in all directions," Claire said, smiling smugly. "There's no way you'd ever catch 'em."

"Having you is enough," Judge Newman said, folding his arms across his chest. He looked over at Becky, then at Edward. "Does my sentence please you?"

Becky silently nodded.

Edward took a step toward his mother and glared into her eyes. "And to think that both Becky and I laid flowers on your grave when there wasn't even anyone there to mourn," he hissed. "When I read your diary and knew the truth, I was sick at heart for days. God, I'm so glad that I came out here and forced your hand. You are a heartless, murdering bitch."

Claire paled. "Even if I did come to save your life by confessing?" she gasped out.

"Do you think that one act of heroism erases everything you did these past years, as though you didn't do any of those heinous acts?" Edward said. He reached out a hand and led Becky to his side. "*She's* the reason I'm being set free. Not *you*."

Edward drew Becky closer to him. "Mother, meet your *daughter*," he said.

A commotion at the back of the room drew Becky and Edward apart. They turned just as Fish Hawk stumbled into the room, gasping for breath.

"Becky, Judge Newman, come with me," Fish Hawk said, staggering toward Becky. "Everyone at the village is ill. We . . . ate tainted flour that trappers gave to us. All of the people are ill. Blazing Eagle, Waterfall, and Whistling Elk are the worst!"

Claire cackled, drawing attention her way again. "You stupid fools," she said, her eyes gleaming. "That wasn't settlers. That was my gang. They planned it well, didn't they? They decided to kill off a few Injuns before disbanding." She frowned. "Seems the flour didn't have enough strychnine in it after all."

Becky stood numbly listening, then she lunged toward her mother and wrestled her to the floor.

Edward took Becky by one arm and forced her away from their mother. "Sis, forget her," he said. "Don't put yourself on her same level by acting like her."

"You're needed at Blazing Eagle's village," Fish Hawk said, gazing at Becky.

Becky wiped her eyes. She looked up at Edward. "Please come with me?" she murmured.

Edward nodded. "Sis, if that's what you want,

yes, I'll go with you," he said, hugging her when she flung herself into his arms.

Judge Newman handed out orders, and Claire was taken away. Then he left the room and quickly mounted his horse as Becky's and Edward's horses were led to them.

Soon they rode from Fort Laramie, Fish Hawk hardly able to stay in his saddle. He swayed, yet kept a firm enough grip as he rode at Becky's right side.

Becky's insides were in a turmoil. She would never forget this day.

Never!

But although it would take some time to forget the pain of what had happened today, she was glad to put this business of her mother behind her.

Now if only she could do something to help Blazing Eagle!

If only he would *allow* it.

If he no longer considered her his wife, what then would she do once she reached the village and saw him so ill?

She firmed her chin, determined not to allow him to send her away again!

Chapter Thirty-seven

Becky's horse had not even come to a complete stop when she slid from the saddle in front of Blazing Eagle's lodge. She could hear moans and groans surfacing from all around her in the village, but her main focus was on Blazing Eagle, Whistling Elk, and Waterfall. They were all three so very precious to her. Should one of them die, that would make the shame that she felt over her mother twofold.

She shuddered, knowing that she would remember her mother's strange cackling laughter for the remainder of her life.

Breathless, Becky ran into Blazing Eagle's lodge. She stopped and paled when she found not only Blazing Eagle and Whistling Elk stretched out on the floor, moaning and clutching at their stomachs, but also Waterfall.

Her gaze swept to the fire pit. She died a slow

death inside when she saw the stack of fried bread that Waterfall had made from the tainted flour. Each loaf of bread was as big as a plate. They looked so nice and brown, they would lure anyone to feast upon them.

She covered her mouth with her hand and held back a sob when she saw the pieces of bread that had been partially eaten.

Tears streaming from her eyes, Becky ran to Blazing Eagle and knelt down beside him. As she lifted his head onto her lap, he gazed up at her with eyes that seemed to be spinning.

"Blazing Eagle," she murmured, a sob lodging in her throat. "Lord . . . lord. . . . "

She glanced over at Waterfall and saw her lying pale and still on the blankets spread across the floor of the lodge, Whistling Elk next to her. She could tell by the position in which they lay that Waterfall had cradled Whistling Elk's head on her lap until she had become too ill herself to sit and comfort him.

Judge Newman came rushing into the lodge. He gasped and took a shaky step backwards when he saw just how ill everyone was. His eyes locked with Becky's as she gazed up at him.

"Are they going to die?" she asked, her voice breaking.

"By the looks of things, I imagine they wish they would," Judge Newman said, sighing heavily.

"What can we do for them?" Becky asked, gazing down at Blazing Eagle, who seemed not even to realize that she was there.

"Their shaman is also ill," Judge Newman said,

falling to his knees beside Waterfall. "And there are no medical doctors for miles. I think the closest one is in Cheyenne."

His fingers gently touched Waterfall's brow, then he felt Whistling Elk's. "They have no fever." He looked over at Becky. "Check to see if Blazing Eagle has a fever."

Becky placed a trembling hand across his brow, finding it damp to the touch, but not abnormally hot. "No, he doesn't either," she said.

"I'll go to the river and get fresh water," Judge Newman said, rushing to his feet. He grabbed a bladder bag and left at a run.

Blazing Eagle moaned and tossed his head from side to side. He was aware of voices, yet the sound seemed to come from deep down in a tunnel.

He could feel a soft hand on his brow, and then on his face. He could hear a soft voice. But he did not know whose hands or whose voice.

The earth seemed to rock and move beneath him.

It gave a sharp turn and kept on turning.

As he gazed up at the face that hovered over him like a sentinel, the face seemed turned upside down.

The face was under him!

"Blazing Eagle, darling, please get well," Becky cried when she saw that he still did not actually see *her*, but something else quite unreal and unnatural as his arms now swung back and forth in the air.

She reached for his arms and gently held them down, then bent a soft kiss to his lips. "It's Becky," she murmured. "I've come home, Blazing Eagle. I've come home to stay if you will have me."

The voice, Blazing Eagle thought to himself. It was getting clearer. It was so soft. It was so comforting.

He tried to focus on the face. Slowly the blur seemed to be lifting. Inch by inch, the face was becoming more distinct. The room seemed not to be spinning as much now. And the ache in his belly that had sent him to the floor was not as gripping.

As he became more aware of things, he realized that whatever had made him ill had left him weak, but he was finally lucid enough to see that it was his wife who sat in his lodge, comforting him.

"Becky?" Blazing Eagle mumbled, his throat dry, his lips parched. "You are home?"

"Blazing Eagle," Becky cried, bending low to cradle his head on her bosom. "You're going to be all right. Thank God, you are not going to die."

"Die?" Blazing Eagle said. He leaned up on one elbow. Fear gripped his insides when he caught sight of Waterfall and Whistling Elk, who still lay so lifeless and pale on the floor.

"They are dead?" he said, his voice tormented.

"No, but they are just as ill from the fry bread as you have been," Becky said. She looked quickly up at Judge Newman when he came into the lodge with the fresh river water.

Judge Newman poured the water into two wooden basins. He handed one to Becky and kept one for himself. Gently, meditatingly, he caressed Waterfall's brow with a cool compress, then Whistling Elk's.

Too weak too stay on his elbow for long, Blazing Eagle crumpled back down and closed his eyes as

Becky ministered to him by caressing his brow with a wet, cool cloth.

"I believe now that this will soon pass," Becky said, her eyes never leaving Blazing Eagle as he occasionally gave her a quiet glance. "Blazing Eagle, I'm so sorry you are so ill."

"You mentioned tainted fry bread?" he said thickly.

"Yes, Blazing Eagle, it was from the flour that was used in the bread," Becky quietly explained. "Those men who came pretending to be friends? Trappers? In truth, they were a part of a disbanding outlaw gang who decided to have some last fun before going their separate ways."

"And . . . how . . . do *you* know this?" he asked guardedly.

Becky swallowed hard and looked away from him for a moment, then gazed down at him with wavering eyes. "How do I know?" she murmured. "Because my mother told me that she knew they were going to do this, that they were going to bring flour to your people that was tainted with strychnine."

Blazing Eagle moved shakily to an elbow again. "Your mother?" he said, his voice hollow.

"Yes, Blazing Eagle, my mother," she said, her voice breaking. "I have so much to tell you. But I should wait until you are stronger."

"Tell me now," he said, his heart glad when he realized that both his son and Waterfall were now awake and talking softly with Judge Newman. That had to mean that the rest of his people would be all right also.

"First I need to know something," Becky said, placing a gentle hand to his cheek and feeling him flinch slightly at her touch.

"That is?" he said, his strength returning with each heartbeat.

"I am back with you in your village," Becky murmured. "Am I welcome? Can I stay? Am I still your wife?"

"There are many things that trouble me about you being my wife," Blazing Eagle said, his eyes squinting into hers.

"I know," she said, nodding. "And I understand. But, Blazing Eagle, none of those things were of my doing. It just happens that my family does not have the best of history now since it is a known fact that my mother led the outlaw gang that massacred your people long ago."

"It was not your brother?"

"I told you before that it wasn't my brother. And I understand why you found it so hard to believe."

Edward came suddenly into the lodge. His eyes met and held with Blazing Eagle's, then he looked slowly over at Becky. "Am I welcome in your husband's lodge?" he asked.

Becky gazed at Blazing Eagle. "Only if *I* am welcome," she murmured. "And only if I am still Blazing Eagle's wife. Is that so, Blazing Eagle? Am I welcome? Am I still your wife? Is my brother welcome now that you know that he is not the outlaw you thought him to be for so long?"

Blazing Eagle's jaw tightened as he continued to glare up at Edward, and then his eyes softened and he reached a hand out for him. "Come and sit with us," he said softly. "This chief is too weak just yet to stand and welcome you in the traditional manner."

Edward sat down. "I checked everyone in your village," he said. "Most are quite ill, but none will die."

"And it was your mother who knew this would be done to my people?" Blazing Eagle said, looking from Becky to Edward.

"Yes," they said in unison, as though they were one voice, one heartbeat.

"And how do you know this?" Blazing Eagle said, welcoming Whistling Elk as he came and cuddled next to him. Out of the corner of his eye he saw Judge Newman cradle Waterfall in his arms, as though love was blossoming between them.

"Our mother made an appearance at my brother's trial. She gave herself up to the law," Becky said, still finding that hard to believe. "She confessed, Blazing Eagle. All these years, when everyone thought it was a man with golden hair riding with the outlaws, it was my mother. After her husband died, she became the gang leader."

She went into further details so that no questions about her mother would be left unanswered once this night was over. She wanted to put it behind her. Now and forever!

"Then she was the golden-haired woman who carried me to safety when the rest of my people had been slain?" Blazing Eagle said, weaving his fingers through his son's thick black hair.

"Yes, at that time she was not so much an active part of the outlaw gang," Becky murmured. "She rode with her husband. I guess it didn't take much for her to learn the wickedness of outlawing and practiced it well."

Blazing Eagle was quiet for a moment, in his mind's eye recalling that day as though it had happened yesterday. When he remembered now, he remembered every second of that day, not only in bits and pieces. And now the memories stayed with him.

But now when he remembered, he would no longer hold his wife in any way responsible only because she reminded him of that fateful day. Her heart was as pure as an early day in spring.

For years now, the golden-haired outlaw had been a torment for him and his people, as well as the white community. But now, the true outlaw was incarcerated. Blazing Eagle was free of the torment brought on by this devilish woman.

His wife was also free of her past, a past that had only recently caught up with her.

Yet he knew from experience that only because something had come to an end did not mean that it was gone from one's memory that fast. It seemed to him that his wife had more to get over than he.

And he wished to be the one to comfort her when the knowledge of who her true mother was hurt too much. Helping her would also help himself. Together they would conquer their tormented pasts!

Fish Hawk came into the lodge, a young and beautiful woman helping him as she held onto his elbow. "Blazing Eagle, I had to see for myself that you had recovered," Fish Hawk said, his voice weak and trembling.

"We are well enough," Blazing Eagle said, gesturing with a hand toward Fish Hawk and the woman. "Come. Sit with us."

Blazing Eagle smiled up at White Water. "Your father?" he said. "Did he come for council?"

"Yes, and we found you all so ill," White Water murmured. "He is outside now helping others."

"He is a good man," Blazing Eagle said. "We will have council when I am stronger."

White Water helped Fish Hawk down beside the fire. Fish Hawk gave Becky a questioning stare, unnerving her.

"My wife is here now forever to fill my heart and home with her sunshine," Blazing Eagle quickly explained. "You were right to go for her so that she could be at my side at such a time as this."

Fish Hawk nodded silently.

"Father, what happened to make us so ill?" Whistling Elk asked, gazing wistfully up at him. "It all . . . happened so quickly."

Blazing Eagle's and Becky's eyes met and held.

He let her explain everything again, and while listening to her soft voice and hearing the caring in it that she held for his son, he knew that he was blessed to have her and felt so foolish for having sent her away!

Never would he be so foolish again!

Chapter Thirty-eight

The "robe season" had passed. It was spring. The Cheyenne women had renewed their lodges, which now stood white and pure in the morning light.

The grass was green. The wildflowers dotted the land in a tapestry of colors. In the trees, the combination of oaks and pine was a favorite haunt of a large-billed yellow bird, the spearfish.

It was a time of new beginnings, but there was much tension in the world of the Cheyenne, for a man named Custer had arrived in Shaiyena country. It was rumored that one day soon he would take up his saber against the whole Cheyenne nation. Blazing Eagle was restless. He did not walk among his people with a peaceful heart.

And being the sort who did not ride down the path of war, he had already told his people that before the next snows began to fall, they would be in the northern land called Canada.

It was not because he was giving up his land that easily, the land they called Shaiyena.

It was because Blazing Eagle did not want to sacrifice any of his people to gain fame for the warmonger white leader.

And he was sad over the loss of Fish Hawk, who had married White Water and taken up his belongings and moved to her village.

This was the first time that Blazing Eagle had been apart from his best friend for so long, and he missed his camaradship during the hunt and all things that friends shared.

Becky sat beside the fire, beading. Her eyes strayed often to Blazing Eagle, who sat opposite the fire from her. He was working on his arrows, filing the sheet-iron arrowpoints to sharp edges, whetting them on a smooth river pebble.

Ribs broiled on a stake jammed into the ground near the edge of the flames, filling the lodge with its tantalizing aroma.

"You are so intent today on what you are doing," Becky said, shaking her hair back from her shoulders. "I know you don't like the idea of having to move north. But darling, I thought you had reconciled yourself to the fact that we were. Are you worrying about something else?"

"My mind is a storehouse of too many things that bring sadness to my heart," Blazing Eagle said, his eyes wavering into Becky's as he looked over at her.

Then he watched his hands at work again. "Too often now I find no answers in my heart where the white pony soldiers are concerned," he said sadly.

"And my heart is heavy over missing Fish Hawk's companionship. But today my attention is on my weapon. The arrows I am fashioning today will have range and penetration they did not have with stone or bone points."

"I see," Becky said, nodding.

"And also I am thinking about Whistling Elk," Blazing Eagle said, pausing in his work to glance toward the opened entrance flap. "He left today for the hills to participate in *a-wu-wun*, to fast for four nights. While there, he prays to receive a special vision. If his dreams are favorable, he will return home no longer a boy, but a man."

"Tell me about it," Becky said, laying her beading aside.

"He must find a place of his choice high on a hill on the right side of the river," Blazing Eagle said, in his mind's eye seeing where he had been blessed himself with his first vision. It had been back with his original people, before the massacre. He had been quite young for his first vision, but it had been proof that he was walking the road to one day becoming a great leader.

"Whistling Elk must lie there for four days without eating or drinking," he said. "He took with him white sage, to lie on as a bed, and filled pipe. He will smoke three times a day, making an offering to *Heammawihio*. If his dreams are favorable, he will remain there four days. If unfavorable, he will return to camp."

"With so much unrest in Shaiyena country, weren't you afraid to let him go so far from our village?" Becky asked softly.

"As long as Judge Newman is at Fort Laramie, we will still have a measure of peace," Blazing Eagle said, shoving his arrow supplies aside. "But there is talk that he will go to make residence in a place called Boston. That is also when we will take up our lodges and travel to our own new place in the sun."

"I miss Waterfall so much," Becky said, then smiled as she recalled how beautiful Waterfall had been on the day of her wedding.

As promised, Becky had readied Waterfall on her special day, when she came to Judge Newman as his bride.

When Judge Newman and Waterfall had said their good-byes, for Waterfall was to live apart from the Cheyenne for the first time in her life, Becky had seen the uneasiness in her eyes.

But Becky and Blazing Eagle had visited Waterfall and Judge Newman's cabin often and seen that Waterfall had settled into her new way of life beautifully. She was even now heavy with child.

Becky reached a hand to her own swollen belly. She thrilled at the thought of soon having their own child to glory over. Four more months, and the big event would happen. Her and Waterfall's children should arrive at almost the same time. She had hoped that one would have a son, the other a daughter, and that the children would grow up loving one another.

But now that their plans were to live thousands of miles apart, she knew that would never happen. She would feel lucky to even get to see Waterfall's child before they both went on journeys that would take them in separate directions.

And she didn't only have Waterfall to leave behind. There was Edward. He now lived in Saint Louis, in the great family mansion. He was following in his father's footsteps, a real estate broker who already had amassed double the wealth of his rich father.

Becky smiled envisioning her brother now married to a pretty young thing who had stolen his heart the first time he had seen her at a debutante ball. Although she was quite young, he bragged about her in his letters, saying that she could make a cherry pie even more delicious than Kathryn's when she was alive.

"My wife?" Blazing Eagle said, framing Becky's face between his hands. "You are the one who is now far away from this lodge. What are you thinking about? Or should I ask *who*?"

"Everyone," Becky said, smiling up at him. "My darling, everything would be so perfect in our lives if we just didn't have to travel to Canada. Do we truly have to? Must we?"

"My people will live better, longer lives once we leave this land that is infested with too many white soldiers and settlers," Blazing Eagle said. "I thought you understood."

Becky lifted his hands from her face, then eased into his arms, resting her cheek against his bare, muscled chest. "I do," she murmured. "But I just wish we didn't have to."

"*Ne-hyo*, I understand," he said, then swept her up into his arms and carried her to his bed. "We are alone. Shall we fill our lodge with whispers of lovemaking?"

"The entrance flap is raised," Becky said, her pulse racing as he gazed down at her with his passion-heavy eyes. "When it is open, it is an invitation for anyone who wishes to enter."

"That is easily remedied," Blazing Eagle said, chuckling. He left her long enough to close the flap. He tied it securely closed, then went back to Becky and stood over her, shoving his breechclout down past his arousal.

He kicked the breechclout away, slipped his moccasins off, then knelt down beside the bed and gathered the hem of Becky's dress into his hands and shoved the dress up and over her head.

When she lay silkenly nude before him, his hands moved over her body, causing her to moan with sweet pleasure. Her insides tightened and grew warm as he filled his hands with her milk-swollen breasts. She saw hidden flames behind his eyes as he lowered his lips to one of her breasts, his mouth moving over her nipple, his hands now moving lower, her tummy quavering sensitively when he stopped and moved his fingers in circles around her navel.

She sucked in a wild breath of pleasure when his hands moved to that place where her desires were hidden beneath a veil of golden curls. Spasmodic gasps shook her body when he plunged a finger into her pulsing cleft.

"Take me," she whispered. "I need you so badly. Please make love to me, Blazing Eagle. I'm aflame inside for you."

His hands slipped beneath her and cupped the rounded flesh of her bottom. He lifted her as he probed with his manhood where she was open and waiting for his thick, throbbing shaft to fill her.

His mouth covered her lips. He kissed her hard and demandingly. His tongue plunged inside her mouth at the same moment that he entered her warm and moist place, thrusting, stroking, each movement promising more, ensuring fulfillment.

He braced himself with his arms, his hands catching hers and holding them slightly above her head. He kissed her feverishly, desire welling up inside him, filling him, spilling over, drenching him with pleasure.

With a groan, she thrust her pelvis toward him.

His body was on fire, pulsing, aflame with longing.

He kissed her, his mouth urgent and eager. He thrust his tongue again into her mouth and flicked it in and out, then moved it along her lips, tasting her sweetness. He felt the passion growing—growing to the bursting point.

Becky gave herself over to the wild passion as their bodies jolted and quivered. She strained her hips up at him, crying out at her fulfillment.

Then their bodies subsided, exhausted, into each other's. They lay there for a moment longer, Blazing Eagle gently stroking her swollen tummy, where their child was peacefully cocooned in slumber.

"Our child," he said huskily. "Our boy child." It gave his heart a fierce pride to know that his wife would soon father his second child.

"Do you truly wish to have a son?" Becky asked, turning to lie on her stomach so that she could look into his eyes as he turned on his side to face her. "We already have one son. Don't you think a daughter would be wonderful? I could bead her such beautiful dresses."

"A son or daughter," Blazing Eagle said, twining a lock of her hair around a finger. "It does not matter. I would love one as much as the other because it is born of our love."

"Yes, and we shall have more," Becky said, sighing contentedly. "I would love to have our house ringing with children's laughter. Wouldn't you, Blazing Eagle? The necklace has blessed us with one child. Surely it will bless us with many more."

He didn't respond at once. Suddenly Becky saw a forlorn look in his eyes that speaking of children had never before caused.

"Blazing Eagle, what is it?" she asked, reaching a gentle hand to his cheek. "What did I say to cause you to take on such a look as that? Don't you want several children?"

"I fear the sort of world we are bringing our children into," he said. "Too many white eyes wish to believe we Cheyenne do not exist, or wish to make it so. What will the world be in the future for our children?"

"The world will be what we make it for them," Becky said, placing a finger to his chin to direct his eyes into hers. "We shall fill their lives with so much love that they will be prepared for anything."

Blazing Eagle placed his hands to her waist and lifted her above him, so that she was straddling him. He shivered with ecstasy to feel the heat of her passion pressed against his stomach. He could feel his own heat building again.

"With a mother like you, how could they ever—"

His words were drawn to a halt when he heard several horses stop just outside their lodge and heard Pebbles barking fitfully. He lifted Becky away from him and handed her dress to her. As she dressed, he slipped his breechclout on, straightened his hair, then waited for her to finish dressing.

They stepped outside the lodge together.

Becky felt him stiffen and grip her hand so tightly that it hurt. She gazed at the woman approaching them on horseback, who was causing such a reaction from Blazing Eagle. She then looked over at the young girl who rode on a pony next to the woman. She appeared to be around eight or nine years of age. She looked guardedly at the warriors who rode with the girl and woman.

Becky looked back at the woman, seeing that she was frail and gaunt. Behind the thin, drawn skin of her face, Becky could see a trace of what might at one time have been beauty. It was obvious that she was wasting away with some sort of illness.

And . . . who was she? Becky wondered, seeing how the woman gazed at Blazing Eagle. It was a pitying look, filled with sorrow.

Blazing Eagle looked past Star Shines at the men on horseback waiting for her, and he knew that she had not come to stay.

His gaze moved slowly to the child. It was apparently Star Shines's child. So then why had she brought her to Blazing Eagle's village?

She did not belong there anymore than Star Shines!

Pebbles sidled up next to Becky's leg and became quiet, but not as friendly as usual. All grown up and no longer a pup, he did not trust as easily as before. His tail lay tucked between his legs as he guardedly watched another savage secret being unfolded.

Star Shines slid from her saddle, then went to the child and helped her to the ground. She then turned and gazed at Blazing Eagle, her daughter beside her.

"Star Shines, what are you doing back in my village?" Blazing Eagle asked warily, his eyes narrowing at the woman who had been his first wife. "When you left, it was meant to be a final good-bye. You are not wanted here."

He gave Becky a quick glance, then glowered again at Star Shines. "Or did you come because you heard that I have taken another wife?" he said. "If so, why would that make any difference? You chose to leave. You are not welcome ever again among my people."

As he spoke, he could not help but see how wasted away Star Shines was and tried not to be concerned over it. She was nothing to him.

Becky's heart skipped a beat when she suddenly realized exactly who this woman was by what Blazing Eagle had said to her. His first wife! She had returned!

Her eyes moved to the child. Whose . . . ? she wondered, suspicions creeping into her heart.

"I have not come to stay," Star Shines said, moving behind her daughter. She clasped her frail hands on her daughter's shoulders and gave her a slight shove toward Blazing Eagle. "But I have brought our daughter to stay with you, her father."

Stunned speechless, Blazing Eagle took a step away from the child, then looked at her more closely. In his mind he was counting out the years Star Shines had been gone. If she had been pregnant when she had left, this child could be his!

"I am your daughter," Snow Deer said, smiling sweetly up at Blazing Eagle. "I have known since I was old enough to know things that you were my father. But mother would not bring me to you. Now she does, and if you will have me, I shall live with you always."

Blazing Eagle's mind was racing, trying to soak up this knowledge of being a father and having been denied the wonders of a daughter these past years.

He turned a heated gaze to Star Shines. "You kept her from me!" he said, his teeth clenched. "You kept my very own daughter from me?"

"I only bring her now because I am dying," Star Shines said, her voice breaking. "I have not married again. So she is yours."

"But why would you keep my own flesh and blood from me?" Blazing Eagle asked, his voice drawn.

"Did you not keep my son from me?" Star Shines said, her voice void of emotion.

"You were the one who chose to leave," Blazing Eagle said, his eyes narrowing into hers. "You were the one who forfeited your son to me by leaving."

"And so you know why I could never tell you about our daughter," Star Shines said. "When she was born, I did not want to give her up to you also, which I would have been forced to had you ever known about her."

Star Shines turned and staggered toward her horse. Two warriors leapt from their horses and helped her up into her saddle.

"This is our final good-bye," Star Shines said as she looked sadly down at Blazing Eagle from her saddle.

"You said . . . that you are dying," Blazing Eagle said, now seeing through his anger to realize what she had said moments ago.

Star Shines gave Blazing Eagle a lingering stare, then motioned toward Snow Deer with a limp hand.

Snow Deer went to her mother and leaned up and kissed her, then hurried back to Blazing Eagle's side.

Blazing Eagle gazed at the child, then looked over at Becky, as if to seek her approval of having a daughter thrust into their lives so suddenly.

When she smiled and nodded, his face filled with sunshine.

She went and stood beside him as Star Shines rode away.

Then Snow Deer turned to face them, her dark eyes smiling. "I do not wish to see my mother go, for I know I will never see her again, but I am so happy to finally be with you, Father," she said. She flung herself into his arms as he knelt to receive her.

Becky knelt down beside Blazing Eagle and ran her fingers through the child's long, jet-black hair. "Snow Deer," she murmured. "That is a pretty name for a pretty girl."

Snow Deer slipped from Blazing Eagle's arms and stared at Becky. "You are a white woman, yet you are heavy with child of the Cheyenne?" she said softly. "Will the child have skin of the Cheyenne or the color of yours?"

"I don't know," Becky said. "Whichever color it is, it will be loved by us. Just as you will be loved by us."

"But your skin is white," Snow Deer said, wrapping her arms protectively around Blazing Eagle's neck, clinging. She gazed into his eyes. "How can you love a white woman?"

"She is white, but in her heart she is Cheyenne," Blazing Eagle said, smiling at Becky.

Then he lifted Snow Deer into his arms. "Come inside our lodge," he said. "Soon you will meet your warrior brother. His name is Whistling Elk."

"Mother told me about my brother," Snow Deer said, still watching Becky with wondering eyes as they entered the tepee and sat down beside the fire. "And she told me about this woman who is now your wife."

"You will love her as both Whistling Elk and I love her," Blazing Eagle said, gazing into his daughter's eyes, marveling still over knowing that she was his.

"You are very pretty," Snow Deer said to Becky, reaching out to gently touch her cheek. "I want to love you. I want to be a part of your family."

"I know that I can never fully take the place of your mother," Becky said softly. "But I shall try to do what I can to make you happy."

"I feel as though I belong already," Snow Deer

said, smiling broadly up at Blazing Eagle.

Blazing Eagle swept her into his arms and hugged her as he smiled over her shoulder at Becky.

Becky was touched by how quickly father and daughter were bonding. She shivered involuntarily when she thought of how many secrets had been kept from so many through the years. They were such savage secrets.

But this secret Blazing Eagle's first wife had kept from him was the worst of all. Her secret had surely been savage, in that she had kept Blazing Eagle from knowing the early, so important years of his daughter's life.

But now everything was going to be perfect for them all. Their lodge would be forever filled with much laughter and love, no matter where that lodge would be. In Canada or in Shaiyena country.

They were together.

That was all that mattered.

And there would be no more savage secrets to get in their way or to tear them apart. There was no reason to hide anything from anyone now. Their lives were rich with blessings.

Dear Reader:

I hope that you have enjoyed reading SAVAGE SECRETS. My next Indian historical romance, SAVAGE PASSIONS, published by LEISURE BOOKS, will be in the stores six months from the publication of SAVAGE SECRETS. SAVAGE PASSIONS will be about the Ottawa Indians of Michigan. This book will be filled with much adventure, romance, mysticism and magic . . . and intrigue. I am anxious for you all to read it! It was such fun to write!

If you would like to receive my latest newsletter, or information about my fan club, please send a stamped, self-addressed envelope to:

> CASSIE EDWARDS
> R#3 Box 60
> Mattoon, IL 61938

I'd love to hear from you all!
> HAPPY READING!
> CASSIE EDWARDS

When I had my first urge to write an historical romance in 1981, I never thought in my wildest dreams that 14 years later I would be seeing my 50th book published! That is what dreams are made of, and this dream came true for me!

I am so happy to write about the Cheyenne Indian tribe in this, the 50th book of my writing career. Not so long ago, my father told me that his grandmother was a full-blooded Cheyenne. I was excited to discover this, for I now understand why I have been so driven to write endlessly about the Native Americans of our country! I am part Indian!

My great-grandmother, who was called Snow Deer by her people, was stolen from her tribe in Kansas and brought to Illinois, where she was given the white name Mame. She soon fit well into the white man's culture, adapting to our customs, but never leaving behind her love for her true people.

In *Savage Secrets* I write about Snow Deer's people, who I am proud to claim as mine!

I hope that you enjoyed sharing my feelings about the Cheyenne as you read this book. It was my intense pleasure to write it! I poured my heart and soul into each and every word.

—Cassie Edwards